# The Kentuckians

# *The Kentuckians*

*by*

JANICE HOLT GILES

THE UNIVERSITY PRESS OF KENTUCKY

This edition published in 1987 by The University Press of Kentucky

Scholarly publisher for the Commonwealth,
serving Bellarmine College, Berea College, Centre
College of Kentucky, Eastern Kentucky University,
The Filson Club Historical Society, Georgetown College,
Kentucky Historical Society, Kentucky State University,
Morehead State University, Murray State University,
Northern Kentucky University, Transylvania University,
University of Kentucky, University of Louisville,
and Western Kentucky University.

*Editorial and Sales Offices:* The University Press of Kentucky
663 South Limestone Street, Lexington, Kentucky 40508-4008

04 03 02 01 00    8 7 6 5 4

Library of Congress Cataloging-in-Publication Data

Giles, Janice Holt.
    The Kentuckians / by Janice Holt Giles.
        p.  cm.
    ISBN 0-8131-1639-2.    ISBN 0-8131-0177-8 (pbk.)
    1. Kentucky—History—To 1792—Fiction.  I. Title.
PS3513.I4628K4    1987
813'.54—dc19                        87-30325

This book is printed on acid-free recycled paper meeting
the requirements of the American National Standard
for Permanence of Paper for Printed Library Materials

Manufactured in the United States of America

# *Acknowledgments*

N O PERSON who writes a book based on historical events and setting does so alone. Many people, many libraries, historical societies and institutions must contribute time and help to the necessary research. I am grateful for every kindness so willingly extended to me. More particularly, however, I am indebted to Dr. Charles G. Talbert of Covington, Kentucky. When I first began the research for this book, Dr. Talbert had just finished his dissertation, "The Life and Times of Benjamin Logan," in partial fulfillment of the requirements of the program for the degree of Doctor of Philosophy of the University of Kentucky. Not only did Dr. Talbert confer with me about my materials and methods of research, he generously placed in my hands his own manuscript and bibliography, with complete freedom as to their use. I am glad to have this opportunity to thank Dr. Talbert publicly for his great kindness to me. I must say further, however, that the results of my use of his material are entirely my own responsibility and none of his.

*To my daughter*
ELIZABETH MOORE HANCOCK

# CHAPTER

# I

I HAVE A WISH that those who come after me should know the truth about our troubles with the Transylvania Company, and the truth about those first hard years in the settling of this country. In time the ones that carried the biggest loads may be forgot, and the things we fought for lost to memory. They ought not be, for in a time and a place that asked almost more than a man could give in strength, there were men, and women too, that stood up to the brunt of it and held on when it looked foolish to hold on any longer. The year of 1777, for instance, when there were but a hundred and twenty guns in the whole of Kentucky and the British were arming and agitating the Ohio Indians against us; when we were scattered in three little settlements, almost out of ammunition and hard put to find food, penned inside three puny little log forts, not able to help one another and for days on end not knowing but that our own stockade was all that was left . . . that year ought never to be forgot, for it was the turning point and those who in time to come live here in this land in peace and plenty can forever be thankful to the ones that stood fast then and would not abandon the country. We've had bad times since, but never again have so few had to make out with such a little. I've been here amongst them from the start, and I know them all as well as men sharing a common burden get to know one another. I want my own, at least, to know what they owe, and the ones they owe it to. Maybe, too, I have a kind of longing that they should know my own part in it . . . not a very big part, to be sure, but it was a man's part and I take a pride in it.

I first set foot in this Green River country in the spring of 1769. Jim Knox, from the Wolf Hills settlement on the Holston, led a party of us into Kentucky to hunt. We stayed better than two years and went back to the settlements as poor as when we'd left, for the Indians cleaned us out of all the skins we'd taken. Folks called us the Long Hunters because we stayed gone such a time.

The country was wilderness in those days. But few white men had ever seen it, and none had settled here. Dannel Boone had made a few trips and had come back with such tales of the country as to make all who listened to him eager to see it. Never, he said, had he seen such a land. The trees were big and thick and clustered in mighty forests, the cane in the flat lands grew taller than a man's head, there was such a plenty of game that a man could take skins by the thousands instead of the hundreds we were used to. He said the land was watered by free-flowing springs dotted all over, and with creeks and streams and rivers on every hand. He said the meadows were matted with rye grass and clover and pea vines, up to a man's knees, and all about were sweet-smelling blooms, wild fruits and berries, nuts, persimmons and pawpaws. And there was always the song of birds, for, he said, there were more birds in Kentucky than he'd ever dreamed of seeing. Dannel called it the Garden of Eden, and it was. It still is, for look where you will, there is no other land like Kentucky. There's no place as green and fair, no place as grand and sightly, and in all Kentucky there's no place as sweet as this country about the headwaters of the Green River.

I learned it well those two years with Jim Knox. We stayed down in these parts mostly for we had no hankering to mix with the Ohio Indians. We hunted all up and down the river, from its head in the hills, where it's no wider than the overflow from a spring, to its mouth where its waters mingle with the Ohio. I learned every twist and turn of it, all its deep places and its shallows, the cliffs and caves it cuts out of the hills, the cane thickets and high-growing grass that border its banks in the valleys and flat lands. But wherever it flows, through hills or valleys, it is rightly named the Green, for its waters are clear and sparkly and as purely green as a jewel. No one can truly tell of the way it catches the heart and holds it, save one who has wandered its course through every season, as I have.

Of its whole length I love it best right here, amongst the hills, where it's had time to widen and deepen some but is still a little stream, not too busy to play about with shoals and ripples, nor too proud to harbor a few deeps where fish can hide. I picked this place even in those days, the stream and the hills, for I've no liking for flat and level lands. I like the hills about me. Not mountains, for they're too grand and broody, but little, friendly hills that break the distance and give a boundary to your living. I like to stretch my legs on their climb and then stand there on a high place and look out across the land. Living on the levels is like forever hunkering down the same. I like the shoulders of the hills pushing against my own. The stream and the hills . . . they go good together.

I was but a lad when I first saw the country, just pushing eighteen, but I'd been on my own several years. My folks came to the Holston from the Shenandoah Valley and my pap settled on Beaver Creek over the Yadkin way. He was ever a restless and wandering man, more at home in the woods than the fields, and likely I come by my own love of the wild places of the earth naturally. I disremember the time when we stayed long in one place. He was always pushing on, west-ward, away from the settled parts of the country. Seemed like when folks commenced to cluster about, Pap got itchy and crowded-feeling, and he'd pull up stakes and move on. Little at a time we left behind us the valley, Draper's Meadows, the New River country, until finally we inched down onto the Yadkin. Dannel Boone was a neighbor of ours and him and Pap hunted together many a time. I first heard the Kentucky lands named by Dannel when he'd sit by the hearth and tell of its wonders. Pap was always aiming to seek it out one day, and it may be I went with Jim Knox on the Long Hunt more on his account than my own.

We'd not been on the Yadkin but a couple of years, though, when Pap's chances to hunt over the mountains were done for. I was big enough to pack a gun, though it weighted me considerably, and to help out with the hunting. It was in the fall of the year and Mam was yearning for the taste of meat. "I'm sick of the sight of garden sass," she said to me one day. "Yer pap's gathering corn this morning, but you take the gun, David, and see can you stir up a young squirrel or rabbit. Mind, though, don't go fur."

I wasn't allowed to go deep in the woods unless Pap was along, for the Cherokee were ever troublesome and it was untelling when they'd be lurking amongst the thickets and bushes. I was overjoyed to shoulder the gun, though, and get away from the clearing. I'd been afraid Pap would call me to help with the corn, and it was a chore I disliked.

I went further than I'd meant, for I saw neither squirrel nor rabbit and kept wandering on in hopes of scaring one up, but I was still close enough to the clearing that I heard the shots when the Cherokee struck, and I heard their screeching and yowling. It shriveled the marrow in my bones and made the skin crawl on my flesh. It froze my feet to the ground where I stood and broke me out all over in a cold sweat. It seemed like an eternity I stood that way, then I broke loose and commenced running back towards the clearing. Pap would have his other gun by him in the corn field I knew, but I misdoubted he'd get much chance to use it.

I pulled up short and out of breath in the edge of the woods. The cabin was already smoking. The redskins were circling it and firing the grass and the outbuildings. I couldn't see but five, but they sounded like twenty, yelling, screeching, howling the way they do. Over near the edge of the corn field I saw my pap lying where he'd fallen, trying to get to Mam and the others in the cabin, and while I looked I saw one of the red varmints drag my mam out of the smoke and heat and cleave her down the middle, like butchering a fresh-killed deer. Something oily came up in the back of my throat, but it didn't keep me from drawing a bead on the Indian who'd already commenced to slip her scalp. He fell sprawling, his arms flung out wide, on the ground beside her. Whilst I was reloading another Indian came through the door dragging my small sister with one hand, clutching my baby brother against his chest with the other. Two redskins leaped at him and jerked them away from him, and I heard my sister scream just once before the tomahawk fell. I aimed then at the one holding the baby, but even as my finger squeezed the trigger the little tyke's brains were spilled out against the log wall of the cabin. It was not much satisfaction to see the red man slither down the wall himself, clutching at it and clawing, but sliding finally into a heap on the ground.

Seeing two of their number killed I reckon they must of figured there was a party of settlers firing on them, so the others lit out into the far woods. I waited several hours before venturing out into the clearing, though, for fear they belonged to a war party and might bring the others back with them. While I waited the buildings burned to the ground, and Patch, our old hound dog, came out of the brush and sat down beside my pap's body and howled. I've never listened to a mourning dog since that I've not been taken back to that shivering, waiting time. The dog howled and it commenced to drizzle rain and a cold east wind blew down my neck. I was twelve years old and my mam and my pap were dead and my home was a smoldering pile of ashes. I've never shed a tear since. Maybe I cried them all that day.

Come evening, I buried my folks. The face of a scalped body is not a pleasant sight to see. The skin, loosed from the scalp, is slack and wrinkly over the face, falling in folds around the eyes and mouth.

With the top of the head gaped open, the brains mushy and bloody and torn, it's like to turn the strongest stomach. It turned mine, for I wouldn't of known my pap and my mam. But I dug a deep grave and put the four of them in it, and gave them as decent a burial as I could. I left out then for Dannel's place.

He was off hunting, but his woman, Rebecca, took me in and I stayed the winter with them. I recollect it was Dannel's oldest boy, James, that said to me that first night, "You're as good a man as ary'n, David Cooper, for you've kilt your first redskin."

I'd killed my first one and I reckon I've accounted for several since, but even though I've never forgot the sight of my mam and pap and the least ones lying dead and butchered, and the cabin and the clearing burnt to ashes around them, and though I've had more cause than most to hate the redskins, I've never killed just to be killing, like some I've known. I don't go so far as to say, like Dannel does, that there's good Indians. I've got no liking for any of them, but I reckon they're human beings and it goes against the grain to kill anything human in cold blood. I've killed when it was them or me, and I've taken my full part in the fights we've had settling the country, but I've yet to draw a bead on one without him having as good a chance as me.

I stayed the winter with the Boones, but come spring I took my gun and went out on my own and for the next six years I drifted up and down amongst the settlements, hunting, trapping and scouting. By the time I was sixteen I was as good a scout as any man on the Holston, if I do say so myself. It was a kind of living I took to like a duck takes to water, natural and easy, free and unhampered, coming and going as it pleased me and beholden to no one. Like the palm of my hand I got to know the undermountain country, up as far as the Greenbrier and even the Monongahela, and down the country through the valleys of the Powell and the Clinch and the Holston into the Nolichucky country.

By the time I was sixteen, too, I had got my growth, the full six foot I've stood ever since, and it was already plain I was going to be lean as a scantling and long and limber-legged. I don't know as legs that can take long strides stand you in any better stead in the woods, commonly, for a short-legged man can be as tireless on the trail as a long-legged one, but if you've got to get some place fast, it stands to reason you can cover a heap more ground in less time if you can reach out and eat it up in sizable chunks. There have been times when I've been mighty glad I was stretched a mite in the legs.

Wherever I went those years, and however long I stayed, it went natural for me to drift back to the Yadkin and the Watauga country in between times. The Robertson brothers had set up for themselves hard by the Sycamore Shoals on the Watauga, and they traded with the settlers and the Cherokee both. They gave a good price for prime pelts, and they kept a fair store of powder and lead, flour and goods and tools and the other necessaries folks wanted. I got in the way of trading with them and whenever they needed a scout or a hunter they mostly called on me. In time I had me all I needed and wanted in the way of possessions . . . a good horse, traps, and a fine Deckard gun. I had no wish for a house and land, for I had no use for them.

But game was ever growing scarcer in the country. It always does when settlements commence to flourish, so when Jim Knox started agitating for a party to go west over the mountains into the Kentucky wilderness it seemed to me like a chance for what Dannel calls a great speck. Everything new and different and venturesome is a great speculation to Dannel.

So it was I first saw the Kentucky country and learned to love it. Like I said, though, our great speck came to naught, for at the last a Cherokee party raided our cache of skins whilst we were off about our business and took them all . . . better than two thousand all told. We went back to the Holston as empty-handed as we'd left it, but most of us went back knowing our days east of the mountains were numbered. None could forget the grandness of the country we'd seen. Not once during the four years that followed, while I was again hunting and scouting for the Robertsons, or while I was fighting in Dunmore's War against the Indians, did I forget this spot on the headwaters of the Green. For the first time in my life I commenced to have a yearning for a piece of land of my own, and it was this piece here I wanted, with the spring down there in the locust grove, and the meadow opening out beyond it, the hills rising up all around closing it in, and the river cutting through the hills. I knew I was coming back here to it some day.

Seemed like by 1774, the year of Dunmore's War, there was a wild craze in everybody to go to Kentucky. I recollect that during the war we used to sit around the campfires of a night and talk about it. It was counted part of Virginia. They'd commenced sending their surveyors into the country and even George Washington and Thomas Jefferson and Patrick Henry were having pieces surveyed for them. The Virginia land law said any man settling in the country and building himself a cabin and raising a crop of corn was entitled to four hundred acres of land. There was a many a eager to take up land under that law and I was amongst them.

One settlement had already been commenced. Jim Harrod from Pennsylvania had hunted through the country, then had worked for some of the surveyors, and finally in the spring of 1774 he'd taken a party of men into the middlemost parts and they'd laid out a town near Salt River and commenced building their cabins. It was about then Lord Dunmore had sent warnings to all that the war was coming and they'd best get back to the eastern settlements. As early as 1773 Dannel had tried to take a party through the Gap to settle in the part he loved the most, on Otter Creek where it runs into the Kentucky River. It had come near breaking his heart that they'd had to turn back. A little band of Shawnee Indians had happened on the party before they even got to the Gap and had so frighted the folks they wouldn't go on. Dannel's boy, James, was killed in the ruckus, but as much as he thought of the boy that wouldn't of turned Dannel back. It was the womenfolks, and the men scared for them, that wouldn't go on.

So there was yet no settlement in the country by the spring of 1775, but the time was ready, and it was that spring a thing happened that hurried it on. It was Charlie Robertson first told me about Colonel Henderson and the Transylvania Company. "He's from North Carolina," he said. "He's a lawyer and a judge back in those parts. He's got several men to back him up and put the money and he's dickering with the Cherokee to buy the whole of Kentucky."

It kind of startled me. "By what rights," I said, "do the Cherokee claim to own the land? Don't it belong to Virginia?"

Charlie shrugged. "The Cherokee claim they had no part in the treaty that give the land to Britain in the first place. It's been their land since time begun, according to them."

As little as I knew about treaties and rights and titles, I knew if Colonel Henderson could buy the land from the Cherokee and make it stick, the whole business of settling in Kentucky would be a horse of a different color. Instead of settling under the Virginia law, a man would have to buy his land from the colonel's company, and the colonel doubtless was aiming to sell on speculation. "How far has he got with the deal?" I asked, for I'd been upcountry a spell and had heard no news of it at all until now.

"Far enough," Charlie said, "that the tribes are meeting here at the Shoals next month to treat with him, and he's might near talked the chiefs into signing."

"What is he offering them?"

"Ten thousand pounds in goods, and the goods are already here."

That pulled a whistle out of me, for it was a heap of goods. It set everything at a rightabout-face and I disliked the looks of it. "I reckon," I said, "this'll go hard with some that's aiming on going out to the country soon. Dannel's not going to take it kindly, for one." Charlie snorted. "Dannel's hired out to him. When the trade is made Dannel is to cut a trail through the country for the colonel and his party."

A punch in the stomach couldn't of flabbergasted me more. Charlie had close-set eyes and one kind of squinted when he looked straight at you. It squinted now as he looked over my pile of pelts at me. "You'd ort to know," he said, "Dannel is so rampant crazy to get back into that country he'll throw in with anybody promising him a start in settling. He'll get his land free . . . the colonel's promised him two thousand acres in payment for cutting the road, and he ain't thinking of nobody else."

I knew better than that, though. I'd not known Dannel Boone all my life for nothing. What I knew was that he was too trusting, and he was never one to think very far ahead. As plain as if I'd listened to them talking I knew the colonel had made him believe in his scheme. And for all I didn't like it I didn't know but what the man had a scheme would work. It was right then I knew one thing for certain. Anybody aiming on settling in Kentucky had best waste no time getting started. And I knew another thing. I aimed to be at the Shoals to see and hear what went on when Colonel Henderson and his partners had their parley with the Cherokee. "Just give me credit for these skins," I told Charlie, "I'll take it up later."

He tallied them up and entered it in his book. "You aiming on staying hereabouts for a while?"

"I might be," I said. "Let me see that entry will you?" Charlie wasn't beyond making a little mistake now and then and I always made sure. "Why?"

"The colonel is needing beeves to feed the Indians during the council meeting and I've contracted to buy 'em up for him. Can use you, if you're a mind to take it on."

I pondered it a minute and decided I could use the extra credit. I'd be needing a heap of things in Kentucky. I handed him back the book and we made a trade. In a couple of days I set out riding around buying cattle for Charlie to sell the colonel and driving them to the Watauga. The whole country was simmering with the news of the council meeting and everybody was planning to go. Half the menfolks were set to leave out right straight for Kentucky, either with the colonel or on his heels, and their women were just as bent on keeping them home. There hadn't been so much excitement in the settlements since the Yellow Creek Indian massacree.

The council meeting was set to commence the first day of March, and by the last week in February the Indians had begun drifting in. They brought their women and young ones with them and set up their lodges down by the Shoals. Wasn't long until the whole countryside was overrun by Indians and Charlie's store was full of them all day long. They'd bring their pelts in and stand around for an hour or two making up their minds what they wanted in trade. Between the smell of the skins and the smell of the Indians that store got pretty high, but Charlie never minded for he was doing a flourishing business. It got better, too, for before long the settlers commenced drifting in and soon I had my doubts if the whole length of the Watauga was going to hold the gathering of folks. What with better than a thousand Cherokee warriors and their families and every white man in the Holston country, it didn't look likely. It was a right smart congregation. Heading it up was the colonel and his partners, keeping a close guard over the wagons of goods they aimed to trade the Cherokee, and keeping a close guard over the Indians, too, feeding them the best they'd ever eat and keeping them from the rum barrels till they'd signed. But there wasn't anybody keeping a guard over the settlers, and of a night around the campfires there was considerable celebrating going on.

The night before the treaty-making was to begin I went down amongst them, seeking out Jim Knox's camp. I knew he'd come on for the council meeting for I'd seen him around a time or two, but I'd been too taken up with Charlie's cattle-buying to spare the time to visit with him. I wanted to have a little talk with him and get his ideas about what was going on, and now that I'd finished up Charlie's business, it seemed like a good time.

It had to wait, though, for when I found his camp Jim wasn't there. But there was nearly the whole bunch of us had been in Kentucky together so I didn't to say mind missing Jim. I just settled myself down to an evening of yarning and joshing and drinking. It was good to be sitting around the fire with them again . . . like old times. Was one new fellow I'd not seen around before. He'd been sampling the jug right freely and was pretty far gone. He kept to himself off to one side with his back propped against a tree. I made sure he was going to have a stiff neck from his head nodding down so far on his chest, but he'd jerk it up again every now and then and open his eyes and blink at the fire. He got up once and walked over to a wolf he had chained to a sapling close by. He was the powerfullest built man I'd ever seen. He was short, but he had shoulders as blocky as an old bull's, thick-muscled and solid-looking. His neck was short and sunk down into his shoulders like a wedge driven into a tree. He had the look of keeping his shoulders hunched all the time, but that was likely on account of his neck being so short. He walked spraddle-legged and, even with as much Monongahela as he was carrying, as solid as if his feet had grown out of the ground.

I nudged the fellow sitting next to me. "Who's he?"

He shook his head. "Dunno. Says his name is Jordan. He just wandered up a little bit ago."

"That wolf his'n?"

"Yeah. Says he caught it in a trap and aims to make a pet of it."

The wolf was on the far side of the fire from me and about all I could see of him was his outline and the shine of his eyes in the firelight. He wasn't to say the kind of a pet I'd of wanted to be having around, but every man has a right to his own likes peculiar though they may be to others. The wolf sat there all during the evening, peaceful enough, squatted back on his haunches just looking on.

The jug kept circulating and we all got to feeling fine. Jordan quit his tree after awhile and came over and sat down closer to the fire. The night had a sharp chill to it and the fire felt good. He took his turn at the jug when it came around to him, but he had little to say, and the rest of us were so taken up with telling tall tales of the old days we kind of forgot about him.

The night wore on and the talk and the laughing passed with it. Some of the men were commencing to stretch out to sleep and I was getting sleepy myself and just of a mind to get on back to the store and go to bed when this Jordan fellow stood up and commenced to make his way around back of the circle. I reckon his feet were clumsy for all he could yet walk straight, for he stumbled over the wolf's chain and the animal snarled at the noise, growling deep in his throat and hackling the fur on his neck. We all turned to see what was going on. Jordan was trying to get his feet untangled from the chain, but he lost his balance and fell flat of his face in the dirt. I don't know what there is about a drunk man sprawling on the ground trying to get up that's so funny, but it is. He looks so foolish and awkward. Everybody busted out laughing and yelling at Jordan, me amongst them. It was me that yelled at him to get up like a cow, hind end first. You could tell he didn't like it. Seemed like his face that was already bloated and swollen with drink turned purple, the way a kid's will do when he's so mad he's holding his breath. He got himself up finally and then he commenced pulling the wolf towards him by the chain. I was standing up myself, ready to leave, but out of the corner of my eye I saw him pull his knife out of his belt. I reckon the rest saw it too, for we all got quiet and waited.

Jordan's backside was between us and the animal but we could all see his arm moving and the knife blade flashing. The wolf yelped suddenly, kind of surprised like, then he yelped two or three more times, sharp and short, before he settled into a high, screeching howling that filled the whole night. It was like a woman screaming with pain. The man stood up all at once and jerked his hand back quick and sudden, flinging it up and snapping something loose. When he stood aside what we saw was too bad to believe. I know I couldn't make a move for what seemed like a long time, I was so stunned. It was pure meanness, what the man had done, for he'd slit the skin of the animal and then stripped it loose from the meat, leaving the wolf all bare and bloody, his pelt hanging loose around his neck. All the bare nerves and muscles were driving the poor thing mad with the hurt and he was leaping and running and clawing, biting at his chain and trying to roll in the dirt. The man Jordan just stood there, wiping his knife on his pants leg, looking on and laughing.

It was more than I could stand. The wolf was his and commonly a man has a right to do what he wills with his own property, but no man could stand aside and see a poor helpless creature so tortured. I jumped and cleared the fire and sunk my hatchet deep in the animal's brain to put an end to its suffering. It crumpled in a heap, its skin-bare legs still quivering and shuddering. I reached out to get my hatchet, but one of the men yelled at me suddenly, "Look out, Dave!"

I turned fast, but Jordan had already lunged and all I could do was roll with him and kick out at the knife in his hand. My foot caught his wrist and sent the knife flying, but we went down in the dirt sprawling, me scrabbling for a hold and him clutching and clawing. The rest of the men circled around us in a ring, giving us fighting room and yelling and howling at us. Men came running over from the other camps close by, but I was too busy to know.

This Jordan was drunk but he wasn't too drunk to fight and he was a big hulk of a man, tough and stout. It sobered me considerably to feel how thick and powerful he was, rolling around there in the dirt and grappling with him. I knew I had me a job on my hands, all right. I didn't want to lose an eye or have the life squeezed out of my gullet and I figured it was going to take some doing to keep from either. I didn't have time to figure much, though . . . I just kept rolling with him, breaking his holds as best I could and trying to stay on top.

I've no notion how long it went on, nor how it would of come out, for I was getting pretty tired, when my foot slipped on a half-burned limb that rolled under me and threw me, and Jordan with me, towards the fire. I twisted as best I could and flung Jordan off, and he landed plumb in the midst of the fire, scattering coals in all four directions. I rolled clear myself. Jordan let out a murderous howl and pulled himself up out of the fire, but his clothes were caught in a dozen different places and ashes and coals were sticking to his hands and arms. He lit out for the river, yelping at every step. I stood there and watched him go, heaving and trying to get my breath back. Everybody was clustered about whooping and shouting and pounding me on the back. One of them said, "By grannies, Dave, that was the smartest trick ever I seen! Don't know as I'd of thought of it myself!"

They thought I'd dumped him in the fire apurpose and I let it go. I was too tuckered to talk anyways. John Baker kicked the fire back together. He was still laughing. "Reckon that'll learn him. Regular Indian trick, skinning a live varmint thataway. But he's finding out right now how it feels to be bad hurt, I reckon."

When I could talk and breathe at the same time I told the boys I'd be seeing them next day at the council gathering and started to leave. Going around the end of the fire my foot kicked against something and when I looked I saw it was Jordan's knife I'd kicked out of his hand. I picked it up and handed it to John. "Here's his knife if he comes back for it."

John took it. "I'll see he gets it," he said. He turned it over a time or two looking at it. "Man, look at the fancy way he's got that handle carved up, will you?" He held it out for me to see.

He'd mounted the blade, just a common, ordinary skinning knife like everybody used, in a horn handle, and he'd carved the horn in deep grooves that made a kind of pattern. Reminded me of one of them stiff-limbed trees my mam had used to prick out on the top crust of her pies. I said so to John Baker. "Reckon them tree limbs gives him a tighter grip," he said.

"Might," I said and went on my way. It made no difference to me how much he carved up his knife handle. I was just wanting to get to bed.

I laid down to sleep that night with one arm achy and sore where the muscles had been pulled, but I figured the Jordan fellow would be nursing worse pains. I wondered some who he was and where he was from, but it didn't matter much. He was drifting and so was I and we'd likely never meet again. But, remembering, I had to laugh over the way he'd high-tailed it down to the river to put out his fire. That would be a tale to tell for a long time to come.

❦

# CHAPTER

# 2

I SAW JIM KNOX at the council meeting the next day.

I went out early, for the proceedings were set to start at sunup. It was still wintery even though it was the first of March and I felt shivery riding along. There were a few signs of spring coming on, but they were meager. Some of the trees along the river and back up the valley had a swollen look along the limbs, like the buds were filling and plumping out, but they had a long way to go yet. Mostly the sycamores were pretty stark-looking, and there's nothing more un-likely looking than a winterbound sycamore tree, all white and bleached, like winter had sucked it dry. Even the bushes and the laurel along the hill line had a used-up look, a kind of brown, speckled look as if the cold had shriveled and pinched them dry.

A close eye could tell, though, that there was a pushing in the earth to stir and break loose, and it wasn't to be held back much longer. There was a patch of green here and there underfoot where cress and dock and purslane were shoving up, and there was a pinky look under the bark of the redbud trees that grew alongside the path. I figured it wasn't going to be long until every limb was blazing with little red blooms, and all the dogwood trees would be spangling out with white. Right now was a sluggish time, but underneath things were stretching and stirring, the bloodstream was thinning and quick-ening and soon the whole countryside would be rampant with color and new leaves and growth. This undermountain country was a sight to see in season.

The mare picked her way along the path kind of dainty, like she didn't relish the wet and frost on her feet, and when we came to a little swale with a run of water iced over with a thin crust and she broke through, she snorted and jerked her head and lunged at the far bank. She was always a mite nervy, but easy quieted. You had only to speak to her, "Come up, now, Beck. Come up, girl. It's only a little ice."

She soothed and pulled up out of the swale and commenced climbing up a long woodsy slope. This was the rim of the valley and from here you could plainly hear the sound of water running strong over the shoals. This was the place of the council meeting, and when we came to the edge of the slope we were in sight of the gathering.

The south bank of the river was shaped like a saucer with the water curving to make one rim and the hill I'd just come up cupping it on the other side. Down at the foot of the hill there were some cabins, three as I recollect, and Colonel Henderson and his partners had been staying in them. In the bowl of the saucer the Cherokee had pitched their lodges and built their camps.

It was but good sunup and the smoke from the Indian fires still hung over the valley, kind of loose and meager-like. The Indian women and children were all bunched together near the fires, but the chiefs and warriors had already taken their places in a big half-circle at the near end of the encampment, sitting on the ground, knees folded and blankets huddled around their shoulders. Like a scraggly fringe along the outside edge of the Indians the settlers were gathering and down front was a table where the colonel and his partners were sitting in chairs. While I watched the colonel got up and walked around the table and held up his hand. He was ready to commence.

I'd seen him around, the colonel, but not to speak to. He was a big man and I reckon you'd have to say a handsome one. He'd dressed for the occasion and he looked right elegant in his eastern clothes. Made right smart of a figure. He began his speech and he had a powerful voice. It rolled around down in the valley like a trumpet sounding off. I could hear him plain from where I was and I decided to stay put. I was close enough I could hear what was going on, but far enough away I needn't mix nor mingle with the crowd. I got off the mare and tied her to a sapling and settled myself against the bole of a big elm tree.

It was a right smart crowd the colonel had got together here at the Sycamore Shoals of the Watauga, a right smart crowd. The Cherokee sat there like Indians always sit when white men are around . . . stony still and moveless. They can sit like that all day and never twitch a muscle. You'd never know what they were thinking of this treaty-making by looking at them. They just sat there, their faces as dark as vat water in a tanyard, as smooth and unmoving as a rock, listening in that starey-blank way of theirs, making like they were uncaring of what was going on.

I didn't know all the chiefs but I figured they were all there. Charlie had said the colonel made sure they would all come. I did know the big chief, old Attacullaculla, and he was right down front. He was the one everybody called the Little Carpenter on account of the way he could make a joining. He'd been one of the main ones pulling for this deal. It had been him had gone back to North Carolina with the colonel to pick out the goods to be traded. He was a little, dried-up-looking man, old now and scrawny, but still a power amongst the Cherokee. Withered as he was he had a pride about him. He had two deep scars gashed down his cheeks and they helped to give him a kind of fierce, eagle look. As Indians go you could come as near trusting the Little Carpenter as any of them.

I knew the Indian sitting by him, too. It was his boy, the one called Dragging Canoe, though I never knew why, and a meaner redskin never lived. He was shrewd and he was clever and he hated everything to do with the whites. I was some surprised to see him, for there'd been talk he wouldn't come. It was said he'd tried to talk the others out of coming. Charlie said the colonel had worried a heap about him. Old Attacullaculla must of bore down on him considerably, for there he was, big as life. That was one Indian didn't try to hide what he was thinking. Right now he looked as sulky as a rain cloud ready to spill. He might of been listening to what the colonel was saying, but he sure wasn't looking at him. He sat there looking over the heads of the people like he was too good to be amongst them. He was a bad Indian all right. He'd always given the western settlers trouble. This treaty-making must be going hard with him.

I stood there looking on, leaning on the barrel of my gun, scratching my shoulder against the trunk of the tree. The colonel was talking big and elegant, stopping every now and then for the interpreter to translate for him. Best I could tell he had Johnnie Vann interpreting for him, but the colonel was standing between me and him and I couldn't see him very good. I knew Johnnie was supposed to come, for the colonel had got ten of the best Indian traders in the country to promise to help out with the translating. If it was Johnnie Vann doing the talking for him now he was commencing with the best. Wasn't a trader from Fort Pitt to the Nolichucky knew the Indians any better, nor one they trusted as much.

There wasn't much use listening too close right then, though, for they had to palaver awhile and get all the polite things said first. I commenced looking for Jim amongst the settlers on yon side, but he must of seen me ride up, for about that time I heard a twig snap behind me and when I turned around there he was coming through the woods. "Howdy, Dave," he said when he reached me and he clapped me hearty on the shoulder. It was the one was sore from the fight the night before and I kind of gave way under him. He commenced laughing. "From what the boys told me you got yourself tangled up in a right smart ruckus last night. I'd love to of seen it."

"You never missed much," I told him. "Reckon I ortent to put my nose in the man's business like I done, but tormenting a living critter that way don't set good with me."

"Me neither. Getting tossed in the fire was good enough for him."

"You know him?" I asked.

"No. Never heared of him before. The word is that him and his woman drifted in a couple of days ago and camped up the river a piece. Claimed he was from up towards the Monongahela looking for a place to settle hereabouts. But he's moved on, I reckon. Folks close by said he broke camp before day this morning and left out."

"Just as well," I said.

Jim eased his weight up against the tree and settled his chin on his gun barrel. He wasn't as tall as me, and he was older by several years, but Jim Knox was a big man in every way, tough as whang leather and as good a hunter and scout as ever lived. I had a heap of admiration for him. I peeled me a sassafras twig and commenced chewing on it, settled myself beside Jim and motioned down towards the gathering. "Right smart shindig the colonel has got going on here, ain't it?"

Jim looked down and ran his eyes over the meeting. Then his jaw set itself and he kind of snorted. "It's a right smart shindig, all right." I could tell he had no more liking for it than I had.

"Are all the chiefs here?"

"Ever' last one of 'em, and all in a notion to sign."

I moved my sassafras toothbrush to the other side of my mouth. "Supposing they do. Does that give him a title he can make stick?"

Jim eased his shoulders against the tree. "It's untelling. He's a smart one, all right. He knows the law and has follered it all his life. He allows the Cherokee have got the right to sell and he's got the right to buy and Britain will have to ratify his title."

"They won't if the country belongs to Virginia."

"He claims that Britain never give it to Virginia. That it still belongs to them and the Cherokee are British subjects and can sell if they're of a mind to."

"You much worried about how it's going to come out?"

Jim grinned. "Not if I get out there and get my land took up first."

That was what I'd been wanting to hear . . . was he aiming on going back into the country too. But there was a stir in the gathering down below and the colonel sat down and the old chief stood up. We listened. I could see plain now it was Johnnie Vann interpreting, and when the chief stopped and waited for him to catch up, Johnnie made his words sound as slow and as solemn as the old man had said them. He commenced by reminding everybody that he was an old man now and that he had been chief of the nation for more than fifty years. He told how he had crossed the big water to see the Great White Father in London and how he had eaten meat with him in his lodge. He said he had always been fair in his dealings with the white man and he told the colonel the Cherokee people had the right to trade the lands of Kentucky to him and to make a treaty with him. He drew himself up straight and stiff as a ramrod and held his fist up over his head whilst he told them the Six Nations had never conquered the Cherokee.

Jim sort of growled in his throat. "Reckon being run out of Kentucky wasn't what you'd call being conquered." He turned his back on the gathering. "The boys said you was looking for me. What was it you was wanting?"

I spit my toothbrush out. "You've done and answered it," I said. "I'm going back to Kentucky and I was just wondering if you wouldn't be heading that way soon yourself."

He grinned. "Me and Ben Logan is aiming on leaving next month. Just go with us if you want."

"I'll be ready," I told him. I didn't know Ben Logan too good, but he was from the same Wolf Hills settlement as Jim and they'd always been friendly. If Jim was traveling with him that was good enough for me. Ben was a Scotch-Irish Presbyterian like nearly all the rest of the folks over in that settlement, and he'd always stayed pretty close to his farm. He had the name of being a thrifty, shrewd kind of man. He'd made good with his farming, leastways, and had a nice piece of property with a good stand of hemp and corn, several head of stock and some Negroes. Being by nature footloose and easygoing I hadn't ever had much in common with him, him being married and settled and all. He was said to be a mite strict in his ways, too, and I reckon I was always one to take my pleasure as I found it. Not that I'm proud of it now, but a young fellow, living free and easy, is bound to be freer and easier in his ways than more settled men. But all I'd ever heard of Ben Logan had been to the good. "How does it happen," I asked Jim, "that Ben wants to take a sashay over thataway."

"Oh, he's heared me tell of it, times without number. I don't reckon you'd know I staked me out a claim close to the Buffalo Springs when I was out there last year, and he's taken a notion to look over the country." He grinned. "I take it you're aiming on going back to the Green?"

I nodded. "I've never forgot that little valley up around the headwaters. That's where I aim to take my stand."

"It's sightly all right. I like over close to the Falls a heap, too."

"Ain't it awful marshy over there next the river?"

"Some of it is, some ain't. Awful rich land thereabouts."

The other chiefs had been talking all this time. We hadn't paid much attention but something of what they'd been saying had drifted up to us. All had agreed to sign the treaty, we knew that much. Jim stretched and yawned. "Reckon the colonel is going to have smooth sailing."

He hadn't more than said the words when, so quick neither of us saw it happen, the old chief's boy, Dragging Canoe, was on his feet, talking short and sharp and angry. Jim stiffened and I eased my gun off the ground. The Indians stirred and several of them got to their feet. The colonel stood up too, but he acted like he didn't know hardly what to do. "What's going on?" Jim said, sharp-like.

I could see that Dannel had moved in closer. He'd been sitting there behind the colonel and his partners all the time. Now he got up and walked around beside the colonel. Fast, Johnnie Vann turned towards Dragging Canoe and talked to him. Dragging Canoe answered him back. Then Johnnie raised his voice and the words came clear to where we were standing. "He wants to talk," Johnnie was saying, "he does not want the signing yet."

The colonel looked at him, frowning. "They've already talked. It's all agreed. He is not one that has to sign."

Johnnie said something to the Indian and Dragging Canoe answered. Johnnie shrugged and looked around at Dannel and the colonel. "He says he has not talked. He has something he wants to say."

It made the colonel so mad he all but exploded. "Well, by the powers he can't say it! We are ready to sign."

Johnnie's voice carried up to us, mild but clear-spoken. "Best let him say it, Colonel."

The colonel looked over towards Dannel and Dannel nodded his head. We couldn't hear what he was saying, for Dannel's voice was ever low and soft, and by now the Indians were commencing to mutter, but it was plain to see he was agreeing with Johnnie. I was thinking myself the colonel had best trust Johnnie Vann and Dannel Boone right now and let the Indian talk. He might not be one of them to sign, but he was the Little Carpenter's boy and if they didn't let him talk it would be taken as a sign of disrespect and might cause considerable of a ruckus.

It seemed like a long time to wait. Nobody but Dannel and Johnnie Vann had moved, but I reckoned every white man there was as tight inside as me and Jim Knox were. All at once the colonel made a motion with his hand and walked over and sat down alongside his partners. Dragging Canoe took his place in front of the Indians, looked out over their heads for a minute, then he commenced talking.

The way he stood the river was at his back and behind him the mist and smoke was hanging over the water, thin and ghosty. It made a kind of wavery curtain behind him and he stood out against it like a clean-carved rock. It was like he had been drawn clear, with all the edges whittled fine. When he started talking his arms were folded across his chest and his voice was low and steady and singsongy. Johnnie Vann stood a little to one side of him, his head bent, listening. When the Indian stopped, Johnnie lifted his head and without looking anywhere in particular translated.

"My brothers," he said, "the Ani-Yunwiya, the real people, have possessed this land of the sunrise. Before memory our people possessed this land. Their bones have made white the war paths. Their bones have bleached in the burial mounds. Before memory the real people lived toward the sunrise. The real people, the Ani-Ketuwaghi, the people of Kitwuha. In peace they possessed the land and there was much for all and there was rejoicing.

"From the west came many. From the west they came saying, 'Let us go to the east; to the sunrise.' From the west came the Mengwe. From the west came the Lenape, and they were many, and they said, 'Let us go to the east,' and they desired the land of the Ani-Ketuwaghi. The Tsalaki, the real people, killed some of them, and all cried together, 'War, war!' Before memory they fought and they killed many, but those from the west were too great, and the real people left the bones of their ancestors and went into the mountains, toward the east, toward the waters.

"Then from the waters came the new men . . . the white men. From the sunrise they came and they said 'Peace, peace.' They cut down the trees. They drove out the game. They fenced in the land and they said, 'This land is ours, you cannot hunt here now.' The real people moved back from the waters and the men with white faces followed them. The real people said, 'We will hunt here.' The white men said, 'You may hunt there.' But again they built their lodges and again they built their fences and again they said, 'You cannot hunt here now, this land is ours.'

"They make words on paper and they say 'You may hunt there,' but they forget the words on the paper and soon they say, 'This land is ours. You cannot hunt here any more.' And they kill many with their guns. They come and they come and they come, like the waves of the waters, and the real people have been swallowed up by the waves. Now, here, in these mountains they say again, 'We want this land. We will pay you in goods, but you cannot hunt here any more.' "

The Indian's voice had kept rising as he talked and now the other Indians were all growling and muttering, swaying like a drum was beating and they were keeping time. Johnnie Vann kept on translating. He made it sound sad and lonesome and mournful, and the way he picked the words kept it sounding just like the Indian was saying it.

Dragging Canoe dropped his arms and he leaned forward suddenly and he spit the next words right into the faces of his brothers. "My brothers, if you put your names to this paper, what shall our children do? Where shall we hunt? How shall we feed our women and children? Where shall we go? This treaty may be all right for men too old to hunt or fight. As for me, I am a warrior. I would keep my lands! My brothers, are the Ani-Ketuwaghi to be told where they shall hunt? Are they to be bought with rum and goods? Are they the real people, or have they forgotten?"

He stood a little time after flinging that question at them, kind of bent towards them, his body as lean as a whip-stick and nearly as taut, then he threw one arm up high over his head and yelled straight at them, "Ani-Ketuwaghi! Have you forgotten?"

Seemed like the words rang out and echoed round and round and came bouncing up over the rocks to where we stood. Everything was quiet, only the echo of Dragging Canoe's words sounding. He stood there like a stone image for a minute, then he turned and stalked away, his back as straight as an arrow. The Indians all broke to their feet and took out after him, yelling and howling, and the whole council commenced to mill around with the settlers piling down towards the front and everybody mixing together and shouting and the colonel trying to shout everybody else down. But the Indians just kept on going, paying no heed to anyone, following Dragging Canoe back to their lodges.

The settlers milled around a little longer, watching them go, and then they clustered around the colonel. I took a good, big breath and I heard Jim let his go in a long gust like he'd been holding it overlong.

I reckon he figured, as I had, that it was touch and go there for a minute, and barely safe over now. I looked at him and he grinned. "Right smart of a speech, wasn't it?"

My throat was still dry, but I pulled out enough wind to say, "Right smart of one."

We shouldered our guns and started walking down the slope. At the gathering Jim went his own way, just turning back long enough to tell me, "Meet us at Martin's the middle of April."

I said I would and went on towards Dannel. I came up behind him. "What now, my friend?"

He turned and saw me. Dannel Boone was no great shakes to look at, being but middle-heighted and getting on in years now. He had a thin mouth and a nose that beaked some at the end, and his eyes were a kind of faded, friendly blue. He always wore his hair clubbed and his old buffalo-skin hat usually sat down on his ears. Easy come, easy go, was Dannel. Hard to rile, pleasant spoke and restless as my pap had been. The ways of the woods were Dannel's ways and a field of corn and a woman and young ones in no way hindered him from following after his own wants. He smiled at me, welcoming. "Howdy, Dave. Kind of a ruckus, ain't it?"

"Think they'll make trouble?"

"I misdoubt it." His tone was mild and untroubled. "They'll ease down."

"Dannel," I said, coming straight to the point, "I'm headed for Kentucky, but I ain't throwing in with the colonel."

Dannel looked at me, then he chuckled and put his hand on my shoulder. "Why, Dave, I reckon that's for you to decide, boy. I hope you well."

I hated to see him hired out to the colonel and I couldn't keep from blurting it out. "Go with us, Dannel . . . me and Jim Knox and Ben Logan. We're all of a kind. Go with us."

He rubbed his hands together. "Well, now, Dave, I tell you . . . the colonel's a good man. He aims to do right by the settlers, and we got to get settlements going out there. It's best for a man with money and backing to give it a push. . . ."

I wouldn't of quarreled with him for nothing in the world. I thought too much of him and he'd been too good to me, and I could see it was no use saying more. He was doing what he thought was best, just like I was. Misled though I thought he was, I knew he was honest in following the way he thought would help the most in settling the country. The colonel came over then, followed by a knot of men which had gathered around him. "Daniel," he said, "can we do anything?"

Dannel squinted at him. "If I was you sir," he said, "I'd spread a big feast. Spread it thick . . . and soon. And set out the goods again. Bring out a power of 'em. Show 'em off. Make 'em look big. But feed 'em first. Fill their bellies and don't say nothing till they're full to the craw."

"Do you think the situation can be saved?"

"I have no doubts of it."

One of the colonel's partners spoke up. "Why are you so certain, sir?"

Dannel looked at the man. "Why, they ain't got much to decide. Dragging Canoe knows as good as the rest of 'em they's little they can do but sign. They can either take the colonel up on his deal and get a little something out of the land, or else wait a few years and have it took away from 'em anyhow. They're smart enough to see that. They just had to act big one more time."

The colonel was impatient. "But this must all be legal, Daniel. It will be no good to us if they don't sign."

"They'll sign. They got sense enough to take what they can get."

Johnnie Vann made a stir then and commenced walking off. The colonel called after him, "We may need you again, sir."

"Not me. You'll not be needing me no more, Colonel. I ain't having no more to do with this treaty-making."

Charlie Robertson laughed. "What's the matter, Johnnie? Your Indian blood showing?"

Johnnie looked at him steady. "They's nary a drop of Indian blood in me, Charlie Robertson, and full well you know it. I'll have no part in this ruckus any further. I'll not be part nor parcel of it. Any way you look at it, it's a shabby deal. If the Cherokee have got title to the Kentucky lands, you're cheating them with your measly little dab of goods. If they've not, you're aiming on cheating the Virginia colony. I'm leaving."

The colonel sputtered like a pan of hot grease, but Johnnie didn't even look around. He just walked off. Dannel watched him go, and when Johnnie had reached the edge of the woods, Dannel turned to the colonel and said, "He is a man of strong feeling, sir, and much sympathy for the Indians."

"Did he translate that speech of Dragging Canoe's right?"

One of the traders spoke up. "He told it right."

"It was a mistake to let him talk. Now we'll be delayed for days perhaps."

"We'd best see about the feast, Colonel," Dannel said, and the whole bunch walked off together. I stood there a minute, watching the place where Johnnie Vann had gone into the woods. I figured the council meeting was going to be hung up for a spell now, longer than I cared to hang around, and I didn't see that it rightly made much difference to me how it turned out now, so I took off after Johnnie. It had come to me that Johnnie Vann knew more about the Ohio Indians than any man alive and it might do me a heap of good to have a little talk with him, especially since I was going to live neighbors to them.

❦

# CHAPTER

# 3

HE WAS LOADING HIS PACK when I caught up with him. "Mind if I go along?" I asked.

He didn't answer save to give a jerk of his head. I lent a hand with his trading pack and when it was tied on tight I went and got Beck and we left the Shoals and the council meeting behind us.

The rest of the day we rode along the Watauga, winding and twisting with it, and Johnnie kept his silence. At sundown we camped on a long, clean beach of sand where the river ran fast and shallow. We cooked and ate and then I stretched out on my back by the fire. The trees didn't quite meet overhead and there was a narrow band of sky left clear and open. I lay there and watched the stars come out, just one or two at first, and then hundreds till the whole narrow strip was full of them, seeded with them like a wheat field after planting time.

Johnnie sat hunched over on the other side of the fire, broody and still not talking. That was all right with me. I was never one to talk much myself and I liked the quiet. I just lay there, letting myself flow into the sand under me, the fire warm and sleepy-looking, and the March chill warded off by its burning. There were things I wanted to ask Johnnie Vann, but they could wait out his brooding.

Of a sudden he had something to say. "I reckon you're going out to Kentucky like all the rest." There was a dryness in his voice near to bitterness and it took me by surprise.

"I'd thought to," I told him.

"With the colonel?"

"Not now or in the next world!"

He grinned and stood up and stretched. He was a little man, lean and withered and drawn by rheumatism from his long travels in all kinds of weather. When he stretched he winced. His face looked like a dried apple, curled around the edges and spotted brown in places. Even his eyes had a dry look, like he'd seen too much ever to wet them again. "Why?" he said.

"Why what?"

"Why are you wanting to go to Kentucky?"

"I like it. It's a fine country . . . plenty of game and good land, room to take a deep breath."

Johnnie bent down and stirred the fire and the sparks cracked and flew out on the sand. I watched them snap and die out. He straightened up. "And how long, my friend, you think it will stay like that? How long you think there'll be plenty of game and timber and good land? There it lies . . . there it is . . . fair and lonesome as the day God made it . . . nothing living there but the beasts and the birds of the forest. It's the way nature made it . . . grand and sightly and lonely."

I waited for him to go on, but he didn't, and after a time I said, "Well, Johnnie, it may be grand and sightly and lonely, but it ain't doing much good to nobody thataway."

He threw me a scowly kind of look. "I reckon you think a land lying free is bound to be turned to some use."

The sand was getting hard under my back and I turned over on my side. "There's no stopping the settlers, Johnnie. Like Dragging Canoe said, they're like the waves of the waters. They'll roll on, with more coming behind 'em."

"And they'll ruin the country."

"How'll they ruin it?"

"They'll ruin it just by going there! Look at you! You said you wanted to make a stand in Kentucky on account of the timber was thick and tall, the land was good and wide, the game was plenty . . . you'll all go there in droves . . . you and Colonel Henderson's company, and Jim Harrod's company, and Dannel and Ben Logan and all the others. You'll all go there, and you'll cut down the trees and fence the lands and kill off the game, and more and more settlers'll come, and then there'll be settlements like in the east, and what you come for will be gone. You'll kill it yourselves. You'll take the death of what you want most with you when you go. Why don't you leave it alone? There's room aplenty here!"

I picked up a pebble. It was cool and rubbed slick and clean save for one horny edge where it had laid against the sand. I turned it round and round in my hand, picking at the rough edge, thinking over what he'd said. There was truth in it, to be sure. But it was true, too, nothing would stop us from going. All I could say finally was what I felt deep inside me to be back of the urging. "It's over the mountains, Johnnie, and folks have got to see what's there."

He rubbed his hand over his eyes. "Aye, that's ever the way. A new land, yon side another mountain, and a path is beat across the mountain, and the land grows old."

I flipped the pebble into the fire. Johnnie sat down and pulled his knees up inside his arms and rocked back and forth. After a time he said, "Dave, you ever wondered why none of the Indians live in Kentucky?"

"Heap of times. They hunt there and cross backwards and forwards all over it but don't none of 'em do more'n camp a few weeks at a time. In the whole time we was out there we never seen more'n a handful, and they was hunting same as us."

Johnnie was studying the fire. "You know why it's called the dark and bloody ground?"

"I've heared different reasons."

"Dragging Canoe was talking true in that speech he made today. Was a time all this land belonged to them. Whatever name they called theirselves, the Allegwi, the Ani-Ketuwaghi, the Tsalaki, it meant the same thing . . . the real people. We call 'em the Cherokee now. They weren't wanderers in those times. They lived in towns and they raised stock and crops, and they were smart, too. They had tools and things made of copper. They built their towns on big mounds, and they dug canals around them. They's some still over where the Ohio runs into the Mississippi . . . still there and you can tell how they laid out their towns."

"What happened to 'em?"

"What Dragging Canoe told. Two tribes from the west . . . the Mengwe . . . what's called the Iroquois now, and the Leni-Lenape, the Delawares . . . they come from the west somewheres, not together at first, but they run into one another when they got to the Mississippi. And they banded together and crossed over and fought the Allegwi. The way the Leni-Lenape tell it, they must of fought more'n a hundred years backwards and forwards, and they tell the Allegwi was giants in size. I misdoubt that. My opinion is they fought so hard to hold onto their land, and the fighting was so fierce and so bloody, times, their size got stretched to equal their bravery. But in the end the two tribes was too much for 'em and they were driven out, what was left of 'em. From a big, powerful nation they were killed off to a handful. They count twelve hundred warriors now, and you seen most of 'em at the Sycamore Shoals today. I reckon a land that was fought over for a hundred years, backwards and forwards, with enough blood spilled to wipe out a whole tribe nearly, could rightly be called a dark and bloody land."

"And that's why won't none of 'em live there? On account of it's kind of haunted?"

"Partly, and mostly. But they's more to the story. In time the Iroquois turned on the Leni-Lenape and conquered them too, and then they claimed the whole land belonged to them and they wouldn't let nobody live on it. Said it was the land where they was going to live 'tomorrow.'"

I thought maybe he'd not finished yet and I waited for him to go on, but he didn't. Just sat there and rocked backwards and forwards and studied the fire. It was burning low. I picked up a log and laid it on and chunked the coals up around it. "It don't go to me like it's always been us white folks pushing the redskins around, Johnnie. It looks a powerful lot like it's always been dog eat dog, and likely always will. We're just a new dog in the country."

I didn't mean it to sound cruel, but I don't know as anything is ever gained by blinking facts. Johnnie's story showed as plain as day the strongest wins out, pitiful though it was. I don't know as the world will ever change in that way. As little as I know about the way things came about in the beginning, it looks to me like the whole business of living has been one long and enduring battle, from men plumb on down to the littlest creatures in the woods. A man who's lived mostly in the woods knows full well the kind of tooth-and-fang struggle goes on there amongst the creatures all the time. But Johnnie's face had a kind of hopeless look on it when he spoke again. "I reckon," he said, "as long as they's two men left in the world, they're both like to want the same thing, and they'll battle for it and it'll go to the one that's the strongest."

I couldn't but say I saw it about the same way. It seemed like a good time to bring up what I'd had in mind all the time. "Johnnie," I said, "I'd like to know more about the Ohio Indians. I ain't fool enough to think a treaty with the Cherokee is going to be worth the paper it's signed on as far as the Shawnee and Wyandots and Mingos go. I figure they're the ones we're going to have the most trouble with."

He looked at me and squinted in the smoke the new log catching on was raising up. "My friend," he said, "why should I tell you anything about the northern Indians? They're my friends and I make my living amongst them."

"Because," I said, looking at him steady, "for all you deal with 'em and live amongst 'em mostly, you're white and I'm white, and I'm going to make a stand out there."

I'd not thought he would like to be so reminded, but I'd not expected him to be as displeased as he was. The look he gave me across the fire was as bitter as gall and came near to being full of hate. Without saying a word he stared at me, and then he turned on his heel and walked off into the night. Gone, I thought, to catch up his horses and ride away. Well. . . there was no help for it now.

I went down to the river and drank, went to see that Beck was easy for the night, then came on back to the fire and settled myself down to sleep. I had dozed off when I heard Johnnie coming back. He came straight on around to my side of the fire. He stood there looking down at me. "All right. You said it. For all I've lived amongst 'em and dealt with 'em, I'm white. You're bound to go, I reckon, and I'm bound to be on your side. Look." He picked up a stick and commenced to draw a rough map in the sand. "Here's the Ohio. Here's where the Scioto runs into it. Right there is a Shawnee town, and here's another one up at Chillicothe on the little Miami." He made quick strokes sprangling out for rivers and dug little holes in the sand for the towns. "Here's the Pickaway town over on the big Miami. Here are the Piankeshaws, over on the Wabash. The Wyandots are up here, on the Sandusky. The Delawares are over here betwixt the Hockhocking and the Scioto. They all move around some but that's mainly where they're settled. The ones who'll make trouble for you are the Shawnee, the Mingos and the Wyandots."

I studied the map. "What about the Delawares?"

He didn't say anything for a minute. His voice was kind of gruff when he spoke. "They're mostly friendly. They have to be stirred up to trouble."

"But they can be stirred up?"

He hesitated again. "Well . . . yes. If old Logan of the Mingos, or Cornstalk of the Shawnee, gets in behind 'em they can't do much else but take to the warpath too. Left alone, though, they'll mostly go their own way."

"They're still redskins, though, and to be taken into account," I said.

His mouth crimped at the corners. "The ones you've got to do the most worrying about are the ones I said. The Shawnee are troublemakers, secret and sly, and they've got an everlasting hatred of the whites. Right now Cornstalk's peaceful-minded, and his word goes a long way. But don't count on him being of the same mind long at a time. Of all of 'em, the Wyandots is the worst. If you ever come up against them, you'll have a mort of trouble, my friend. They're the only redskins I ever seen would fight as hard as a white man, and as long. Start giving the others a good licking and they'll quit. They'll thieve and they'll plunder and they'll pick off lone settlers and burn 'em out, but they can't abide a long fight. They get fearful when they commence losing men. The Wyandots are of a different cut. They'll lose ever' man in a war party ere they quit. They can last just as long as you can, and maybe longer. Never forget it. They won't cut and run."

I grinned. "If I run into a Wyandot war party, Johnnie, I'm like to cut and run myself."

"It wouldn't be a bad idea."

I have good reason to remember what Johnnie Vann said about the Wyandots that night, for years later it was the Wyandots gave us the worst licking the Kentuckians ever took, at the Blue Licks, when they outsmarted and outfought us and killed off most of our best men. But that was still eight years in the future, and that night on the Watauga there was no way of knowing it. I did know Johnnie Vann was telling me things would stand all of us, all those going into the country to stay, in good stead, and from the look on his face I knew he had been hard put to decide to do it. "I'm obliged to you," I told him.

He threw the stick down and rubbed his foot over the map he'd drawn in the sand. "If you ever name it to me again," he said, "I'm like to fill you full of lead."

He moved over to his pack and took a couple of buffalo skins out. He threw one to me. "I stir soon of a morning."

"Me too."

Each to one side of the fire we rolled into the skins and stretched out. The next thing I knew it was morning.

꧁≈꧂

# CHAPTER

# 4

I RODE WITH JOHNNIE as far as the Long Island of the Holston the next day. I had some skins cached there and on down the valley I wanted to pick up. Neither one of us did much talking. Johnnie was nipping right steady at a jug, but I reckoned he had to ease his mind some way. At the Island, still saying nothing, we parted company. Johnnie motioned his way towards the north, then he waved in a kind of large westerly direction, which I took to mean me good luck in Kentucky. He didn't say where he was going and I didn't ask. I just watched him tug at the lead of his pack animal and ride off. I didn't even wonder where he might be heading. A man follows his own bent and eats his heart out over his own miseries. Whatever Johnnie's were, I figured they belonged to him. I watched him out of sight and then I turned Beck south towards my cache of skins.

Time I got back to Charlie's with my skins a week later the council meeting had simmered down and they'd taken up where they'd left off when Dragging Canoe had upset things, but it was getting on towards the middle of the month before they got the chiefs to sign. I was pretty busy but I took time to go out and keep an eye on what was going on from time to time. I recollect the day they signed Dragging Canoe was looking on, bitter and glum, and when it was over he turned around and told Dannel, "Brother, we have given you a fair land, but I think you will have trouble keeping it." I made no doubt of it myself.

The colonel sent Dannel and his bunch of men on to cut the trail as soon as the signing was over, and him and the rest stayed on to pay off the Indians and to provision their party. Ten thousand pounds in goods sounds like a heap, and it looked like a heap piled up in six big wagons, but when it was given out to the Cherokee they came out with not much more than a shirt apiece. Reminded me of that fellow in the Bible sold his birthright for a mess of stew.

In less than a month I'd wound up my affairs, which, since I wasn't a family man, were few. I didn't say anything to anybody about my intentions, and if the folks in the Watauga settlements guessed, they were free to guess the way they would. I'd decided to take just one pack animal with me and I had to pick and choose what to take along. Even so it was going to be a right smart load. Mainly I had to have plenty of powder and lead, some axe heads and a couple of extra knives. Man could make himself a shelter and find his food with no more than that. Then there was seed corn. I was aiming to get me in a crop right straight. Ammunition and seed made a hefty load, but I tucked in a whetstone, some horseshoes and nails, some flints, and a little bar of iron for whatever use it might come in handy. I figured to pick up a poke of meal and some salt and maybe an extra pair of moccasins at Martin's.

So I was ready to go, and by first light one morning the second week in April I left out. It was cold and foggy. I left just like I'd left a hundred other mornings to go hunting. Just caught up the animals, loaded on my pack, got on Beck and rode off. Wasn't nobody but Charlie Robertson to say me farewell and I don't reckon you could call that much of a farewell. He stood there in the door of his place with his arms folded over his chest to keep warm, and all he said was, "Take keer of yourself."

Had it been handier I might of rode over to the Yadkin and said goodbye to a girl I'd been talking to over there, but it was too far off the trail and I thought too little of her, so I made out with Charlie. Rode away from the Watauga without looking back, to say it true, for all my thoughts were ahead.

I could of followed the trail in my sleep, it was that known to me. Up the Holston to the Moccasin Gap where the path hits the old Indian trail and from there Dannel and his party had been ahead of me. They'd widened and marked the way plain with fresh slashings. I was plumb dumbfounded, though, when I saw wagon tracks. There'd been some talk around the council meeting that the colonel had a wish to take wagons to Kentucky with him, but I'd not thought he'd be so foolish as to try. It looked like he aimed to, though, for they'd sure been over the road ahead of me. And in trouble, too, all the way. I misdoubted he'd get further than the Powell Valley with them, if that far, for there were places a horse was hard put to get over. And I was right.

The road followed Moccasin Creek up the valley, then over a range of hills to Troublesome Creek and up it to the Clinch, over another range of hills, down another valley, then up and over Powell Mountain and down into Powell Valley. The colonel's wagons had been strowed from the Clinch to the Powell, him having had to abandon four all told. I couldn't keep from laughing. That underslung jaw of his had showed him to be a stubborn man, but the trail to Kentucky was stubborner.

I came up to Martin's Station in the Powell Valley the evening of the fourth day. This was Joe Martin's place. It was little more than a clearing, squatting in the shadows of the high cliffs that barred the way to Kentucky, but it was the farthest west of any settlement. Joe had come here first in 1769, but he'd been driven out and had just come back to make a fresh try this spring. The place was still grown up and untidy looking, with but a small cluster of buildings, but he was making headway on getting it cleaned up. Joe's was the jumping-off place for the western country. Jim and Ben Logan hadn't yet got there, as I soon found out.

Joe fed me and gave me the news as I eat. He was powerfully excited by all the traveling past his place. "Dannel and his party come by the twelfth day of March," he told me, "but they never stayed but overnight. Hastened on the next day."

"Any word of 'em since?"

"They got there all right, but they run into a little trouble the last day before making Otter Creek. Redskins ambushed 'em and kilt one of 'em and hurt another one so bad he died a couple of days after. There has been several parties through here since, making tracks back to the settlements."

"Any of Dannel's men? Or the colonel's?"

"Well . . . no, not exactly. One of the colonel's partners quit on him, but that was whilst they was still here . . . before they got started. Hasn't been none come back through since they left out."

"Which one of the partners was it?"

"Fellow by the name of Hart. My opinion he wasn't skeered to go on . . . him and the colonel quarreled about something and he's going later on his own."

I laughed. "So they're quarreling amongst theirselves already."

Joe filled my noggin with ale again and I drank it down. "None of Dannel's has been by," Joe went on. "Mostly the ones passing had gone down the Ohio from upcountry. Said they had business back in the settlements."

"There'll be more than one has got business to tend back in the settlements if the redskins commence pestering out there," I said, laughing, and Joe joined in. He was an old hand at Indian trouble, so he knew as good as I did what it was like to feel lonesome and chickenhearted at the sight of the redskins. Wasn't nobody could say the truth but had felt the sweat pop out all over him when an owl or whippoorwill called untimely just before day, and wasn't nobody but the glimpse of a slithering, oiled body behind a tree didn't give the creeps. It would take some doing to stay it out in a country so far from neighbors with the redskins all about. But it had to be done if the country was ever to be settled.

I'd got through with my supper, so we took chairs over to the fire and I spread my hands out to the flames. "Any word of Jim Harrod?"

Joe poked the fire up. "He's there," he said, "with a right smart party . . . forty or fifty men all told, on Salt River where he made a start last year. They're commencing to work."

The heat of the fire loosened the chill in my hands and I could feel the blood limbering and warming my fingers. It felt good. Joe filled a pipe and lit it and I watched the smoke curl up around his head. Times like that I wished I liked a pipe myself. But it was too much bother the way I'd always lived on the trail, and too much danger. A man couldn't let himself get in a habit he couldn't do without. It was bad enough to be in the habit of eating sometimes. But all those I'd ever known that smoked seemed to take a mortal comfort in it. Joe did now, sitting there sucking on his pipestem, drawing in the warm smoke and blowing it out.

"When was it," I said, "the colonel come through here?"

"Not more'n ten days past. He come on ahead, but he had to wait here several days till his wagons caught up." He commenced chuckling.

"I seen what was left of a few of 'em on the road," I told him, joining in with his laughing. "Was he thinking he could actual take 'em all the way?"

"He was. And it takened considerable persuasion to talk him out of it. I reckon he figured Dannel was going to build him a toll road. He was right put out over having to leave 'em here and considerably flusterated over having to change his plans."

"I'd reckon he would be. From what I seen of him at the council meeting he struck me as a man used to running things to suit hisself. Who persuaded him?"

"You might say I had a hand in it, but the trouble they had getting this far convinced him a mite."

"Did he happen to name what his price for the land was going to be?"

"He did. Said he was aiming to get twenty shillings a hundred for it. You aiming to buy you a piece of Kentucky from him, Dave?" He grinned at me.

I grinned back. "Not so's you can tell it, I ain't."

"You going under the Virginia law?"

"I'm going under the Virginia law. The colonel may have got hisself a Cherokee title, but I figure the Virginia title is a little more powerful."

"It may be," Joe said.

I asked him then if Jim Knox had been around yet.

"No," he said, "I ain't seen hide nor hair of him."

"I'm traveling with him. I'll wait here till he shows up."

"Wait and welcome, Dave. Sleep you in the shed or here by the fire. Just suit yourself."

I told him the shed would do and I stood up ready to seek it out, for a full stomach and the heat of the fire was making me sleepy. The door to the back room opened just then, though, and a girl came in. She went over to the table where I'd eat and commenced to stack up the empty bowls and platters. I watched her. I'd never seen her before, but of course Joe hadn't been back in the valley very long and I hadn't been over this way in a time and a time. I always did fancy a redheaded girl, though, and this one had hair the color of a new-turned penny. It hung down her back nearly to her waist in big, fat curls that made a man want to reach out his hand and get hold of one and give it a tug. It wouldn't stay under her cap at the sides and front, either, but flew about her face in what some folks would of thought was an untidy way, but I liked it. It made a kind of frame for her face. She was rounded out without being fat, and when she leaned over the table to pick up the dishes she bent easy and graceful, like a willow sprout curving towards the water. Lordy, but she had a waist would fit snug into a man's arm!

She didn't say a word whilst she was in the room . . . just gathered up the dishes and went out. "You got you a new bound girl to help your wife?" I asked Joe, knowing he had no girls of his own.

He was covering the fire for the night and he didn't look up. "No. That's my sister's girl. Just staying with us a spell."

I wished there was some way I could ask her name, but it came awkward to me so I left it off. I figured if Jim happened to be a day or two late I could make my own chances to find it out. I said my good-night to Joe and went on out to the shed.

It didn't work out much like I thought it would, though. I had little to do the next day. Beck had cast a shoe on her right forefoot and I put a new one on. I got meal and salt from Joe and packed it away, and then I was through. But I kept on hanging around the house. Joe's house had four rooms, two in front, one on each side the dogtrot, and two in back. One of the back rooms was the cookhouse. It appeared like she was keeping herself there, for I could hear her talking and laughing with Joe's woman once in a while. When the day had more than half gone and I'd not had a chance to talk to her, I thought me up a little scheme. I got my gun and took a little sashay out into the nearby woods and killed a mess of squirrels, then I took them around to the cookhouse. She came to the door all right when I called, which was what I'd hoped she'd do. "I've got a mess of squirrels here," I told her.

She held out her hand, but I didn't give them over. "I'd be proud to skin 'em for you," I said. My intentions were for her to help and maybe I could make a little headway while we were skinning the squirrels.

But she just kind of nodded her head. "There's the bench," she said, and she turned around and shut the door in my face, leaving me standing there. With ten squirrels to skin. I'd got a good look at her though, and she was fairer than I'd thought. She had white skin with little blue veins showing through at the temples, and there was a sprinkling of freckles across her nose. Her eyes were brown, which went queer with red hair . . . a kind of light brown, like leaf-rust water in a shallow pool, and her teeth were even and white, not yellowed from snuff and rotted like most women's. There was a nice smell about her, too, like she was just fresh-washed and her clothes new-ironed . . . a kind of starchy, soapy smell that put me in mind of the way my mam used to smell when I was a youngun and used to run and hide my head in her lap. I felt kind of mortified to be stood off so neat, for girls mostly took to me, but then, I thought to myself, it showed she wasn't trifling and loose in her ways, taking up with every buckskin shirt passing by.

When I'd finished with the squirrels I left them on the bench and ambled on around the corner of the house. Joe was sitting there with his chair leant up against the wall, taking in the late sun. I hitched me up a chair and sat down alongside. The sun set early here in the valley on account of the west mountains, leaving a shortened day with a long twilight even this soon in the year. There wasn't much heat left in it, but it felt good, shining straight on my face. "Your sister's girl ain't very conversational, is she?" I said to Joe.

"I ain't never noticed," he said. "Reckon she's conversational enough when the notion strikes her. Never seen a woman yet that wasn't."

"I just takened her a mess of squirrels and she didn't hardly more'n say much obliged."

He laughed. "Oh, Bethia's always a mite awkward with strangers. Gets to know you, she can talk as good as ary other woman."

Bethia. Now I knew her name. I said it over a time or two to myself. I'd not ever heard such a name before, but I liked it. It sounded like a good, sensible name, such as a good, sensible girl ought to wear. Bethia. It went kind of easy, too.

"Don't reckon you seen ary sign around?" Joe said in a minute.

"None," I told him. "It's not likely you'll be pestered for a spell."

"No. Pays to keep cautious, though."

I agreed. The Cherokee weren't likely to commence troubling for several months after the colonel's council meeting, but Joe's place was far enough west the Shawnee might take a little sashay over his way any time.

We both heard the sound of horses at the same time. "That goes like a right smart party," Joe said, getting up.

I stood up, too, and we went around the corner of the house to see. A sizable bunch of men were riding up towards the house.

"Heading for Kentucky, I'll bound," Joe said.

I saw Jim and Ben Logan amongst them straight off, but I'd never seen any of the others. They were total strangers to me, and I reckoned there must be at least thirty in the bunch. They rode on up to the house and commenced getting off. Jim waved at me and then him and Ben and one of the others walked over to where Joe and me were standing. "Howdy," Jim said, and then he made us acquainted with the stranger. His name was not strange, though, when Jim named it, for everybody had heard tell of Cap'n Floyd who had any knowledge of Kentucky. He was a surveyor for the Virginia colony, and it was him had done most of the surveying for the colony in the western country. "He's heading for Kentucky again," Jim said, "and me and Ben thought it might be a good idea to travel with him and his men. Part of this party is surveyors, under orders to Cap'n Floyd, and the rest is adventurers aiming to settle in the country. Seems like Dannel stirred up a little hornet's nest out there and it might not be too safe for a few to be on the trail by theirselves."

"Might not be," I said. "Howdy, sir."

Cap'n Floyd bent over a mite at the waist. "Your servant, sir."
He was dressed like all other men dressed in this country, in buckskins and moccasins, but he was elegant even in buckskins. He spoke
pleasing and quiet-like and he was, I thought, just about the prettiest
man I'd ever seen. Not to say pretty the way a woman is pretty, but
almost. He was tall and slim and limber-looking. One time I saw a
sword that looked slim and limber like that, and held it in my hands
and bent it. The steel gave but when I let it go it sprung back straight,
twanging with its temper. Cap'n Floyd put me in mind of that sword.
It was plain to see he was a man of education and manners. He acted
like he was used to being waited on and looked up to, but in a nice
kind of way, just taking it for granted he would be served. I've heard
that folks that's always had servants take on that manner.

"You recollect," Jim went on saying, "me and him surveyed together in Kentucky last year."

I'd forgot but I remembered it when Jim called it to mind. Then
Jim and the cap'n commenced talking to Joe about putting up the
party for the night and I spoke to Ben. I'd not seen him in a time. He
was a man about the same height as me, one of the few men I could
look at level in the eyes, and we were built a lot alike. We both had
shoulders so wide it took one more skin than common to make us a
shirt, and we both were waspy in the middle and had long-boned legs.
Ben, though, was a heap handsomer man than I ever hope to be.
You'd never of called him pretty, for it wasn't that kind of hand-
someness. It was more a kind of strongness in his face. He had eyes
that were blue, like deep water, and they held steady when they fixed
on you, and his mouth was full and curvy, gentle-looking, but I guessed
that in a pinch it could firm up as thin as my own. Like I said, I
didn't know him too good, but all I'd ever heard of him was to his
credit. He was counted a good woodsman. Wasn't any man ever
amounted to anything in this country but had to be, naturally, but he
was held to be better than most. In a fight he was said to be a power,
strong and coolheaded. He'd always done his part in the Indian fighting, and he'd come out of Dunmore's War with a captain's rank.

"So you're aiming on trying your hand in Kentucky, too," I said to
him.

"Well," he said, "I've heared so much about it I thought it wouldn't
hurt none to take a look at it myself. Don't know as I'll settle there,
for I've a good place already, but a man is always wanting to better
hisself, I reckon, and if it's as rich as Jim says it is, seems like it would
be a betterment."

"Jim's not led you astray," I told him. "Once you've saw it, you'll be staying."

Behind us we could hear Cap'n Floyd talking to Joe and we turned around to listen. "We understand we are traveling just behind Colonel Henderson, sir. We are eager to have news of him."

"Well," Joe said, "they's not been no news of him saving word he sent back by a feller going home to the settlements after Dannel's little fracas. The colonel said he was making haste to get to Otter Creek as fast as he could."

Jim laughed. "He's game, all right. He ain't turning back at the first Indian skeer."

Cap'n Floyd spoke up politely. "He has too much invested in this venture to turn back."

We went inside then, the rest of the men going around back with the horses. The smell of food cooking was heavy in the big room and a haunch of deer meat was roasting on a spit in the fireplace. The womenfolks used the fireplace in this room for cooking as much as the one in the cookroom. The redheaded girl, Bethia, was tending the meat, and her face was hot and red from the fire. When she bent over to ladle the melted fat over the roast her skirts were hoisted in back so that her stocking showed past the calf of her leg, and beyond that you could see the white underskin of her knee. She sure had a shapely leg. She had a shapely figure, too, bosomy and curvy . . . the kind that made a man's hands want to stray. Mine, leastways. They fair itched.

She looked up when we came through the door and hastened to spoon the last of the drippings over the meat and scurry out the back. I watched her skirts swish out of sight and then I followed the others over to the long table.

Joe brought hot rum and we all drank. His woman brought food and we set to with good appetites. Not until we'd done and all set back and Joe and Cap'n Floyd had filled their pipes did the talk commence. Hungry men don't mix food and talk, but once we'd eat the talk flowed fast for the happenings of the spring were uncommon and made a teasing kind of subject. We talked mostly about Colonel Henderson's venture at first, and whether he had a chance to make a go of it.

When we asked Cap'n Floyd he just shook his head over it. "I would not venture an opinion. It's too soon to know. There is good likelihood of some mixing up of titles, I'd think, however. We have been surveying for certain Virginia gentlemen under the law of the province, but if Colonel Henderson's title is valid, I should think all land would have to be purchased through him." He shook his head again. "It is going to be most confusing to say the least."

"It may be for some," Jim said, "for there's them that has already takened their stand and are proving their lands right now . . . like Jim Harrod and the McAfees and others. I don't reckon they'll be overly anxious to pay the colonel twenty shillings a hundred for their land when they're already entitled to four hundred acres apiece. Far as I'm concerned it ain't confusing at all. I just don't aim to throw in with the colonel."

Ben Logan nodded. "I'd ruther take my chances on my own hook, too."

I had my say, then. "That's my opinion, too. I don't aim to be beholden to the colonel neither. I figure I can do my own settling and abide by the provisions of the Virginia law. Looks to me like the colonel is aiming to set up a colony of his own over in Kentucky."

The cap'n sucked on his pipe. "Well . . . you may all be making a wise decision. And then again you may lose out. Only time can tell."

"A man don't get nowhere," I said, "without taking a chance, and I'd ruther take mine without no Colonel Henderson mixed in with it."

The talk turned to Indian troubles, then, and speculations as to how much bother they'd give in Kentucky, especially this year. News coming back over the trail was given out by Joe, and as always when a bunch got together those days the talk turned finally on the rich land, the great forests, the game in such plenty and the fine streams of Kentucky. As ones who had spent the most time there, Jim and me told tales of our adventures, stretching them as men will to fit the telling.

"I mind the time," Jim said, chuckling, "we'd been out there nigh on to two years and was hunting in the Green River country. It was the best season we'd had and we'd got a mort of skins. More'n we could take keer of. We built us a skin house on a little creek along there and cached them away and then we went out on a little sashay for upwards of a couple of months. When we come back to get the skins, by grannies the Indians had tore the camp down and made a ruin of the whole place! Even the dogs we'd left to stay by the stuff was gone wild. Hit was plumb disappointing, I can tell you."

"What did you do?" the cap'n asked.

"Wasn't nothing to do but give 'em over as lost and come on back home."

"Tell what Skaggs did," I put in.

"Why, he was so damned put out and riled up he walked over to a tree and got out his knife and he cut big letters in the bark of the tree, best I can recollect, '2300 skins lost, ruination, by God!' "

Cap'n Floyd was laughing. "Well, I'd agree that twenty-three hundred skins lost would come pretty close to ruination."

"It did, at that."

Just recalling those times and talking about them made me itchy to be on the way. I stood up and stretched till I could touch one of the rafter beams. Seemed like I couldn't hardly hold myself and of a sudden I grabbed the beam tight and swung up high and skinned my legs between my arms. I had to be doing something to let off steam. The others commenced laughing. "He ain't full-grown, yet," Jim said, "still likes to skin the cat like a youngun."

I was hanging there, head down and dizzy from the rush of blood, when I got a glimpse of a skirt going past the door. It looked a heap like Bethia's starchy one. Then I heard the back door slam. I thought to myself she'd gone outside, and hasty I finished skinning the cat and picked up my hat from the floor. "Well," I said, "I reckon I'd best be getting some sleep. Be leaving soon in the morning, will we?"

"Break of day," Jim said.

"I'll be ready," I said, and I went on outside.

I turned around the house and circled into the fenced lot at the back. Little by little my eyes got used to the dark and I looked good, but there wasn't a trace of a swishy, starched skirt. I wandered around the house, too, but she wasn't there, so I figured she'd just ducked out and back, quick. I gave it up and headed for the shed.

There was a gate betwixt the lot and the shed and I fair stumbled into the girl before I saw her, she was standing so still and quiet. It scared her when I bumped into her, I could tell, for I heard her get her breath quick-like, and then she turned around and started to run away. I grabbed her by the arm and stopped her. It shames me to remember it now, the way I treated her, but I had ever been bold and daring with girls, and like I said, mostly they liked it and took to me. I had no reason to think she would be any different, so I pulled her back towards me and slid my arm around her waist. "Ain't you afeared," I said, "you'll ketch cold out in the night air thisaway? Leave me warm you a little," and I put my other arm around her.

She was stronger than I'd thought and she commenced turning and twisting to get free. "Let be," she said, kind of fierce-like.

I just laughed at her. "Oh, no," I said, making a band of my arms and holding her tighter, "not till I've had a kiss for barter."

She didn't waste no more breath on words, saving it all for struggle, but she was like a kitten trying to get loose from me, for I had strength and to spare to hold her. "Give over," I told her, "what's a kiss or two?" Then I pulled her up close and hard next to me and held her with one arm while I turned her head so's I could find her mouth. It was warm and full when I touched it, but she had turned to a block of stone, unyielding and ungiving, and the kiss was like wine gone flat. It surprised me, and then it made me mad, for that was not the way I was used to kissing. By grannies, I said to myself, she'll kiss me right or strangle, and I kissed her again, holding it long and hard. Of a sudden she quit her struggling and went kind of limp, and her mouth was soft and quiet under my own. I thought she'd given up, and what with being kind of dizzy and out of breath from the kiss myself, I let up on my hold of her. Quick as a flash she twisted loose, catlike, and drew back before I could move and slapped me hard on the mouth with the back of her hand. Her knuckles slammed against my teeth and cut clean through my lip. The suddenness of it and the pain brought the water to my eyes and I jerked my head up. She broke free then and slapped me again, this time on the cheek, and she wasn't fooling. The palm of her hand hit my face like a whip cracking and fair made my ears ring. Before I could think to do a thing she was gone, and gone so fast her skirts made a breeze in their passing.

I just stood there, dazed and shaking my head to clear it. My cheek stung and I felt of it, easy. I run my hand over it and it was like all her fingers had left their print there, and they were rising up in whelps. By grannies, I thought, that wench can wallop as good as a man! Then my mouth felt full of salty sweet stuff and I knew it was blood and I spit. I touched my tongue to my lip and it was ragged and split. I commenced getting mad. By grannies, I thought, I'd ort to have just carried the little wildcat out to the haymow! But then I couldn't help laughing. She'd sure put one over on me. That one had fire, now. Wouldn't nobody ever get the best of her. She didn't have that red hair for nothing! She'd given me just what I deserved, making free with her the way I'd done. Still, how was a man to know the difference between them that would and them that wouldn't unless he tried. She was one that wouldn't, no doubts about it, and deep down inside me I was glad she was. Right then and there I made up my mind that one way or another I was going to get to know her better, and maybe in time she'd let me court her proper.

I felt of my mouth again. It was already swelling. Likely, I thought, I'll carry the scar of that backhanded lick to the end of my days. I'm right, so far.

# CHAPTER
# 5

MY LIP WAS A SIGHT to see the next morning, all swelled up over my face and as sore as a boil when I touched it. I couldn't help wondering if a man's own tooth could poison him. My face sure felt like it was all mouth. That backhanded wallop of the girl's had might nigh run it plumb down my throat. I would ruther not of appeared in public right then, but there was no way out of it, so I put on a bold front and went over to the house for breakfast. The others were just drawing up to the table when I showed up. Jim was letting himself down into his chair when he looked up at me and spoke, and then seeing my mouth pushed out like a shelf over my chin, his own mouth hung open and he dropped the rest of the way with a thud. "My God, Dave, you been tangling with a catamount?"

I could feel my face turning hot, and likely reddening, but I hitched me up a chair, careless as I could, and heaped my plate. "I fell over that damn woodpile of Joe's in the dark last night," I said, "and landed on a stob. Been a mite closer it would of rammed clean down my throat. You'd ort to be more careful where you leave them stakes when you rick up your wood, Joe. Somebody's liable to kill theirselves, and then you'd have it on your conscience how careless you'd been."

Joe looked at me kind of queer-like over the steam from the hot food, then he just went "humph" and commenced eating. Reckon he knew as good as I did there wasn't no stob out back, but he wouldn't give me away. The others all gave my mouth a good look and the talk turned to the odd ways a man could hurt himself when he wasn't thinking. But it was soon forgot, for we had to eat and hurry. Except Joe kept looking at me, funny and queer, and it made me feel ashamed.

I figured he knew I'd been fooling around Bethia and it was her had given me the cut lip. The girl was his own sister's . . . he'd told me so, and I hadn't ought to treated her lightly. I didn't see any way to mend it, though, so I just kept on eating and let it go.

It was Bethia served us, but she paid no heed to me at all. Far as I could tell she never even looked to see what she'd done to me. Just went on about her serving, never resting her eyes on me. Out of the corner of my eye I could see her bending and stooping over the fire, her red hair falling thick about her shoulders and tumbling across her face when she bent. When she straightened it was like a young sapling rising up again, green and slim and tender. I couldn't keep from looking at her mouth, and I couldn't help remembering how soft and warm it had felt, and I couldn't help, either, being glad I had the remembrance of it.

She didn't to say go to the trouble to avoid me. She served me as good as she did the others. She just paid me no mind. I might as well of been a horse for all the notice she took. I made me a vow right then. All right, I thought to myself, all right, Miss Redhead. The day'll come when I kiss you and you'll like it. You just wait and see. Be just as proud as you want now, for I like it in you. But pride's got no place in love, and I aim to make you love me before we're through. I ain't ashamed of making that vow, for I meant it in the right way.

The packs had been made ready and the animals loaded before we eat, so when we'd done the men strung out for the start. The sun was not yet up, but it had lightened the sky with a pink glister in the east. As always of an early morning, the mist floated in the low places of the valley, and the way the pink light showed through the mist reminded me of the inside of an oyster shell, kind of purply blue around the edges and pinky white inside. I've always liked the early morning, with the sun coming up slow and the night chill still lingering. Everything has got a new-born feeling, like the world was starting fresh, and it always gives me the feeling of starting fresh with it.

I swung up on Beck and took a look down the string of pack animals. Jim and Ben Logan were already up, waiting. Cap'n Floyd was saying some last-minute words to Joe. I looked at Ben. He was sitting there, ready, but with no sign of eagerness or hurry in him. Patient, steady, like a rock, and as solid. Jim's horse was dancing around, nervy and restless, and I knew Jim was feeling the same inside. Good as I liked Jim Knox I knew him to have a kind of fretfulness in him that disliked slowness and waiting. He liked to keep moving and stirring and he could never hide it. His horse felt it now. Me, I was nervy inside too, but it didn't show I reckon. I could always appear to be steady even when my whole body was aquiver.

I looked over towards the mountains. That's where we were heading. Over the mountains. Like a dog sniffing the trail I looked at them, and was eager to be off. The trail went there, through the heart of the mountains, through the Cumberland Gap and down into Kentucky. Seemed like I could feel it and taste it and smell it. Like it was already in my hands I could feel the rich grain of the whole country, the blood of it and the bones of it. It was a land that had been hard held and would always be hard held. It was not a land to be bought and sold, like the colonel wanted. It was a land to be sweated for and bled for and maybe died for. Unthinking I pulled my shoulders up like I was already facing whatever it asked.

"There's the signal," Jim said, and when I looked Cap'n Floyd had mounted and had lifted his arm to us in the lead. I turned around again and as I turned I ran my eye over the cluster of buildings we were leaving. Joe stood out front and I waved to him. He waved back. Then I caught the movement of a skirt at the corner of the house. I wasn't hardly sure, for it was just the edge of her dress showing, but while I looked the red head peered around the corner. She looked down the whole long line of men and horses and when her eyes finally found me I grinned. She'd not been so indifferent after all, then, I thought. I started to wave, but she saw she'd been noticed and cut back around the corner. Ben's voice chipped in, quiet and too low for Jim to hear. "I was wondering if you'd see her."

I looked at him. His eyes were twinkling and his mouth had a quirk at the corner. He was a heap more noticing than I'd thought him to be. I grinned. "I ain't likely to forget that one soon."

"So I thought."

"Let's move," Jim said, and he kicked his horse and strung out ahead. I fell in and moved up alongside. We were started. Come what may, now, we were started. Ahead of us were the mountains, the Gap, the wilderness, the rivers and meadows and forests, the land, the redskins, all of it, known and unknown, and it was all fine and all good. Like a river, flood-loose and swelling, running full and heavy, the thought of it ran all through me. It was all fine and good. I was heading for Kentucky and a red-haired girl had looked goodbye at me.

We traveled fast that first day. Except to the new men in Cap'n Floyd's party, the trail was familiar. From here to the Gap and some beyond, it had always been used by the Indians and Dannel had had to do little chopping or widening. It was well beat down, free of brush

and undergrowth, and to us Holston men was a good road. The ways
of traveling the trail were known to us too. We were old hands at
packing tight and light and at ever taking care that the animals didn't
break loose and head into the woods, drag their packs and break them
open and scare the others into bolting. I knew this was the easiest
part of the journey, though. There'd be fords to make across the
streams, and there'd be loads getting wet and lost in the currents.
There'd be the packs of the new men that hadn't been well made and
they'd gall the horses' backs. We'd all have tired bones and flesh and
muscles ere long. There'd be the sameness of riding, broke only by the
need of forever having to take care. There'd be rain and cold yet, and
wet camps and sleeps, and there might be, likely would be, an Indian
scare or two. It was all part of what most of us had been used to, more
or less, all our lives, though. No need borrowing a bit of the weariness
or wetness or even the fear that would choke up in your throat and
strangle when the Indians came. Time enough to deal with those
things when they happened. Now it was good enough to ride easy
and fast the twenty-odd miles to the Gap, and to camp there come
night, feeling fine over the day's distance.

The next day we crossed the mountain through the Gap. The
trail wound upwards, steep in places, slight in others, and while we
made slow time on account of having to walk to save the animals, we
plugged along steady. The path passed right under the overhang of the
big white cliffs in places, and I had a feeling of their weight and their
oldness on my shoulders. When I looked up at them I thought of
how the Indians spoke of old things . . . beyond memory. These cliffs,
I reckoned, went beyond memory. Beyond the memory of any living
thing, likely. They'd been there a time and a time and would be there
when all that was left of me was bare bones. I never liked that pass
through the mountains. It was a gloomy place and it always gave me a
shivery feeling that what the Indians said of the land beyond being
dark and bloody was true. It was like that pass had been set there to
forbid the coming of men. I'd felt it, going to Kentucky before, and
had been glad to leave it behind. I felt it again, now, and was just as
glad when we came out on top and could look down the other side.

One of the new men pulled up beside me. "That Kentucky?"

"That's Kentucky."

The man snorted. "Don't look none too promising to me."

"Wait," I told him. "That's but the beginning."

"It had better be."

About four miles yon side the Gap we met a party of some fifteen
men heading back to the settlements. They were hurrying fearfully

and their fright showed in their faces. They stopped just long enough to pass on their news. "The Indians are rampaging," they said. "There's no telling how many of 'em has took to the warpath. You'd best turn back now!"

I made sure Dannel and the colonel and maybe Jim Harrod had all been wiped out. Cap'n Floyd listened. "Has there been fresh trouble since Boone's party was attacked?"

"No, but they's sign all around. Ever' day a body comes on new sign. It ain't safe, I tell you."

"Is Jim Harrod still at his improvement? Are Boone and Colonel Henderson at Otter Creek?"

"Yes," they said, "but they ain't enough to stand them redskins off, and they ain't no settlements for protection."

"There never will be settlements if everyone is afraid to try it," the cap'n said.

But they paid him no heed. "Not me," they kept on saying. "I'll not risk it."

The fellow guiding them was an old graybeard with one good eye, and it squinted, and a tight-buttoned mouth. I made a chance to talk to him. "They just got chickenhearted?" I asked him.

"Just got chickenhearted," he said. "Ain't been but the one skeer."

"They right about fresh sign?"

"They's always fresh sign in Indian country in the spring and summer. No more'n usual, I'd say. They ain't pestered none to speak of."

"How come you're going back?"

"I'm getting paid for it." The old man winked his good eye. "You know ary better reason?"

I laughed. "I reckon not. You'll be back, likely."

"Soon as I get this passel of fools safe to the settlements. I got a clearing close to Boone's I got to tend."

They pushed on, looking back over their shoulders like the redskins were hot on their heels, and I wheeled Beck around and caught up with my own party. The talk of the settlers' fears was running through the new men like wind over a field of barley. But it wasn't till we camped that night in the Yellow Creek bottoms that we found out two of them had got cold feet and turned back with the other party. The cap'n didn't act put out about it. All he said was, "It's their own business. If men haven't the courage to take their chances it's best for them to turn back."

We made a cold camp that night. From Yellow Creek on they'd all be cold, for while no Indians made their home in Kentucky, from all sides, north, south, east and west, they hunted over it and traipsed across it. It was never to be taken for granted there weren't redskins about, for they hunted sometimes during the coldest spells of the winter, and come spring they were liable to commence fighting one another and big war parties would take to the trail. The country was crisscrossed with their paths, and one, on account of it being used so constant, angling to the north and east, was called the Warrior's Trail. We were camped not too far from it that night.

Myself, I didn't look for any big trouble. There were too many of us traveling together for a little band to attack, and while there was always the chance of running into a sizable war party, it wasn't so likely as to be much feared. What we had to keep watch for mostly was four or five Indians out hunting that might run onto us and steal some of the horses. There was no use drawing them to us with the light of a fire, so from here on we'd eat and sleep cold.

But the orders to build no fires, the telling off of guards to keep watch, the fear of the party we'd met that day and the way both Jim and Cap'n Floyd cautioned everybody about their animals made the new men pretty nervy. As the dark settled down they huddled around together and kept looking over their shoulders into the bushes. It wasn't cowardly of them. Matter of fact I reckon most of them were stouthearted enough, but they came from the settled parts of Virginia and Carolina and Indian fighting was kind of new to them. We were through the Gap now, and every day was going to take us further and further from the settlements and help if we needed it. I knew how they were feeling, for I'd felt the same many a time . . . shaky and shivery and fearful.

Jim and Ben and me threw our packs down together and after we'd seen to the hoppling of our animals me and Jim talked of it together, and we went around amongst the new ones and tried to hearten them. "There's no call," we told them, "to be scared. It's but common sense, though, to take care. Them that takes care usually has little to regret, for they're ready. We're in country the redskins pass over and it's but to be expected we could have a little brush with 'em. We don't look for it, but it could be and we'd best be ready."

They took heart from what we said, knowing we were old hands and not talking idle. They stirred about, taking off their packs and hoppling out their own animals. The way things were in the party, every man was held responsible for his own riding horse and pack animal, if he had one, save amongst the surveyors. Cap'n Floyd was the leader of them and they came under his care.

Jim went off to talk with Cap'n Floyd then and I went on back to my own pack. Ben was hunkered down by his pack, mending a broken bridle. I got out some meat and a chunk of bread left from the day before and commenced making out my supper. Ben kept on at his work steady, boring his awl deep through the leather and pulling the whang tight. He was a quiet-turned man, hardly ever speaking unless spoken to, and then giving no more than an answer. Didn't seem like he ever talked just to be talking, and I liked that in him. But talk didn't fret him any, for he'd always listen. "They're some nervy tonight," I told him, nodding towards the new men.

He looked over that way and then bored his awl through the leather again. "It's a mite unsettling," he said.

"You ain't never been in these parts before either, have you?" I asked.

"No," he said, pulling the thong tight and looping it and knotting it, then cutting it with his knife, "but I don't figure Indian trouble in Kentucky will be any different from Indian trouble anywheres else. I been mixed up in Indian trouble most of my life."

I went on eating till I was through, then I closed up my food bag and tied it. "Way I see it," I said, "is that any person with a itchy foot and bound to settle in Indian country stands to risk losing his hair. I'm like to lose mine, you're like to lose your'n, but no need worrying about it ahead of time."

Ben put his awl and the leftover piece of whang back in his pack. "The ones that's steady enough will simmer down after a time, and the ones that ain't will give it up. It's a natural kind of weeding out the good from the bad." He stood up and took his gun from alongside his pack. "I got the first guard down this end. Best be settling down to it, I reckon." And he walked off in the dark. That was the most I'd ever heard him talk at one time.

The next day we traveled down Yellow Creek following an old buffalo trail. It was heavy-trampled and was a good, wide road, but the cane grew thick and wild on both sides. The cane stalks were green, thick as a man's thumb, jointed, with little slim leaves like willows branching off at the upper joints. They grew six to eight feet tall and as we rode along the wind blew through their tops in slow waves, like the sea pushing up slow rollers on the sand. They rubbed together and even sounded like the sea, kind of sighing and licking and whispering. The cane was so thick you couldn't see farther than five or six foot through it. I was riding alongside of Ben and he looked around at the thicket curious-like. "Ain't no place to do any Indian fighting," he said.

"Worst in the world," I told him, "and awful easy to get lost in

yourself." I reached out and cut off a stalk of cane and handed it to
him. "Mighty good feed for animals though."

He looked at it. Cane is hollow, and it's tough and pithy, but it
runs juicy and we'd found out what good feed it was when we'd been
in the country before. Ben ran his thumb over the sharp cut, watched
the juice ooze, then dropped the stalk on the ground. "Looks like
good fodder. Grow everywheres in the country?"

"In all parts, far as I know, but mostly in the bottoms close by the
streams."

He nodded his head, like he'd heard good news.

We came to the Cumberland late in the evening. It was in flood,
flowing swift and deep and over its banks in places. Jim shook his
head when he saw it, and him and Cap'n Floyd went down to take a
look at the ford. When they came back the cap'n said we'd camp on
the near bank for we'd have to raft the provisions over and it would be
best to wait till morning.

I had the first watch that night and when I called Jim at midnight
everything was quiet. I turned in and went straight off to sleep, not
knowing another thing till Jim woke me towards morning, shaking
my shoulder and whispering, "Dave, get up. Something's skeering the
animals."

I came awake and on my feet at the same time. We'd hoppled the
horses back from the river a piece in a kind of meadowy place where
they could feed. The cane grew right up to the edge of the meadow on
yon side of it, but the horses couldn't more than browse along the
rim of it on account of being hoppled. "You call any of the others?"
I asked Jim.

"Cap'n Floyd and Ben," he said, "they're coming now."

When they came up the four of us divided and commenced angling
around the bunch of horses. Jim and the cap'n took the down side
nearest the river and me and Ben started making our way along the
outside. The horses were bunched together, like they will when something frights them, and in a kind of ring towards the middle of the
meadow. They were restless, stomping their feet and blowing and
snorting every now and then. It wasn't good day yet but there was
light enough to see. Ben and me crept along without saying anything.
Wasn't any use talking. Horses will scare like that in the night for a
number of reasons. Something wild, like a bear or a fox, sniffing
around will cause them to take alarm, but so will a redskin. My bet was
it was redskins, for riding all day through the cane like we'd done had
given them an awful good chance to watch us without our knowing

they were within a hundred miles of us, and a bunch of horses the size of ours was mighty tempting.

We'd got about halfway round the circle when the animals milled together all of a sudden and started trying to run, which they couldn't on account of their hopplings, and there was a high, scared whinny from yon side. It was Beck. I knew every sound she was given to making and there was no mistaking that whinny of hers. Something was after her. I started towards her on the run, but about that time she broke loose from the herd, running, and an Indian was bending low over her neck, whipping her up with a limb. I hadn't more than seen him till three more horses tore loose, every one of them with a redskin astride, and they were running hard towards the cane. I fired, and it was but natural I picked the redskin on Beck, and from behind me Ben fired, too. We heard Jim and the cap'n firing from the other side, but the horses kept going and there was no way of telling whether we'd hit any of the Indians. I saw they were going to get away and I grabbed the first horse I could lay hold of and commenced slashing his hopplings. Ben grabbed him a horse, too, and then Jim and the cap'n came running up. "How many were there," the cap'n asked, "we saw two from where we were."

"We seen four, but two of 'em could of been the same ones you seen. They broke out the horses from over that way," I told him. I was up on the animal I'd caught by that time.

"Not more than half a dozen at the most, then," the cap'n said. Jim had caught him a horse by then and was crawling up. "Hadn't we better take two or three more men?"

"No," Jim said, "the three of us will be enough. You'd best stay with the party yourself, Cap'n."

Cap'n Floyd looked at us, regretful-like, but what Jim had said was right. The cap'n was the leader and his place was with his party. "All right," he said. Then, "We'll make our crossing and wait for you on the far side."

"Best mosey on up the trail," Jim told him. "I misdoubt we can recover the animals, but it'll take us a time anyways. We'll ketch you up tomorrow or the next day, though."

I didn't know about Jim, but I wasn't aiming to lose Beck without making an awful good try to get her back. She was too good a mare to fall into the hands of any Indian.

It was easy enough to follow the redskins through the cane, but they were smart enough to head back to the buffalo road soon, and there our own passing had trampled the ground till we could barely tell one mark from another. It slowed us up considerably having to keep watch for prints and likely would of slowed us more except for Beck's new shoe I'd put on at Martin's. It made a deeper print than the others and we took to keeping an eye out for it. It would show up every so often, in a soft patch on the road, over to one side where the prints were fewer, or maybe printed deeper over another one. I sure gave thanks for her casting that shoe when she did. It helped a right smart.

It was me, riding a little bit ahead of the others, saw the splotch of wet in the road and was off looking at it time they caught up. It wasn't more than a spoonful of blood had made the patch in the road, but it looked good to me. "One of 'em is hurt," I said.

Ben nodded. "That'll slow 'em up."

I reckon we followed the blood spots a couple of hours. Times, there'd be a mile or so without any, but they hadn't time to stop and bind up the man's hurt, and likely he'd get weary of stanching it himself and let go and it would commence bleeding afresh. "He's hit in the leg, likely," Jim said, "from the blood he's losing."

It was about then we figured it was the wounded one riding Beck. We came across a puddle of blood right alongside her new shoe print. I pointed to it. We studied it. "In my opinion," I said, "he's easing that hurt leg by lifting it up on her neck."

The others said so too, and we could tell by the blood being fresher and newer we were gaining on them.

It was another mile before they turned off the buffalo road. We came to a little creek, and since redskins are a big hand to take to water to hide their tracks we went a piece downstream and then upstream to see if they'd done so. Upstream about half a mile we found a blot of blood on a rock sticking up out of the water.

"Either he don't know he's bleeding now or else he's hurting too much to care," Ben said.

"My guess is he don't know it," I said. "It's draining down his leg and seeping through his moccasin. I've left a trail that way myself."

We came up on them five miles upstream where they'd stopped, thinking they'd thrown us well off the trail. We came around a bend and they were strung out on the bank, doctoring the leg of the one that was hurt. They saw us about the same time we saw them, and they fired almost as quick. The horses scattered when the firing commenced, but one of the Indians grabbed hold of one as it went past him, and pulled himself up on it. Then he reached down and dragged the one with the bad leg up behind him and they made off through the woods on the run. The rest of the Indians took off on foot, gone and lost to sight as soon as the brush closed round them.

We followed them a piece but gave it up soon and came on back to round up the horses. I found Beck standing peaceful in a sassafras thicket, cropping the little new green buds. She looked mighty good to me, and though we'd lost one horse and hadn't accounted for any of the redskins save one pinked, I was glad to get out of it that easy.

We caught up with Cap'n Floyd and the others the next morning, at the Big Flat Lick. Up to here Dannel had followed the natural road made by the buffalo and the Indians in times past, but from here he had to leave it and cut fresh trail, angling off towards the north and west. It was rough country, hilly and broken up with thickets and heavy growth and crisscrossed with narrow, fast-flowing streams. He'd left a plain-marked trail, but he'd not taken time to do more than slash a path through. Some of the new men thought it powerful rough going, but the rest of us knew what a heap of work it had taken to do that much. Jim kind of snorted when they grumbled and told them, "You'd have something to complain of if you was having to cut trail for yourselves." But there was no way they could know.

We kept to the path, bearing ever north and west with it for several days, then we came to the spring near the hazel patch. This was a thicket of hazel bushes, and it was here me and Jim and Ben would leave Dannel's trace. That night we told Cap'n Floyd. "We take our old trace here," Jim told him, "the one we always called Skaggs' Trace. It goes by the Buffalo Springs where Ben and me are heading and into the country where Dave aims to make his stand."

"How are those springs located in relation to the colonel's stand on Otter Creek and Harrod's stand on Salt River?" the cap'n wanted to know.

"I'll show you," Jim told him, and he picked up a twig and drew a map in the dirt. "Dannel and the colonel went due north from here . . . Otter Creek empties into the Kentucky River about here, and that's their location. Here are the Buffalo Springs, westerly and not so far north . . . some forty mile, I'd say, from Otter Creek. Jim Harrod is about twenty mile straight north of the springs."

The cap'n cupped his chin in his hand and studied the map. "I think," he said then, making up his mind, "we'll turn here with you. We're to survey in the Dick's River country and the springs would make a good camp for us, if you have no complaint."

"Nary a one," Jim said. "I got a claim staked out there, and Ben wants to look around some, then him and me is going on over to the Falls. If I'm of the same mind as now, I'll likely settle at the Falls. Dave has got his place picked out a mite south and west of the springs."

The cap'n stood up. "Well, I'll tell the boys. We'll turn with you."

When we turned off Boone's path the next day our old trace was barely to be seen, so thick had it grown over. We stopped and tightened packs and loosened knives and hatchets and then we headed into it. It was still broken, hilly country, the woods thick and scraggly with underbrush. "Does it get any better?" Cap'n Floyd asked when we stopped to eat at mid-day. We'd spent the morning cutting brush, dodging branches and winding in and out amongst prickly, thorny scrubs. It was hard work all right, and we were all of a sweat. "We'll come out of it tomorrow," Jim promised him.

"Tomorrow," I said, putting in my word, "we come to the crab orchard."

"I've heard of it," the cap'n said.

"Now, that," I told him, "is a sight to see. It ort to be in full bloom about now."

"If the season ain't been too cold," Jim said.

Next afternoon we came to it. We topped a long rise and then there it was, stretching out in front of us, a wide, sweet orchard of wild crabapple trees. This was the third time I'd seen it in bloom, and it looked prettier every time. There's no bloom in the world as sightly as the crabapple blossom, pinky white and thick-clustered on the branches, but floating down like little plumey feathers in the least bit of a breeze. They have a spicy smell, sweet but mixed with sharpness. Of its own accord the whole party stopped to look. No one said anything for a minute, then the fellow who hadn't liked the view from the Gap spoke up, "Now," he said, "I'm commencing to like Kentucky."

"You've not seen nothing yet," I told him. "We're just now getting to the Kentucky part."

We went on down the hill to the spring near the orchard, and we camped there although it was yet early in the day. Nobody wanted to go on past the orchard for a while. It was in a kind of swale and all around the ground was already thatched with young pea vines. We hoppled the horses out amongst them and they fell to cropping like they'd been half starved. Under the trees the blooms had fallen so thick the ground was covered with them and looked like a pink coverlid. Everybody was in a good humor, and we all lazed around in the sun, and rolled in the apple blossoms and stuck them in our hats and laughed and forgot about Indians and cold camps and saddle-sore muscles. We just turned into a bunch of younguns and had ourselves a fine time.

But we had to get on, so we left out early next day. We'd come out of the broken country now. The hills had been getting lower and the levels in between were broader and flatter. The land was richer and there were wide stretches of grass and young pea vines. We'd not seen much cane since getting into the hills, but it commenced to show up again, now, green and tender, along the watercourses. We came into grand stretches of woods, with no undergrowth matting the way, and we could pass through riding two and three abreast, under the mightiest trees a man ever saw, elms and poplars and walnuts, sugar maples and ash and oak. Lord, but they fair touched shoulders with the sky. I saw Ben looking at them and I knew he'd never seen their like before.

Along towards noon we came up on a little run wandering down a shallow valley, and we turned along its course, for it led to the springs and overflowed from them. The springs lay in the swale, a hill rolled back away from them on each side, just a gentle, rising slope, like. Already the grass was thick up their sides, and the trees that topped them were leafing out. "That is the place," Jim said. It was the evening of the first day of May.

I got down, tied my animals to the bushes and walked up the slope of the near hill. I walked on through the woods and came out where the hill sloped down again. From there I could see a far piece, and I stood and took a long, long look. The grass was standing high enough for the wind to bend it in blowing and there was a smell of the earth in the air. The sky was high and blue and far away, shiny like it had been polished. The shadows laid flat from the trees, and down near some marshy place a frog cleared his throat. It was just like I'd remembered, only better, and I wondered what had kept me away so long.

There was a sound behind me and when I turned I saw it was Ben had come up. I motioned out towards the meadow. "Well, Ben . . . there she is."

He didn't say anything for a time . . . just looked, and then he spoke, quiet and soft, " 'But made his own people to go forth like sheep, and guided them in the wilderness like a flock. And he led them on safely, so that they feared not . . . And he brought them to the border of his sanctuary, even to this mountain, which his right hand had purchased.' "

I'd heard my mother read that psalm out of her Bible, and it was kind of like Ben had said a prayer over the land. We turned around then and walked back down the hill.

WE BUSIED OURSELVES the rest of the day throwing up some shelters and that night around the campfire we had a talk about somebody going on to the colonel's camp. Cap'n Floyd said he was of the opinion somebody ought to go and find out what his plans were.

"It might be a good idea," Jim said, "but I don't know as it makes a heap of difference."

"You don't want to go, then?" the cap'n said.

Jim shook his head. "Not me. Soon as Ben takes a look around here we aim to be moving on. The season's getting late and we got a clearing to make, corn to get in, plenty of work to do. We'll have to hustle without taking time to call on the colonel."

"Dave?" the cap'n turned to me.

"I'm in the same fix as Jim and Ben. And anyways, it seems to me somebody had best go that can talk with the colonel on his own level. You've got learning, why don't you go?"

His own men thought he ought to go, too, and they spoke up in favor of it. The new men, the ones coming into the country to settle, were all going on either to Harrod's or the colonel's and they were eager to have him lead the way. He thought about it a time and then he said he'd go. He named John Todd to take charge of the surveying whilst he was gone.

They left out early the next morning. Jim and Ben spent the day looking at the land laying close around the springs. I rested my horses and lent a hand in finishing up the shelters for the surveyors' camp.

Early the following day Jim and Ben made ready to leave and I caught up my own animals. "Just go with us, Dave," Jim said to me when we were all mounted.

"Nope," I told him, "I like these parts."

"I like it here awful good myself," Ben said. "How far is it to the place you aim to clear?"

"About ten mile . . . maybe twelve. Not far."

"It's sightly," Jim told him, "but hillier'n I like. Let's move, Ben."

Ben pulled his horse around. "I might be back," he said, and then him and Jim rode up the knoll and over the top of it and out of sight.

I hollered and told the men at the camp I was leaving and then I headed west from the springs, following the valley that laid between the two hills. For about an hour I followed the valley, then it pinched out on a level plain. Now there was only the rise and fall of the land, like long, far-rolling ocean swells, gentle and easy-curved, and ahead where the hills rose up again, it was like the land broke against the hills, in the way of the sea against the shore. Some of the rises were topped with woods, and down between little creeks meandered across the path.

Finally, over to the left, I saw the line of trees breaking from the hills, the way I remembered them, and I knew I had come home. There flowed the Green. I pulled towards it, leaving the rolling lands off to my right, and another hour's ride brought me up under the trees and to the banks of the stream. It rose further up in the hills and even here it was still narrow, but it was commencing to feel its power and it flowed swift and certain. It caught the sunlight and sparkled back, like green glass, light and pale as the underedge of a sycamore leaf. Lordy, but it was fair and pretty.

I got off and led the horses into the stream to drink, and myself, I drank my fill. It was cold, icy cold, and tasteless save for the pure freshness of clear, clean water. When the horses had done drinking I turned downstream, following the windings and twistings of the river. The cane was tall and thick along the banks and well back into the valley. This was the valley I'd had in mind . . . narrow, with the Green on one side, and a high cliffty hill on the other, but with the rolling lands opening out before it.

It wasn't far till I came to a little run that emptied into the river. I turned back up it about a quarter of a mile and there was the spring I'd remembered. It gushed out clean and cold, ever-flowing, from a rock ledge that banked up against the foot of the knoll. Back behind the knoll the hills crowded in close, for it was but a shelf jutting out at their feet. Its sides were smooth and grown over with clover and pea vines, and it was topped with a grove of high-standing walnut trees.

Here at the spring I unloaded my pack and hoppled the animals out to feed.

It's not changed a lot. The wild ferns still grow along the water's edge, and in the spring they're as young and tender and curly as they were that spring, and the water hyacinths still grow with their roots deep down in the damp and head up into proud, purply blooms. The spring is boxed over now, and there's a well-beat path leading down to it, but crow's foot and bloodroot and red trillium still sprangle out where the locust trees make a heavy shade. It was a sweet place then, and it's a sweet place now, and never has the water failed to flow, clear, cold and good-tasting.

When I'd eat a bite I made a close circle all around. Wasn't a mark on a tree far as I could tell. But few knew this country through here and I'd not expected anyone would come this far from Harrod's or Boone's to make a stand, but I felt a relief when I found no sign of a claim ahead of me.

I slid my hatchet out from my belt and blazed the tree nearest the spring. Then I fixed a green pole, cut from a sapling, in the edge of the spring and wrote on a piece of paper I'd brought along special, my name and my claim to the land. I split the end of the pole and wedged the paper in. Now it was mine. The Virginia law said I could have it, did I build an improvement on it and raise a crop of corn. I reached down and took up a handful of the soil and drifted it through my fingers. It's mine, I thought. My land. My dirt. I rubbed it between my hands and smelt it and tasted of it.

And all at once I had a funny, mixed-up feeling about it, like this land somehow put chains on me. I'd never owned anything of my own before. Nothing, but a gun and a horse and the clothes on my back, and that had been enough for me. I'd thought to have a real excited feeling when I marked out my own land, and in a way I did have. I'd been looking forward to this minute since I'd headed towards Kentucky. I wanted this land. I knew I wanted it. Four hundred acres of it. But of a sudden I had to shake the dirt loose from my fingers. It clung and I wiped my hand across my shirt front. I had a scared feeling like I couldn't get loose of it, like the land wouldn't belong to me, but I'd belong to the land, now.

I looked all around, at the spring and the meadow and the knoll topped by the walnut trees, and at the hills back of the knoll. I thought how it would hold me in this one place. It takes time to build a cabin and daub it and fence it in. It takes time to plant crops and tend them. It takes time, even, I thought, to get married and live with a woman and raise up young ones. It takes time . . . and all the time it takes is time not your own any longer . . . time give over from yourself and your own free ways. While you're planting corn you could be in the woods, your old Deckard under your hand and the trees sky-high and sun-thick over your head. You could be drawing a bead on a white-tail deer, the Deckard steady on its rest and the day hung up somewhere, not counting the hours against you. While you're building a cabin and chinking it and fencing it, you could be trapping beaver over there on the Green, or fishing for the speckled fish that hide out in the cool places under the rocks, or listening to the gobble of a tom-turkey over in the little swale on the far side of the stream. All the things I was used to doing with my time piled up inside me and crowded me and choked me and scared me till I could feel my breath coming short and fast like I'd flushed a redskin out of the cane. Of a sudden I thought I must of been out of my mind to want land and a corn crop and a cabin, and I grabbed the paper out of the wedge in the pole and tore it into little bits. My time wasn't going to be sucked up by four hundred acres of land, nor was I going to be chained down to it. Not me, not David Cooper! My time wasn't going to be spent getting married and living with a woman when I could be . . . I could be . . . and like she had turned the corner of a cabin built right up on the knoll amongst the walnut trees, I could see that redheaded girl standing in front of me. While I was getting married and living with a woman and raising up young ones. . . . I stood there and looked at the picture my thoughts conjured up in front of me, and time, my time and all the rest stood still while I looked at it.

Then I sucked in a big breath. I was beat and licked, and I knew it. A man can't go his own free way all his days. Comes a day when he has to divide himself up and give part of his time and his ways to somebody else, and to things that count for two people and maybe more. I pulled out the other piece of paper I had and wrote my name on it and put it in the wedge of the pole. It was like I'd wrote myself a letter, I thought, telling the David Cooper that used to be goodbye. I couldn't help wondering if I was going to like as good being the David Cooper that owned four hundred acres of land.

But I shook off my sad feelings and caught up Beck and took the rest of the day riding over my land, marking it as best I could, the way I wanted it to lay. I figured to get some of Cap'n Floyd's men to ride over soon and lay it off proper. There was a wealth of timber on the hills, and the meadow opening out of the valley had a good-lying length to it. There had always been a plenty of game in these parts and I thought if a man had to own four hundred acres of land, I'd just about picked the best.

When I came back to the spring in the late evening I made camp and then walked up the knoll just back of the spring. Like the knoll over at the Buffalo Springs, it had a long look. The walnut trees were the biggest I'd ever seen, the biggest one measuring, when I stepped around it, more than twenty steps. He was a monstrous old fellow, that tree. Made two twenty-foot sill logs in this house, two foot square, and that's its stump in the front yard, grown over now with honeysuckle vines. I decided that night to put the cabin here in the middle of the grove. If you notice, the trees are like hands folded over the roof to keep the weather off. I brought my horses up and slept that night under them, listening to the wind in the topmost branches. I thought how I'd hear that sound when I laid down all the rest of my life, till it would be a sighing forever in my ears. I watched the stars shine through and thought how I'd see them so often it would come to be the way I'd always think of stars shining. I laid my hand against the ground and thought how I'd walk on it and build on it and plow it, sweat over it and maybe curse it and hate it, and maybe love it and bleed over it, till it would come to be part of my own bones and sweat and blood. And I've done all those things, like I thought I would that night. And the land has got to be part of me, till there's no separating us one from the other.

But there was no need building a cabin straight off, so I took several days making me a shelter down by the spring so as to be handy to water. I sharpened the ends of sapling poles and rammed them deep into the sloped side of the knoll. At the outside edge I notched them and built them up, end over end. I made it some six foot deep, facing east, and left the front half open. Come winter I could hang skins there or close it up with some more poles. Now all I wanted was a kind of makeshift to keep my belongings out of the weather and to count as an improvement this year.

When the shelter was done and moved into, I commenced clearing a patch out of the woods for the corn. It took a mort of sweat to clean out the brush and sprouts and girdle the trees, but I kept at it. Day after day I got up before good light, made my breakfast and tended camp and had my axe swinging by sunup. Sometimes when I'd look in front of me at the work yet to be done I'd groan that I'd set out to clean up ten acres. But when I'd look back of me I couldn't help but take a pride in it. I'd thought my hands were calloused and hard, but they got axe-sore and tender just the same, and the muscles in my shoulders and back ached me so bad sometimes I couldn't hardly stand to lay down at night.

The best part of the day was late of an evening when I'd go down to the river and strip and plunge in. It wasn't deep enough to swim in, but it was a good place for washing the sweat and the dirt off. It would be cold and would make me feel tingly and rested all over. I liked best to lie on a little spit of sand with about six inches of water flowing fast over it. I'd lay my head on a big rock and stretch the rest of myself out in the water and lie and watch the sky turn pinky dark over the hills. When it came on to gloom I'd dress and go back to the spring and eat. Sometimes, then, I'd walk up to the top of the knoll and sit with my back against one of the walnut trees and watch the lightning bugs come out in the tall grass down in the valley, and listen to the chuck-will's-widows and the frogs deep-croaking over by the river. It was so peaceful a body was like to forget the need to keep watch . . . only you couldn't ever. Taking care and watching out had to be as much a part of a man's nature as eating and sleeping, and you couldn't no more cease to be cautious than you could leave off those habits. Too often I'd seen it happen that when peace and quiet had lulled a settler into carelessness, the redskins struck, and there'd be nothing left but a hairless dead man, to be forever careless. My gun was always with me. I never left it at one end of the clearing whilst I worked at the other. Every yard I moved, the Deckard moved along with me. I'd have felt stripped and naked without it, and helpless as a babe. But it was powerful still and peaceful those evenings, and made a man wish it could always be so.

It took the best part of two weeks to clear that ten acres. The soil, being woodsy, was loose and loamy and before dropping the corn I just scratched it around a little finer with a pronged stick. In time I meant to bring out a plow from the settlements, but for this first crop going into new land a little scratching and stirring would have to do. Main thing was to meet the requirements of the law and raise a crop of some kind this year.

When I'd got the last of the corn dropped and covered I was tired of the whole thing. I hadn't stirred off the place for more than two weeks. Hadn't even hunted very far off, for I'd contented myself with small game to eat. I wanted to get free of it for a time and I decided I'd take a turn over to the Buffalo Springs and see what had been going on there.

I moved my goods from the shelter and took them down close to the river and buried them there, covering over the hole so as to leave no sign just in case some prowling Indians happened by. Then I left out. I got to the Springs about midmorning, and it was like the camp had always been there. The horses had tramped down the grass around the springs and the men's packs had been strowed about the shelters, making the kind 'of mess was always made where men camped for long at a time.

Not many men were in camp though. I figured the surveying party was out at work. I rode up in front of the shelters and hollered, and Cap'n Floyd stepped outside. I wasn't much surprised when Ben Logan stepped out behind him. "Howdy," I said, "when did you get back?"

Ben came over and held Beck's head while I got off. "'Light and tie," he said. "I got back yesterday."

"Didn't like over there?"

"Not as good as here. Me and Jim made a trade. I staked out four hundred over there alongside of him and then traded it to him for his rights here."

"We'll be neighbors, then." I felt glad it would be so. I was beginning to think a heap of Ben Logan and it would go good to know he was living you might say door-neighbor to me. From all appearances he was a man you could tie to and put your dependence in, and likely we would have need of one another many a time. "Jim ain't coming back?"

Ben shook his head. "No. He likes over there."

I would of liked to see Jim settle close by but a man has to follow his own mind. I knew we'd not be seeing much of him, for the Falls was too far away for neighboring, but little did I know that his business and the war would take him out of the country at a time when we could of used him best. The fact is, when him and Ben Logan had ridden out of sight over the knoll at the Buffalo Springs that day, it was my last sight of Jim Knox for several years.

I hoppled Beck out and then the three of us, Cap'n Floyd, Ben and me, walked down to the springs and sat down there on the rocks to talk. They both wanted to know if I'd found the place I had in mind and was pleased with it and what I'd been doing.

"You think you'll stay there, then?" the cap'n asked.

I told him I had no doubts but what I would. "Did you find out anything from the colonel?" I asked him, then.

"I was just telling Ben, here. I wasn't in camp when he got in last night. We're running some lines over on the Hanging Fork and we're camped over there until we get through, but I came over this morning after some salt and other things. Found Ben here and thought we'd better talk awhile. Yes, I learned a few things. The colonel is open and frank about his intentions."

Both Ben and me were listening. "It's this way," the cap'n went on. "The colonel has got a valid title if the crown recognizes it. Virginia and North Carolina have both repudiated him, but he hasn't sought recognition from them and isn't depending on it. He has bought the land from the Cherokees, and it's his opinion that under the terms of the treaty at Hard Labor it was recognized by Britain as belonging to them. He intends to set up as a proprietor under the crown. He's purchased the land from the mouth of the Kentucky River along the boundary of the Ohio to Powell Mountain, down the ridge of that mountain to the Cumberland River, and down the Cumberland to where it flows into the Ohio. That takes in just about all of these lands. He's already started entering claims in the name of his company, which he calls the Transylvania Company, and he says he will not recognize any claims lying within his boundaries save those that are registered with him. If he proves his title, he is within his rights."

I looked at Ben and Ben looked back at me, as sober-faced as a judge. I reckon we were both thinking the same thing. The colonel and his partners were setting theirselves up as lords-proprietors of a colony all their own, and if the crown recognized their title instead of being freeholders under the Virginia law, we'd be beholden to them and paying quit-rent to them for the rest of our lives. It gave me a sinking feeling just to think of it. Didn't either one of us say anything, though, and Cap'n Floyd went on talking. "They've begun their buildings where Otter Creek runs into the Kentucky, and they have a kind of fort started. Not much of one, yet, but the colonel intends to complete it soon. I was just telling Ben of what happened while I was there. You know Jim Harrod?"

"I've seen him around."

"Well, he's made a stand about six miles from Harrodstown, where the rest of his party are located . . . a place he calls the Boiling Spring. A man by the name of Slaughter, from North Carolina, has pre-empted land all along near Harrodstown. The two of them showed up at Colonel Henderson's three or four days after I'd got there, and they'd been quarreling over their claims. Slaughter said Harrod's men had already got all the best land, and Harrod said they hadn't. They'd come to talk it over with the colonel."

"What in the world for?" I said.

The cap'n shook his head. "I don't know, except that the colonel is a lawyer and a judge and they probably thought he'd be impartial between them."

It went queer to me and I said so. "Jim Harrod's made his stand

and got his improvements built according to the law. Don't look to me like he'd want to have any dealings with the colonel."

"Jim don't know much law, Dave. He's fitful as the wind about it, and worried. In my opinion, if the colonel is here to stay, Jim would rather throw in with him than not."

That didn't sound very good to me. I'd been thinking Jim Harrod would take the same stand as Ben and me. It was pretty unsettling to learn he was blowing hot and cold about it and might throw in with the colonel. "Well, what happened?"

"The colonel talked with them, and he made a suggestion that each one of the settlements elect delegates to meet together at his place some time this month and form a civil government and make some laws. He said, and I must admit I think it is well taken, that this kind of argument would keep coming up continually, and of course it stands to reason the more settlers come in, the more need we are going to have of civil and restraining law. The game up around their settlements is already getting scarce from wanton killing, and there is more drunkenness and fighting than needs to be. However the land title turns out, we need law and order here, and it seems to me the colonel is being very fair in suggesting the government be formed by a delegation of freely elected men. He and his partners could make the laws themselves, you know."

"Not," I said, "till that title of theirs is proved. They've got no more right to make laws than Ben and me here have got."

The cap'n shrugged his shoulders. "Well, at any rate he suggested a reasonable plan to follow."

Ben was rubbing his chin. I didn't know then but in time I learned that when he was studying something over in his mind he had a way of rubbing his chin. He said, "Is he aiming on trying to set up laws about the land?"

"Well, yes . . . after all the land belongs to the company, and he said they'd recognize the titles already staked out if they were registered with him."

I couldn't keep from snorting. "Now ain't that kind of him!"

Cap'n Floyd picked up a twig and commenced turning it end over end in his hands. "Well, what was finally done . . . he made out commissions for four settlements . . . Boonesborough, Harrodstown, Boiling Spring and St. Asaph's."

"Where's St. Asaph's?"

The cap'n pointed the twig downwards. "Right here," he said, laughing. "I thought we'd better be represented, and I told the colonel we had a considerable party encamped here and some of the men were intending to settle nearby. He was ready and willing to give us a commission. When he asked what name to make it out in, I thought of how we'd arrived here on the first day of May, and being of Welsh descent I remembered it was the name day of the Welsh saint, Asaph, so I took the liberty of naming this encampment, St. Asaph. You are therefore members of the settlement of St. Asaph, gentlemen."

Seemed to me the cap'n had taken a right smart into his own hands and I didn't care much for it. It looked pretty clear that he was aiming to throw in with the colonel, and he'd made sure his own camp was commissioned. I eased myself up off the rock. "Well, Cap'n," I said, "I don't know about Ben, but I don't aim to be beholden to Colonel Henderson nor any of his company. I don't consider myself a member of any settlement commissioned by the colonel, either. And I'll take no part setting up any kind of government headed up by lords-proprietors. I have staked out four hundred acres of land and I have built an improvement on it. My corn is in the ground. Under the Virginia law I am entitled to my land, and I don't aim to register it with nobody but the Virginia land office. I'll have no part of Colonel Henderson or the Transylvania Company, now or any time."

Ben and the cap'n stood up then, too. It was not my intention to rile Cap'n Floyd, for I liked him fine, but feeling as strong as I did I felt like I had to say plain out the way I was thinking. "What Dave has said is my way of thinking, too, Cap'n," Ben said, as quiet as could be, but firm.

Cap'n Floyd broke the twig he had been holding in two pieces and let them both fall to the ground. He smiled at us to show there was no hard feelings. "Well, you may be right. I take it, however, you do not wish to be nominated as delegates to the meeting?"

We both said no.

"That leaves it entirely within the body of my surveying party, then," the cap'n said. "I would not have wished that."

"It's best so," Ben said. Then he grinned at the cap'n. "I don't want to appear unmannerly, Cap'n Floyd, but I'll have to remind you these springs are located on my land. Your party is welcome to camp here long as need be, but I'd best make it clear it's with my permission."

To save my life I couldn't help laughing. The cap'n's St. Asaph settlement was right smack in the middle of Ben's claim, and Ben wasn't having nothing to do with it. Cap'n Floyd looked a mite startled and then he commenced laughing, too. "All right, Ben. I think we understand one another." He started walking away, then turned back. "By the way. The colonel is to send word about the meeting. I'd be obliged if you'd send his messenger to me on the Hanging Fork."

Ben said he would and Cap'n Floyd went on away. We watched him till he went inside the shelter. "Well," I said then, "looks to me like the two of us is about all that's holding out on the colonel."

Ben pulled his hat down firm around his head. "It looks that way. Well, I got work to do."

"I'm kind of caught up," I told him. "Be glad to help out if you want."

"Be obliged to you," Ben said. He pointed up the rise to the top of the knoll. "I aim to raise my cabin up there."

# CHAPTER

# 7

WE HADN'T BEEN WORKING but a couple of days felling trees for Ben's cabin when the messenger came from Colonel Henderson: "He says to name your men, and they're to be at Boonesburg come sunup on the twenty-third."

"Cap'n Floyd ain't here," Ben told the fellow. "He's over on the Hanging Fork. You'll find him there and him and his men will hold their election."

After feeding and resting, the man went on, and we went back to felling trees. The next evening Cap'n Floyd and three of his surveyors rode into camp. Best I recollect now it was John Todd, a fellow named Dandridge and one named Wood that was elected delegates along with the cap'n. They aimed to start the next morning, going by Harrodstown and traveling with the ones elected from there.

Me and Ben were laying the sill logs of the cabin when the thought came to me that about the only way the two of us would ever get a straight story about what went on at that meeting would be for one of us to be there. Not as a delegate, but just looking on. I said so to Ben.

"It's a good idea, Dave," he said, "but it'll have to be you that goes. I got too much to do to spare the time."

"Don't reckon the cap'n would care if I rode along with them."

"I'd not think so."

"I'd feel a heap easier to know for myself what takes place."

"It would suit me better, too."

Cap'n Floyd didn't mind when I said I'd like to go along. He was as pleasant-spoke as always and said I'd be welcome. "You can't take part in any of the proceedings, though."

"I wouldn't want to," I told him. "I'll tend to my own business."

We rode the next morning to Harrodstown, covering the twenty miles by midafternoon. I was surprised at how much they'd got done to their fort there. I knew they'd laid it off the year before and had built some cabins, but I'd not had any notion they'd built as solid as they had.

We rode out of the woods plumb upon the site, which was laid up on a low hill with a long stretch of view. I would of thought Jim Harrod to be smart enough to do that. The cabins were all built alongside one another with their backs making a solid wall along three sides of a square. The stockade wasn't done, but the cabins made a fair barricade already. He'd built around a fine spring and it looked to be a place meant to stay.

It was Jim Harrod himself came out to welcome us. Like I said, I'd seen him around during Dunmore's War, but I didn't to say know him. He was another big man, full as tall as Ben and me, and built the same way, lean and long-legged and full-spanned in the shoulders. He had dark skin, both from nature and the weather I judged, and his hair was nearabout as black as my own. He was a man with as pleasing a look on his face as I've ever seen, and he was grinning when he walked across the square. "'Light and tie, Cap'n," he called out, "come in and rest yourselves."

We followed him into the nearest cabin, which was the one on the corner. "I've seen you somewheres," he said to me, then.

"At Point Pleasant," I told him.

He laughed. "Why, sure. I recollect now. You was with Evan Shelby's company. You from Sapling Grove?"

"The Watauga."

He poured us noggins of Monongahela and I drank mine down fast. It was raw and fiery. Cap'n Floyd kind of sipped his. I wondered how he could manage it so slow. Monongahela was made for a quick down and over with. No use keeping your gullet on fire any longer than need be. But I reckoned a man's ways of drinking were his own and set early according to what he was used to. The cap'n was likely more used to fine Madeira than Monongahela.

We drank and talked and Jim told us who the delegates from Harrodstown and Boiling Spring were. The talk rambled around over the coming meeting and I took care to keep my opinions to myself. I did say I wasn't a delegate but was just going along. I thought I'd ought to make that much clear. "It's a free country," Jim said, filling up my noggin again, and I wondered if he'd given any thought to how long it would stay that way if the colonel won out, but I didn't say so.

Next day, riding towards Boonesburg, I was glad to listen to what the men were saying amongst themselves. They were all full of talk, some appearing to be for the colonel, some not knowing and worried about what might happen, some just plain against the colonel. Lord Dunmore had come out with a proclamation against Colonel Henderson, and the men were disturbed and upset over it. "He come plain out and said the colonel didn't have no right to treat with the Cherokee, didn't he? Don't stand to reason he'd say so without the law back of him."

"What law?"

"The Virginny law!"

"What's the right of Virginny having any say over Kentucky?"

"Why, man, they've always had a right to it, ain't they? Ain't it part of Virginny?"

"That's what I'd like to know."

"What I don't like," Azariah Davis put in, "is him calling us thieves and criminals. That don't set good to me. I ain't no thief nor criminal and I ain't beholden to nobody and have got no liking to being so named!"

"He was talking about them two hundred the colonel aims to bring on to settle, doubtless," Isaac Hite said.

"If he was, he'd ort to of said so. The first ones here has been good men, and I'll take my stand on it. What kind of riffraff they got over at Boonesburg I wouldn't know."

"Some of 'em ain't riffraff. They's Dannel and Richard Calloway and others as good men as you'd want."

The Reverend John Lythe, who was one of the delegates from Harrodstown, spoke up to make peace. "Gentlemen, gentlemen, let there be no quarreling. The purpose of this meeting is to bring peace and order amongst us. Let us come together in harmony, and leave the quarreling to those of lesser stature."

"Sure, sir," said Azariah, "and I'm willing. But I've no liking for being lumped with them the governor names as thieves and convicts from debtor's prison."

"None of us have a liking for that, Azariah. But being named a thief does not make us thieves. We have a duty to disprove it and by our actions to make a lie of the words."

Jim Harrod rode along amongst the men saying nothing, but I thought his face wore a troubled look. I misdoubted his mind was very easy, and I thought, too, that men such as these were going to be pretty hard for the colonel to handle. You take a man tough enough to pull up stakes and head into new country, country that's way out and beyond the settlements and open to Indian trouble on all sides, you take such a man and you've got one that don't usually bend very easy to a yoke of any kind. Likely if he hadn't found a yoke galling he wouldn't of headed for new country in the first place. I figured that in time, when they got done milling around and deciding, the colonel was liable to find he'd bit off a right smart chunk of trouble.

We made camp that night a few miles this side of Boonesburg so as to have an easy ride the next day. The colonel had set six o'clock as the time to commence the meeting.

I didn't think too highly of the fort when I saw it in the fog drift early the next morning. It was a lot smaller than the one at Harrodstown and not built too securely. There wasn't any stockade yet, nor any barricade of any sort, and the cabins weren't much more than shelters. The location didn't look very good to me, either. It was on the bank of the river and the ground on the other side was high, which made me uneasy just to look at. Bad shots as most Indians were, they could do a heap of damage from over there. It went foolish to me that Dannel should of picked such a place, but then Dannel wasn't cut out to be a settler. He was a woodsman, and likely he'd admired the place for the way it curved into the river and looked sweet and sightly. The river made the clearings have to be strung out, too, not bunched so as to be of protection to one another.

I saw Dannel but not for much longer than to say howdy. "You a delegate?" he said.

I shook my head. "Just come along to look on. I done told you my stand, Dannel."

"Thought you might of changed your mind."

"No."

The colonel called the delegates to gather under a big elm tree then and we didn't have time to say more. That was the biggest elm tree I ever saw. It was a good four foot through and a full nine or ten foot to the first branches. I reckon it stood near sixty foot tall. The colonel called it the Divine Elm on account of he meant to have church under it in time. The whole gathering could sit under it without crowding.

The reverend opened the meeting by praying and then they named a chairman and a clerk. After that the colonel made a speech. I was sitting on the outside edge of the gathering and I could hear every word was said. You could sure tell the colonel was a man of learning, and you could tell he was used to the courtroom, too. "You are called and assembled," he commenced by saying, "at this time for a noble and honorable purpose." He went on to talk about prudence and firmness and wisdom in council and conduct, and peace and harmony in deliberations. He talked about laws and edicts and how important it was for everybody to have his full advantage. "You," he said, "perhaps are fixing the palladium, or placing the first cornerstone of an edifice, the height and magnificence of whose superstructure is now in the womb of futurity, and can only become great and glorious in proportion to the excellence of its foundation. These considerations, gentlemen, will, no doubt, animate and inspire you with sentiments worthy of the grandeur of the subject."

I grinned. I could just feel the nobility rising up inside of me, and I made sure Jim Harrod was being inspired. My, but the colonel was an elegant speechmaker! Especially here where he didn't need to have it translated for him, only I wasn't sure but it needed a mite of translating for some. I wondered, now, if Dannel knew what a palladium was, or Azariah Davis. Azariah was likely thinking it some newfangled way of calling a man a thief by some other name.

The colonel was talking now about the governor's proclamation. He was saying, ". . . an infamous and scurrilous libel lately printed and published, concerning the settlement of this country, the author of which avails himself of his station, and under the specious pretense of proclamation, pompously dressed up and decorated in the garb of authority, has uttered invectives of the most malignant kind, and endeavors to wound the good name of persons, whose moral character would derive little advantage of being placed in competition with his, charging them, among other things equally untrue, with a design . . ." and he looked at a paper he held in his hand and read from it, "'of forming an asylum for debtors and other persons of desperate circumstances.'"

There was a stir amongst the men and a general muttering and mumbling. It was plumb clever of him, I thought, to stir them up that way, including them in the governor's proclamation. He let the muttering grumble its way through them and then he held up his hand and went on to talk of laws and such, naming some the proprietors thought would be good, like courts and tribunals for the settlement of quarrels of all kinds, the organizing of a militia, laws to protect the game and so on.

When he'd finished his speech he left the meeting, and I left, too, figuring I'd heard as much as I needed to. It was plain enough the way things would go. Not that I never thought the laws wouldn't be good for the country. It was certain sure we'd be needing laws in time. But they'd ought to be the Virginia laws under which we were bound as people of the Virginia colony. There was law and a plenty already. This country was the westernmost part of Fincastle County and Fincastle County had its own rightful delegates every year to the General Assembly meeting in Williamsburg. For law and order we had only to appeal to our own delegates, and ask them to petition the Assembly in our behalf. It was a denying of everything I held to be law and order to be setting up a government in hand with the proprietors of the Transylvania Company. But the colonel was slick-tongued and the men were uneasy and bothered.

I saddled Beck and passed the rest of the day in the woods, hunting. I took my own uneasiness and bother with me, too, but being by myself in the woods was a comfort and helped me settle my own thinking. Let the meeting go the way it would. The laws they'd pass would be all right, saving, maybe land laws according to the colonel. For my part I'd abide by them and stake my faith that in time the Virginia colony would do right by its westernmost boundaries. I'd abide by them all saving any land laws passed. Nothing could make me register my clearing with the colonel nor pay him in any manner for it. If it came to the worst and the colonel's title was held good and the country was set up as a colony separate from Virginia, then I'd get out . . . go back to Virginia proper. I couldn't come out any other place and have any peace with myself.

I camped that night with Dannel and his brother, Squire. The whole gathering was kind of divided into two groups. Cap'n Floyd, John Todd, Dandridge and Preacher Lythe ate with the colonel and his nephew, Samuel. Jim Harrod joined them, too, and the Slaughter man. The rest of the men scattered out amongst the ones as rough and unlettered as themselves. Dannel chuckled to himself when I named it to him. "The colonel has been some troubled over Jim and Cap'n Floyd," he said. "He's shining up to 'em."

"I'm afeared it's going to work, too," I said.

Dannel was cooking a piece of meat on a forked stick and he leaned over to turn it. "Dave, you'd ort to be a more trusting feller."

"I'm trusting. I'm trusting of what I think's right."

"The colonel is a right shrewd man, Dave. It could be he's got the right of it."

"He's got Kentucky, for ten thousand pounds of goods offen the Cherokee. He's got one of your great specks up his sleeve, and you've fallen for it. How can you be so blind, Dannel?"

Dannel waved the smoke from in front of his face. "I want to see the country opened up. The colonel has got ways and means of opening it up. He's taking the risks, Dave. It's but fair he should make a profit. He means well, to my notion."

There was no use talking to Dannel. He'd figured it his own way, and he had a right to. I just hoped he'd have sense enough to look after his own interests, which he didn't. Neither of us sitting by the fire together that night could look ahead and see the time when Dannel Boone would lose every acre of land the colonel deeded to him, and the thousands he staked out and claimed by his own sweat. There was no way of knowing he would leave the country, bitter against it and so poor he had naught but his own gun to provide his living again. I'm glad I never knew it that night. I felt bad enough the way it was.

They took two days getting the meeting organized. The delegates made speeches and the proprietors made speeches and all were trying to outdo one another in politeness. Times I wondered if they ever would get down to business. Reminded me of the palaver had to be got through in dealing with the redskins. I stayed around long enough to get the feel of the meeting every day before going out to hunt, but I never did sit and listen close like I'd done that first day. I could pick up what had gone on at night around the campfire.

It was Thursday, I think, they named the country Transylvania. It looked to me like every man there had lost what mind he had and forgot he'd come to Kentucky! Transylvania. The colonel said it meant "across the mountains." Any fool knew it was across the mountains. But it was Kentucky that was across the mountains and no need to dress it up. And it was Thursday and Friday they made most of the laws. Dannel was the one told about them. "John Todd," he said, "was named the head one to write up the law on the courts, and that Dandridge feller, on account of them knowing the law. And Cap'n Floyd was named to head up the committee on the militia, and Jim Harrod along with him. Me, I got to draw up a law preserving the game." He laughed. When Dannel laughed he never made any sound, just kind of chuckled down inside himself, and his shoulders would shake with the chuckling. "Only game I ever preserved was what I kilt and skun," he said, "but I reckon I'll make out. And the preacher, now, he's to head up one to stop swearing on the Sabbath."

"My God," I said, "you mean we can't cuss on a Sunday?"

"That's it."

Squire Boone laughed at the look on my face. "That ain't exactly the way of it, Dave. The preacher don't want no profane swearing at all and the law is to prevent it and to make sure we don't break the Sabbath."

"And what am I going to say when I mash the hell out of my finger, pray tell!"

"You," Dannel said, drawly as was his way when he was having fun, "ain't going to mash the hell outen your finger no more, Dave. You're just going to mash it."

"And I reckon I'll say, 'Land sakes!'"

Everybody laughed and we fell to and eat supper. "That part about breaking the Sabbath, though," Squire Boone said when he'd finished, "is all right. They's no need to work seven days a week. We'd ort to take a day of rest and when the preachers commence to come we'd ort to take a day of worship."

I recollected Squire liked to do a little preaching himself on the side, but I figured he was right and I said so. "It'll be a good thing, especially when the women and younguns commence coming. We'd be pretty rough, elsewise."

"Speaking of women and younguns," Dannel said, "I'm aiming to bring mine here soon. This fall, I'd thought."

I was surprised. "Hadn't you best wait and see what the redskins are going to do first?"

"I don't figure we'll have a heap of trouble with 'em. No more than common back home. I'll risk my woman and younguns here same as there."

Dannel had always got along pretty good with Indians, and never bore a grudge against them, not even when he'd lost his own boy. Seemed like he fought them when he had to, and got along with them when he didn't. And it was ever Dannel's way to be hopeful. I could hope right along with the best of them, but it went foolish to me to think this quiet spell we'd been having meant a thing as far as the Ohio Indians were concerned. I figured they'd had their eyes on us from the minute we'd crossed the Gap, and were watching to see what we were up to and what we aimed to do. In my opinion we'd been lucky to have a little breathing spell to get our crops in and our clearings made and it wouldn't of surprised me a bit to have them break loose any day. There'd be trouble and plenty of it, I thought, and likely for more than one year to come. I couldn't see those Ohio Indians giving up this land so easy. If I had a woman and younguns I wouldn't of brought them into the country until the forts were finished and there was a sight more protection . . . but it was purely Dannel's affair.

When I left Boonesburg on Saturday the delegates had made and passed nine laws, and they'd agreed to meet again in September. I studied on the laws while I rode along. They were fair enough . . .

better than that, they were plain good if they hadn't of been laws for the new colony of Transylvania of which Colonel Henderson and his partners were the proprietors. There was a law setting up courts; a law for setting up a militia; one for punishing lawbreakers; one to prevent profane swearing and Sabbath-breaking; an act for writs of attachment; an act for setting sheriffs' and clerks' fees; an act to preserve the range; one to preserve game; and an act for improving the breed of horses. I have to laugh when I remember that last law nowadays, for it wasn't but a few years later, when we'd been made a state, they were trying to get laws passed to stop horse racing. We always loved a fast horse in this country, but back in the beginning it was a need as much as a love. Sometimes whether you kept your hair or not depended on how fast a horse you had.

Well, those were the laws. The colonel hadn't tried to ram any law about land titles through. Wasn't actually any need for him to, for the whole business was as good as admitting the Transylvania Company had a right to all of it to sell as they pleased. Jim Harrod and some others had talked with the colonel and had got his word that the company would abide by the rules they'd first set up about registering with them, and wouldn't go up on the prices to the ones already in the country. It wasn't put in writing but it was understood the colonel gave his word. Not that it mattered to me, but for them registering with the colonel it was but fair. And it looked like everybody was going to throw in with him. It looked like Jim Harrod had such intentions and most of his men had been pacified and were following him. Cap'n Floyd had named his intentions, too, and had been made the head surveyor for the company. John Todd had laid him off a piece he liked and staked his claim near the fort. The wind was blowing the colonel's way right now. Well, I thought, let it blow. Me and Ben will just have to sit tight and wait it out.

I felt kind of lonesome, though. The delegates weren't leaving till Sunday, so I was traveling a day ahead of them. I was eager to talk with Ben. Man had to follow his own judgment, naturally, but it made me feel better to remember Ben's judgment was like my own. I got to the Buffalo Springs around sundown of the second day. Ben was making supper. He had a pot of stew hanging over the fire I could smell as soon as I came in sight, and I was hungry as a wolf. From across the fire he yelled at me, " 'Light and tie! You're just in time."

"Past time," I said, "as far as my stomach knows."

"Well, pitch in, then. It's ready."

I did so, and Ben joined me. When we'd done, he said, "You're from the meeting, I reckon."

"I'm from the meeting." And I told him all that had taken place. He listened and his face took on a sober look, a kind of solemn, judging look. After I got to know him better I always called it his Presbyterian look. When Ben looked like that he was weighing and deciding, trying to think where his duty laid. "Well," he said, when I'd finished my telling, "I reckon they've got it all fixed."

I could joke about it now that my mind was eased from talking it over with Ben. "Yes," I said, "I reckon you'd say they have done fixed the palladium."

He raised one eyebrow. "The what?"

I had to laugh. "That's what the colonel claimed we were all aiming to do out here in Kentucky."

"Humph," he snorted, "the rest can fix palladiums if they want to. I'm aiming on proving four hundred acres of land and raising me a crop of corn and making a home for my folks."

It sure was a comfort to hear him talk so, but speaking of a home reminded me I'd noticed he had nearly got his cabin raised. I named it to him. "I been working on it steady," he said, "you want to take a look at it?"

I did, so we walked up the rise where he'd located it. The cabin was rough, but stout. He'd made the walls eight logs high and he had several stacks of staves already rived out for shingle boards. He hadn't bothered to cut windows yet, nor to lay a floor. It was little more than a shelter, but it would serve till he could better it. "I got to get my corn in now, and then I'm aiming on going home for a spell. I figure to bring some stock out before the weather breaks, and I got to keep hustling."

"Dannel is aiming on bringing his woman and younguns out soon," I told him.

He shook his head. "I don't think to bring mine till I get things fixed a mite safer. Maybe by spring, though."

Dark was coming on and the air was chilling. We walked back down the knoll to the fire, tended the animals and then rolled in our blankets. Just before I drifted off to sleep I thought of something. "When is it you're aiming to go home, Ben?"

"July, I'd thought. Ort to be able to get done here by then."

I said no more but I'd come wide awake. Ben would be riding by Joe Martin's place. And he'd surely see Bethia. I rolled over, and I told myself, Now don't commence thinking of her or you'll get no sleep tonight. But in spite of myself I kept seeing her and thinking and wishing I was going when Ben did. And my tongue kept licking out to feel of the scar I carried on my mouth. It had healed quick enough but there was a little rough ridge where it had been split. Every time I thought of her that had done it, the tip of my tongue would reach for it. Seemed like I carried around in my own flesh a living reminder of her.

I thought Ben was asleep but of a sudden he spoke up, so soft and teasing I could barely hear him. "I'll tell her you're abuilding her a cabin over on the Green."

Like I'd been stung, I jumped. "You'll do no such," I yelled at him. "I'll do my own telling when I get ready!"

He commenced laughing and then smothered it out in his blanket. I knew I'd given myself away by being so quick. "Aw, go to sleep," I growled and turned over myself.

But I was grinning in the dark. Ben would let fall a word where she could hear it, I knew. Not much of one. Just the naming of me, likely. Just enough so's she wouldn't forget, and that'd do till I could get back and do my own talking. I rubbed my thumb over the scar. By grannies, I thought, she'd ought to have to look at it the rest of her days just for giving it to me!

❦❧

# CHAPTER
# 8

IT WAS A PEACEFUL TIME that followed the meeting at Boonesburg. Peaceful beyond what we had a right to expect, seemed to me. Not a sign of a redskin had been seen for weeks. It was like the lot of them had disappeared, leaving no trace. It didn't go natural and there was no settling into ease because of it. There was no knowing what to make of it, but I made sure it wasn't to be counted on, and when I worked in the corn field I kept my gun as handy as my hoe.

The corn was up now, green and tender down the rows. That was my first corn crop . . . the first living thing I'd ever planted and tended on my own, and I admired it a heap. Used to stand and look at it and listen to it. Folks that say growing things don't speak a language of their own don't know what they're talking about. Corn makes a rustling sound, even when there's no wind blowing, like the blades unwrapping sigh on leaving the seed. And if you look close you can fairly see it taking on height, shooting up slim and tall. Corn is a proud-growing thing.

The spring wore into summer and the days got longer and hotter and the nights had less chill in them. The rye grass and clover on the slope of the knoll grew close and high and was a thick mat to my knees when I waded through it. The honey locust trees down near the spring bunched out in clustery blooms that brought the bees swarming around. Sometimes I'd stand there and listen to them. They made a steady buzzing sound that went like a hundred little drums all rolling out together. When you stood still enough and listened long enough it got in your head and went buzzing through your whole body until it was a shaking clean through. It gave me the idea of having a stand or two of bees someday when I could get around to it. So many blossoming trees about had ought to make the honey ripe and good, I thought.

I had time now to wander off the place and I went hunting several times over in the hills that lay to the west. We'd called them the Knobs when we'd been here before, on account of they were little knobby hills that looked like they'd been tumbled and dropped helter-skelter any whichway. There was a plenty of game in the hills, squirrel, turkey and deer, and for a time I could roam as wild as the game, taking pleasure in the roaming. I aimed to make a good settler, and I figured I would. I knew I could stay with anything I commenced. But there is something loosening and freeing about being in the woods, and I never had any doubts but I'd always love it best, and I never had any doubts but what I'd take to the woods when I could.

I wondered if Bethia would be the kind of woman didn't want her man off wandering around. I didn't much think she would be. She'd know I'd have to kill so's we'd have meat, and she likely wasn't flinchy or easy-scared at being left. Anyway, a woman had to take her man the way he was. I had to grin, though, as I thought it worked the other way around too. To hinder or help was in a woman's power, and some I'd known I wouldn't of shook a stick at. But I didn't figure Bethia was that kind. She had spunk and gall, as I had good reason to know, and it would stand her and me both in fine stead.

I rode over to Ben's several times and he came over one day to look at my place. He thought it was sightly and said I'd chosen well. He had some news that day. Dannel was leaving soon to go for his family and Colonel Henderson was going back to have a meeting with his partners. "Claims he'll be back in the fall," Ben said. "I reckon you've heared George Rogers Clark is at Harrodstown."

"No. What's he doing out here?"

"Taking a look around. He's been out thisaway before a time or two, and thinks highly of the country. Says he aims to settle here hisself."

"I've never seen him," I said, "but I've heard talk of him."

"I knowed him in Bouquet's campaign," Ben said. "He's a right good man. Good soldier . . . but I'd say he's a mite ambitious."

"Wonder if he'll throw in with the colonel too."

"No way of telling."

He was getting ready to leave and was already on his horse when I recollected I'd meant to ask him whether he'd been seeing many buffalo over his way. "Not many," he said. "Not near as many as I'd expected from the talk of their numbers in the country. Dannel said there was a plenty up on the Licking, though."

"Let's you and me take a sashay up that way. I got a hankering for buffalo meat."

"Wisht I could," he said, "but I look to be going back to the settlements in another day or two. I hope you well, though."

When Ben had ridden off, I made up my mind to take a turn up around the Licking by myself, and to start out right then. But riding along I wondered if Jim Harrod wouldn't like to go. From the talk I'd heard around the campfires during the war I knew he was a good hunter and loved it. Him and his brother had hunted over in the Illinois country for a time, out of Kaskaskia, and had roamed free amongst the Illinois Indians. They'd trapped and hunted and shipped their furs down the river to the French, on account of the British not allowing any hunting and trapping west of the mountains. He had a big name as a hunter and I figured if he wasn't tied up with something else he'd like to go.

The path lay within a few miles of Jim's Boiling Spring claim and I veered that way to see if he might be working there. I guessed right for he was chopping trees, alone and hard at work. I shouted to warn him of my coming and he dropped his axe and came to meet me, a grin stretching his mouth all over his face. "Howdy," he said, "get down."

"No time. You're getting on with your clearing, I see."

"I'd ort to, for sure," he said. "Facts is, I been so busy lending a hand to new folks coming in and laying off their pieces for 'em I've not got as much done on my own as I'd like."

"Reckon there's been a considerable number come since it's warmed up," I said.

"Several."

I looked around me at the clearing. He'd picked a nice place for his own. "You aiming on bringing your woman out in time?" I asked him.

"When I get one," he said, laughing. "I'd have to find me one first."

I laughed too. "Not broke to harness yet, huh? Me neither."

He rubbed his hands together and dusted the dirt off his palms. "I've not thought a heap on it. I'd thought to bring on the rest of my brothers and folks, if they'd come. Reckon that'll be family enough for me. I'm kind of woman-shy."

"Like a gun-shy dog."

"Well, I ain't to say been that skeered, but they make me a mite uncomfortable. Whyn't you get down?"

"I got to go on. Don't reckon you've had much time to hunt lately."

"I've always got time for that," he said, grinning up at me. "I can't settle myself down to this clearing and building for long at a time. Always ruther to be out somewheres. But," he went on, sobering, "they's been sore need of game amongst the folks too. Hit gets skeercer and skeercer nearabouts."

"Always does," I said. "Folks come in and skeer the game off . . . what they don't kill off. Go with me. Let's take a real sashay and come back with a load of buffalo meat for 'em."

He didn't say a word. Just threw his axe in the shelter nearby, picked up his gun and untied his horse. When we'd headed off through the woods he commenced laughing. "Man, I'm glad you come by! Where you heading? The Blue Licks?"

"I reckon. Dannel told Ben there was buffalo there."

"Never seen the time they wasn't. I've seen herds that would run into the thousands there. Let's go by the fort and pick up a pack horse."

We made our way east and north, fording the river which some called the Louisa and some the Kentucky, leaving Boonesburg to the right. The country was level to rolling here, the stand of rye grass and clover high and sweet. It was the first time I'd ever been up in this part of the country and I had the feeling of being on a kind of upland or plain. There were no hills, just a gentle roll of swelling land and a high blue sky overhead.

"You ever hear," I asked Jim, chuckling at the remembrance, "what Dannel said of this country?"

"No. Can't say as I have."

"He said he reckoned heaven must be a Kentucky kind of place."

Jim laughed, and then he looked around. "Does seem," he said, "like it's might near too good for men."

From the start I'd felt at home with Jim Harrod. He was an easy man to be with, and an easy man to like, and, it might be, too easy led by those he thought to be more knowing than himself. He was agreeable and pleasant, and I'd heard that when there was quarrels and ructions amongst his men it always bothered him. I wished he'd not been so quick to take up with the colonel and I couldn't help thinking that in time he'd weary of the Transylvania Company. He'd worked too hard to get his settlement going and he was a man of too free and independent a nature. What a power he'd be if he could come to see things the way me and Ben saw them. Thinking so, I asked him if the men at Harrodstown were still feeling pretty good about the agreements made at Boonesburg.

"Some is. Some ain't. Looks like there's no suiting all. Isaac Hite is about the worst disgruntled of the lot. He says we got took in. I don't know . . . don't know what to think. I reckon you've heared Cap'n Clark is stopping with us lately?"

"Ben told me."

"He's some of the same opinion as Isaac. He's from the east and he claims they's a heap of talk that things betwixt the colonies and the British is worsening all the time. He says if they's war with the British, the colonel can't never prove his title on account of it resting with the crown."

"By grannies, Jim," I said, "that man's talking sense! Is he still at Harrodstown?"

"No. He's went on to Williamsburg. He aims to see what he can find out in Virginia."

"And he thinks there's likely to be war with the British."

"So he says. So does my brother, Will, from what he hears up around Fort Pitt. The feeling that we've got to be free of Britain is strengthening all the time . . . they both say."

I'd not given it much thought. To say the truth not many of us out beyond the seaboard towns and settlements had given it much thought. We were too far removed from the hardships the taxes and abuses worked in those parts for them to seem very real to us. We knew the pot was simmering . . . we heard of it and we talked of it, some. As a rule men take concern over the things they bed down with day to day. In the east it was taxes and tea and shipping and tariff and so on. On the Holston it was making clearings, planting crops, killing meat to eat and fighting Indians. There were times when not even London seemed any further away than Philadelphia. But . . . if war came between Britain and the colonies, I made no doubt every man in the western country would be for the colonies.

At the moment, though, and because it was closest home, I have to admit I paid more attention to the fact that the colonel might be done out of his title than to any reasons and aims for the war. And I feel no shame for admitting it. It's but the way of men.

But Jim was talking again. "Cap'n Clark said a thing has been troubling me some. He said whyn't we pull off from Henderson and set up for ourselves. Said we had first rights and hadn't ort to pay him any mind."

"What's troubling about that? Some of us has been thinking that right along."

"Well, that ain't actually all. He didn't to say advise it, but he hinted right strong that the facts is we can set up free of Virginia, too."

That pulled me up short. "Free of Virginia! Why, that's where we've got our rights. What would we want to be free of Virginia for?"

"Now, just calm down, Dave. I ain't the one saying it. I'm just telling you. It went like he thought we could just as well set up a government of our own and sell off the land to get the money to back it up. That way we'd not be beholden to nobody."

"No," I said, and I tried to make it stout, "we got no right to do that. Jim, you wouldn't actually go along with Clark on a scheme like that, would you?"

"Dave, it ain't a scheme. He just kind of hinted like it could be worked."

"Well, let him keep his hints to himself. Ben said he was a ambitious kind of fellow. Ten to one if he could get enough to follow him in a plan like that he'd set himself up to run it!"

Jim started laughing. "My God, don't be such a firebrand. What are you and Ben Logan aiming to do? Run it yourselves?"

I had to laugh, too, but I was serious about it at the same time. "No, we ain't aiming to run it ourselves. But there's one thing you can put in your cud and chew on, Jim Harrod. We sure as hell ain't aiming for nobody else to run it either. This country is part of Virginia and we'll abide by the Virginia law."

He took it good-humored. "Well, anyway, Cap'n Clark is good friends with Patrick Henry and he said he was going to have a word with him about Colonel Henderson and try to find out which way the wind is blowing back there. He can do us that much good, leastways."

I was glad to hear him say *us.* I took it to mean he was commencing to see the light a little.

We came the second night to a clearing on the Elkhorn. "This is Joe Lindsay's stand," Jim said, "we can take the night with him."

He had a good cabin, tight and well built, and a crop of corn, beans and turnips growing in his field. But it wasn't Joe Lindsay came to the door when we hollered. I was never so surprised in my life. It was Johnnie Vann. "Johnnie!" I yelped, "what you doing in the country?"

He came out wiping his hands down the sides of his pants and grinning. "Just moseying. 'Light and tie. Howdy, Jim."

"You already know Jim Harrod, then."

"Knowed him . . . how long is it, Jim?"

Jim stuck his tongue in his cheek and figured. "Fifteen years?"

"About that. Get down. I got a stew on boiling. My horses is in that little pasture out back. Reckon you can put yours there too."

When we went inside Jim asked where Joe was. "Got no idea," Johnnie said, dishing up the stew, "I was passing . . . just made myself at home."

Joe had whittled him some bowls out of buckeye, and we joshed about how fancy it went to be eating out of dishes. We ate and talked. Johnnie wanted to know where we were heading. "To the Licks . . . after buffalo," Jim said, "just go with us."

Johnnie pondered it a minute. Then he slapped his knee. "I'll do it. I've not been on a hunt with you in a time and a time."

That started them off and I sat back and listened to two men talk that had something to talk about. Seemed they'd known one another since they were both yearlings, and Johnnie had come from the Conococheague country up in Pennsylvania same as Jim, and before he'd commenced trading with the Indians Johnnie had trapped and hunted all over the Illinois country. Him and the Harrod boys had had many an adventure together. They told of some of them, and while I allowed for the stretching we all did telling tales, they still made good listening. They'd covered a lot of country and been in a lot of tight places.

They'd about run down and I was beginning to think of turning in when of a sudden Johnnie commenced talking to Jim in Indian. I was never much hand to pick up Indian talk and all I knew was a little Cherokee, but it wasn't Cherokee Johnnie was talking. Jim answered him and they went on for quite a spell in what sounded like a lot of jabber to me. Whatever they were talking about it must of been kind of sad, for their faces looked that way. Finally when they stopped I said, "What kind of Indian talk is that?"

It was Jim answered me. "Delaware."

I reckon I showed my surprise. "You've mixed and mingled with the Delawares enough to get to know their talk?"

"Well," he said, "they're right friendly, and back when Will and me hunted out of Kaskaskia I used to get along real good with 'em. Stayed with 'em several times out hunting. Facts is," he went on, "I've stayed amongst 'em two, three months at a time. You can't help picking up their talk when you're around 'em a spell. Johnnie was just telling me some of their news."

It was then I did a thing that makes my face turn red to this good day, all unthinking and meaning only to joke. "You two," I said, "being around Indians as much as you've been, you sure you never took you a squaw amongst 'em? I've heard there's some real handsome ones, if you don't mind 'em being kind of dark."

There was a stillness so quiet that if a mouse had skittered across the room it would of sounded like a buffalo. Then Johnnie stood up and without saying a word walked past us and went outside. I stared after him. "What's got into him?" I said.

Jim looked at me without saying anything either for a minute. "Dave," he said, then, "that was the foolishest thing I ever heared a man say. Didn't you ever know that Johnnie's woman is a Delaware, and he's got two or three kids? And he lives amongst 'em when he's not out trading."

I believe a feather could of pushed me over. "I swear I never knew it," I said, and I commenced scrambling to my feet to go outside and find Johnnie. Jim laid his hand on my arm.

"Leave it lay," he said.

But I shoved his hand off. "Well, by grannies, I think a heap of Johnnie . . . I never meant . . . well, it's a man's own business and I don't aim for him to think I'm looking down on him. . . ."

"You'd best leave it lay, like I say, Dave."

I wouldn't, though. I went outside and stumbled around trying to find him, but he wouldn't answer when I called and I didn't run across him anywhere. I did know he hadn't left, though, for his horses were still in the pasture. I gave it up and went back inside finally and rolled up in my blanket. It was a long time before I slept. Wherever my thoughts settled they always came back to trouble me for having spoke out of turn. I'd of cut my tongue out before treading on Johnnie's feelings. It just went to show how big a fool a man could be with loose talk.

I thought Jim was asleep but when I'd turned and tumbled for a good hour trying to get off myself he spoke up. "Don't worry no more, Dave. If he's not gone in the morning I'll make a chance to tell him you didn't know and didn't mean nothing. It's just he's had it throwed in his face by so many he's touchy about it."

"He'd ort to know I wouldn't."

"Likely he will. It just hit him wrong."

It was a big relief to me when Johnnie showed up next morning acting like nothing had happened. It was like I'd never said a word and Johnnie had never walked out the door. There was just morning talk about catching up the horses, the chances of finding a sizable herd of buffalo, whether to leave Johnnie's pack in the cabin or take it along.

We got off at first light and rode all day. Along towards evening we came to the Blue Licks. I thought I'd seen signs of big herds before, but I'd never seen nothing could compare with what I saw then. The banks of the stream had been trampled till no grass grew anywhere. Animals seeking salt will lick the ground where they find it bare as the palm of your hand. These banks were furrowed and grooved like they'd been plowed, graveled out and worn slick by thousands of rough tongues.

"They've been lately," Jim said.

Johnnie nodded. "Likely they'll be seeking water come morning."

We made camp and turned in without any talk.

It was Jim waked me. It was still dark but I could feel morning all around. You can always tell early morning. You feel it in the lightening and freshening of the air. Night air has got a heaviness to it, and just before day it thins and shifts and its weight is rolled back. You can tell early morning, too, in the way little things start stirring in the woods, little waking animals, stretching and turning and making ready to commence their day. And you can tell it in the smell. The night damp brings the earth smell out, and it's strongest just before day. Jim shook my shoulder. "Listen," he said.

I listened. Before I could hear it, I felt it. Down in the earth and under me, quivering and trembling, nothing yet to be heard, just to be felt. Like apple jelly, held solid in a glass, but shaky if you touch it with a finger . . . that's the way the ground under me felt. Then I could hear it . . . a sound like a storm wind gathering, commencing to heave and rumble and the quivering in the ground turned into a heavy jar. The thoughts of the size of a herd that was causing it made me shivery all over. "It's time," Jim said.

We rode through the woods towards the sound and came out on the edge of a wide, endless meadow. Out of the woods it was lighter, and we pulled up a minute to look. Then we saw them, coming up over a long rising swell of land. Hundreds and hundreds and hundreds of them moving slow and cumbersome together, big shaggy beasts with their heads low and their humps rising and falling. I didn't even know I was holding my breath till I let it out with a gust. There was no end to them. As far as you could see across the meadow they kept coming, the ones behind pushing the ones in front, and you had the feeling they'd move on like that forever, one great, solid pack, something inside them pushing them to hunt for salt and water, as unstopping as a slide of land down a mountain. We waited.

"Ready?" Jim said finally.

I looked to my priming. "Ready."

Johnnie kicked his horse up beside us. "Ready," he said.

We took off at a run, making straight for the near flank, and all of us yelling and shouting like redskins. At the noise the leaders of the herd stopped and raised their heads, snorting and blowing. Then they commenced milling and when we got closer they bore left, turned and began running, the rest of the herd following blindly where the leaders went. The meadow was long and flat and gave them room to turn.

Soon we were alongside and I picked my animal. Before I could fire, though, I heard another shot and from the corner of my eye saw one of the beasts drop. Then I took my own shot and when I saw the animal go down a kind of crazy wildness went through me. I pulled up to reload and then went tearing down the flank of the herd again, and again and again until I lost count of the times. Not till the last of the herd was disappearing over the hill at the far end of the meadow did I pull up and stop. Beck was breathing hard and so was I, the excitement still running plumb out to the ends of my fingers. I sat there and watched the last of them out of sight. Buffalo, I thought. There wasn't any other hunting like it. Lordy, Lord . . . the sight of a herd, the feeling of size and bigness, the fast run down the flank . . . all of it just plain set a man on fire.

I rode back then to where Jim and Johnnie were. Jim was already down making ready to skin out the first animal. "Man, that went good," I said. "I know I got five shots, but I think I missed the last one."

"I missed one of mine, too," Jim said. "Too big of a hurry. But we got a plenty. Too many, in fact. We'll just take the tongues and humps and hearts and livers. All we can pack."

I set to with my knife to help, but Johnnie just stood there looking out over the meadow spotted with the beasts we'd killed. "Fifteen," he said, after a spell. "We killed fifteen."

I was bubbling over. "That's pretty good, I'd say."

Johnnie pulled his knife out and commenced to work on a carcass nearby. "It's too good. Three would of been a plenty. Hit's so good there'll be none left, soon."

I just stared at him. No buffalo left? When there were herds that size in the country? "You're crazy," I said.

"Am I? What happened to the deer and the elk and even the small game over on the Holston? What's commencing to happen to it here?"

"But they've never run in herds the size of buffalo!"

He just lifted his shoulders and let them drop. "You'll see. They'll go, too."

I reckon I knew he was right, for I couldn't help looking over the meadow at all of them we'd killed and would leave lying there for the wolves, saving their best parts. We hadn't made a dent in that big herd, but let enough folks come into the country, all of them shooting as careless as we'd done, just for the pure excitement of it, and I could see what would happen. And it did. There's not been a buffalo in Kentucky for years.

But that day I just felt a little sorry and pitched in and helped skin out what we could pack. Johnnie took enough for a meal or two, and left us then, riding off to the north without even looking back.

When we got back to Harrodstown the first piece of news we heard was that Colonel Henderson had been by on his way back to the east. The place was buzzing with the talk of what might come out of the meeting of the proprietors. It was too late for me to ride on, so I took the night at the fort and we sat around after supper and talked. The men were all uneasy. "It's untelling," they said, "what'll come of it. They's talk from Boonesburg they're aiming on raising the price of the land, and some talk they'll even commence charging a surveying fee."

Jim tried to be pacifying. "It stands to reason," he said, "they'd have to meet together sometimes. The colonel ain't out here by hisself. He's got to report back to the company. No need of getting troubled and bothered about it."

"What's the worst of it, Jim," one of the men said, "is, they're gobbling up all the good land over at the Falls, and you know in reason around the Falls is the best location in the country."

"Who says so? Right here is the best location to my notion."

"John Floyd said so. Said it was but sensible to think the Falls was the best place for a town. Said river trade was bound to build up there, and land would be powerful valuable when it done so. Said he aimed on staking him a piece over there."

"So let him. I like right here."

"So do I, Jim. I like it fine for myself. But if them greedy hogs takes all the best land around the Falls, they can set up for theirselves and have the say of all the trading. Seems to me like it ort to be open to all alike."

Jim agreed, "But it's no use crossing the river till we get to it. We'll not be knowing what they aim to do till the colonel gets back. All we can do is wait and see, ain't it?"

"Yeah. Wait and see. Set here on our backsides and let them hog up all the best land, fix the price of land to suit theirselves, get rich offen the folks that's got to sweat for it. I don't like it, Jim."

Jim's face showed he was bothered and I thought it was a good time to put in my oar. "Well, one thing . . ." I said, "don't look like the colonel could have that meeting of the delegates in September like he aimed to. I misdoubt he'll get back in time."

"That's so," Jim said. "I'd plumb forgot that. Reckon he'll have to put it off."

"Gives a kind of breathing spell, don't it?"

He looked at me. "Breathing spell for what?"

"Well, for thinking on something to do. Something like sending a petition to Virginia, maybe."

"A petition to Virginia! What for? What kind of a petition?"

"A petition," I said, giving it to him straight, "telling 'em we are part of Virginia and deserving of their protection and interest! And a petition telling 'em we don't like the colonel and don't aim to knuckle under to him. How long you men aim to bow and scrape around him, anyhow? Government, yes. I'm for it, same as you. But we got a government . . . Virginia government. We don't need the colonel's government, and we don't need the colonel setting himself up over us and setting up his own kind of laws."

"But the colonel's here. And he's got the rights to the land. Looks to me like we got to deal with him."

"We don't have to deal with him at all. He's got no right to the land till that title of his is proved, and I'll lay you my four hundred to a coonskin it's never proved. Think on it, Jim. If enough of us get up a petition and sign it and send it over to the Assembly, they'll come out for us. We got to tell 'em we ain't beholden to anybody in this country but them, Jim, and we got to show 'em!"

Some of the men commenced to mutter and talk amongst themselves, but Jim just rubbed his chin. "It's a confusing time. Nobody can tell what's best or right to do. I don't see nothing, myself, but to wait."

I could of punched him in the nose, but it wouldn't of done any good. He had a right to make up his own mind. But he was so slow-moving, so easygoing and pleasant and agreeable to all, it tried a man's patience. Looking at it one way I could see how he'd have to make sure, for he'd led a big party of men into the country and they looked to him as the one heading them up. I could see how Jim couldn't just make up his mind for himself like Ben had done, and like I'd done. But in another way, it was on that account as much as any other he'd have to take a firm stand soon or late. Men don't follow a leader that blows with any wind, and the men that had trusted Jim and come into the country with him were already commencing to be fretful and restless. In time he was going to have to choose, and slow as he might be I didn't think Jim Harrod was one to bow and scrape long, either.

Well, I'd said my say, for whatever it was worth. There's times a man's called on to do that and I'd felt this was one of the times. I thought maybe the idea of the petition would give Jim something to ponder on. What happened next would just have to wait.

◆◆◆

# CHAPTER
# 9

WHAT HAPPENED NEXT was just one slow, hot day after another moving the time along through the summer. It rained a lot that year and the days it didn't rain the air was so heavy and sticky it was like a steaming blanket thrown all over the country. The sun would come up, looking like a fried egg, orange-colored and fat with heat, and it would scorch down through a kind of muggy haze, and a heavy, rank growth stewed and spread everywhere. The cane down by the river got so thick and high that not even my passing every day kept the path clear. I had to keep whacking away at it, and weeds and grass matted and tangled waist-high all over the meadow. The sprouts and bushes in the corn grew faster than I could hoe. I'd get it cleaned out one week and the next one I'd have to start all over again. Some days I was about ready to cuss a land where the weather pushed the green stuff up so fast. I mortally never saw stuff grow like it did that year. Of course, you get a hot rainy summer any time in Kentucky and you get a full, rank growth.

Ben's wife had given him some bean seed and some squash to bring along and he'd passed a few on to me, which I'd dropped in between the corn. Some woods varmint got the most of the beans while they were yet young and tender, but a few grew and filled out into sizable beans. I gathered some along and cooked several messes of them, not caring much for them but not wanting to see them waste. Once I tried the squash. I don't know whether I fixed it wrong, or whether that's the way squash is supposed to taste, but it was a dish I couldn't say much for, and I've never tried it again. I gathered the things up fast as they yellowed and fed them to the horses. They appeared to think highly of them and eat hearty, but the mare had a puny spell about then and I've always laid it to the squash. Apparently it's not a fit food for man or beast.

I recollected that my mam used to lay beans by for the winter by snapping them and drying them out in the sun. Thinking back I recalled she always waited till the vines were just about ready to quit bearing, so when the leaves on my vines began to wither and turn yellow I took a morning and picked off all the beans. Then it took me all afternoon to string and snap them. When I'd done I spread them out on my blankets to dry. I never thought to bring them in every night out of the dew wetness, and the next time I went to see about them they'd all mildewed and softened and turned green with mold. They stunk worse than a polecat. I had to take the blankets down to the river and wash them to get the mess off. I figured I'd better stick to meat from then on till I had a woman knew how to take care of such.

I built the cabin that summer, too. We use it for a cookhouse now and it's as stout as the day I built it. But it was the kitchen, parlor, sleeping room and workroom all, for many a year. I'd promised Ben to keep an eye on his place while he was gone and every week or so I'd ride over there and take a look around. Worked his corn out several times, and I'd always make sure his cabin hadn't been tampered with. I reckon it was being around his cabin so much made me think of going ahead with my own. I didn't to say need one, for the shelter served me well enough, but my thoughts kept turning to it and one day when I got back from Ben's I just set to and commenced work on it.

I felled the biggest walnut first. If I had it to do over I wouldn't cut that tree, but I thought it stood right where the cabin had ought to go. I could of put the cabin to one side or the other, but it was such a big tree and made such a heavy shade I thought it would darken the house too much. But I was sorry the minute my axe bit into it. I'd swung hard and the axe went in to the helve, and it made a kind of thin, whining sound, like crying. When I pulled the axe free the sap oozed out of the gash, slow and in big drops, like blood from a hurt too deep to bleed fast and free. I had a queer feeling of hurting something alive and knowing. I'd always wondered about the things of the woods that were supposed to be unreasoning and unknowing . . . the trees and bushes and even the rocks. Seemed to me that no one could say for sure if they felt and hurt or not. Sometimes I'd thought how could it be that anything that was alive and growing didn't know and feel its life and treasure it. I'd never named it to a soul, for of course it went foolish to be thinking so, but I'd had the feeling many a time in the woods and by the streams of being bound all around by things that knew and felt just like me.

Now it was like the walnut tree had cried out and bled, and I felt a pity for it. When I laid my hand against it, it was still shuddering from the axe blow. Seemed as if I'd ought to comfort its grieving and give it some word of explanation of what was happening to it. I couldn't think of any, though, and feeling like a whipped dog I went on and cut it down.

I chopped down five more to make this clearing here in the grove, then I left the balance of the walnuts standing for shade and for the nuts. Most of the logs from those trees hewed out close to two foot square. I laid the sills from them, then I let the rest of them lie and season out for doors and cupboards and shutters and the like. The cabin is twenty foot square. I wanted it roomy. I figured Bethia would be a finicking woman and I aimed to build a cabin would suit her. From the start there was no need hiding from myself I was building for her, and once I commenced, it surprised me how the thoughts of her ceased pestering me, like doing something real and actual made them solid under hand, and instead of buzzing around in my head and tormenting me, they fell into place like the logs of the cabin walls. The house was for her, and like she'd been there telling me what to do, I made it nice for her.

I picked oak trees for the wall logs, for they're stout and lasty, and I squared them up all of a size. Then I adzed them smooth and notched them and levered them into place. It was slow work, but there was a pleasure in doing it and now that the corn was laid by I had all my time to give to it. There was sixteen hours of daylight that time of year and outside of doing a little hunting for something to eat, I spent them all working on the house.

I cut locust saplings for the ridgepole and rafters, and I peeled them and seasoned them in the sun awhile, then rubbed them with bear grease until they were slick and shiny. The shingle boards were made of ash, for it don't curl too bad, and I tied them down with slabs of hickory laid across. I had the time and the notion to lay a floor, too, and I made it out of ash boards that I'd adzed smooth. To whiten it I rubbed it everyday with sand I got from the river bed. By the time I got through with it, it was so slick and polished you couldn't raise a splinter with a knife blade. Then I cut windows on two sides and made shutters out of the walnut that had been seasoning, and I made a big walnut door and hung it in place with hinges made out of buffalo skin.

What kind of a chimney to make puzzled me for several days. The easiest would be the cat-and-clay kind, for there were sticks aplenty close by and mud handy at the spring. But the prettiest and the best kind would be one made of rock. I'd done so good on the house itself I couldn't content myself to settle for a cat-and-clay chimney, so in spite of the extra work I decided in favor of rock. There was plenty of rock, too, on the hillside, but it handled heavy and had to be hauled. Took me two solid weeks to haul enough rock to build that chimney. I built me a sled out of poles and took turns between Beck and the pack horse pulling it. That chimney is a good six foot wide and three foot deep, for I didn't skimp. I allowed Bethia would be the kind disliked smoke in the house and I made her a good-drawing chimney while I was at it. The hearth is made of two big slabs I hauled out of the river, and the water had smoothed them and turned them gray. There's not a rough place on that hearth.

I finished up around the last of August, and I can tell you I took a deal of pride in what I'd done. I don't know of anything makes a man feel more of a man than building himself a house, unless, and I reckon after all you could put it first, it's when he looks on the face of his first youngun. But I had that ahead of me yet. For the time my pride was content with the house.

I didn't move into it, though. I wanted it fresh and unused for Bethia, and I knew a man's ways would soil and tarnish it. But I liked to walk up and sit in the doorway of an evening and look out across the meadow and think of the time when she'd be there too and we'd be using it together. One night when I was sitting there, turned side-ways so's I could look inside or out, whichever way I wanted, I got to thinking of the way the fire would burn in the chimney and flicker its light all over the room and warm it with a good, thawing heat. I thought how there'd be snow outside, all down the side of the knoll and across the valley, and likely ice around the edges of the spring. But inside Bethia and the youngun would be safe. I thought how she'd likely keep the cradle near the hearth, and the cradle would be dark and shiny, hewed out of a piece of the walnut and smoothed with bear oil and the rubbing of my hands. Almost I could hear the rockers creaking, and the youngun crying. Thinking on it I wondered if the mixing of Bethia's red hair and my own black wouldn't give it hair the color of a chestnut horse. And what color would blue eyes and brown stirred up together turn out.

Then I laughed at myself for my foolishness and got up and pulled the cabin door to, shutting out my thoughts and my notions. It would be a time before there was e'er youngun rocking in a cradle on that hearth, and I'd best be occupying myself with something to show for my time instead of puling around like a lovesick boy.

There was no Indian sign all that summer. Not in my parts, anyhow. I hadn't seen any near Ben's place, either, and I knew somebody would of ridden out with the news had there been trouble elsewhere. With the cabin done, the corn laid by and time hanging heavy on my hands I felt restless and I decided to take a little sashay up to Harrodstown and listen to some news and talk with folks for a change. I rode by Ben's and found it quiet, then I headed north. The squirrels were thick in the woods and I killed several to take along. They'd swell the stewpot a little, although I was mortally sick of squirrel meat.

I was about halfway between Ben's and the fort, riding along slow and easy, when all of a sudden Beck pricked up her ears and balked, spreading her front legs and trembling all over. I slid off quick and knowing she'd be snorting or whinnying in another minute, put my hand on her throat to choke it off and commenced talking to her. "Easy, now, Beck. Easy girl," and at the same time I backed her off the trail into the bushes. She stood quiet but quivery, and I had time to see to my gun.

But it wasn't a redskin that had scared the mare. It was a white man, so worn out he was stumbling and beyond taking care, for he was noisy with his walking and not looking to either side of the path. Just the same I called out a warning before stepping out of the bushes. "Howdy, friend."

He stopped and his gun came up quick. I stood out where he could see me then and walked towards him. "You'd best take more care, mister," I told him. "You'd of been a powerful good shot for a Shawnee."

He kind of run his hand across his face and then like his legs had just given out on him he crumpled down on a stump. "Man, am I ever glad to see somebody! I'm just about used up."

"Well, rest yourself a mite," I said, "it's safe enough I reckon. You been on the trail?"

"Yes. I'm making my way to Harrodstown. My party is behind. There's four families of us and we've come over the trail with Dannel Boone. Arrangements have been made for us at Jim Harrod's place, so we left Dannel at Dick's River. He gave us directions how to get on to Jim's, but I reckon we lost the way. We've been wandering around in the woods three days now, not knowing where lay the trail."

"Where are the others?"

"Well, we've got stock with us and to save it in this heat we left it with my boy and some other lads on a little creek. That was two days ago. The rest of us were trying for the fort. We came up on the trail last night but the womenfolks were so pegged out we made camp and I set out by myself this morning for help to bring them in."

"You got womenfolks and younguns with you?"

The man was middle-heighted, with a brush of sandy hair and a trail-grown beard that bordered on red too. "Yes, we've got our families and our stock and as many of our belongings as we could bring. My name is Hugh McGary."

"Did Dannel bring his family?"

"He did. And Richard Calloway has brought his."

I started laughing. "Well, I reckon this'll really fix the palladium! Womenfolks and younguns in Kentucky!"

He looked at me, not understanding, and it brought to my mind how worn out he was. I hurried to get Beck. "Here, now," I told him, "first off we got to get you to Harrodstown. You're too tuckered to do a mortal thing but stretch out somewheres and rest your bones. Get on my horse, here."

He didn't want to but I made him, and when he finally crawled on the mare he let out a sigh. "It sure is a pleasure to take my weight off my feet."

With me leading the horse we started on. "You run into any trouble?" I asked him.

"Trouble? Nothing but trouble! All day . . . every day! Packs slipping, sink holes . . . we had to shoot one of the pack horses. Stepped in one and broke its leg. Creeks and rivers to ford, mountains to climb, brush to fight and heat, and worst of all women and younguns to see to. Crying women and puking younguns. Lord keep me from ever journeying with a pack of women and younguns again!"

He said it so strong I couldn't help laughing. But I hadn't meant that kind of trouble. "See any sign of Indian?"

"None. You been peaceable here?"

"So peaceable you wouldn't believe it. Too good to be true, but it's been right kindly of 'em to let us get a head start."

When we got to Harrodstown there were plenty willing to go back and help bring McGary's party in. Jim wasn't there, but the arrangements had been made all right and cabin room set aside for them. The whole fort had been waiting for them. The news that womenfolks and younguns had actually set foot on Kentucky land stirred up a heap of excitement. Not a married man in the fort but commenced thinking of bringing on his own woman and younguns, thinking if these could risk it, his could too. Truth to tell I got to thinking that since there were other women in the country for company, I might take a little sashay over to Joe's before cold weather started in and bring Bethia back with me. I'd not counted on it so soon, but my cabin was stout and we could weather the winter as good as anybody. I could easy go when I got my corn in and Ben got back. Traveling light I could get back to the stand before frost time. It made me feel lighthearted and good just to be thinking on it, for I hadn't thought to see her till spring.

The McGary fellow gave us directions how to find his two parties and we set out about midmorning, part of us heading for the boys and the stock and the rest of us heading for the women and families, but traveling together for a spell. I was leading the ones going for the families. The man had said they were camped on a little run just off the trail a piece and he'd slashed a big tree at the place to turn. We found it without any trouble and came up on their camp just as it was coming on towards dark. From a considerable distance we'd been smelling their supper fire and had seen its blink through the woods. It was foolish of them to have a fire, but folks have got to learn.

They had out a guard, though, for a little distance from the fire a man stepped out of the bushes. "You folks from Harrodstown?"

I answered him. "Yes. Hugh McGary is safe there and we have come to lead you in."

He slid his gun to the ground. "Obliged to you. The women and younguns have bedded down for the night. Reckon it'd be best to wait to travel till tomorrow."

We said it would. The man said his name was Hogan and he went with us on to the fire. There was another man sitting there and the Hogan fellow called his name as Tom Denton. Hugh McGary had spoken of three. "Where's the other one?" I said.

"Done turned in," Tom Denton said. "I'll rouse him if you want."

"No need. I just wanted to make sure you were all here."

They talked a spell of their journey and troubles and then we all bedded down.

The camp stirred at first light the next morning, the men hustling to bring in the horses, the women making breakfast, and the younguns milling about in everybody's way. I saw to my horse, went to the run and washed my face, took a look around the camp into the woods and then went back to the fire. It was then I saw Bethia bending over the fire, looking almost exactly as I remembered her bending over the hearth at Martin's, shielding her face from the heat with her arm thrown up in front of it, her red hair falling forward and swinging about her shoulders as she moved. I was never so glad or so surprised.

Nobody had said she was here amongst the families . . . kin to some of them, likely. I picked up my walk to a near-run and was just ready to call out to her, but she turned away from the fire and went over among the other women and one of them came to take her place. Bethia went towards some packs laid to one side. I started over that way, for she'd never seen me, but just then a man came out from behind some bushes and walked in her direction. I stopped dead in my tracks, stunned by recognizing the man. It was the one who'd already turned in when we'd got to the camp the night before and I'd not seen yet this morning. Not in a lifetime would I have looked for it to be who it was . . . things just don't run that way as a rule, and I'd not once thought of the man since I'd last seen him, his clothes burning and him hurrying to the Watauga to put out the fire. But I'd of known Judd Jordan anywhere I saw him, in spite of the fact I'd not noticed before he limped a little in his right leg when he walked.

I stood there and looked on while he went to where Bethia was rolling up some blankets. He said something to her and she answered him, and then he took the blankets and commenced tying them up, her helping. A cold shiver started making its way down my back. "Him and his woman are camped up the river a piece." I could hear Jim Knox telling it again, just the way he had that morning when we'd met at the council meeting. Judd Jordan and his woman. There's four families of us. That's what Hugh McGary had said. That was Judd Jordan over there. And Bethia was helping him make up his pack. But she'd do that, likely, anyhow, I told myself. She'd help out where she could. That never meant she was . . .

She must not of been doing to suit him, for of a sudden Jordan let out a string of cuss words and gave her a shove that made her stumble and fall over the pack, and that angered him more so that he jerked the pack loose and kicked out at her, hitting her on the leg. And that told the truth, for a man only did such things to his own woman. It made me sick and I turned around and went back to the fire.

The cold had spread to my hands and I warmed them over the blaze. In a kind of lightheaded way I thought how these mornings in early September had a chill in them and a damp from the mists in the low places that fair settled in a man's bones. I kept hearing a queer clicking sound and I looked around to place it. Then I knew it was my own teeth chattering and I set my jaws to hold them firm. I was shivery all over. And then all at once instead of being cold a hot flush ran over me and my face commenced burning and my neck and the insides of my arms felt on fire. I pushed my sleeve up and laid my hand there, but the skin was cool to touch, only it tingled where I put my fingers.

*She couldn't be Judd Jordan's woman.* I wouldn't think it. And my mind skittered around here and there. We'd best make a quick start soon as breakfast was done. We'd have to travel slow with women and younguns, and it was a good twenty miles. It would take all day at least, and might be another night. *Was she already wedded to Jordan in April?* Well, but she had to be. Jim had said him and his woman. *She was Judd Jordan's woman then that night at Joe Martin's.* Don't think of it. Think of something else. Think of . . . time we eat and got the packs tied on and everybody ready it would be a good hour past sunup, if not later. But the trail was fair between here and Harrodstown. Harrodstown. *There was cabin space lotted to Judd Jordan and his woman at Harrodstown. There was two cabins right next the corner.* Cabins. *There was a cabin on Green River. There was a cabin built specially for her and waiting for her. But she was going to stay in a cabin at Harrodstown.* Jacob Harman had said it, "These are the cabins for Hugh McGary's party." *That wasn't Bethia, though. That was somebody else.* Don't think. Think how the younguns are milling around and the women piddling till it's like to be noon before we get out of here.

I looked at the woman by the fire and saw her mouth was moving. She was talking but the words went through my head and made no sense at all. I felt like I'd been standing there by the fire since time began, everything stopped and moveless and me hurting inside like a big hand was squeezing in my chest. For the woman to speak was as astonishing as if the trees and rocks had suddenly commenced talking. And it was just as astonishing when I heard myself talking. "What did you say?"

"I said I reckon you're awful hungry. My man is always sour-spoke of a morning till he's eat. Reckon most others is the same."

I was going to say "yes ma'am," but what came out was different. "Who are those people?"

The woman looked where I was pointing. "That's Judd Jordan and his woman."

Well, now I knew. I stood there a minute longer and then I turned around and walked off. My legs felt stiff and numb and it seemed like the trees and the sky were whirling round. I ran into one of the Harrodstown men. "I'll meet you all at the trace," I told him, "or if I'm not there I'll be a little piece on ahead, looking out."

He just stared at me, and then when I pushed past him he said, "Ain't you going to eat?"

"I'll eat going," I told him. "This outfit's as slow as molasses. Hurry 'em up if you can."

I got on Beck and we hit the trail. Just to show you how much habit can be counted on to lead a man, I had no more notion of directions than a blind dog in a meat house. I paid no heed with my mind to which way I was heading, but I headed right. I never even bothered to duck the branches, just let them whip where they would, not seeing or heeding them. There was a kind of a dark veil over everything and I was in the middle of it. I barely knew I was riding, and that not until Beck stumbled and nearly threw me. Mean-like, I jerked her head around, too hard and quick and she snorted and sidled, being unused to such. That kind of brought me to. I'd never mistreated any animal I'd ever owned and likely I'd cut the mare's mouth jerking on the bit. But I'd not known before that when you hurt all over, almost too bad to stand it, you want to grind something else down and make it hurt too. This was like a toothache or a broken leg. My chest was so tight it pained me to draw breath, and I wanted to smash out with my fist, hit something hard and keep on hitting it till my arm went limp and all the tightness was worked out of me and I could feel slack and limber again. I got off and made my peace with Beck, and then decided I'd walk awhile.

When I got to the trace I thought I'd better wait, so I squatted against a tree. My stomach was empty and I thought maybe I'd feel better if it had something in it, so I got out some dried meat and commenced chewing on it. Without thinking I kept looking around. That was habit too, but the woods are always full of life if you've got eyes to see. There was a little brown bird sitting on the topmost branch of a shoemake bush. Light as the bird was it weighted down the limb and it swayed up and down under it. Something decided the bird to move on, and the commotion of its leaving stirred up a storm of shaking in the whole bush. What a to-do over one little bird's flight. There was a nuthatch circling up the trunk of an ash tree. Around and up, until he got to the first limb. Then he turned around and commenced circling back down again. Crazy bird. Didn't care whether his head was up or down. A flock of parakeets flew down and settled in a thicket, chattering like a bunch of silly women with their high-pitched scoldings. The parakeets are gone from Kentucky too, now. There was never a bird colored so bright and pretty, but they were like magpies for noisiness. There was a fox squirrel ran across the ground in front of me and up the bole of a tree, and another one ran along behind him. They barked at each other, quarrelsome and hoarse. I saw a snake twisting its way along through the leaves until it reached a green vine covering a log. It slithered under the vine and then turned so its head was but barely hidden.

I saw all those things and I heard them, but it was like looking at a picture, standing off and looking and seeing and hearing, but seeing nothing or hearing nothing inside myself. When I'd done eating I rubbed my hands together the way you will when you've been holding food, and there was a tender spot that had just healed from where I'd torn the palm of one hand against a jagged rock when I was building the chimney. *The chimney. I'd built a chimney and a whole cabin for her. I'd sit in the doorway of an evening and brought all the remembrances of her and piled them up, scant as they were and made rocks under my feet of them. I had sit there and dreamed how a fire would feel, come winter and cold, with two people to sit beside it, and I'd thought how the light from it would gleam on her red hair. Time and again I'd felt the scar on my mouth, glad it was there to recall her, and time and again, feeling it, I'd felt her mouth, soft and cushiony underneath my own.* And thinking of it now my senses drained away again and my face felt swollen and hot with the want of her. *But Jordan was the one that had her!* That block-shouldered, bull-headed, mean-tempered, ugly-streaked animal that passed for a man. *It was him could lay hand to her any time he pleased. I'd built her a hearth and had looked to see a cradle there . . . a cradle even! And it'd be Jordan's younguns she'd bear.* Goddlemighty, how much thinking and feeling can a man do and not go crazy!

Tormented beyond sitting still any longer I got up. The snake forked its tongue at me from under the vine, and suddenly, fired beyond any anger I'd ever known before I hacked a sprout off a bush as thick as my arm and I walked over to the snake. I pulled it out of the vine with the leafy end of the sprout and then I clubbed it to death, pounding it till it was soft and mashy, and keeping on pounding it till it was shredded and mixed with the dirt. Then I felt sick and I threw the club away. It wasn't even a poison snake.

I heard the sounds of their coming long before they got to the trace. They were a clumsy-moving party. I got on Beck and rode on, keeping out of sight but within hearing distance. Killing the snake had eased the tightness and numbness, and the cold and the heat of first hurt were passing. I could begin to see what a fool I'd been. The biggest damn fool that ever was. I reckoned hadn't anybody ever built as much on as little as I had to go on, and I thought that's what happens when a man departs from his own ways. David Cooper had gone his own way since he'd been a man, loving easy and never lingering, dipping here and yon into pleasure with a careless arm around every slim waist it found. It took a redheaded married woman to make a fool of him, and a double-dyed, simpleton idiot fool at that. Passing a tree I hit out at it with my fist and the pain ran the full length of my arm and felt good. That was over. Done with, and the hurt would pass like the hurt in my arm.

They traveled faster than I'd hoped or expected and got to Harroadstown around sundown. I rode in about fifteen minutes ahead of them. I meant to pass the news on to Jim and leave before they got there, but he kept me talking and they trailed into the square before I could get away. There was nothing to do but stand my ground.

Tom Denton and his folks were in the lead, and the Hogans came next. Last of all *they* came. They were walking, Jordan leading their pack horse, and I noticed the bloody froth around its mouth where he'd jerked at the horse's head. That went like him, I thought . . . mean-natured to animals and folks too.

She was worn out, I could tell. Her face was white and her shoulders sagged down. Her dress was sweaty and it hung slack and clung to her. There wasn't no swish of starch left in it now, and it was dirty and briar-torn. I felt a pity for her . . . a kind of sickening pity, but I hardened it as soon as I felt it. She'd picked her man, and it's a woman's place to go where her man goes. If that meant walking better than two hundred miles over rough wilderness trail, wearing herself down, suffering his ill-treatment, it was still her affair and none of mine. I wouldn't let myself feel soft towards her.

She stood there, patient, the only thing about her not changed being her hair. I reckoned nothing would ever change that. Not weariness or trail-dirt or time could ever tarnish its brightness. Jim came out to welcome the party and they clustered about him, all but her. Jordan handed her the lead rope of their animal and she stood off to herself, holding onto it. She looked around over the square and the cabins, and then her look rested on this man's face and that one's, and I waited, knowing it would find me soon. It did, and it passed on without giving any sign. If she was even a little bit glad to see somebody she'd seen before, she didn't let on. Just traveled her eyes across me like I wasn't there. And her not even batting an eyelash at me was all I needed to finish me off.

I slipped away. Not before, however, I provided myself with a jug of Lisha Evans' best fermented spirits. I wasn't aiming to lie awake all night thinking of Judd Jordan and his redheaded woman.

‎⟨§§⟩‎

# CHAPTER

# 10

IT WAS A BLEAK home-coming I had the next day . . . mighty bleak. The sight of the cabin topping the knoll rankled me into fresh anger with myself. "I'd ort to burn the damned thing down," I thought when I rode into sight of it, "setting up there so pleased with itself. Just ort to burn it into a pile of ashes."

I was more than half minded to do it. My head felt the size of a piggin and it pounded till it was like to bust my skull. Enough of Lisha's raw spirits to souse a man like I'd been soused the night before was full guaranteed to split his head next day. My mouth felt like it had grown a lining of lint, and my tongue was pure beaver pelt, furry and swollen and might near as stinking. I was dry as a drought-baked rain barrel, but all the water I drank did me no good, and besides my stomach was roiling in a way to make me heave up every drop I put in it. I was in a mood of plain disgust, with myself, and everybody else, with Kentucky and with life in general. I'd never before known such a flat gloom, and I thought it was like to last to the end of my days. Seemed like all pleasure and joy had fled from me, and there was nothing but gray flatness dooming me forever.

I started to get off at the spring but instead I rode on up the knoll to the door of the cabin, and there I sat staring at it. It was new and clean and it graveled me afresh to recollect, looking at the log walls and the fine barred door and shutters, how it had pleasured me to build it. It looks like a empty grave, I thought, just a stone-cold empty grave, and the words of a sad song-ballat came to my mind. *When I lie in the ground, stone-cold in the grave, scatter roses around, and with tears do them lave.* The words were so woeful and they made me feel so lonesome that a lump came in my throat and my eyes stung with a sudden wet. Not even the grave could make me feel any deader, I thought, so I turned and rode back to the spring, misery covering me over like a dark cloud.

I felt like that for several days, not finding comfort anywhere. But little by little it commenced lifting. My head cleared up and my stomach rid itself of the whisky poison, and one evening a rainstorm worked up and blew the heat and stickiness away and the air felt fresh and cool, and I was hungry and wanting to eat again. I went down to the river and fished awhile, and then washed all over, and when I came back to the spring along towards dark I felt stretchy and light-footed once more. I cooked my catch and while I was eating it came over me I'd been acting just like a youngun that howls over a splintered toe overlong, on account of he's feeling so good howling. I couldn't help chuckling.

I went on a long sashay the rest of the month . . . down the river almost to the barrens, the place the Indians had burned over till there was no growth of trees left. The way followed the twistings and turnings of the river, and it pleasured me again to be seeing all of its deeps and shallows, its shoals and its quiet places, and always its glass-green color. Was no river ever half so pretty. I reckoned that was on account of it hardly ever ran the same more than half a mile at a stretch. It was forever changing, running through the hills and across the valleys. The only thing never changing was the color.

I wandered Beck along, stopping where and when I pleased, fishing when it suited and cooling myself in the waters when I felt the need, kind of soaking up into myself the quiet and stillness. I've not ever had any name for the kind of feeling the woods bring me. All I know is that in the woods there is nothing to chafe or tighten, nothing to rile or compel. You can come and go as you please . . . you can do your own bidding. The woods that September were soothing to me, as ever. They were deep and shady. The river was forever winding. The sky was high, and no where was there a human voice to hear. It was like spreading salve on a fiery burn.

I found the limestone cave we'd come across before and I stayed a week there. There was an underground stream that flowed at the back of it and I'd lie for hours listening to it and watching the beads of water that formed on the roof of the cavern and dripped down the sides of queer-shaped rock slabs. I counted once and it took to sixty for a bead to form and drop. If it's true, like I've heard, that the water dropping carved out the rocks into the shape they were in, it must of taken an eternity to do it at that slow rate.

There was a meadow of white clover on just beyond the cave, and one night when I'd taken Beck there and hoppled her out so she could feed on the clover, I laid down on my back in it. It rose all around me and covered me over so I could only see by looking through it. It was damp from the dew and sweet-smelling and soft as a cushion under me. The katydids were fiddling away in the woods and so far off it was like listening to an echo a mockingbird was singing. The moon was full and bright and while I lay there and looked a scud of clouds raced across it, like a strong wind had sent them hurrying. I felt so peaceful and so quiet that I knew the time had come I could turn back. I knew I had freed myself of my tempers and ructions and the soreness was passing and I could think steady again. The grayness and flatness were going and I could even think with calm of living out my life with some hope it would be good. The next morning I headed home.

The month had turned and there was a feeling of fall in the air. The leaves of the trees were commencing to rust a little and show signs of fading, and the shoemake bushes were red. In the meadowy places the broom sedge was turning brown and along the watercourses the sycamore trees were whitening and shaking down their leaves. When they fell on the river they floated like sails, weightless on the water. The persimmons were withering. The summer heat had swelled them and now the sharpening chill was blueing and shrinking them. Soon they'd be dropping, loosened by the wind. The walnuts were falling, too, and, times, I'd ride through swirls of leaves the wind caught up and sent flying. I've often wondered if that season of the year is called the fall on account of things falling . . . like persimmons and walnuts and leaves. It could well be, seems to me.

When I got home I moved my packs and belongings into the cabin. There was no need keeping it fresh any longer and no need letting it be a empty grave. I thought I'd fill it and use it and lay Bethia's ghost by keeping house with it. There was no denying that when I thought of her, and it was often, there was still a hurt to it, for you can't break the habit of holding a person in a given place without it troubling you, but I figured I'd tamped it down where it belonged and I had the comeuppance of it.

Ben didn't get back until late in November. By that time I'd gathered in my own corn and his. My yield was fair, for I'd tended it pretty good. Ben's was a mite scant, but I figured if he wasn't aiming to bring his family out till spring we had enough between us to last us out the winter. I built a crib for mine, but I cribbed Ben's in his cabin.

The first I knew he was back was when he rode up one day. It was snowing that day, a fine, dry snow that was powdery in the wind. It was a time to stay indoors and I had a good fire going and was mending a pair of moccasins when I heard him call. I went out, feeling happier than I'd thought I'd be to hear him again. His face was stung red by the wind and the snow had powdered his shoulders and hat brim. " 'Light and tie," I yelled at him. "Man, this is a day, ain't it?"

"It is for a fact," he said. He got off and we took his horse around back to the shelter I'd built for my own animals. Ben looked around him at the cabin and the corncrib. "You been right busy since I been gone," he said.

"Some," I told him.

Inside the house he shook the snow off his hat and brushed it off his shoulders. "Mite early for snow," he said. Then he looked all around the cabin room. "It sure is a sightly place, Dave."

"It'll do," I said. "I was fixing to eat soon. I'll bound you're hungry, bucking that storm." I had a pot of stew hanging in the fireplace. "I got everything but my extry pair of moccasins in this stew but it'll fill you up, I reckon."

"Smells good," he said. He pulled up a stool to the fire and stretched out his feet towards the heat. "Much obliged for getting in my corn. I thought to be back in time to do it myself."

"Wasn't nothing," I told him.

We eat and then settled to our talking. I told him what meager store of news I was acquainted with. Had been but precious little happening. Looked like most had left out for the settlements, either to sell out and bring their families back, or to winter at home, or, in some cases, making their choice and going back for good. Hadn't been but a handful of folks in Kentucky all summer. The colonel was still in North Carolina . . . hadn't been no meeting in September on account of him not being in the country. There was some new settlers had come . . . early in September. I told of the coming of the women-folks, not mentioning, though, that Bethia had been amongst them.

Ben looked at me when I told that. "I reckon," he said, when I'd done, "you'd best know that girl you was so took with at Martin's is done wedded and has come to Kentucky with her man."

I just nodded my head and there was no more said of it.

"I sold my place back home whilst I was there," Ben said, then. "Got a fair price for it and was satisfied to sell."

"So? You aiming on wintering here then?"

"No. Not without I have to. We can stay with Ann's folks till spring. Did you aim to stay the winter at ary one of the settlements?"

"I hadn't thought of it. Why?"

"Well, I brung my cattle and hogs this trip and I was kind of hoping I could get you to see to 'em for me. Suit you as good to stay at my place during the cold?"

I felt some disappointment that Ben was going back to the Holston. I'd kind of planned we might hole up together for the winter and do some trapping down the river, but no need saying anything of that now. That was the way of a man that was married, though. He always had to go back home. "Sure," I told him, "might as well be there as here."

"I wouldn't of named it," Ben said, "but I allowed that now . . . well, I figured you'd be. . . ."

"You figured right," I told him. "My time's my own."

He looked kind of uncomfortable and changed the subject. "I reckon you've heared that the Transylvania Company is sending their own agent to the country."

"No. When?"

"Next month if it goes according to plans. We heard of it a short time ago in the settlements. They had a meeting, reckon the same one the colonel went to, and they hired a feller name of Williams to handle their dealings here. I wouldn't swear to the truth of it, but they're saying the company has went up on their prices. They're aiming on asking fifty shillings a hundred now, and charge a entry fee besides."

I let out a whistle. "By grannies, that ought to bring Jim up short! His men has been grumbling a heap over things, and if a company agent comes into the country and they go up on their prices they'll just about start a war!"

"Reckon it might swing 'em clean away from the company?"

"I wish to hell it would! Jim hates to make trouble, he says. He wants to do what's right for all. He ain't sure what's best. I give him credit for being a good man and I like him a heap, but I wisht he could see for himself he's got no call to be beholden to anybody!"

"Takes some men a time to make up their minds."

"If anything'll make Jim Harrod make his up, this had ort to do it. I give him up if it don't."

Ben stayed the night and the next morning I closed up the cabin and rode back to his place with him. He took several days to rest up and get things tidied around, and then he headed back to the Holston. "You can look for me," he said just before leaving, "as soon as I figure we can make it through. Should the winter be mild, it might be as soon as February or March."

"I'll look to things," I promised him, and he rode off down the shoulder of the knoll and was soon lost to sight amongst the black-limbed trees.

It was maybe a week before Christmas that Jim Harrod came. He was a little surprised to find me at the springs. "I was hoping I'd catch Ben before he left out," he said, "and then I was aiming to ride on over to your place. The womenfolks are fixing to have a kind of shin-dig for Christmas, and wanted all to come that would. I said I'd ride out and give the invite, but that ain't my prime reason. Things is troublesome, Dave, and we got to do something." Then he sat down and told me the same news Ben had brought.

I couldn't keep from telling him it was no more than I'd expected. "They're speculating, Jim, and they've not got the good of the country at heart. They'll make all the money they can. It stands to reason. That's what they counted on doing when they made the deal."

Jim was gloomy. "They have thought to pacify us by promising to move the land office to Harrodstown. They know in reason we have been anxious to turn settlers our way, as who wouldn't. It's but natural we'd ruther see ourselves grow as Boonesburg. But makes no difference where they put their dratted land office! The colonel give me his word they wouldn't go up on their prices, nor change any of the conditions they first stated. And now they're doing it. My men are riled up a heap over it, and ready to pull out."

I was sure glad to hear it, and to hear Jim talking so. "You got anything in mind?" I asked him.

"Well," he said, "I don't know as it would do a heap of good, but I been thinking on that notion of your'n to get up a petition. I don't see as it could do any harm, anyways. Like you said, it would give the folks in Virginia the idea of where we stood and might stir 'em up to take some kind of a step."

"What was it you wanted me to do?"

"I thought if you was coming to the Christmas party we could have a kind of meeting and maybe work out the petition. I was hoping Ben'd be here and go along with us, too."

I studied on it. I'd been ducking going to Harrodstown, no two ways about it, since Bethia was there. A man don't go putting his hand back in the fire of his own accord once he's been burned. But I couldn't keep on sidestepping her the rest of my days. She was in the country and so was I and we were bound to cross paths soon or late.

Besides this was a chance to get Jim Harrod to take a stand that might not ever come again and I was too pleased over it to risk missing out on it. "Well," I said, "Ben's done left out, but I'll sure go with you."

We talked things over some more while we rode towards his place. "The petition had ort," Jim said, "to tell just what the scoundrels is doing, and how they are aiming not to allow no claims excepting to them that's registered with them, and how they've gone up on their prices so's most can't register with them, and how they have hogged up all the land over at the Falls. They's some over at Boonesburg displeased, too. Likely we could get them to sign. William Poage and his woman have moved to our place just lately. They ain't many, Dave, has got the entry fee in hard silver, to say nothing of fifty shillings sterling."

He was full of talk of it and I let him talk on. "It don't suit," he said, "it don't suit none of us. I was willing to give the colonel his dues, and try to get along with him, and over at the meeting in May he all but give his word he wouldn't go up on the prices, and he'd take notice of our claims, seeing we was already here. He's went back on his word, and I got no use for a man don't keep his word." He was so worked up he just kept on muttering. "I allowed he had a good education and knowed what was right. I figured he'd be fair."

"Them kind is often the slickest-talking, and seldom overly fair," I said. But I didn't want the petition to be just our quarrel with the colonel and his company. If we got anywhere with it we had to let the Virginians know we counted ourselves part of them, and wanted to be represented amongst them and intended to bide by their law. I said so to Jim. "We can only hold our lands with our guns unless Virginia comes out for us. We must make certain we say that strong in the petition."

We'd said it all by the time we got close to Harrodstown, and my mind then commenced running on Bethia. As we came nearer to where she was I felt like something was in back of me hurrying me on, and I couldn't hurry fast enough just for the sight of her. Seemed like my stomach chunked plumb up in my throat when I thought of seeing her again. At the same time I wanted to hold back and dig in my heels and balk, turn around and run as hard and fast as I could back to Logan's. I didn't know which pushed or pulled the worst, but I was commencing to wish I hadn't come. Still, I made myself ride on.

The fort was crowded now. The men had come in from their clearings for the winter, and what with the womenfolks and younguns and some from Boonesburg either visiting or changing places, every cabin was full. Jim lived in the near corner cabin along with a bunch of fellows that either were not married or didn't have their families with them yet. Anyhow, there were no women in that cabin and that's where we held our meeting. Jim sent word around and had all the men come. Amongst them of course was Judd Jordan. Seemed to me I saw him plainer and clearer than the others, but I reckoned I'd always be seeing him like that when our paths crossed now. It was but natural.

The meeting went smooth as molasses. Jim talked first and then he had me to say what our ideas about the petition were. The men were worked up a plenty, bothered and uneasy, and ready and willing to take steps. Soon as they heard what we had in mind they were for it, the only talk being how soon we could get it done and over with. "We can get it wrote up in the next day or two," Jim said, "and signed and then send it over to the Holston to Billy Russell and let him take it to the spring meeting of the Assembly at Williamsburg."

It was decided that way and the vote was taken to petition the Virginia Assembly in our favor. Then they named Jim and me and Isaac Hite to put it in writing. The meeting ended with the agreement that when we'd got it ready we'd let them know and there'd be another meeting for the signing. I don't know when Judd Jordan left the gathering, for he'd not opened his mouth the enduring time. Just sat and listened with a kind of sully look on his face. I couldn't help wondering if he ever laughed or thought things pleasant enough to light up his face. I misdoubted it, but then I'd never seen him enough to judge. I didn't expect him to come up and speak to me, nor didn't want him to. I knew in reason he'd never forget his shame on the Watauga nor cease to hold it against me. That was but human. I looked for him to go his way and me mine and little love ever to be lost between us. I thought it likely we'd mix again in time, him being the kind of man he was . . . but I didn't aim to let that trouble me. Come the time and I'd know what to do about it.

I never saw Bethia that night, naturally, nor for the next two days, for we stayed housed up that long struggling with the petition. That was a job, I can tell you, for none of us had much learning. We knew what we wanted to say . . . there was no trouble about that, but saying it in an elegant and proper way came close to being beyond us. "I never knew before," I said, along towards noon of the second day when we'd just about worn ourselves down, "it was so hard calling a man a scoundrel in a mannerly way."

"Or trying to explain," Jim growled, "I was fool enough to let him outtalk me."

We got it done finally. Not that we felt satisfied with it, but we got all the things Jim and me had talked about into it and in a way that put it plain, and we thought we'd best let it go at that. We had another meeting and everybody signed. Then we celebrated Christmas. All, that is, but me.

We finished up with our business about noon of Christmas Eve and cleared out of the cabin so's the women could make it ready for the shindig that night. I don't know as there was much making ready to do, for the womenfolks had been cooking for days already, but anyway they picked up after the men who slept in the cabin and swept it out and stuck up some cedar branches around the room. It looked right cheery that night and with a plenty to eat and drink and Hugh McGary fiddling it was a right festive occasion. The first Christmas in Kentucky . . . I recollect we drank to that, and to many more of them.

It was right after that the whole party went sour for me.

I saw her when she came in . . . a little later than some, and looking as pretty as the first redbird of spring. Judd wasn't with her. She came in with Miz McGary and another woman I didn't know at the time but found out later was Miz Poage. I figured they'd been redding up after the supper. Right off she was partnered for the next set, and it was plain to see she loved to dance and was good at it. She looked to be light as a feather on her feet and her face had a glad look on it, like a little girl's. She kept laughing all the time. All the women, being so few, had more partners than they could manage, and danced till they'd be so weary they had to rest a spell. Not Bethia, though. She danced every set and appeared to be enjoying every minute of them.

I paid my respects to the other women first, but all the time I was thinking soon I'd be dancing with her and dreading it, at the same time not even knowing which woman it was I was swinging, for wishing all of them were her. I kept thinking ahead how it would be to touch her again and to step through a set with her and put my arm around her waist and swing her lightly. But I made myself wait till I'd squired every other woman in the room onto the floor.

When the music was starting up for the next set, then, I went over where she was and made my bow. "I'd be obliged if you'd dance this next set with me, Miz Jordan," I said.

She looked straight at me and the only sign she gave that I was something human and alive was that her face colored up a little. "I feel honored, Mister Cooper," she said, "but I've been dancing so much I feel the need of resting a spell."

And I knew she was lying. I'd not once thought she wouldn't dance with me and knowing she was taking this way of getting out of it made me mad clean through. I reckon I must of had just enough rum toddy to make me more tempery than usual or else it wouldn't of run all over me the way it did. The set was formed and they were about to commence. I just reached out and pulled her up off the bench she was sitting on. "You can rest next time," I said, "right now you're dancing with me."

There wasn't anything she could do without causing a commotion. As graceful as if she'd accepted my partnership willingly, she laid her hand on my arm and took her place opposite me in the set. But if the look she threw me had been a dagger it would of killed me deader than four o'clock.

There isn't much chance dancing a quadrille for talking, but going down the center the first time I said to her, "I been wishing to tell you I never knew you was married . . ."

Her hand barely touched mine when we crossed arms, like the feel of mine was too disgusting to her. "I reckon," she said, "if I hadn't of been married what you done would of been excusable in your thinking."

I had to wait till we do-ci-doed then. "I wouldn't say it was excusable," I told her, "but anyways it's more understandable."

She didn't say anything, just tossed her head.

Going back down center my dander was up. "Who was it you was looking for the morning we left Joe Martin's?"

She snipped off a few words. "I wasn't looking for nobody. It was just curiosity."

"Well, don't look so grim about it. You'd best smile and make out like you're enjoying this dance whether you are or not. Folks'll think we're having words."

She slanted me another deadly look but she turned her mouth up at the corners and finished out the set looking a little less glum. I walked her across the room then, and bowed her to her seat. "It's been a pleasure, Miz Jordan."

There were others around so she kept her voice low, but I could hear every word she said just the same. "It's been no pleasure to me, Mister Cooper, and in the future I'll ask you just to keep your distance. You picked a quarrel with my husband and fought with him and threw him in the fire so he's been lamed ever since. And then you made light with me at my uncle's. The less I see of you, the better I'll like it."

There wasn't time to tell her I'd not picked the quarrel with Jordan, and doubtless she wouldn't of believed it anyway. A woman usually takes her man's words, and if he'd told her I'd picked the quarrel,

that's what she'd believe. Besides I was too mad to say anything more
saving I'd try to see to it she wasn't troubled with me no more. I
walked off and left her then, and left the party too. I didn't feel like
celebrating Christmas or anything else right then.

# CHAPTER

# II

I WAS FIXING TO LEAVE the next morning when Abraham Hite rode in from Boonesburg with the news they'd had an Indian scare. A fellow by the name of Campbell and two lads had crossed over the river to hunt and had been ambushed. One of the lads was killed and the other one taken captive, but the Campbell fellow got away.

"How many Indians?" Jim asked Abraham.

"Best we could make out, not more'n six."

"Not a war party, then."

Abraham shook his head. "No. Likely just some out hunting and they run across Campbell and the boys."

"Dannel followed 'em I reckon."

"Yes. But they headed back over the Ohio."

"Get any stock?"

"No. Just fired on Campbell and the boys and lit out."

Well, it was the first scare since we'd come into the country, and overdue to my way of thinking. Only a fool could of thought the quiet we'd had all summer was going to last much longer. From now on, seemed to me, we could look for trouble and plenty of it. I said so to Jim. "We'd best keep scouts out," I told him. "I'll keep an eye out around Ben's place and over towards mine and come in ever' couple of weeks with word."

Jim thought like I did and he named off some others to commence keeping watch, and that's the way we spent the rest of the winter, riding a circle about twenty miles out from the stockade. On account of Ben's animals I had to come back to his place pretty often, but I took little time to rest there. I'd take several days to circle west to my place, and then on around north to the fort. Then I'd circle south and east back to Ben's place. It made me riding into Harrodstown oftener than I'd thought to be, but it was the handiest way of keeping a close watch. It gave me a good chance to hunt, too, and they needed food bad there. Usually I had a pretty good load to take in with me.

But the party of redskins that ambushed Campbell and the two boys must of been the last ones out hunting our way, for we never saw a sign the rest of the winter. We didn't cease keeping watch, however, for there's never any way of knowing where or when Indians will strike, and in the dead of winter with us least expecting, it would be just when they might pick. We kept on with our riding and circling all through January and February, cold and miserable as it was for us.

I saw Bethia sometimes when I'd be at the fort, but not often. It being wintry and cold, and wet underfoot a big part of the time, the womenfolks stayed inside mostly, and usually when I'd see her she'd be either on her way to or from the spring. The women carried water by putting a yoke across their shoulders so's they could pack two pails at a time. The yoke and the buckets, empty, made a heavy load and full they must of been a cruel burden. Times I'd see her, her shoulders dragged down under the yoke, I felt a pity for her and if she'd been anybody else I'd of stepped in and helped her out. But I never offered to with her. I made no doubts she'd of slung one of the pails in my face had I of.

Sometimes I'd see her chopping wood. The menfolks snagged up logs and piled them in the middle of the commons and everybody used from it, the womenfolks as a rule seeing to their own needs. She was too slight to be a good hand at chopping, and was awkward, but she made out. Sometimes, too, on a fair day I'd see her washing out her clothes down at the spring, and she took her full part in cleaning and dressing the meat all of us brought in. She was a good stout worker and she never slacked for all she was little and on the slim side. But for all I'd see her around, I never once went seeking her out. I left her purely alone, and I wasn't seeking her the next time I had words with her.

Judd was in and out of the fort just like all the rest of the men, taking his part in the hunting and scouting. Sometimes he'd be there when I was, and sometimes he wouldn't. When he was we paid no mind to one another beyond nodding when we passed. The word had got around of our fight and didn't anybody expect us to be very friendly. Not that I told of it, nor him, but things like that get told all over the country and too many on the Watauga had passed it on. I did tell Jim about it, for I wanted him to have the truth of it, but that was all. I don't know whether Jim passed it on to anyone else or not, and I don't know if that had anything to do with the fact Judd wasn't too well favored amongst the folks. I misdoubt it. I've always thought it was more because he was short-tempered and mean-natured in general. Nobody denied he was a good man in the woods, better than most. He was a dead shot and he could trail good as a red-skin. He always came in from hunting with a full load. And he was stout and could turn his hand to any needed thing. Everybody gave him full credit for that. But like I said, he was tempery and unac-countable, and he was mean to his animal . . . and the womenfolks said he was mean to Bethia. I didn't doubt it, for I'd seen his mean-ness to her. Lord knows we've not all been angels in this country . . . most of us were rough and tough and there was many a one with a streak of meanness in him, but taking it on the whole we treated one another as good as it was in our nature to do, put no more on our womenfolks than we had to, and thought of our animals as being just about as human as we were. So when Judd lit in and beat his horse to a frazzle, or shoved Bethia around in front of everybody, it didn't set well and it caused talk and dislike of him. It was that mean streak in him laid the cause of me speaking with Bethia again.

It was about the middle of February, and the days had lowered till the span of daylight was but a few hours. I'd come in off the trail towards midafternoon and had unloaded the game I'd killed and then I'd sat and talked to Jim awhile. It was coming on dark when I went to stable Beck and settle her down for the night. There was no one else in the shelter and I took the time to rub her down good and talk to her. She was always finicking and I'd spoiled her a heap. She liked to be rubbed and talked to. Reckon there's womanly ways that carry over even to animals, for sometimes Beck put me in mind of a woman wishing to be made over. I humored her when I could.

Good dark came on whilst I was soothing and petting the mare and I heard but couldn't see when somebody came in the far end of the shelter. I paid little mind to it, for the shelter was a common stable for all the animals in the stockade and there was a right smart coming and going around it. I never even gave a thought to who it might be till I heard Judd cussing his horse out. I reckon the horse stumbled and displeased him the way he talked, for he commenced letting out a string of cuss words ought to of lit all the straw in the stable with the fire he put in them. Then he commenced beating the animal . . . what with I don't know, but whatever it was I could hear the blows, and the horse, scared and hurt, stomping around and whinnying and trying to get away.

It was just about in the worst of it that I realized Bethia was with him, for she screamed out for him to quit, and I heard her over the sounds him and the horse were making. "Quit, Judd!" she screamed out. "Quit! You'll kill him!"

"That's what I aim to do!" he yelled, and kept on with his beating.

I know now that what Bethia did next was to get hold of his arm and swing onto it to stop him, but then, standing there in the dark and only hearing, all I made out was that he left off beating the animal of a sudden, and there was a noise of scuffling and scraping around. Then I heard Judd again. "You goddamned witch you! I'll kill you, too!" And I thought he would from the way it sounded.

I don't know how many times he hit her before I got there, but it must of been anyway three or four good hard licks. I picked up a clout of wood I'd seen leaning up against the end of the feedboxes and made for him. I'd always heard it said that if a man gets mad enough he sees red, and I reckon that's as good a way of saying what happened to me as any, for I don't rightly recollect what I did. But I can still feel the madness shaking all through me when I remember it. I must of hit him pretty hard with the piece of wood I was carrying, and it must of been in the right place for he went down like a pole-axed ox. He didn't even make a sound, just slid down into the straw and laid there.

I couldn't see Bethia but I could hear her. She was whimpering and kind of sobbing, off to one side, and I made my way towards her from the sound. The sounds of her crying muffled whatever noise I made getting to her and I was afraid I'd scare her, so I called out her name. "Bethia . . . Bethia."

But she was too scared and too hurt to hear. I crawled closer and put my hand on her. It was her shoulder I touched, and she sucked in her breath quick and squirmed out from under. "Don't be frighted, Bethia," I told her. "It's me . . . Dave Cooper. I was here in the stable seeing to my mare when you all come in. I couldn't help over-hearing . . . are you hurt bad?"

She snubbed her crying down, but she didn't make any answer.

"Listen, Bethia," I said, trying again, "he'll not hurt you no more tonight anyways . . . I reckon I've knocked him senseless. . . ."

She was lying in the straw where he'd pushed her and I could hear it rattling like she was turning, maybe. Then her crying overtook her again. She kept trying to muffle it but the misery inside her had slipped beyond her controlling. I let her cry, thinking it would be best. "I ain't going to touch you," I told her when she could hear again, "I'm just aiming to set here till you're quiet."

It was warm in the stable from the heat given off by the animals, and we sat there in the dark with just them around us making their feeding and breathing noises and stirring once in awhile. She didn't cry long and directly I heard her blow her nose and figured she was done. "First off," I said then, "how bad hurt are you?"

She kind of hiccuped, then spoke. "Not much. No more'n . . . I ain't hurt much."

She'd cut her words off but I knew she'd started to say she wasn't hurt much worse than usual. It made me sick to my stomach that she was so used to his mistreatment. "Look," I said, "I reckon you'll hold this against me too . . . hitting him over the head that way . . . but couldn't no man of stood there and let him beat you up like that."

"No," she said. She was still getting her breath between little sobs the way a youngun does when it's trying to leave off crying. "I'm obliged to you. He was awful drunk. He might of . . . I ortent to tried to butt in like I done. I ortent to come down to the stable, but when he unloaded the game I seen he was awful drunk and I knew he'd take it out on the horse . . . maybe kill it. I just felt like I couldn't stand no more of it."

I had to know and I just exploded the question at her. "Why?" I said to her, "why in the name of all that makes sense did you pick him to marry? Wasn't there no way of telling before hand what you'd be getting yourself into?"

She stirred and I thought I'd made her mad and she was leaving. But she was just easing herself in the straw and when she spoke again there wasn't any anger in her voice. It was just dull and flat. "I never picked him," she said. "My pappy give me to him. I didn't have no say in it. I wasn't but fourteen."

"What kind of a man was your pappy to do a thing like that?"

"About the same kind of a man Judd is. He never actually killed my mammy outright, but he made her life so miserable she died of it before her time. Then he got shut of me by giving me to Judd. That was two year ago."

So she was but sixteen even now. No wonder I'd mistaken her for a girl at Joe's place. "Did your pappy know Judd was like he is?" I said.

"He never knew nothing about him. Judd just happened along that day and Pappy made a trade with him. He'd never saw him before. But Judd give him a horse and some powder and lead."

"Are you wedded to him, or was that all there was to it?"

"Oh, I'm wedded to him all right. We got married the next settlement we come to."

"Where was that?"

But of a sudden she shut up. "I've talked too much already. It's no matter where it was. I'm wedded to him and that's the end of it."

She stood up and I got up too. "I'd best be getting on back," she said. "You reckon he'll come to any harm down here?"

"No," I told her, "it's warm from the animals. He'll be all right."

We walked outside the shelter. The night was clear, with no moon. A million stars seeded the sky and from their light I could see her. Her hair was tousled from falling and she reached up with both hands and pushed it back to kind of set it straight the way a woman does. She pulled at her skirts and commenced brushing the straw off. She let me help. "Bethia," I said, "I don't reckon you'll believe it, but I never picked the quarrel with Judd that time on the Watauga . . . and him getting throwed in the fire was a pure accident. . . ."

"You needn't to say no more," she said. "I know Judd. But a woman has got to try to stand by her man. . . ."

I felt encouraged enough to go on. "And I wish you'd believe, too, that I've been sorry about that time at Joe's. A man tries things. . . ."

She laughed a little. "I reckon it never made me as mad as I let on. I've thought some of what I done, too. But I took note your mouth got well all right."

Oh, I wouldn't of traded that minute for all the riches of the earth. For her to be saying she'd thought of it! Like a drink of wine the joy of it rocked all through me, and without thinking I laughed out loud. Quick as a wink she put her hand over my mouth to still me. "Sh-h-h-h."

She left it there only a second, but it was long enough for me to feel it. It was warm and the palm of it against my mouth was rough, and it smelled of woodsmoke where she'd tended a fire. It smelled of corn, too, where she'd patted out hoecakes, and it smelled of meat where she'd been stripping out venison. Mostly though it smelled of her, like her blood flowing had an odor, and her flesh caging the blood-stream picked it up and carried it and spread it out into her skin. It was a sweet woman-smell and it set me quivering and yearning to reach out and pull her up close against me . . . so strong a yearning that I had to flatten my hands against my thighs and claw my fingers in deep to keep them from reaching. One way or another I managed to get my voice up out of my chest. "It got well," I told her.

"I'm glad," she said.

Then she went past me and was gone. In the starlight I could see her cross the run and make her way up the slope towards the cabins. Watching her, it came over me with a bitterness like gall how foolish

I'd been to think I'd made a ghost of her. Like the scar on my mouth she was grown into me, and I'd never, never in this world or the next, be rid of her.

But she'd said it herself. "I'm wedded, and that's the end of it."

# CHAPTER
# 12

I T WAS IN THE FIRST WEEK of March that Ben came back.
I'd just got done riding a full circle around and had got back
to his place about midafternoon. It was early to be eating but I
was hungry, so I'd built me up a good fire and hacked some meat off
a haunch of deer and set it to roasting on a pronged stick. I was sitting
there watching it sizzle and brown, the fat around the edges melting
and dripping into the fire, keeping up a continual popping and crack-
ling. Waiting and watching, turning the meat every once in a while
to keep it from burning, I got to thinking how, a year ago almost
exactly, I'd been at the Sycamore Shoals for the treaty-making. Just
a year . . . but in a way it seemed a lot longer than that. A lot of
water had run under the bridge since then and it was hard to recollect a time when I hadn't been busy the way I was now . . . tending Ben's stock, seeing to my own place, scouting and riding and
hunting, trying to get shut of the Transylvania Company, keeping
watch for redskins and listening for news of the breaking out of the
war in the east. Except for that last it was like this little piece of
Kentucky we'd staked out for ourselves was the whole world and we
were the only ones living in it. It went queer to think of folks outside
going their own ways, some in comfort and peace and even richness,
deciding things in Williamsburg and Fort Pitt and Philadelphia, and
even over in London, that would make things harder or easier for us
here in the western country. I reckon it's always hard for a man to think
out beyond his own affairs. Hard for him to realize that the wants
and dissatisfactions of folks can be added up and stacked until they
reach out and touch every living being in a whole land. As well,

maybe, he doesn't think of it too often, for his own wants and dissatisfactions might then get to be too important.

The meat got done and I ate. I shucked out some corn for the hogs and foddered the cows and horses. I was dipping out a pail of water to take up to the cabin for night when I heard the shout from down the trail. "Halloo-o-o, Dave!"

It was Ben. He'd seen the glint of the fire and had known I was there and called out. I answered him and then went footing it down to meet him. He was riding ahead, and man, was I glad to see him! He looked as broad as the cliffs in the Cumberland Gap sitting up on that big bay horse of his, and might near as steady. He got down and we clapped one another on the back and grinned and said howdy half a dozen times. He sure looked good to me, and I reckon I must of looked as good to him. "I've brung my folks," he said, "they'll be on."

There was just about time enough for me to tell him everything was fine at his place and that I'd not lost a head of his stock for him and we'd been peaceful enough during the winter, before his party hove in sight. At first glance it looked like a considerable party. In the lead was his woman, packing their youngun who was still in arms. Next came a Negro woman, and behind her, three Negro boys ranging in size from one that was nearly full-grown to a pint-sized little fellow not more than six or seven years old. The boys were herding the pack horses, and there looked to be almost as many as we'd had coming on last year. There were pots and kettles and quilts and blankets and bundles tied all over the animals, and then Ben of course had been foresighted enough to bring in salt and flour and more seed and ammunition. Ben Logan's folks had moved into the country, for a fact.

When they came up Ben made me acquainted with his wife. "This here is Dave," he said.

It was plain to see she was tired, but she smiled. "Ben has talked a heap of you," she said, and then she motioned to the youngun. "This one's Dave, too."

"Honest?"

"Honest," Ben said, "but we call him Davey, which is just as well, seeing we might have trouble telling the two of you apart."

The Negro woman was called Mollie and she belonged to Ann. Her father had given the woman to her when her and Ben got married . . . the woman and her three boys.

We went on to the cabin and Ben helped Ann and the youngun down and they went inside. Ann Logan was not what you'd call a handsome woman. In a manner of speaking, I reckon she was actually what would be termed plain, but her face had a quiet, firm look on it, like she'd be hard to fluster, and was, in most cases, pretty certain of herself. It had a pleasing look, too, kind of composed and smiling. She was a little on the tall side with nothing, even after the days on the trail, of the slattern about her. She was as trim and neat as a well-kept mare.

I felt a mite apologetic about the cabin, for there was no doubt it was in disorder, but if it troubled her she didn't show it beyond making a little clucking sound and a commencing at once to set things right around the fireplace so's she could bed down the child. I took note that Ben was quick to do what she asked, but like a sensible woman she never asked beyond the needs of the youngun and left us to ourselves to exchange what news we had.

We talked till up in the night. The first thing any man abiding in the wilderness wants of a traveler from the outside is news of what was happening there, and the first thing any traveler returning to the wilderness wants is news of what's been going on during his absence. There was a deal of it on both sides that night. But when we finally turned in I felt some relief to be giving the care of his place back to Ben. I'd not minded tending it for him, but I was glad to be free of it now.

Ben's coming was but the first of a steady stream of settlers that came pouring into the country that spring. Some went due north from the hazel patch to Boonesburg and those parts, some branched off and followed the path that led past Ben's to Harrodstown, and some settled close around us. Ben Pettit took up a stand over on the Hanging Fork and brought his family out. William Whitley settled down by the crab orchard . . . him and his brother-in-law, George Clark. George Clark, mind, not George Rogers Clark. Looked like the country was making a fine start towards getting settled.

All the new ones had a call on the help of those of us already there and what with getting our own crops planted and helping the others we had a right busy time of it. Ben and Ben Pettit worked together putting in their corn, first at one place then at the other, and they offered to come over and help me out. Not being a family man, though, I wasn't putting in as much as they were and I figured I could make out by myself, and I lent a hand with all of them when I could. Ben was busy too laying off tracts for his three brothers and for Ann's father and brother. They wanted to be close to him, so he ran their lines nearby and planted a little corn for each one of them. Worst part of Ben's location, to my mind, was it being right on the trail to Harrodstown. His time was taken up a heap by the folks passing. I've always been willing to help folks, but all that passing and commotion wouldn't of suited me. I was just as glad I was out of the way over on the Green. I liked being off to myself. But most didn't care for the knobby, hilly country over that way and didn't anybody settle in that direction for a time and a time.

Things were pulled up short in April when word came of an Indian scare. Fellow by the name of Willis Lee on the Elkhorn, up north of the Kentucky, was killed. Fright flurried through the country and some folks, timid maybe anyhow, were afraid enough to load up and make tracks back east. There'll always be those easy enough to scare to quit at the first mention of Indian trouble and they're no loss to the country. But when several weeks had gone by and nobody had seen any further sign, things quieted down and the killing was laid to a little party bent on plundering and stealing horses. Most went back to their planting and clearing, taking care, of course, but not too bad scared.

The fort at Harrodstown was a different place nowadays. The Indian scare made the men pitch in and commence strengthening it. They finished up the stockade and built a heavy gate for the opening. The folks in the fort weren't the same either. The ones there during the winter had gone to their own clearings now and the cabins were full of newcomers staying till they got located. It was a bunch that shifted and changed all the time, never the same two weeks hand-running, and it seemed to me they were awful uncaring of appearances and cleanliness. The commons inside the square took on a littered, untidy look most of the time and the smell of the slops and animals and crowded folks was foul and unpleasant.

I didn't go much any more. There was folks enough there now to take care of their own needs, and . . . well, I might as well say it, Bethia wasn't there any longer, and it made a heap of difference. Judd was one of the first to leave out for his own stand, taking, naturally, Bethia with him. For all I cared, the fort could of stood empty after that.

I saw her to talk to just one more time before her and Judd left, and it came about purely by accident. I was riding up to the fort early one morning and I came up on her driving some cows out after milking. She was driving them past a little thicket that was close-grown and commencing to leaf out and I was quick to see a chance to talk to her without all the eyes in the fort looking on. I pulled Beck up and got off and Bethia stopped, waiting. I had no notion what I wanted to say, but I felt pushed by a need to talk to her one more time for when she got out on Knob Lick where Judd's stand was there'd never be any good reason to see her again. But once I'd got off the mare and stood beside her I was so tonguetied I couldn't think of a thing to say and I just stood and looked at her.

The winter had gaunted her some . . . not much, just a kind of honing down. Her freckles had faded and her face looked whiter without them. The sun was up, more gold than red at that time of year, and she stood there with the light shining through her hair turning it brighter than glory. She never let it go tangled and uncombed like some of the women. It was always as tidy as its way of curling would let her keep it. It looked warm that morning, and I wished I could of touched it to see if it felt as warm as it looked.

She had a long willow switch in her hand that she'd been driving the cows with, and while we stood there, neither of us finding anything to say, she commenced stripping off the little leaves that had but barely started showing. Like she was counting them she pulled them off and let them fall to the ground. They fell slow, floating, and they settled down around her feet. It made me feel sad, watching them, like there was no use to anything. Spring and new leaves, and so soon come to their end. Oh, not that I felt sentimental about the leaves, but they put me in mind of how short a time every man has got on this earth, and the same end to all. And the circumstances being what they were between me and her, my own time seemed kind of useless.

She turned like she was going back and just to keep her from leaving I busted out with the first thing that came to mind. "I reckon," I said, "you'll not be staying at the fort much longer."

I knew she wouldn't. I knew in fact from the talk around the fort that Judd was aiming on leaving the very next day, but like I said, I was just talking to hold her. She shook her head. "Tomorrow will be our last day."

"I know where Judd's clearing is at." And then still seeking something to say I stumbled on, "Was you bad scared over the Indian trouble on the Elkhorn?"

"No."

"No need to be. . . ." Goddlemighty, I was talking like an idiot and I might not get the chance to talk to her again for a year . . . no telling whenever, and all I could do was blather like a fool. Then I knew what I'd been wanting to say. "Look, Bethia . . . if there's ever anything . . . if you ever need anybody . . ."

"I'll come in to the fort," she said.

"Promise you'll do that . . . or get to Ben's, or my place. This is the lie of the land." And I took her willow switch and drew a kind of map in the dirt. "Here is Judd's clearing, on the Knob Lick. It lies south and west of the fort here at Harrodstown. Here's Ben's place, nearly due east of it. And here's my place on the Green, south. Any one of 'em is about the same distance from you. But likely," I said, and for the first time felt some regret that my place lay out of the way, "you can reach Harrodstown or Ben Logan's place easier. You got to come over to the trail anyway, and it won't matter much which way you turn."

She studied the drawing. "I've got it in mind," she said then, "and I'll remember." She took the willow out of my hand and sunk the butt end of it deeper into the little hole I'd dug for my place. "Is it sightly where your clearing's at?"

"It's sightly," I told her. "To my notion it's the prettiest place in the whole country. . . ." And I told her about the river and the hills. I even told her about the cabin, though I made no mention of having built it for her. It eased me to tell her of it.

When I'd done she rubbed the drawing out with her foot, circling her foot over the tracks till they were smoothed and leveled down. It was like she'd heard what I'd said and was now rubbing it out. I couldn't stand it, and I kind of groaned and pulled her inside my arms. She didn't pull away. She just leaned there against my chest and I kind of rocked her back and forth, feeling nothing but misery poured all through me. It was so useless and so hopeless to love her.

Didn't either of us say anything. There was nothing more to say. And after a time she pulled away and I saw her eyes were wet. She wiped them with the backs of her hands, like a youngun. "I've got to go," she said, and that was all. For she went, without even once looking back. I watched her go, feeling like somebody had tied me hand and foot and turned me loose to make my way so hampered. There wasn't a thing I could do, save squirm and twist in my bonds. Wishing never made anything so, and wishing she was free, wishing Judd Jordan had died when he was birthed, wishing I'd never started to Kentucky and laid eyes on her . . . oh, wishing ten thousand things, none of them made any difference. They just twisted me tighter.

When I got to the fort that day George Rogers Clark was in Jim's cabin with him. I'd not ever seen Cap'n Clark before, but I'd had the news he was back in the country and was glad to see him. He turned out to be a tall, gangly, sandy-haired, blue-eyed fellow, younger than I'd expected. Jim made us acquainted and told the cap'n I was to be trusted and they went on with their talk. Cap'n Clark was trying to get Jim to call a meeting at the fort soon.

"Colonel Henderson has sent out a call for a meeting at Boonesburg in June," he said. "Now the thing to do is to forestall him by holding one here. A majority of these people in the country now will follow a strong leader against Henderson. Patrick Henry will take office as Governor of Virginia next month. He is much interested in this country, for as you know Captain Floyd laid out a considerable claim of land for him over by the Falls. He is a man of vision and he is also prudent. War is a certainty now and he well understands the importance of securing this country to Virginia."

"I have heard," I put in, "that both Mr. Henry and Mr. Jefferson lent a sympathetic ear to Colonel Henderson. Have they changed their thinking?"

Cap'n Clark looked at me in a sharp and shrewd sort of way. "Yes sir," he said, "I believe that is true. You must understand that they are politic, sir. They have the good of the country at heart, and it may be that for a time it seemed to them Colonel Henderson's scheme held out the best interests of the people. They no longer hold that opinion, however. I have it straight from Mr. Henry himself."

It looked pretty clear to me and I said so. "Seems to me they kind of listen whichever way the wind blows and sway with it."

Cap'n Clark laughed. "You might say that, but that is part of being politic, sir. We can count on Patrick Henry's good counsel and action. He gave me his word. I talked with him in Virginia, and now is the time to act. But act we must. Neither Patrick Henry nor Virginia can do a thing for us unless we give them something to act upon. The initiative lies with us."

Jim was looking a little puzzled. "Well, we just sent off a petition a little while ago. Sent it to go by Arthur Campbell and Billy Russell on account of them being the delegates to the Assembly from Fincastle County."

"What concern have Campbell and Russell for you people west of the mountains?" the cap'n said with some heat. "Call a meeting of all Kentuckians, write a new petition and elect men of your own choice to take it and present your cause to the Assembly. That is the only way you can get action. Campbell and Russell are concerned only with the Holston settlements, which is natural. That is where they live, and my friend, there is a good bit of jealousy on the part of the Holston men for Kentuckians, don't forget that."

Well, it all set me thinking. I remembered what Jim had told me when we'd gone buffalo hunting . . . that Clark had said if Virginia didn't recognize us we could set up our own government, free and independent, and make ourselves a country in our own right. He made no mention of such, now, but watching him as he sat there and talked and egged us on, I couldn't help thinking it was likely he still had the notion in the back of his head and would regard such a scheme right highly, especially if he had the running of the country. Ben had said he thought Cap'n Clark was a man of ambition. Listening to him, there was no misdoubting the fact he was used to giving orders, and was impatient of any opinion but his own and liable to be displeased with those who went against him. He was not to say unpleasant in any way, nor snobbish or unmannerly. It was just that he talked so sure and certain, and kind of down his nose.

Still, I thought it more than likely he was right about Arthur Campbell and Billy Russell. Besides, both had been hand in glove with Colonel Henderson, along with the Robertson brothers, in the treaty-making. Even if they presented our petition they might do it in such a way as to enfeeble it. A new petition, our own elected delegates, not obligated or biased in any way saving towards the best good of our people . . . that looked to be the way. I thought I could see how to tie Cap'n Clark's hands, too, when the time came, though naturally I said nothing at the moment. I just looked at Jim and said, "Whyn't we do it, Jim?"

Jim had been studying too and he looked back at me, frowning, but I winked at him out of my off eye and his face cleared up. "Well," he said, "all right."

The cap'n's face cleared too and he stood up. "Now make haste to call the meeting, Jim, but don't say what it's for. Just say it's in the interest of all settlers in Kentucky. There's no need letting the colonel get wind of what we have in mind. Time counts and Henderson consolidates himself with every passing day."

"All right," Jim said.

The cap'n picked up his hat and pulled on his gloves. "I have business at the Falls and must be going. Good day, gentlemen." And he closed the door behind himself.

"What do you make of him?" Jim said as soon as he was gone.

"Well, in my opinion he's a man don't let his left hand know what his right one's doing, but both of 'em is always doing."

"He gives me an uneasy feeling, too."

"I don't know what he's got up his sleeve, but I'll lay you six-forty to a coonskin he'd ruther see this country set up for itself as to come under Virginia, and that's what lies back of his egging us on to hold this meeting."

"That's just what I was afeared of. But you give me the sign."

"Sure. He'd *ruther* to see the country set up for itself, but if he can't have that, he'd ruther see it come under Virginia than for the colonel to get a stranglehold on it. If we can tie his hands sufficiently that he can't act free and get what he'd ruther have, he'll serve us well getting what we'd ruther have, for he's a shrewd, noticing man and he's got too big an investment of his own in the land of this country not to look out for its interests."

"How'll we do it?"

"Doubtless he is counting on being named to represent the country to the Assembly. That's fine. Let's elect him . . . but let's make sure he's elected as a delegate acting under the strict orders of the people, and not as a free agent to represent us. He's got the ear of Patrick Henry, no doubts about it, and he can do us a lot of good. He will, too, for he's a good man . . . but let's not turn him loose."

If I do say so myself, Jim looked at me with his mouth hanging open and admiring. "I'd not of thought of that."

"Yes, you would," I said, "in time. Let's go along with him, but make sure he goes our way, not his'n."

So it was decided to send out a call to all the men in Kentucky to meet together at Harrodstown. The time was fixed for the sixth day of June.

I was right surprised, though, when I rode by Ben's to give him the word. He was scapping weeds in his corn and he rested on his hoe handle to listen. When I'd done telling he studied a minute and then he said, "I reckon I'll tend my own business, Dave. Leave the politicking to them that knows more about it."

I'd thought he would be in a big way to stand on the side of the settlers and I was caught off balance. "It's to your own interest same as ours, Ben."

"I know it is. But it's my belief if we are law-abiding and respectful of the Virginia government they'll do the right thing by us and we'll get our just dues."

It made me rare up, a little hotheaded. "That's as may be," I said, "I believe in being law-abiding and respectful of the government, too, but there's times, seems to me, when you got to remind 'em a little of what just dues are. Sometimes if you don't venture nothing, you don't get nothing."

He chopped down a cockleburr, but he was grinning. "Every man to his own notion, Dave."

Well, was no use quarreling with him. I thought too much of him to do that anyway. It was just Ben's Presbyterian way to go slow and take things as they came. We turned the subject and commenced talking about his plans for the fort he was aiming to build at the springs. We needed one there, for a fact. Everybody passing on the trail stopped and Ben stood in bad stead of a way to shelter them. Besides, another fort would be just that much more strength in the country. I gave him my word to help out on it.

It must of been just a couple of days before the time set for the meeting at Harrodstown that Johnnie Vann turned up at my place, him and his Indian woman and three younguns.

I'd been down at the river cutting cane all morning and hauling it up to the place. It was hot and steamy and I'd stopped at the spring to get me a drink and rest a spell when they rode into sight, coming in from the hills over to the west instead of down the meadow. I didn't know him till he got within hailing distance. I figured it was some newcomer with his family, maybe lost on the trail and wandering far to the west. But just about the time he called out, I recognized him. I was glad to see him and made him welcome.

"Could we camp here at your spring a day or two?" he said, after we'd spoken.

"Why, sure, Johnnie," I told him, "but you'll not to do no camping down here at the spring. The cabin'll hold us all. A mite crowded, maybe, but we can squeeze in."

His face got red. "I'd ruther not misput you."

It kind of made me mad. If he thought I was the kind to hem and haw over his Indian woman he was plumb crazy. The way I looked at it if she suited Johnnie Vann, it wasn't nobody else's business. "I'd be proud," I told him, "to have you. You'll be the first to take the night with me, outside of Ben Logan."

Him and the woman talked a minute in Indian and then he said they'd stay. I took them up the hill to the cabin. The woman was timid, like all Indian women I ever saw, and she trailed along behind us up the slope. But when we went inside and she saw the way the cabin was fixed up she commenced walking around looking things over and clucking to herself like a little banty hen. I'd hewed me out some tables and stools and had put up a pole bed in the corner farthest from the fireplace, and there was a skin or two on the floor serving as rugs. Johnnie laughed at her. "She says," he told me, "your woman has many pretty things."

"You tell her," I says, "it don't take a woman to have pretty things if these is pretty. For I've got no woman. What's her name?"

"We-to-mah. One who Laughs."

She was a handsome woman, as Indian women go . . . on the dark side, as was to be expected, but little and slim and sightly, not fattened up the way most were. What got me, though, were her eyes. They were so big and black they made her face look all eyes, and she had a way of looking at you that made you wonder if they were going to melt and run over. Put me in mind of a doe's eyes.

I helped them get settled in the cabin and showed the woman where things were so's she could cook or bed the younguns down. Like I said, there were three of them, all boys. The oldest one looked to be about ten, the next one about six, and the least one was maybe three or four. None of them favored Johnnie that I could tell, except they all three had blue eyes, and if you don't think that don't go queer in an Indian face you'd just have to see for yourself. The least one was fussy and whiny and We-to-mah sat herself down to let him nurse. I reckon it's true that Indian women let their younguns nurse as long as the youngun wants to, for the kid was way beyond the age a white woman would of let him hang on.

Johnnie and me went outside and back down to the spring. I figured something was on his mind, but knowing the way Johnnie was turned I didn't hurry him. He set to and helped me haul up the rest of the cane and stack it and by that time the day was wearing on towards evening. We watered all the animals and turned them out to crop, his along with mine, only he hoppled his, seeing it wasn't their home pasture and they might stray. It wasn't till then he said what was on his mind. "Dave, I've come by to give you news. The British have treated with the Six Nations and the Indians are going over to their side in this war."

I never doubted him for a second, seeing who it was was doing the telling, but it flabbergasted me so that I couldn't help blurting out and asking him how he knew.

"The word has been passed down. All the tribes north of the Ohio know of it and will take their part."

"The Delawares?"

"The Delawares."

"That's where you got the word, I reckon."

He nodded.

"What are they aiming to do?"

"They're aiming to strike at the settlers in Kentucky, hard and often, with British guns and powder backing 'em up, and in time even British officers to lead 'em. Henry Hamilton has put up a bounty for ever' scalp they take."

"Who," I said, "is Henry Hamilton?"

"He's the British governor at Detroit."

Only somebody that has seen the way Indians fight, what they do to the folks they kill, and worse, what they do to the ones they take, could have any notion of the kind of horror Johnnie's words held. The picture that was ever in the back of my mind, of my own folks butchered and scalped, rose up before me, and like it was spread out in front of me already I could see a hundred cabins in Kentucky burned to ashes and the clearings laid waste and the people left hairless and mutilated. It was almost more than the mind could stand.

"My God," I said, "I wouldn't of thought even the British could be so scoundrelly! Don't they know what Indians turned loose in the country will do? Haven't they got any pity for women and children? We got families in the country now!"

"Well, it's their notion of war, Dave."

"A pretty uncivilized notion, I'd call it. Did you come by just to pass the word on?"

He didn't say anything for a minute, just stood there fingering his chin, then he came out with it. "I'm not taking no sides in it, Dave, neither white nor Indian. But I couldn't stand off and see it happen without giving you warning. I'll not pass on no more, but this much I figured I had to tell."

"Looks to me," I said, "you'll be siding with the Indians that way."

"No. I'm leaving the village. I'm taking mine down the river to the Illinois country. I couldn't stay on, knowing they was warring against my own kind of folks."

Speaking out as quick as I thought it, I said, "Just throw in with us, Johnnie. Whyn't you just stay close here?"

He just looked at me steady. "You think the womenfolks would make We-to-mah welcome? You think they'd have her around and treat her decent? You think the men would put their dependence in me?"

I was sorry I had spoken so hasty, for of course he was right. When he took an Indian woman for his wife and raised up younguns by her and lived in her village with her folks as relations, he put himself outside the limits of the settlers' understanding and liking. He went against their ways and they'd not forget it. The men would of mistrusted him, and the women would of mistreated his woman. Nothing but hurt would of come of it. An Indian trader has his uses, naturally, but if he's got an Indian family it don't go so far as to take him in as a door neighbor. It made me sad, though, to think of Johnnie leaving the village that had been his home for such a time, and his wife pulling up the roots of her own folks and relations, and going into new country and new ways. "Where did you think to go in the Illinois country?" I said.

He shrugged his shoulders. "Some place around Kaskaskia, I reckon. I thought to do some trapping till I'd got the trust of the Indians over that way."

"Well," I turned it off light as I could, "I've heard it's good country out there."

He said no more and we went inside.

Johnnie's least boy was sick that night, feverish and whiny and he kept everybody awake most of the night with his crying. He was still sick the next morning, so I told Johnnie they'd best stay on till he got to feeling better. He thought so, too. The lad's face felt parchy hot to touch, and he took on like something was hurting him bad. The woman left him on the bed all day and brewed up some kind of a physic from bark and roots she went out and gathered, but seemed like it just made the boy sicker.

Johnnie and I cut cane again and hauled it, but it was plain to see he had his mind on the youngun, for every time we brought a load to the place he'd go in to see about him. The woman was bothered, too, but she held her feelings in better than Johnnie did. Not knowing much about kids I didn't to say worry much, for I figured it wasn't anything but a bellyache and would wear off soon or late, but when the little fellow went clean out of his head along in the afternoon even I knew he was bad off. We-to-mah heated rocks and wrapped them in a blanket and laid them on his stomach and seemed like that helped him more than anything, for just about sundown he got easy and straightened out his legs that had been cramped up in a knot, and dozed off to sleep. We all heaved a sigh of relief.

We-to-mah fixed us some supper and we all eat, and then Johnnie and me went outside to cool off. We were sitting there talking about the kid and how good it was he'd finally dropped off and was getting some rest, when right in the middle of it the woman let out a screech you could of heard plumb down to the river. We leapt up and ran inside. She had the youngun up in her arms rocking him back and forth, with her head thrown back stiff and her eyes walled up till only the whites showed, and every breath she was moaning and screeching.

Johnnie grabbed the kid from her and looked at it, and then he just walked over and laid it down on the bed, gentle and easy, and covered it up. That was the first I knew it was dead. And it puzzled me how it could of gone so quiet and none of us knowing. Johnnie put his arm around the woman's shoulder and talked to her, but if she heard a word he was saying she never let on. She just kept moaning and crying and talking some kind of gibberish herself. Finally he gave it up. "She says she went to the bed to see if she could wake him enough to feed him. And his spirit had left him . . . in his sleep."

If there's any harder words to find than those to comfort a grieving person, I don't know of them, and I've ever been awkward with words anyhow, but I must of stammered out something, for Johnnie held onto my hand and told me I was good and kind.

We buried the kid that night . . . about midnight, I reckon. What made it so bad was he had to be laid away without the ceremonials of the tribe, and it came close to killing the woman. She did her best, and Johnnie helped out and I felt so everlasting sorry I even raised up my own voice, though I can't tell one tune from another, not that it mattered singing those chants and death songs of theirs. She painted the boy's face with ashes, and her own and the other younguns', and Johnnie and me dabbed some on ours too. I reckon all of it pacified her a little, for when the time came we took him away and she gave him up without any more fuss. It sure went hard with her, though. Shoveling in the dirt I thought how the most homeless feeling in the world is to be cut off from the known ways of your own folks. You can stand almost anything if you've got people and customs that are part of your own blood and ways around you. But cut yourself off from the tribe and something withers and dies away. We-to-mah and Johnnie both had done that. They didn't belong with the whites or with the redskins, and they'd wander the land, now, shifting and restless, and rootless.

They wouldn't stay on. They left out the next morning, soon, and I rode a piece of the way with them, then turned back and went my own way towards Harrodstown for the meeting. The last thing Johnnie said to me was, "Dave, I'll not forget how good you've been."

I told him it amounted to no more than he'd of done for me. Which was true.

## CHAPTER

## 13

I TOOK THE SHORT WAY to Harrodstown, not going by Ben's place. It wandered through the hills and came out on the Knob Lick, and I reckon I must of had some notion of riding past Judd Jordan's clearing when I took it, although I didn't name it so. But when I came to the Lick, instead of crossing it and going on, I turned Beck downstream, the way towards Judd's. I didn't know whether he'd be going to the meeting, or already gone, or if he was going whether he'd take Bethia or not. I didn't collect my thoughts and figure on it one way or the other. I just had a notion to ride past and look at the place where she was living.

It wasn't much of a place. He hadn't cleared more than five acres and it looked like he hadn't even bothered to make rows for his corn . . . just scattered it helter-skelter, and he had a skimpy stand at that. I didn't look for him to of built a good cabin yet, but the thing he'd thrown up for a shelter would of put a puny youngun to shame. It appeared he'd just tossed a bunch of saplings together and laid some branches across for a roof, without tying them down. A wind and hard rain would of collapsed the whole thing like a pack of playing cards. It was open-front and I could see how Bethia tried to keep their things in order and neat, for nothing was strowed or laid about careless like. There was a place to cook, outside, with some rocks built up to hold the fire and kettles and such, and there was a fire going and a kettle on. Somebody was there, so I stood Beck in the edge of the clearing, not aiming to ride out and be seen. I don't recollect how long it was I sat there, just looking and thinking what a sorry way it was for her to be living . . . sorry now, and likely to be sorry forever, for I didn't see much reason to believe Judd Jordan would ever make much of a settler. It looked to me like her hopes for any betterment were mighty slim, and it came over me how little she deserved such fortune. It had just been bad luck that she was fathered by an ill-natured man who had given her to another ill-natured and do-less man. She'd had nothing to do with any of it. Sometimes when you think of the way things happen to people it seems like their fate is decided by a chance as uncertain as the throw of the dice in a game of rattle-and-snap. There's no way you can make it appear sensible, and oftentimes nothing to be done about it.

I was just fixing to leave when Bethia herself climbed up the bank of the Lick with a bundle of wet clothes in her arms. She dumped them in the kettle and gave them a stir and then she chunked up the fire. I changed my mind about leaving and rode out into the clearing, calling to her to keep from scaring her. But it startled her just the same, for she flung up one arm and scurried towards the shelter like she meant either to hide or get a gun. "It's me, Dave," I yelled at her, getting off Beck at the same time. "Nothing to be scared of."

She came back, laughing, but still trembly a little. "My sakes, Dave, you give me a fright. I wasn't expecting nobody."

"Well, it's just as good to be cautious," I told her, "it might of been a Shawnee. Where's Judd?"

"He's went to the meeting. Left at daylight this morning."

"Whyn't he take you?"

"He never said . . . but then I didn't to say want to go . . . I had my work to do up . . . . I'd laid off to wash today. . . ."

The plain truth was, of course, he hadn't taken her because he didn't want to. "Is he aiming on coming back by night?"

"Likely."

"Did he say he was?"

There was a sizzling from the fire and she brushed past me. "Oh, the water's boiling over . . ."

I didn't know how long the election would take, but with as much Monongahela as there would be flowing that day, and with Judd liking it the way he did, I had my doubts he'd get back that night. "Bethia," I said, "you ortent to be here by yourself. It's not safe even daytime. Look how easy a redskin could ride up on you. You couldn't of got to a gun awhile ago . . . a tomahawk would of split your head before you'd taken six steps. And you sure ortent to be here by yourself of a night."

She left off stirring the clothes and looked at me. "It would be no more than I'm used to, for he's gone the biggest part of the time, and if you want the straight of it, it's a relief to me for him to be gone!"

"Where does he go? Jim's got a plenty to do the scouting now without calling on him."

"I don't know. He don't say, going or coming. Hunting, I reckon, for he usually brings in something. He likes to be in the woods."

It flew all over me, him wandering the woods and staying out overnight, leaving her by herself to come to no telling what end. "Listen," I said, "get your things and go on into Harrodstown with me. There's womenfolks there that'll help you out. You don't have to stay out here running risks and putting up with him!"

She just went on stirring the clothes around. "Yes, there's womenfolks there, and likely they'd take me in . . . for a time. But what would I end up doing? Everybody in this country has got his own self to look after and nobody is going to want to be burdened with a woman won't live with her man."

"Whyn't you go back to Joe's? He'd take you in. He's your own uncle, ain't he? There's always passing on the trail and you could go with the first party happened to be heading that way. Or I'd take you myself."

She laughed, and as serious as I was talking it sounded good to hear her, for she threw her head back and laughed as lighthearted as a girl. "Now, wouldn't that be a pretty sight? David Cooper squiring Miz Jordan back to the settlements! That would give the country something to talk about, wouldn't it?"

"They'd not talk long," I said, heating up.

She shook her head. "No, I'll just stay on. Uncle Joe would make me welcome, and don't think I've not thought of it. But his woman would begrudge me ever' bite I eat, and I'd have to pay for it with the lash of her tongue. Besides," she said, looking at me slyly, "there's a heap of stopping there and a mort of men to keep warded off."

"I'd not worry none," I said, giving her back as good as she sent, but chuckling, "about that, unless you lost the use of your right arm."

We both laughed, but she sobered up quick enough. "It ain't so bad, Dave. Mostly he keeps to hisself, comes and goes to suit hisself, and says but little. He ain't to say downright mean except when he's been drinking. There's many a woman has worse to put up with."

"The difference being," I said, "that I don't happen to love none of the others. Bethia . . ." and I started towards her.

"You'd best be going," she said, putting the kettle between me and her. "I take it kindly that you've got my interests at heart."

She took it kindly! Lord love you . . . when I'd just said I loved her. But she didn't reproach me, anyway. And she was right. I did have to be going. I'd be late to the meeting the way it was. There was just one more thing. "You promise me," I said, "you'll not stay out here and endanger yourself more than common, or put up with anything more than you want to. Ben Logan's place is not more than ten miles from here, and his woman is as goodhearted as they come. I know she'd take you in and never give you a harsh word nor begrudge you a thing. Just don't be foolish, Bethia."

"I'll not," she said, and seeing I was in earnest, she lifted her right hand, "I swear I'll not."

I left her, then, not much comforted, but some. I couldn't lay my finger on any one thing I was afraid of for her, because there were so many. It seemed to me like a whole cloud of things were hanging over her, and I didn't know which, befalling, would be the worst.

It was as hot as the inside of Bethia's wash kettle by the time I got to Harrodstown. Felt a heap like it, too, steamy and smothery and I figured a rain was storing up and would be upon us in the next few days. But for that day, anyhow, the sky was clean of clouds and the sun beamed down. The fort was bulging with folks and they milled around the commons with their faces streaming with sweat and their clothes wet and sticking to them. But they didn't seem to mind the heat, for a gathering together of any sort was an occasion for celebrating. It meant laying off work for a day or two and seeing your neighbors. The women bunched up in little droves and let their tongues clack, and the men herded together and passed a jug around and, to tell the truth, let their tongues clack too. What difference did the heat make.

It wasn't to be expected that all who'd been notified of the meeting would come. There were plenty of folks up around Boonesburg loyal to the colonel, and thought those of us around Harrodstown were purely troublemakers. Cap'n Floyd didn't come, for instance, nor John Todd, nor Dannel nor Richard Calloway. None of those up on the Licking came, or for that matter not many north of the river. Seemed like the river was a kind of boundary line. Still, it was a right smart gathering . . . enough of folks to fill the square to running over, and my guess was, better than two-thirds of all the folks in the country.

I saw Jim in a bunch of men, laughing and talking, and I went over. "Where," he said, grinning when I walked up, "in the hell have you been?"

"We'll go into that later," I told him, not wishing to say Johnnie had been at my place, or anything of the word he'd brought, till we were by ourselves. "You about ready to hold the election?"

"Well, whatever it was kept you I'm glad you're here finally. Cap'n Clark ain't showed up yet and I'm getting uneasy. Most of the folks will have to be leaving out by midafternoon, but I hate to commence without the cap'n."

It was getting on towards noon, by the sun, so I told him if I was him I'd go on and start. No telling what was holding up the cap'n and he'd likely expect us to go ahead, anyway. So he called all the men together under the big tree down by the spring and explained to them what the meeting was about. Jim wasn't a fancy talker, but he could make things plain. He told them we'd thought it best to write up a new petition and send it this time by our own delegates we'd elect right then. Everybody was for it. So then he got Jack Jones, a fellow who'd just been in the country a few months but who was a lawyer and mighty slick with his tongue, to read out loud the new petition. Jones had mostly written it, too.

It sounded mighty elegant and he'd written it up in fine style. It said over again a lot we'd put in the December petition, but it was stronger worded. For instance, Jack Jones just came plain out and said if all of us western folks hadn't of fought at the Battle of Point Pleasant and licked the Shawnee, likely the country would still be a wilderness and uninhabitable. And since we aimed this time to send the petition by our own delegates we got Jack to close it by requesting that the Assembly recognize the delegates. We made sure he used the word "delegates" too, not "representatives." If Jones noticed the difference he made no mention of it, but from what happened later I misdoubt he noticed it.

There wasn't much discussing of the petition. Most were in favor and when the vote was put it was passed in short order. But when the voting commenced to elect the delegates it took a little longer. Finally wound up by electing George Rogers Clark and Jack Jones. Cap'n Clark hadn't showed up even then.

We closed up the business by setting up a Committee of Safety to maintain law and order. We figured that since we were pulling out of the Transylvania government and not yet under the Virginia government, we'd best set up something to go by till we heard from Virginia. So we named twenty-one men. I was amongst them, and just before the meeting dwindled off Jim asked us to stay on a day or two, if we could, to decide on some things.

I saw Judd around during the day and he voted along with the others, but naturally I didn't seek him out. I didn't see him again after the meeting broke up. No way of knowing whether he'd ridden off with a bunch of fellows and would be laying the night out somewhere in the woods drinking with them, or whether he'd headed for home. But he was gone, there was no doubts about that.

Cap'n Clark didn't get to the fort till past dark. We'd had supper and the Safety Committee was gathered in Jim's cabin and we were just getting down to business when he came in. He gave his excuses for being late. I forget now what they were, but it was some kind of private business had come up and delayed him. Between Jim and Jack Jones he was told what had happened and it suited him fine till he looked over the petition. He spotted what we'd done right off, and he slapped the paper against his hand, showing his dislike for it. "Why did you elect us as delegates, gentlemen? We shall have no standing as delegates. The Assembly will not recognize us, for Fincastle already has two duly constituted delegates and it would take a vote of the Assembly itself to change that. You should have elected two men and deputized them to treat with the Assembly, free and independent."

Jim looked mortified . . . so mortified that I almost believed it myself. "You said delegates."

The cap'n fidgeted with the paper and studied it. "Well, it's done, now. I should have been here myself."

"I sure wish you had of been," Jim told him. "I hated to go on without you, but we didn't see nothing else to do."

"No. Let it go. We'll do the best we can . . . and we'd better leave soon, Jack. The Assembly may be adjourned by the time we arrive in Williamsburg now."

I thought this was the crowd of men, the ones who'd been named to head things up in the country, and this was the best time to pass the word on of what Johnnie had said. "Before you leave the country, Cap'n," I said, "there's a thing we've all got to hear and think about." And I told them.

At first they couldn't believe it, just as I couldn't . . . that the British would arm the Indians and turn them loose on the settlers. But I told them how the word had come and there wasn't a man there didn't know Johnnie Vann was to be trusted to tell it straight. It just went too awful to believe, was all. It was Cap'n Clark recovered first, and you could tell he was a military man all right from the short, crunchy way he took over and commenced making plans. "This news must not get out over the country. It will create panic and undue fear. It might even lose us the country! We shall have to stand firm. You gentlemen here tonight . . . tell no one else!"

Lordy, but it was something to watch that man's mind commence to work . . . and it was working straight, now. This changed everything, and if he had any ambitions of his own he put them behind him, only saving the country mattered now. "This committee, speaking for the people, should petition Virginia to establish the country as a separate county . . . Jack, write it down!" Like military orders he snapped out what he was thinking. "Begin by telling them of the Indian danger. Mention our concern over the war with the British. Say to them that as a new county, of Virginia, we could prevent the region from becoming a haven for Loyalists." He paced back and forth across the room, fingering his chin, ordering his thoughts and speaking them out until he'd covered everything. The rest of us listened, putting in a word now and then, but he could see so plain what our dangers were and the steps we needed to take that there wasn't much need for anyone else to remind him of anything. He wound up by having Jack write that it would be impolitic for Virginia to allow such a respectable body of prime riflemen to remain in a state of neutrality. That let off a siege of shouting and yelling and joshing and laughing. "That's telling 'em," Jim whooped, "that's sure putting it to 'em. If they want us crack-shooting, backwoods, rip-snorting Kentuckians on their side, they'd best get a move on and do something about it, or else we'll fight our own war and stand on our own when it's done!"

Jack made a fair copy of the petition and we signed it that same night. It was decided, too, that Cap'n Clark and Jones would try to get as much powder and lead as they could. We'd be needing every pound we could lay our hands on, and we were a far piece from where it came handy.

The Safety Committee met the next day again and laid out some plans for keeping scouts moving, and made some general rules for keeping law and order, then we dismissed. I stayed over another day and rode down the trail with Cap'n Clark and Jack who were heading without any more delay for Williamsburg. Jim rode piece the way, too.

It was foggy and drifty when we left Harrodstown, but it turned into rain before we'd gone five miles, and Jim went on back. I thought maybe it was just a shower, for usually rain following fog don't last long. But the mist was just sort of eaten up by the rain and it settled into a steady, heavy downpour that was liable to last all day. And it did. It made a full day's journey to Ben's place, where we all took the night. The cap'n must of decided to let Ben in on the news, even though he'd not been at the meeting, for he told him before we bedded down. I was glad he did, for Ben's place was located right on the trail and was important in the safety of the country, and in my own mind I thought, whether he wanted it or not, Ben ought to be counted one of the leaders. Folks thought of him as such, anyway. He took it quiet, even though his own woman and youngun were amongst those exposed to the danger. He didn't say anything one way or the other while the cap'n was talking . . . just nodded his head over the plans and when Cap'n Clark had finished, said, "It sounds to me like you've done the best that could be done. We'll make out."

"We decided, also," the cap'n went on, "to send word to the leading men at Boonesburg, warning them to take care that the news did not get spread around."

So all the leaders knew, now. And we'd taken what measures we could. All we could do, now, was go on about our affairs and wait for things to start. Which they did soon enough, and, for me, at least, in a little different way than I'd expected.

It was still raining when I left Ben's place the next morning, but not as hard as it had the day before. It was more of a fine drizzle than a rain. I didn't hurry Beck any, for the ground was slushy underfoot, but we made pretty fair time anyhow and came to the stand by mid-afternoon. I had a surprise waiting for me. The roof of the cabin was burned off and fallen in, and there was nothing but a pile of ashes where the stable and corncrib had been. The field had been burned over, too, and there wasn't a stalk of green corn left. At first I didn't take it in. I'd been riding along, hunched down under the drizzle, and was plumb up on the spring before I noticed anything different. I'm not proud of telling that, for a body ought never to be so careless, and I laid myself open for an ambush for which I'd of had no one but myself to blame. What brought me to, actually, was Beck snorting and sniffing, smelling the dead fire. I could tell in a flash it had been burned several days, for the rain had wet down the ashes and they had a kind of damp, moldy smell.

I looked the cabin over first. It had been wrecked inside . . . the bed torn down and pulled apart, the stools and tables hacked up and partly burned, and it looked like they had just willfully sunk their hatchets in the floor to rough it all over. Big chunks had been gouged out and splintered off the boards. I didn't mind the furnishings so bad, for they'd just been makeshift anyway, but it made me sick to see the floor, for if I do say so myself it had been as pretty a floor as there was in the country. It would take a heap of adzing and rubbing to smooth it up again. From the way things were wet down I figured I had the rain to thank for saving the cabin. Otherwise it doubtless would of been a pile of ashes, too. I thought likely the redskins had set the stable and crib first, trying to draw somebody from the house, and then when nobody was flushed out, they fired the cabin. Having done their damage they'd left, then, and the rain commencing soon after had put the fire out with only the roof burned. Bad as it was, it could of been worse, and I was thankful not to have to raise those log walls again.

The crib and the stable weren't much loss, for they'd been kind of thrown up and could be rebuilt easy. I hated losing the corn, though, and it was too late in the season to plant again. I was glad I'd taken the pack horse over for Ben to use earlier, for they'd of stolen him, sure as shooting.

I took a look around for tracks, but the rain had beat the ground down hard and any prints they might of left had been washed out. I gave it up and set to work to clean out the shambles left in the house. It took me the best part of a week.

Then I went up on the hillside back of the cabin to cut saplings to start building a new stable and crib. There was a ledgy little limestone cliff ran all around the brow of the hill, and I've got no idea now what made me climb all the way up there, but I did. And I found Judd Jordan's knife up there.

The first thing I saw after I'd clambered up was the ashes of a fire and a couple of spit sticks where somebody had roasted meat. I looked them over, then, not far from the ashes I saw the hide of a deer. I walked over and poked around what was left of the carcass, and on a flat rock, handy to the kill, laid the knife. I knew it before I even picked it up. There was no mistaking that horn haft, carved up like a stiff-limbed tree. It was plain he'd laid it there when he'd finished slicing up his meat, and had gone off and forgot it. It was plain, too, that no redskins had fired my place. He'd known I was staying on at Harrodstown after the meeting and had sneaked over and set the fire, counting on me thinking redskins had done it. But for him forgetting his knife, that's the way it would have gone, too. There's no man so careful but what he don't slip once in a while. Judd had slipped and I had the proof on him and intended to have it out with him.

# CHAPTER

# 14

THERE WAS NO EXCUSING the sneaking, underhanded way he'd taken to get even with me, and without waiting around to cool off, I headed straight for his clearing. I have no idea what might of happened had I found him at home that day. I make no bones of the fact that I had little doubts one of us would finish off the other one, and it may have been the Lord's way of keeping me from killing . . . making me too late to catch up with Judd. I don't know. I have always been glad, since, he wasn't there, but at the time I felt let down and bitter disappointed. The clearing was as empty as if it had never been lived in at all. There wasn't a sign of Judd or Bethia either, although I rode all around and looked for traces and tried to raise somebody by shouting.

It wasn't till after I'd done that, that I noticed their things were gone from the shelter. It brought me up short and broke me out in a cold sweat, for it meant they weren't just off somewhere for a few days, but had likely left the country. Judd must of missed his knife and reasoned out where he'd left it. He'd be bound to know I'd find it sooner or late, and he must of figured I'd be on his trail when I did. It was good riddance of Judd. I didn't know of anybody would grieve over him being gone, but it made me sick and heavyhearted to think of Bethia . . . not knowing where she'd been taken or what was in store for her or whether I'd ever see her again. Not that I had any right to want to, but a man can't help his feelings.

I satisfied myself they hadn't buried their things to keep them safe while they were away for a few days. They hadn't. They'd just plain packed up and left. Their tracks headed towards the trace, but that told me little, for they'd have headed for the trace no matter where they were going. I rode along, following, with my spirits lower than a wet flag.

At the trace, though, my hopes were raised, for their trail turned north and I broke Beck into a lope for Harrodstown. The first person I saw when I rode into the square was Bethia herself, pounding hominy at the big block in the middle of the commons. Such was my relief that without giving thought to the talk it might cause I jumped off the mare and made straight for Bethia . . . at a dead run. I had been too bad scared to think of anything but my joy at seeing her again, and I told her so, barely able to keep from reaching out and touching her to see if she was real. She laughed and shook her head. "No . . . we've not left the country. Leastways I've not, and Judd ain't gone for good. He brung me to the fort to stay awhile. He's went back to the settlements on some business and he thought to be gone several months."

I came close to blurting out the reason I thought he'd left, but in the nick of time I caught myself. Was no use bothering her with the trouble between us. Something else occurred to me, too. "It would of been a good chance for you to go back yourself," I said.

She stirred the hominy in the block and made ready to commence her pounding again. "We've done talked of that. There's no place for me to go. Anyway, Judd wouldn't of took me. He said he had to travel light and fast."

I reckoned he did, for a fact, but I didn't say so. "Are you making out all right here?" I asked her.

"I'm making out fine," she said. "The McGarys made room for me in their cabin. Go on about your business now before the women-folks have something to talk about. . . ."

"Well, I knew," I said, "you didn't look with favor on staying with none of them when I named it to you before."

"This is different. I wouldn't want to burden nobody for a long spell, not knowing any end to it. Judd'll be back before snow flies."

That was the bitter along with the sweet . . . that he'd be back. For there's no denying I felt lighthearted to know he was gone, and Bethia's face showed she felt the same. It looked like a hand had been passed over it, smoothing out the worry and trouble it commonly carried. For the first time since she'd come into the country she looked as young as she had at Joe's place . . . no older than the sixteen she was. It was the way she deserved to look all the time, unburdened and untroubled, and I couldn't help wishing it lay within my power to keep her so. "For a time, things'll be easier on you," I said. "I'm glad."

She reached up and pulled the big, heavy pounding-block down. It made such a noise squashing down into the hominy in the hollowed-out stump that I couldn't hear for sure what she said, but it went like she was saying she was glad, too, and would get to see me oftener. When I asked her, though, she just motioned me away and said, "Shoo!"

I shooed, but with the happiest feeling I'd had in a long, long time. Not even the worst Indian scare we'd ever had, happening just a couple of weeks later, could take away all the happiness, for though it sent a terrible fear through all of us and threatened us with a troublesome time to come, Bethia was safe inside the fort at Harrodstown and Judd Jordan was out of the country.

I remember well it was the twentieth day of July. I was over at Ben's place helping to cut trees to commence building his stockade. It was nearing midday when Jim Harrod rode up, his horse lathered like he'd run it every step of the way. Both Ben and me knew he had trouble to tell and we moved about as fast as we ever had in our lives to meet him. He commenced talking before we got to him, swinging himself down off his horse between words. "Ben, you'd best bring Ann and the youngun to the fort right off. There's trouble."

"Where?"

"At Boonesburg. Dannel's girl and the two Calloway girls was took captive right under their eyes at the fort, there, and carried off."

I reckon our mouths dropped open and our eyes bugged out, for he motioned us to be quiet. "Wait," he said, "wait'll I get my horse tended, and I'll tell you."

But Ben took the horse and hoppled it and turned it loose to crop nearby. "We'd best talk down here," he said, when he came back. "No need scaring Ann till it's time. Now, what happened?"

"Well, seems that Dannel's girl, Jemima, had cut her foot on a cane stob and was limping around with it paining her a right smart and she talked the Calloway girls into going on the river with her in a canoe so's she could dangle it over the side in the water and ease it. Nobody thought nothing of it, and I misdoubt any of us would, either. They never once got out of sight of the stockade, but they let the current drift 'em to the far side and float 'em right up next the bank. Next thing they knew a redskin had reached out and dragged the canoe into the canes and a party of 'em pounced on the girls and carried 'em off."

I reckon Ben and me both had the same impatience with Jim's slow way of talking, for together we asked the same thing, "Did they ketch 'em?"

"Yes, they caught 'em," he started laughing, "it must of been right exciting for a time with everybody milling and stewing around. Flanders Calloway has been courting Jemima, and they said he had about as much sense as a chicken with its head cut off till Dannel quietened him down some, and the colonel's nephew, Sam, has been courting Betsey Calloway, and he was in about the same state."

My sympathies were with those two boys, for had it been Bethia carted off by redskins doubtless I'd of done some circling around myself. With some dryness I told Jim, "You can laugh about it, but had you ever been in love, it's unlikely you'd find it very funny."

He stared at me in astonishment. "I didn't know *you* had."

Ben came to my rescue, for I was too confused to think of an answer. He laid his hand on my shoulder. "Oh, yes," he said, "times without number. Dave would of probably been grieving over all three of the girls, being such a ladies' man."

Jim chuckled and I growled at him to go on. "Well, the upshot of it is that under Dannel and Cap'n Floyd they got a party organized to go after 'em, and they come up on 'em in several days. The girls was smart. They tore off pieces of their skirts and dropped 'em along, and then when they had to quit that they'd dig their heels in soft places to make marks."

Ben asked the sober question we both wanted to know. "Had they been harmed?"

"No, and a God's blessing they wasn't. The girls told Dannel that there was three Shawnee and two Cherokee and they could all talk a little English. They told 'em they was taking them to their village on the Scioto and aimed to sell 'em to whoever wanted 'em for wives."

What happened to white women in the hands of the Indians was always enough to make a man shudder. Sometimes they used them and then killed them. Sometimes they took them to their village and sold them into slavery to some Indian woman that wanted a servant. But the worst was when they were sold to be some redskin's wife . . . or woman, for it was far from being a marriage. More than one poor thing had killed herself rather than be so used. Jim was right. It was just a God's blessing Dannel's party had come up on the girls and rescued them in time. "Both Dannel and Cap'n Floyd think they accounted for a redskin," Jim said, "so that's two that'll not pester no more. But they're all around, Ben. Feller up on the Licking was killed last week, and one over on Drennan's Creek, and there's fresh sign every day. I wouldn't lose no time getting the folks to the fort, if I was you."

That night Ben Pettit rode in. He'd found sign over on the Hanging Fork, and the next morning, soon after Jim had gone on to warn others, William Whitley and his woman, Esther, and their two little girls rode up. Billy had seen sign down near the crab orchard and was taking his family to Harrodstown. That was enough for Ben Pettit. He lit out to get his folks and came back before sundown with them and William Manifee and his woman, Jane, who'd built close to him on the Fork. That was everybody in our parts, and they all took the night at Ben's. He did his best to talk them out of going in to Harrodstown. "As many of us as there is," he said, "we can pitch in and throw up a stockade right here that would stand a right smart siege. We could have it built in a couple of weeks time, and we wouldn't have to be crowded up at Harrodstown and so fur off from our crops. Whyn't we just light in and get our own fort built right now?"

But they wouldn't listen. The womenfolks were scared and they wanted to get behind a stockade soon, and seeing it was the girls the redskins had pounced on at Boonesburg I couldn't to say blame them for wanting to be safe. I know I took a mort of comfort in knowing Bethia was at Harrodstown.

Ben gave in and set to work packing to take Ann and the youngun in, too. Ann wouldn't of gone except she was expecting again and was slowed up some on her feet. "If it wasn't for that," she said, peartly, "I could outrun ary Indian happened around!"

"You'll not try it," Ben told her, setting her atop a horse. "You'll go to Harrodstown and you'll stay there till the others come back and the country's safe again."

I went with them that day, helping to drive the stock, for they didn't want the redskins to steal their cows and hogs. It made a slow two days of the twenty miles, but we finally got there. Then there was a shuffling around to make room for the four families of them. The way it turned out, some of the others moved and doubled up and gave over two cabins to them. Ben's family and Billy Whitley's took one, and the Pettits and Manifees took the other one. Knowing I'd be coming and going, I bunked in with Jim.

Now, being forted up is a wearisome thing. There's too many folks in too little a space. You're like a big family, everybody knowing down to the last twitch of an eyebrow the ways and habits of everybody else, and the women's tongues clattering, and the men quarreling over the jobs to be done. It's not ever pleasant, but it was uncommonly trying that first time. For one thing it was hot as hell, and the flies and the mosquitoes swarmed all over, and the heat beat down, and the grass on the commons dried up and got mulched in with the dust, and the spring got down to a thin little trickle and the women couldn't wash, the younguns ailed and whined and ran wild around the commons till they came near setting everybody crazy with their screeching and milling and yelling. Folks got nervy and cross-grained mighty easy and gave way to flarey tempers and hot words too quick.

If it hadn't been for a few that kept steady and calm it's untelling how we'd of made out. Miz Coomes started a school with the oldest younguns and kept them from underfoot part the time. And Anne Poage, who had shifted with her man, William, from Boonesburg, had brought her spinning wheel with her across the mountains and she let all the women use it that wanted. It was Anne Poage figured a way to make cloth, too, when it had all the others stumped on account of there being no flax yet in the country. She went out and gathered some nettles and soaked them in the water trough, and then she broke them out and wove the fibers with buffalo wool. She had William to make her a loom, and first thing we knew she was turning out a good strong cloth. It wasn't fancy, and it rubbed the hide off, times, but it was tough and lasty and a lot better than nothing, which some of the women had been facing.

And there was always the cooking to be done. The womenfolks had to grind hominy every day, dress out the meat we killed and brought in, and see to it there was something to fill empty stomachs with all the time. Ann Logan was one of those that went her way with patience and calm in the midst of everything. I never saw the time when her heart wasn't stout and high. And Bethia was another. Redheaded she might be, but she kept her temper through it all.

The first few weeks Bethia was staying with the McGarys and Dentons but as time went on she and Ann got to be good friends, and one day when I came back from hunting and took the meat to Ann, Bethia was there, helping out. From then on she stayed in Ben's cabin. I figured it was Ann's doing and it pleased me. I wondered if Ben had told her anything. He could of, for Ben knew the straight of things clean back to Martin's, and he had a good heart. But then Ann was a kindly woman and it would of been like her to take to Bethia and befriend her on her own account.

One thing her being in Ben's cabin did, it gave me more of a chance to see her. Though I slept in Jim's cabin along with the rest of the single fellows, I came and went at Ben's and usually took my meals with them. The Whitleys were there, of course, and we all mixed and mingled together. It seemed like Bethia kind of bloomed out there in the midst of them. Billy was a teasing kind of man, goodhearted and easy-natured, and Esther, though she was forthright and quick-spoken, was goodhearted, too. They all acted like Bethia belonged to them.

In one way it wasn't easy for me to sit around talking to Ben and Billy with her coming and going nearby, but it was easier than having her out on the Lick with Judd, and I reckon every man that ever loved a woman liked having her under his eye. She made no difference in the way she treated me and the other men, saving sometimes when she looked at me it was like she'd reached out and touched me, which she was careful not ever to do. There wasn't ever a chance to be alone with her, with so many around and underfoot, but I figured she wouldn't of been a party to it anyway.

As the fall drew on and Ann got heavier and more cumbersome on her feet, Bethia took over the care of Davey more and more, saving his mother the bending and lifting of him, for he was a stout, heavy boy. Seeing her so one day, with the child in her lap, I couldn't help thinking how it would be with one of her own. But it was a thought that soured even as it skittered through my mind, for any youngun she ever had would be one of Judd's, not mine, and there'd be nothing but soreness for me to bite on did that ever happen. I wondered though why she had none. Usually folks married as long as they had been, had several. I just gave thanks she didn't.

Ben was watching her with Davey that same day and he spoke of it. "She's got a easy hand with a youngun."

I didn't say anything, just nodded.

"It's a pity . . ."

Before he could say any more I broke in, "If you say it's a pity she's not got any of her own, Ben Logan, I'll lay you flat of your back!"

He looked at me, and kind of lifted one eyebrow in a way he had when something amused him. "I was just aiming to say it was a pity she was wedded to that Jordan feller."

I felt like a fool, of course. So I just blew my nose and walked off. I was getting tempery, myself.

The Indians kept up their pestering and plundering. Though no one else was killed, there was always too good chance for folks to risk getting back to their clearings. And those in the outlying parts of the country, not wishing to fort up, just took to the trail and went back to the settlements. Some have said that more than two hundred went back that summer and fall. I don't misdoubt it, for there sure was a steady flow of them. We took a pride, Jim and Ben and me, though, in knowing that it was mostly the come-latelies the colonel had brought on that panicked and left in such a hurry. But few of ours left. And the steady ones around Boonesburg stayed on . . . like Dannel and Squire, John Todd and Cap'n Floyd. The colonel wasn't in the country that summer. He was in the east, in Virginia and North Carolina, working hard to get the ear of any public man he thought could help him, but his business was carried on at Boonesburg by his agent, and, I reckon, Cap'n Floyd as the head surveyor. Business had fallen off considerably, though, since we'd pulled away.

We took risks that summer, and some of us knew exactly how big the risks were. We had to risk Cap'n Clark and Jack Jones being able to convince the Virginians to give us a title and repudiate the colonel. We had to risk being able to hold off the Indians should the British be ready to turn them loose on us while we were yet so few and low on ammunition. We had to risk losing the country itself if time ran out on us. We talked about it sometimes, between ourselves, and I'd not be telling the truth if I didn't say that some were nervy and afraid. They were. I was myself, times. The risks were too big for a sensible man not to be. I think even Ben was once in a while and commonly he was like a granite rock for steadiness. But we stayed on, and there was never any talk of leaving.

We kept on working on Ben's fort, those of us who lived close by . . . and that was Ben himself, Billy Whitley, Ben Pettit, William Manifee and me. It's right interesting the way a place changes names. When we first came into the country on the Long Hunt we spoke of the place as the Buffalo Springs, and that's what Ben had named it for a time. Then Cap'n Floyd called it St. Asaph's, but that never took hold. After that we got in the way of saying Logan's Place or Ben's Place, then when we commenced building the stockade everyone spoke of it as Logan's Fort, and for years that's what it went by. Now, it's the town of Stanford, but nobody had any notion there'd be a town there when we built that first stockade.

Ben picked a rise about fifty yards west of the least spring for the location, and he stepped off the stockade a hundred and fifty foot long and ninety foot wide. We didn't build our cabins on all four sides, or even three sides, like the other stockades. We built them on two sides, facing each other, and we left a kind of wide street down the middle. Of course we filled in the ends with a stockade fence. We put a blockhouse at three of the corners, and a regular cabin at the fourth one, so that on one side of the street was two blockhouses and three cabins, and on the far side was one blockhouse and four cabins. By building the fort on top of the rise we had a good view, but it put the springs outside the fort. Ben came up with an idea that took care of that. He said we'd make a tunnel from inside the fort down to the springs and cover it over good with puncheons tamped down with dirt so it would be stout and steady. And that's what we did.

But of course we didn't throw up that fort overnight. It took time, the balance of the summer and the fall and most of the winter, with us riding backwards and forwards from Harrodstown in all kinds of weather. And we couldn't always be working on the fort. We had to take our part in the scouting and hunting, cribbing the corn, getting up wood and so on. Sometimes a couple of weeks would go by and none of us able to ride down and lay a hand to the fort, but we kept plugging away at it.

We weren't the only ones fortifying that fall. There was a fellow named John McClellan up on the Elkhorn had a station he was strengthening and stoutening. There were several families clustered around a place called the Royal Spring there, and they figured to throw in with McClellan and have their own fort. Every fort meant a stronger hold on the country and we wished we could get, say, half a dozen good stout stockades built in the next few years, so it was heartening news to us when we learned John McClellan was holding out, though we couldn't help having our fears over the place he'd picked. It was north of the river and way off to itself. It would be hard to hold.

Judd Jordan had left in June . . . the last part of the month. By September I was beginning to look for him back, and I could tell Bethia was too. With as much hanging over the country as there was, I'd still felt a kind of peace that she'd been free of him for a time, but I figured it would come to an end soon. Unless he had awful lengthy business, three months was time enough for him to go and come. But September went by, and then October, and still no sign of him. I took a sashay over by his clearing on the Lick several times to see if he'd been there, but I never saw or heard a thing. The place stayed grown over and deserted. My own stand stayed grown over and deserted, too, and sometimes when I rode over and looked at it, it made me feel kind of sad and forlorn, seeing the roof of the cabin still fallen in and the weeds and briars tangling around the doorstep. It seemed a long time since I'd stayed there. But mostly I felt cheerful enough about it, being certain the time would come again when the country would be peaceful enough a man could take up his usual ways. For now, though, we had to cluster together and see to one another.

It was along the middle of November when Ben and Billy Whitley and me were working down at the fort, and the weather was so mild and warm we decided we'd just camp there until it broke so we could get to work soon of a morning and put in a good, long day. Ben asked me to ride up and tell Ann we intended to stay on. I took along some meat and a little parcel of salt. It was getting powerfully scarce, but Ben still had a little, and Ann had told him to bring it next time he had a chance. She was awful glad to get it, but troubled over it running so short. "Is this the last?" she asked when I handed it to her.

"It's the last," I told her.

She made a little face. "I just don't relish meat without salt, but I reckon I'll have to when this is gone."

"If the redskins'll stop pestering long enough," I said, "we can get over to a salt lick and boil out a batch."

She laughed. "If the redskins'd stop pestering we could do a lot of things."

Bethia was washing up the bowls and things and she'd not stopped when I went in except to speak. Seemed her feet were mighty light and airy, for she was flying around and kind of humming a little song while she worked, and her eyes looked twinkly and her face was sweet and happy. Ann motioned to her. "She's been awful gay the last day or two. Must be getting shut of you menfolks makes her that way."

"Do we make such a lot of work, Bethia?" I asked her.

"You make a plenty," she said, "but I reckon it's just the weather. It's more like summer than fall."

Davey was fretting and whining and pulling at Ann's skirts and she bent over to lift him up. Bethia flew at her. "I've told you not ever to do that. He's too heavy. I'll take him."

Ann was within a month of her time and so bulky that just bending over was something of a chore for her. She gave over the child, pushing her hair back in a limp way that told how listless she felt. Beside her, Bethia looked as slim as a willow wand. "It's warm enough you could take him outside, Bethia," she said, "and get him from underfoot awhile. I'll finish redding up if you'll take him. He wearies me so."

Bethia put a cap on the lad and pinned a shawl about him, though she had hard work of it with him dancing first on one foot then the other with the excitement of going out. When she'd done I opened the door, and Davey shot through it like a stone released from a sling shot. Bethia ran after him. "Davey! Come back here! You have to stay where I can watch after you."

He came back but he had springs in him and he had to bounce till he wore them down. Funny how a youngun lets go his joy mainly by running in circles. Satisfied as long as he stayed where she could see him, Bethia let him run and settled herself on a stool by the wall. I squatted on my heels alongside of her. "What's happened?" I said, then.

She leaned her head back against the wall and folded her hands in her lap. "How do you know anything has happened?" she said.

"By the way you look, and by the way you act. It ain't just the weather."

She laughed and turned her head so I could look her full in the face. "Dave, he ain't coming back for a while."

So she'd heard. "How do you know?"

"Was a man through here yesterday from the settlements. He brung me the word. He said Judd told him he'd not finished up his business yet and it might be till spring before he got back."

It was foolish of us, I reckon, to take such comfort from the news, for if we looked at the facts it was a meager kind of comfort, the end just put off and not changed. All the news meant was a little more time of peace from Judd . . . that's all the words said. But when we looked at each other, our looks said something different. Wrong as it may have been we both had the same hope. Maybe he'd never come back at all. That's what our eyes said, though neither of us named it. And, looking at each other, it was like we'd made a promise . . . that until he did come back, we'd keep on hoping. As if to seal the promise she put her hand on my arm, just for a second, the way I'd seen Ann touch Ben, and Esther Whitley touch Billy . . . the sweet, owning way of any woman with her man. It burned my arm through the sleeve. Then she took her hand away. "How soon before the fort is done?"

I shook my head. "It'll be a time yet, but we'll likely get it done this winter."

"You reckon Ann and Ben would let me go with 'em when they move?"

"Would you like that?"

She nodded.

"I have no doubts," I told her, "they'd be pleased to have you. You're a sight of help to Ann."

"Would you care?"

I couldn't help smiling at the way she asked it, as if she didn't know it would please me more than anything. "I'd feel a sight better," I told her, "to know you were in kindly hands."

We didn't say, though we both knew, the real reason of her asking and my answering was that we had to go on being close together.

A howl from Davey made an end of our talk. He fell down and skinned his knee and Bethia had to see to him. From the way he was taking on you could tell it was going to take a mort of comforting to hush him, so, yelling to make myself heard over Davey's screeching, I told her I had to be getting on. She nodded to let me know she'd heard and carried the lad inside.

I went on over to Jim's cabin, thinking to have a word with him before heading back to the stockade. And I was glad I did, for he had news. "Billy Bush was through yesterday," he said, "from the Holston. He brought word of Cap'n Clark and Jack."

We'd all been wondering what was keeping the two men and worrying some over the state of our powder and lead, worrying, too, over what might be taking place at Williamsburg. "What did he say?" I asked, settling myself down with the drink Jim poured.

"Well, Jack's got folks on the Holston and he turned up there during the summer. He said they'd got to Williamsburg too late for the spring gathering of the Assembly, so they had to wait over for the fall meeting. Jack took a sashay around to visit his folks but aimed to meet Clark in plenty of time."

"What was Clark doing during the summer?"

"Working on Patrick Henry, from what Billy said. But it was too soon to tell what success he'd have."

"Well," I said, thinking it over, "there's no need looking for them back till up in the winter, now. Likely the Assembly is just now meeting. We've not got enough powder and lead to run us that long have we?"

"Not if we was to have any trouble. We've got barely enough for hunting."

"Looks like some of us had better make a trip to the Holston."

Jim grinned. "Who did you have in mind?"

I grinned back at him. "Why, me and you, naturally . . . and Ben, if he cares to go."

"You think we could risk all three of us going?"

"Would you want to ask anybody else to take the risk?"

"Nope."

So it was settled and we left out the next morning. We told no one but Hugh McGary where we were going so the folks wouldn't take alarm. I didn't even tell Bethia or Ann. Just left like I was going back to help on the stockade, and Jim just going along. Ben went with us, though Billy Whitley tried hard to persuade him not to, with Ann so close to her time. Billy just wanted to go himself, and Ben could see through it easy. There was plenty of time to go and come back before Ann's time. "I'd hate to try," he told Billy, "to make my peace with Esther was I to let you go, Billy."

Billy bristled up like a fighting cock. "Well, don't think," he said, "I'll try to make yours with Ann!"

Ben just laughed at him and made ready to ride with us. "No need to tell her anything as long as the weather holds. She'll think I'm down here working. If we run into trouble, you'll find a way to break the news."

But Billy wouldn't be pacified and we left him still grumbling.

We made a fast, easy trip, with no trouble going or coming, and we got back to Harrodstown two weeks from the time we'd left. We brought on a hundred pounds of powder and a little over a hundred pounds of lead. We'd got it from Arthur Campbell. We also got the word from him that the colonies had finally declared themselves free and independent of Britain and had written out a paper saying so. It had been signed on July the fourth, and the war had commenced.

That was big news, and soon after it got circulated around over the country, several left out for Virginia to take part in the war. Cap'n Floyd was one that left. The word was that he intended to outfit him a privateer and sail the seas for a time. But most of us thought we could serve the colonies, as well as ourselves, best by staying with the country, and we did so.

We just got back in time, for it was early in December that Ann Logan took to her bed. That was the first time I'd ever been around when a birthing was taking place. Esther and Bethia shooed us out and I went with Ben over to Jim's cabin to wait. Ben appeared to take it easy enough, except that he kept going to the door and looking out. That was the first time, too, I'd ever thought what a little part a man has to do with the birthing of a youngun. Just his pleasure, you might say, and the rest is up to the woman. I've never rightly rid myself of the notion it don't quite balance out.

It was another boy, and they called it William, after Ann's father, Will Montgomery. I'd seen my own little brother when he was newborn, of course, but I didn't recollect he was as little and as red and wrinkled as this one was. But Ben seemed to take a deal of pride in him. "Look at that chest," he said, pointing, "and look at them fingers."

Well, he had a chest and ten fingers, and I saw nothing for pride in that. Most babies did have. Then Ben got to figuring. "You know, he's but the third youngun to be born in Kentucky. There's just Harrod Wilson and Chenoa Hart before him."

That kind of awed us. To be the third youngun born in the country. Now that was a thing to be proud of! Then I did a little figuring on my own, counting off on my fingers. I nudged Ben, "Looks to me like," I said, "according to when he was birthed he must of been planted in the country, too, or else on the trace coming in. Don't that set you up as the first of something, seeing as the others were all in the family way before they come into the country?"

He just grinned and said he didn't reckon that was a fact you could publish and claim. But he was sure proud of that boy.

# CHAPTER
# 15

WE COMMENCED GETTING READY for the Christmas shindig soon after little William was born. It was Anne Poage that set things going. "We aim to have a fine Christmas feast this year," she told us men, "and we're plumb tard of deer and buffler and elk. You men just kill off the big game on account of you can't hit the little. Why," she snorted, "even I can hit a cow elk as good as a man. Git out there and see if by chance you can hit a few turkey and pattridge and dove. Now, them would be fine eating!"

She didn't mean it, of course, but she had a sharp, peppery tongue that could sting plenty, and that part about the cow elk stung. She'd given us a target to shoot at, for sure.

You had to ride fifteen, sometimes twenty, miles to find any kind of game nowadays, and it was troublesome trying to round up enough birds to suit the women, but we were bound to. By taking chances on going nearly to the Falls, clean up on the Licking, and by me spending a week down on the Green, we did it, too. It was worth it, though, when we sat down to the feast the women spread on Christmas Eve. Not only had they cooked all the birds we'd brought in, but they'd roasted whole haunches of venison, buffalo humps and tongues, and there was even bear meat for those who liked it. With flour so short you wouldn't of thought they could have puddings and duffs and such, but they did, and Bethia said they used wild honey for sweetening and meal for thickening. They were tasty, too. There had been a plenty of pumpkins and squash and snap beans raised, and the table was loaded with them, and there was a kind of a jam the women made by taking berries they'd dried during the summer and mixing them with honey and stewing them down. Anne Poage had named it right when she'd said they aimed to have a fine feast, for that's exactly what it was.

After the supper we went over to Jim's cabin, it being the biggest, for the dancing. We had two fiddles now, Hugh McGary's and William Poage's and they sounded fine. Jim called the first set. Us men had been wetting our whistles considerably during the day and we felt good. But with or without a drink there never was a man more sociable or easygoing than Jim, or one that wanted to see folks pleased and having a good time. He stood up there at the end of the room with his black hair falling down over his forehead and his black eyes snapping, clapping his hands together to the music, throwing his head back and raising his voice like he was calling hogs. The roof might near fell in.

I led out Esther Whitley first and then Jane Manifee, but I kept my eye on Bethia. When she'd been partnered twice I went over to claim the next set for myself. Like a queen she put her hand on my arm and walked out on the floor with me.

We took our places and bowed and Bethia spread out her old patched, fringy-grayed linsey dress as full as it would go. When I looked down on the top of her head while she was curtsied, it was like my blood had turned to water of a sudden. Even my stomach felt shaky and it churned like it had a dasher going around in it. She was such a little bit of a girl, and she did so good at making out with things the way they were. I wished I could just sweep her up in my arms right in front of everybody and walk out the door with her and keep right on going.

"Form fours and circle eight!" We straightened up and joined hands in the circle.

"Swing your lady, twice around!" She was light as a feather, and under my hand her waist was soft and curvy. I could have broken every rib in her body with just one bear-crushing hug, and it was a temptation not to. Not to break her ribs, of course, but to hug her tight.

We made a fine couple, for if I do say so myself I was always a good dancer, and Bethia stepped light and easy, keeping her waist steady to her partner's hand. She swung wide on the corners, her skirt sweeping out and her hair flying. We made too fine a couple, I reckon, and no doubt I acted foolish, dancing with Bethia as often as I did. But neither of us thought of how it looked till Ann Logan called it to mind. Ann and Ben were there, though neither of them danced. They didn't hold with dancing, but of course they wouldn't of turned their backs on the Christmas party. The evening was wearing on when I walked Bethia to where Ann was sitting, the new baby asleep in her lap. She slid down the bench to make room and Bethia leant over to lift the corner of the shawl that was covering the baby and take a peek at him. Ann spoke low enough no one else could hear. "I wouldn't dance with Bethia no more if I was you, Dave."

Bethia caught on right straight and she sent a hasty look towards the flock of women gathered in the far end of the room, her face reddening. But I was slower. "Why?" I said.

"It's causing talk. You been singling her out right often and after all she's a married woman. The fact that her man's not here just makes it look worse."

I don't know of anything that leaves you more helpless than to be caught between what you want to do and what you can't do. I'd of liked to get up on a bench and tell everybody what lay back of Bethia's being wedded to such a man as Judd Jordan, and how he'd treated her. I'd of liked to tell them my own feelings. But no amount of telling would change the circumstances, nor make my own feelings look right and proper in the eyes of others. Wherever there are people, even inside the walls of a stockade in the wilderness, there are always those ready to think and speak ugly things. We knew, and some others like Ann and Ben and Esther and Billy Whitley that knew us best, how little had passed between us. But even while that was passing hotly through my mind, I knew, and looking at Bethia's troubled and bothered face I reckoned she knew too, that the joy we'd felt in dancing together . . . the joy, itself, was something we were not entitled to. The cold, hard fact was not to be altered. My head, that had been up in the clouds, now felt dull and achy and the music was too loud and the room was too hot and there were too many folks. "I'll leave," I said, "for you're right."

"No," Ann said, "go on dancing awhile longer. But not with Bethia."

I had no chance, though, to follow Ann's advice, for I'd no more than turned around to walk away when through the door stepped George Rogers Clark, like a ghost conjured up out of the dark. Everything stopped all at once, the music, the talking, the singing and dancing. Folks stopped right where they were and stared at him, some, new since he'd left, not knowing who he was, and the rest of us, remembering but not yet believing. He looked tired and he was muddy and trail-worn. His face that was always lean, was pinched in at the jaws and his eyes were sunk, like he hadn't slept in a long time. But he re-

membered to be gallant. He bowed, in that stiff, unbending way that
appears to be the elegant way of acting mannerly, and said, "Don't let
me interrupt the festivities, gentlemen. Go on with the merriment.
But if I may see you . . . Jim, Ben, Dave, Hugh . . . those of you
who are members of the Committee on Safety . . . I have a report to
make."

Hugh McGary laid his fiddle down. Jim took his arm from around
Jane Manifee's waist, where, unthinking, he'd kept it after the music
stopped. Ben handed young Davey, whom he'd been holding on his
knee, to Bethia, and my stomach, which had ballooned up into my
throat at the sight of Cap'n Clark, settled down where it belonged.
Everyone started moving and talking at once, but those of us on the
committee pushed our way through to the door. When we got outside
there was some milling around till we settled on where to go to talk,
for we'd always used Jim's cabin. Ben offered his and we gathered
there. It wasn't till then any of us thought to ask the cap'n whether
he'd had anything to eat. "No," he said, "and there are three men
with me. Simon Butler, who guided us here, and two of the men who
came down from Fort Pitt with us."

Simon Butler was a fellow who had a clearing up on the Licking.
He'd been in the country as long as any of us, but he always went
along on his own hook, not throwing in with anyone else. He was
probably the best scout and woodsman in the country, better even
than Dannel or Jim, but none of us knew too much about him on
account of him being such a lone wolf. Of course, in time we found
out his name was actually Simon Kenton, not Simon Butler, and that
he'd fled his home back over the mountains thinking he'd committed
murder in a hasty quarrel over a girl he loved. He'd taken the name
Butler for safety. But none of us knew that then. He'd come and he'd
go, and we all had a respect for his ways in the woods. He didn't come
down in our parts often, mostly taking his news to Boonesburg and
spending what time he wanted to be around other folks with them
there.

Jim sent to have him and the other two men accommodated, and
he sent for food for the cap'n. We waited with what patience we could
muster for him to eat and refresh himself, and he didn't take long
at that. When he'd done Jim told him, "Now commence with the
beginning."

He did so. He told how he and Jack had had a terrible journey,
with weather all the way like it was the day they'd left. How they'd
lost one of their horses before they ever got to the Gap and had to
take turns riding, and how, from their feet being wet all the time

both of them had got scald feet and had had to lay over and doctor them at Martin's. Only it wasn't Martin's any more, for Martin had been scared off again and they'd found the station abandoned. How they'd kept going, though, and finally got to Williamsburg, only to learn they were too late and the Assembly was already adjourned.

"There was nothing to do, of course, but to wait over for the fall meeting," the cap'n told us. "Jack went back to the Holston for a visit with his people, but I busied myself around Williamsburg. I made several trips to see Governor Henry, who was ill at his home. He was entirely sympathetic to our cause, and when I presented our plea for powder and lead to defend ourselves with, he gave me a note to the executive council urging them to honor my request for five hundred pounds.

"The council expressed its interest and concern, and agreed to furnish the powder. However, since the Assembly was not in session the executive council hesitated to make us a gift of the powder. They agreed to furnish it as a loan, and they required that I, personally, should be responsible for its repayment in the event our petition to the Assembly was not successful. On those terms they sent me an order for the powder, and they further required that I should be at the expense of transporting it thither."

"I hope," I said, butting in, "you didn't agree to any such terms."

"I did not." The cap'n rubbed his chin, but his eyes were twinkling. "It was not to my liking at all. And I felt so certain that Kentuckians would concur with me in the establishment of an independent government should Virginia fail us that I was bold enough to use that knowledge in a small matter of . . . shall we say, coercion." He smiled, and when George Rogers Clark wanted to, he could smile very winningly. "I took the liberty, as badly as we needed the powder, gentlemen, of returning the order. With it I sent a letter which explained that I felt myself unable to bear the expense of transporting these military stores to such a distant point, and in the letter I also expressed my great sorrow that Kentucky should have to stand alone. I concluded by stating that it was of general knowledge that a country which was not worth defending was not worth claiming." He minced the words in a kind of drawl so that he made his meaning clear. Lord, I thought, but the man was bold. We'd tied his hands so he couldn't legally do just exactly what he had done, for he had come out plain and told them if they didn't help defend Kentucky, they'd get no part of her. He'd had no power to threaten, but he had.

The other men caught it as fast as I had, and the whole room exploded. It was exactly the kind of bald courage and bluff they admired most and it tickled their fancies to think Cap'n Clark had pulled it. Hugh McGary reared back and whooped and pounded the man sitting next to him on the back. "By God, he stretched 'em right across the barrelhead, didn't he? Man, man, but I would of loved to see that!"

"So would we all," Jim said, laughing himself till the tears rolled down his face.

When the commotion died down the cap'n went on. "Well, then, having made my thrust there was nothing to do but wait. I thought I could count on their fear of losing us, and I presume that fear worked mightily, for on August twenty-third they issued me another order, which provided us the powder outright and carried with it a provision for the transportation of the powder to Fort Pitt at the government's expense. I sent you a letter, Jim, telling you of this and suggesting you send a party to get the powder, since Jack and I had to stay on for the meeting of the Assembly, but I learned before we left Williamsburg that you had not yet sent for it."

"There's been no letter," Jim told him. "None at all. Why, me and Dave and Ben made a trip back to the Holston to get powder on our own hook, not knowing whether you had succeeded or not."

"I judged you had never received it."

I was eager to hear what had happened to our petition. "What took place at the Assembly?" I asked.

"Well, we were not received as delegates, as I feared would be the case. As you know, Fincastle County is already represented and there is no county of Western Fincastle. But they heard our petition and were very courteous to us generally, although we were not allowed to sit. By the way, did you know that Mr. Slaughter also sent a petition asking that militia commissions be issued to the inhabitants of the country, and Captain Floyd has been in constant correspondence with Colonel Preston regarding the state of the country. He had suggested that a campaign against the Indians be conducted by Virginia. Oh, believe me, gentlemen," he laughed, "this session of the Assembly was very much taken up with the question of Kentucky and its people!"

"What about the colonel?" I said.

"He was there, and he worked mightily in the interests of the Transylvania Company. He laid a petition before the session stating that we were a small and rebellious group, disgruntled and with no standing, and he made bold to suggest Virginia would not wish to deal with such ignorant and insolent people."

It was not to be expected, of course, that the colonel would do otherwise. He had a big investment in the country, and he'd naturally pull every string he could to save it. But it gave me an anxious feeling to hear the cap'n's words. "I don't reckon you know how it turned out yet?" I asked him.

"No. We did all we could, and I can tell you that Governor Henry was sympathetic and that the Assembly itself was kindly disposed toward us. But when we'd done what we could and had then learned the powder was unclaimed at Fort Pitt we felt we must leave in order to return by Fort Pitt and claim the powder. We could not risk losing it. The Assembly was still debating when we left, and was not yet within sight of a vote."

"So we still have got to wait," I said.

"We still must wait."

"Did you bring the powder safely?" Jim thought to ask, then.

"There," the cap'n said, shaking his head, "we ran into some difficulty. At Fort Pitt we had intelligence that the Indians knew of the powder and intended waylaying us and taking it. How they learned of it is a mystery, but some way they did, and we should have run straight into an ambush save for our friend, Johnnie Vann."

"Johnnie Vann!" It was Jim that shouted first, but my own voice mingled with his before the words had time to echo.

"Johnnie Vann. He sought me out with the information, although he would tell me no more than the bare facts. They, however, were enough to warn us, and we enlisted several men to man two boats and come down the river with us."

"Johnnie said he was going into the Illinois country," I said.

"He did. He told me he was trapping and trading out there. But Johnnie is a roamer and he still gets around in a wide circle."

"He said, too," I said, mentioning for the first time what Johnnie had told me, "he didn't aim to give us any more information."

The cap'n looked at me and shook his head. "It's pitiful, isn't it? He is a man torn between loyalties. Apparently the word reached him we were to be ambushed, and he could not bear to withhold such information. At the same time, he would not tell us anything about the Indians . . . which ones they were, how they had learned of the powder, or anything else. I think he only spoke one sentence regarding the matter. 'You're to be ambushed going down the river,' he said, and that was all."

"For which," I said, "we can be everlastingly grateful."

The cap'n nodded. "We managed to evade the Indians as we came downstream, but we never entirely lost them, and at Limestone we decided the risk was too great to continue, so we abandoned the boats, hid the powder and marched overland on foot. We came to a cabin on the South Licking and we camped there night before last. While we were there, Simon Butler happened by. He told us it was Hinkston's old station. Since we did not know the country too well in those parts, I asked Simon if he would guide us in. We divided the party, I coming on with two of the men, and Jack staying at the cabin with the others. He will wait there to guide a party to the powder. We must send immediately."

Well, there it was . . . and a brave and stirring story it was, giving us a lot to think about. They'd got the powder and had a time getting it into the country. They'd presented our petition to the Assembly and had done the best they could for us. And while it was untelling what the Assembly would do and we had to wait yet to know, we couldn't of asked more of the men we'd sent. I still thought we'd done right to tie the cap'n's hands so he wouldn't be free to deal with Virginia save through the lawful channels. He might of been too bold had he been unhampered, but I couldn't help chuckling over the use he'd made of the meagerest kind of a threat. He was a shrewd and clever man, no doubts about it.

Jim asked me to lead the party to recover the powder and five of us, with Simon guiding, left early the next morning. There was an overcast sky, lead-colored and soggy, and I figured it was breeding weather. I was right, for within half an hour after we'd put the fort behind us it came on to snow, a fine, misty snow with a wet, keen wind slapping it in our faces. We hunched down into it and rode on. It was a miserable way to spend Christmas Day, but we couldn't take a day off to celebrate. Already the Indians might of found the powder.

We had gone some six or seven miles, I'd reckon, when Simon, who was running trail ahead, blocked the path and held up his hand. We pulled up short and waited. We could hear something blundering along the trail and we were off our horses and into the bushes in a split second. Then we heard Simon laughing and heard him call out. He had a funny voice for a man . . . soft and high and womanish. "Well, friends," he said, "what brings you here?"

A party of six men rode into sight. They looked frozen and gaunt, whittled down with cold and tiredness. Then I saw that the lead man was John Todd, and as fast as I could I got to him. "John!" I said, "what's happened?"

I was afraid the fort at Boonesburg had been wiped clean out. I couldn't think of any other reason John would be in these parts, for he commonly stayed close to his own stand. He was swaying so he could barely stay on his animal, so I braced him on one side and Simon steadied him on the other. "Indians," he said, his voice hoarse.

"Where? Boonesburg?"

He shook his head, and even that much movement made him lose his balance till he nearly fell off. "We went for the powder. Five of us out hunting yesterday . . . ran across Jones and men at Hinkston's. Made ten of us . . . thought . . . enough to bring powder. Attacked. Mingos . . . Pluggy. Jack killed . . . three taken."

Pluggy. Pluggy was the Mingo chief. I shook John again, afraid he was dozing off from the cold. "How many?"

"Thirty . . . forty, maybe."

That rung a bell clean through me . . . a bell of fear. That was a war party, and it was well down in the country. I thought fast, and decided. "Simon, you take a couple of men and make haste over to the Elkhorn and pass the word to the folks at McClellan's, then circle on over to Boonesburg. We'll take these on in to the fort and give the word there."

Simon nodded. "But I don't need nobody else. Get along faster without."

"Suit yourself," I told him. No need saying more. He knew as good as I did the need for hurry. The way it was he might find nothing but ashes at McClellan's or Boonesburg either. He faded into the woods before I'd done speaking, and I knew he'd not stop till he'd made the circle.

We got Todd and the others to Harrodstown, and when they'd been fed and had rested a little, Cap'n Clark called the Safety Committee together to make plans. By the redskins attacking, he didn't think they'd found the powder yet. It was his opinion that they'd been following him overland in the hopes he'd lead them to the powder.

Hugh McGary, being redheaded, hasty-handed and roostery, was all for leaving out right straight and tracking down the red devils with a sizable party. I must admit I favored that myself. "There's enough of us," I said, "if we all take the trail to wipe out the bunch of them."

"It would take every man we have to do that," Cap'n Clark said. "There'd be no one left to defend the fort."

"If we wipe out the scoundrels the fort won't need defending," Hugh said, with more than a little heat.

"No," the cap'n said. "It's too risky. We have to remember, gentlemen, that this may be the beginning of the British plan. Pluggy's band may be only a part of a much larger band. Instead of thirty Indians, we might easily run into three hundred. Or it may be part of the plan to draw all the men away from the fort and then swarm over it and take it. It's too risky."

We said no more, for he'd thought straighter than we had. It made cold chills run down your back to think of the things he'd named, but we had to think of them. We talked and talked. There was no doubt a big party had to go out to stand off Pluggy and recover the powder, but there was also no doubt we couldn't leave the fort too shorthanded. It was finally decided Jim should head up thirty men to go for the powder. That was equal with the redskins we knew of. And Cap'n Clark would stay at the fort and head up the defense. We were mostly single men told off to go with Jim, which was right, seeing it was the greater risk and we'd leave no widows and orphans.

I've always been sorry we took two days to strengthen the fort and bring in more corn and drive up the stock, but hindsight is always better than foresight and we had no way of knowing what the need would be. It looked like our first duty lay with our own. Anyway, when we'd made the place as secure as we could against attack, we made ready to leave the next morning and laid down that night feeling we'd done all we could. We'd have to risk, now, whatever happened.

I went to sleep straight off, but I came awake suddenly along in the night, hearing a shaking and pounding at the big gate. In the light of the fire I saw Jim already up and fumbling for his gun. Cap'n Clark, who stayed in Jim's cabin, too, was getting up. We all found our guns about the same time and made for the gate. Hugh was running across the square and I saw Ben taking the slope in long strides. Silas Harlan was on the gate and he was drawing the bar when we got to him. It was Simon Butler that slid through the crack of the opening. Silas dropped the bar behind him. "What is it?" the cap'n snapped at Simon.

Simon's voice was whispery from running. "McClellan's."

"Pluggy?"

Simon nodded. "Attacked at sunup. Fought all day."

"Did they take the station?"

"No. Somebody put a bullet through Pluggy hisself and they left out."

"Our losses?"

"Four hurt. John McClellan and Charles White are mortally hurt, in my opinion. Ed Worthington and Robert Todd but slightly."

John Todd shouldered his way through the crowd that was gathering. "What was that about my brother?"

Jim put his arm around John's shoulder. "He was hurt at McClellan's, John, but not bad."

"They had but twenty guns all told," Simon said.

Twenty guns . . . and they'd stood off Pluggy's band all day. Stood it off and saved their own, for the redskins'd had to withdraw. It made me sick to think we had been bringing in corn and stoutening our own fences whilst they were fighting all day long. But we didn't know. That's the way it always was those first years. We just had to do the best we could, and each little settlement had to be, to some extent, like an island all to itself.

Well, with Pluggy killed doubtless the redskins would make tracks for the Ohio and their own towns. We could recover the powder in peace now, likely. But they'd done a lot of damage, Pluggy and his Mingos. Jack Jones was dead, a smart man and a loss to the country . . . John McClellan and Charles White were doubtless dying. Three had been taken captive, and two men had been bad hurt. We could ill spare one man, to say nothing of eight, there were so few of us left in the country. But we had to spare them, and fewer by eight we had to keep on, maybe sparing more.

I stood there in the night thinking of it, and shivering, not altogether from the cold. The thought came to me that the powder hadn't all been paid for by the Virginia Assembly. It had cost more than that, and the paying couldn't be done by the Virginians. It had to be fought and paid for, and dear at that, by these in the country themselves. Likely it would always be so.

# CHAPTER
# 16

THE ATTACK ON McCLELLAN's STATION changed our plans some-
what. Those folks had to be helped, so Cap'n Clark took six of
us from Jim's party and sent us to the Elkhorn. "Bring them in,"
he said, "as soon as they can travel. The station is too weak and stands
too lonely and far from help. We cannot scatter our strength to defend
it."

I disremember now who all of the six were, but I do recall the two
Johns, John Kennedy and John Martin, were among them, and I was
named to head up the party. We left and traveled part the way with
Jim's bunch, but once we'd crossed the river they had to angle east-
ward and we kept headed north.

Before we ever came to the puny little stockade itself we passed
several clearings . . . nothing left of them, of course, but ashes and
ruins. The folks were safe enough, for they'd been forted up at Mc-
Clellan's since early winter, but Pluggy's band had left them little more
than themselves to go on with. The land was still there, but their
homes and whatever belongings they'd had to leave were gone. When
we got to the stockade we learned that all their stock had been killed
or driven off, too. Their lives, their guns, and the clothes on their
backs were about all they had left. And some had forfeited their lives.
They were burying Charles White when we arrived, and it was plain
to see John McClellan was lingering by a thread.

It was a sad and sorrowing handful of folks clustered there, and
the attack had shaken them up considerably and scared them, but by
grannies, they weren't panicky, and they didn't want to give up . . .
not by a long mile. We gathered them together, women, younguns

and all, when the burying was over and told them what Cap'n Clark had said. They didn't want to go to Harrodstown. And at first they said flat out they wouldn't go. "We can make out," Ed Worthington said, though he was carrying his arm in a sling at the time. "Just give us enough powder and lead, and we can hold on."

Well, he didn't know, of course, what some of the rest of us knew, and I didn't have leave to tell him. All I could do was point out that their station stood by itself, north of the river, handy to the Ohio tribes, where they'd have to take the brunt of the Indian trouble it was but sensible to expect with spring and summer coming on. "Besides," I told him, and the others listening, "there's so few of us left in the country it seems best not to be too scattered."

They didn't give up to leave, though, till after John McClellan died on the sixth day of January. That was the day Jim rode out to see what was keeping us. He said they'd had no trouble finding the powder, nor had they seen any redskins going or coming. All was well at the fort, too. "But," he told me, privately, "the cap'n is fretting over these folks and wants 'em brought in soon."

"Well, let him come get 'em himself, then," I said, not liking to be nagged. "McClellan was too bad hurt to be moved and he's just this day passed on. Besides, there's not but two horses amongst 'em. Tell him to send us some pack animals."

He did, but it was another two weeks before we could get them moving, and they were slow on the trail, then, partly because the weather was so cold and miserable, but mostly because their hearts were glaumy and heavy. There is no way to comfort and cheer folks driven out of their homes, especially when they must also leave unmarked graves in a wilderness that will soon grow briars and weeds over them. It was sure a relief to me when the last of the McClellan's station folks passed through the gates at Harrodstown.

That night, when finally we were all safe inside the walls of the fort, Cap'n Clark had a meeting of the Safety Committee. I remember sitting there in Jim's cabin, crosslegged on the floor by the fire, listening and thinking. Mostly I was thinking how the year before the folks had swarmed into the country by the hundreds, and how, by the hundreds, they'd swarmed back faster than they'd come in. Now, what was left of us could be held in two settlements, we were so few. Two settlements. But Cap'n Clark was telling it. "We count eighty guns, now that McClellan's people are in. Simon Butler told me that Boonesburg can count in the neighborhood of sixty."

One hundred and forty guns . . . in the whole country, one hundred and forty men.

"There are forty families of women and children in the country," the cap'n said. "And across the Ohio are five thousand Indians whom the British are arming and agitating. The situation will not get better unless Virginia comes to our aid, and we do not know whether she can, or will. For all practical purposes, we stand alone. We have on hand enough ammunition for our immediate needs. We may or we may not be able to get more. We are crowded together in two small forts. We may all lose our scalps shortly. Or," he added dryly, "we may save the country. Gentlemen, what shall we do?"

Hugh McGary was the head of the committee. "How do you vote, Cap'n?" he said, taking up the roll.

"I vote to stay," Cap'n Clark said.

"Jim Harrod?"

"I vote to stay."

"Ben Logan?"

"To stay."

"Isaac Hite?"

"Stay."

"Silas Harlan?"

"Stay."

"Dave Cooper?"

"Stay."

Right on down the list. To a man we voted to stay, and Lord, what fools we were to do it. What reasonless, senseless, crazy, glorious fools we were. Any way you looked at it, it was foolish. We had such a little chance of holding on, it was already practically gone up in smoke. By any line of reasoning we'd ought to of skedaddled and left the country to the British and the redskins. But we didn't. Mark it down that we didn't. Even with women and younguns to risk, we didn't. Even knowing the folks at Boonesburg might not hold out and we'd be left alone, we didn't. Even knowing we might be fighting with hatchets and knives in the end, we didn't. Oh, I know the country would have been settled in time, anyhow, no matter what we decided that night. I know that in a few years the settlers would have been back. But it was us that stayed and gained those years. It was us . . . George Rogers Clark and Jim Harrod and Ben Logan and Hugh McGary and Billy Whitley and Silas Harlan and Isaac Hite and Abraham Hite and me, Dave Cooper, and all the others . . . it was us decided and it was us held on. And up at Boonesburg it was Dannel and Squire Boone and John and Robert Todd and Richard Calloway and Nathaniel Hart, and the others. Never forget who the few were, for they held the country for all who were to come. They were the first, and in some ways the best, of the Kentuckians.

When the voting was done we settled down to talking of ways and means and Ben put the question whether we'd best go on building our fort down at his place. We were in favor of it, of course, but the good of all had to be thought of, and while it would help the over-crowding at Harrodstown for us to move out, it would also weaken that fort by as many guns as we took with us. Finally it was decided we should go ahead, on the grounds that it was but twenty miles away and to the south where it wouldn't run so much risk of attack. "I don't aim to sound unhospitable," Jim said, "but it would help with the room. Since the folks from McClellan's have come there'll be eight to twelve in every cabin."

"My God," one of the men moaned, "it was already so bad I had to have the help of everybody in the house to be with my woman. Reckon I'd just as well move in with the boys up here, now."

Everybody laughed, but it was the truth. It did take considerable maneuvering for the married couples to have any place or time to themselves. The number of women in the family way, though, told they managed it one way or another.

We pitched in and worked hard on the new fort with the women-folks crowding and pushing us all the time. When one of us came in the whole pack of them, Ann and Esther, Jane Manifee and Ben Pettit's woman, all jumped on us to know how much we'd got done. Finally, about the middle of February when we told them the cabins were roofed and chinked and the stockade fence built, Ann and Esther commenced packing.

"There ain't a door hung yet, Ann," Ben said, "nor a winder cut, nor a chimney finished. To say nothing of no floors laid. It's awful rough, and it might be you and the younguns had best stay on here till the cold breaks."

"It might be," Ann said, not stopping her packing, "but it ain't going to be. I don't care how rough it is, it'll be better than staying here in this mess of folks."

Ben looked at me and laughed. "You'd think she plumb hated the folks here."

"I don't hate 'em," she said. "Of course I don't. But I sure am tard of living amongst 'em."

When Ben went out I followed him and stopped him before he could make off to some chore or other. "Ben, has Ann said anything about Bethia going with you all?"

"Why, sure," he said, acting surprised. "I'd of allowed she'd done told you . . . Bethia, that is. That was settled a time ago. She's more than welcome to go."

"Bethia and me don't get much chance to talk," I reminded him, and then without thinking I said, "I'm obliged to you, Ben," just like Bethia had been my wife and he was doing her a favor.

He grinned. "Oh, it's nothing, Dave. Glad to oblige you."

"Look, Ben," I said, "you know . . . you've known from the start . . ."

He made a motion with his arm, stopping me. "Dave, there's no need you saying ary thing. I reckon me and Ann both knows. We wouldn't hold with such in the common run, for the Scriptures says thou shalt not covet . . . and that's bound to mean thy neighbor's wife as well as other things. But we know you . . . and we know Bethia . . . and we know the ways of you both, and . . . well, we aim to do what we can for Bethia. Ann thinks as much of her as if she was blood kin."

"Well," I said, "in my opinion it's stretching it a mite to speak of Judd as my neighbor, but I reckon mostly what the Scriptures says is right. I wouldn't of wished to covet anybody's wife, had I had my druthers. It's sure not a comforting thing to do. And the Lord only knows what's to come of it. But anyhow, I'll feel better about her knowing she's safe with you and Ann and not left here amongst these folks that might talk and mistreat her."

"You can rest easy," Ben said. "She'll be safe with us. Till he comes for her, leastways."

Till he comes for her! That was what goaded me almost beyond bearing . . . the thoughts of her ever being with Judd again. Whatever peace of mind I had about her now would come to an end then, and it had to be expected and looked for. I turned away and walked off, seeking some chore to do that might take my mind off it. Thou shalt not covet thy neighbor's wife. The Scriptures never said anything about what misery it would be. They just said thou shalt not, and made it a sin. But I figured the misery kind of paid off the sin.

Not caring to risk the women and younguns of a daytime, it was decided for us to move down to the fort at night, so two days later, come good dark, we filed out of the big gate. There was a little knot of folks gathered around to say goodbye and wish us well. Any leave-taking in this country was liable to be forever and was always sobering. Miz McGary, who was likely to be teary any time, cried while she said her farewells. "You're all going to your deaths, I just know it!"

Jane Manifee sniffed. "Well, we'll not be crowded to death, that's one good thing." But she reached out and patted Miz McGary's hand. "Just save your tears, honey, for we'll be all right."

All day it had snowed and the ground was thick with a white coverlid that muffled the sound of the horses' feet. Along towards evening, though, it had cleared, and a half moon showed. There was just enough light to reflect on the snow and to throw out shadows like ghosts in front of us. Ben led off, with Billy Whitley. Right behind came Ann, carrying the least one, William, in her arms. He was asleep and bundled till not even his face showed. Ann's Negro woman Molly and her three boys came next. Behind them was Bethia with young Davey held in front of her. He was bouncing like a jack-in-the-box with his excitement. She had to hold onto him hard to keep him from falling off. I was counting the folks through the gate and when she went past and I saw the trouble Davey was making her, I called out to her. "Hang onto him."

"I aim to," she said, "but if he don't calm down I'll be wore to a nubbin time we get there."

Next after Bethia came Esther Whitley and her two little girls, then her brother and his family, then the Ben Pettits, the William Manifees, and the James Masons. That was all the families. Strung out in back, driving the stock and guarding the rear were the single fellows that had thrown in with us . . . John Martin, John Kennedy, Azariah Davis, Burr Harrison, William May, and a free Negro named Daniel Hawkins. I name them all so there'll be no mistaking who it was that made the first stand on the headwaters of the Green . . . our own part of the country. I, myself, rode last.

There were thirteen men, but we counted fifteen guns, for Esther Whitley and Jane Manifee could shoot as good as any man in the country. That was fewer than had been at McClellan's, and it might be we were making too bold a move. But there was a lot of difference. For one thing, giving John McClellan all due credit for his courage, Ben was a lot shrewder man than John had been. The way they'd picked their locations showed that. John had picked the riskiest place in the country . . . off to himself up north of the river . . . the first place the Indians would find once they crossed the Ohio. Of course it was mighty rich land. Ben had picked his place along in the middle, satisfied with land maybe not so rich and level. John's fort had never been more than a makeshift, while Ben had planned his down to the last stockade pole, taking everything into consideration and building stoutly. There was a tidiness in Ben's nature that made him do everything he turned his hand to well . . . and a cleverness that made him look far ahead. He took care, and he was patient and steady and sure.

It was a long night. The hours wore out slow and quiet. Ben and
Billy set a pace accommodating to the women and the stock, not too
fast but steady and going right along. When the moon went down it
was darker, but the stars gave enough light to keep to the path. The
younguns dropped off to sleep soon as the excitement wore off, even
Davey, and when they were no longer chirping and cheeping like
little birds, all the other sounds were quieted and softened down. A
pack train along the trail at night. Do you know what you can hear?
You can hear the sluff of the horses' feet, sounding like sea waves
dragging over sand. You can hear the creak of leather, whangy like a
fiddle string plucked and turned loose. You can hear a pot or kettle
jostle against another one when a horse rubs against a low-hanging
branch or steps in a hole. You can hear a man speaking out now and
again, his voice kept low and deep in his throat, asking his woman
likely, in a married man's way, how she's making out. You can hear
two women, riding close, murmuring, and their voices, running together, sounding like creek waters flowing. You can hear a youngun
whimpering in his sleep, and his mother shushing him and comforting
him. Homey sounds, all of them . . . the sounds of folks and their
belongings, going some place, together.

The sun was up when we came in sight of the fort. There it was,
on top of the knoll, empty, new, raw, ugly and patched with snow.
But nothing had ever looked better or handsomer or stouter to those
folks. The women stirred and straightened and the younguns waked
and stretched and were amazed to be still riding. Clear down at the
end of the line I could hear young Davey's voice, shrill and high,
"Aren't we there? Aren't we there, Bethia?"

I don't know what she said to him, but Ben rode back and took
him and led the way into the stockade with Davey astride the pommel
of his saddle ahead of him.

They drew lots for the cabins. The Whitleys, the Manifees and the
Masons drew the southside cabins, and Ben, the Clarks and the Pettits drew the north ones. "That leaves," Ben said, "the blockhouses
for the boys and one cabin left over."

Jane Manifee walked up to the cabin she'd drawn and poked her
nose in the door. "Lordy," she said, drawing in a big breath, "fancy
a whole cabin to yourself again! I don't know as I'll know how to
act."

"I do," Ann Logan said, herding her younguns and Bethia across
the street. "I know exactly how I'm going to act. I'm going to spread
out all over and take up all the room I want."

"You'd best do it while you can, then," Ben told her, grinning, "for likely in time it'll be as crowded as Harrodstown."

"Save the day," Ann said. "But you can't spoil my pleasure, Ben Logan. I've got my own to theirselves again, and when the folks commence crowding in, it'll still be my own cabin, and me making free of it for them. Not the other way round."

Glory, but it was something to watch those women take over. They went around for two or three days just sniffing the new clean smell and spreading out their blankets and robes to air and dry in the sun, hanging up their belongings and setting out their pots and kettles and settling themselves and their younguns down. "I don't know," Esther Whitley said, spreading her blankets out, "if I'll ever get the smell of that fort outen my things. No matter how clean-handed a body tried to be, the dirt and the filth and the stench got rubbed in."

Me and John Martin were standing by the corner of the blockhouse watching them one day and I said to John, "You ever watch an old hen making herself a nest? Ever notice how she's got to squirm and turn herself around six, seven times, and peck at the straw and shake it up, and ruffle up her feathers and scratch herself a place? Them women reminds me of a hen. When they get done airing and spreading and ruffling up their feathers, they'll likely settle down in them cabins and set there, blinking their eyes and clucking."

I never saw Jane Manifee till she had me by the ear. "That's right, young man," she squawked at me, "that's right. May take a old hen a time and a time to get her nest to suit her, but you never seen a rooster taking the bother, did you? Oh, sure, he's a good hand at strutting around the barnyard crowing his fool head off, but did you ever take notice it's a hen that lays the eggs and sets on 'em and hatches out the young, and gets things done generally. Now, you can just quit your crowing."

John had ducked around the corner slicker than an eel wiggling through a mud flat, but Jane had me fast. "Now, Jane," I said.

She shifted her hold from my ear to my shirttail. She had a mouth full of tobacco juice and she had to spit before she could say anything more. "Don't now Jane me," she said when she'd laid a stream up against the bole of a tree, "you come on with me. I need me a hand. I got to get my chimbley done. William's off sashaying around, and I can't be up on the roof and down on the ground all to oncet. Takes two to build a chimbley."

I was hooked so there was nothing to do but go along. Behind me I could hear John cackling. No doubt he'd have a lot to say about roosters crowing when I next saw him.

We had room and to spare in the blockhouses, too. We wanted a watch kept in all three, so the six of us fellows that weren't married spread out, two to a blockhouse. When we drew lots, John Martin and me were partnered in the southeast corner. John Kennedy and the Negro Hawkins drew the northeast corner, and Burr Harrison and Billy May had the southwest. The gate was in the middle of the stockade at the east end of the street, and the slope angled off southeastward from it towards the springs. The blockhouses were built just like those at Harrodstown, two-storied, with the upper floor extending about four foot beyond the walls on the outside. Standing at a loophole, then, you could see all along the fence and the redskins couldn't creep up and make an unexpected assault directly on the stockade itself.

The cabin on the northwest corner was the one left empty, but it didn't stay that way very long. Within a week's time we had another family with us. These were Sam Coburn's from on Gilbert's Creek. Sam had come into the country with Dannel's trail-cutting party, but in time he'd quarreled with the colonel and had withdrawn from Boonesburg. Gilbert's Creek was about the same distance from any one of the three forts, but of course Sam wouldn't of wished to take his family back to Boonesburg, and I reckon he figured Logan's wouldn't be as crowded as Harrodstown. Anyhow, we were pleased to have him. We had room, and he made one more gun. But, Lordy, there were times when I wondered if his gun was worth the commotion his girl caused amongst the folks.

Besides Sam and his woman, there was with them this girl of theirs. She'd been married, but her man, Jim McDonald, was killed up on Drennan's Creek the year before. He'd been up there with a salt-making party. He left her with a youngun, a babe still in arms. It was but natural she'd take the child and go with her folks. Now, women free to wed were so scarce in the country that no widow had to stay free of choice. No matter what she looked like, or how shrewish or slack-handed she was, there were a dozen men clamoring for her. Commonly they didn't wait more than a week or two after burying one to take up with another, for not only were there a dozen men to one woman in the country, a woman just couldn't make out by herself. She had to have a man. You can imagine, then, what a stir there was when Sam Coburn rode into the fort with a widowed girl who was as pretty as a picture. She was little and round-faced and she had dimples in both cheeks and her chin, and she laughed a lot, which showed them off. The womenfolks stood and watched while she got off her horse. They'd come out to welcome her, but it's my opinion she was so different from what they'd expected, and so sightly looking, she made all of them feel kind of old and frowzy. They were patched and work-hardened and weathered by the country. She'd been in the country a time, too, but Sam was a man of property back on the Yadkin and he had the means to make life easier for his womenfolks. Ann had the look of never having done much work. She had the look of always having been waited on and cared for.

Then I don't reckon the way the men clustered around her set very good with the women, either. There were six of us not married. Dan Hawkins, being a Negro, was excluded from courting her, and I certainly paid her no mind, Bethia to the contrary. To this good day I'm accused of having swarmed with the rest of the bees after the honey, till a firm hold was taken on me, but I never. I don't deny I thought she was pretty. Man with eyes in his head don't quit noticing the difference between a pretty girl and a plain one, just because he's in love with one woman. But there's a heap of difference between noticing a pretty girl and wanting her. I wouldn't of traded Bethia's little finger for the whole of Ann McDonald, as little chance as I had of ever having Bethia's little finger.

But there were sure four other fellows that sat up and paid attention. There was a terrible shaving off of old beards and cutting of hair and of trying to scrape and clean up smelly old buckskins, and one at a time or all four together they took to hanging around Sam Coburn's cabin most of their free time. It didn't help make the women like her any better, either, when the boys commenced taking the extra-fat birds and tenderest humps of meat to Ann McDonald. Commonly what was killed was brought in and divided up amongst all the folks, share and share alike. The six of us without families did most of the hunting, and ate where we pleased, being welcome in any of the cabins. I eat at Ben's, which would of been natural for me even if Bethia hadn't been living with them. But, like I said, it wasn't long till the others got in the way of holding out partridges and turkey and taking them over to Miz McDonald as presents. They took to drifting over there to eat right often, too.

The way I got into trouble was like this, and I was as innocent as a newborn babe. Jim Harrod rode down about a week after the Coburns had moved into the fort. He'd been out hunting, and since we'd decided the two forts should keep in touch with one another about once a week, he'd come on in to take the night with us and exchange news.

The sun was getting low and the women were commencing to do up their night work, like bringing up water from the springs and milking and getting in wood. Jim and me were standing talking not far from the mouth of the tunnel, when Ann McDonald came out lugging a heavy kettle of water. She came past us and stumbled over a root, nearly falling, and nearly losing the water. Now, what, I'd like to know, is any man to do when a woman stumbles right into his lap? Just let her fall? Well, I didn't. I grabbed her and held onto her until she'd steadied herself. I'd of done the same even if I'd known Bethia and Ann Logan had just come out of the tunnel themselves and were looking on. But I didn't see them and I didn't help them with their kettles of water, and I did take over Ann McDonald's and me and her and Jim walked on over to her cabin.

As if that wasn't bad enough, when we got to the cabin she asked the two of us to come back for supper. I had no intentions of going, but Jim was terribly smitten with her and wanted to go. While he was shaving and cleaning up he kept begging me to go. "Go yourself," I told him, "I don't want to."

"I can't go by myself," he said, "she asked both of us. It wouldn't look right for me to go without you."

"She'll never notice I'm not there," I said. "She only asked me to be polite. It was you she was wanting to come."

That pleased him, but he still held out for me to go. And it pleased me for Jim to be taking notice of a woman finally, so when he came flat out and said he wouldn't go unless I did, I gave in and went. I thought nothing of it save that the evening stretched out long and tiresome and I missed seeing Bethia at all.

Jim left early the next morning, full of talk about Miz McDonald and as moony-eyed as a lovesick calf over her. I rode out with him and was gone all day, scouting over towards my place and around and not getting back to the fort till nearly suppertime. When I'd tended to Beck I went to Ben's to eat. Ben spoke and we sat down at the table. Ann was at the far end feeding young Davey and she didn't look up or speak when I went in. Bethia was busy at the fire and she didn't turn or speak, either. But I thought nothing of it, for often when they were busy they didn't stop to talk till they'd finished whatever they were doing. I watched Bethia spooning up the stew, just glad to have her in sight again after not seeing her for a little spell. The room was warm and the stew smelled good and I was tired from riding all day. I felt fine.

It didn't last long. Bethia set the bowls of stew down in front of us with a clatter that almost spilled them over and swished around on the other side of the table. "I don't know," she said, "as we've got anything will suit you tonight, Mister Cooper."

"Why, you'd ort to know I ain't finicking," I told her, puzzled. Mister Cooper!

"Well, you never used to be," she sniffed, turning her nose up in the air, "but the company you been keeping might of changed you. We ain't got no pewter cups and plates, neither. Will these here whittled out of wood be good enough for you?"

I looked at Ben, but he was bent over his stew and didn't raise his head. I thought his face looked kind of red. Ann was still busy feeding Davey and she wouldn't meet my eye, either. I commenced to burn. I didn't know what it was all about, but apparently me going to supper at Miz McDonald's was at the root of it. I stood up and shoved the stool back so hard it rolled clean across the room. "You come outside with me," I told Bethia, going over and taking a firm hold of her arm.

"I'll do no such," she said, jerking loose. "I got my work to do."

"Let it wait. Either you come outside with me or I'll carry you out!"

Neither Ann nor Ben appeared to take any notice, and half pushing, half jerking, I got Bethia outside and planted myself in front of her. "Now I aim to get at the bottom of this," I told her, so mad I was boiling. "What's the matter with you?"

She stuck her chin up in the air. "There's nothing the matter with *me!*"

"There is so. Calling me Mister Cooper, like I was a stranger! Accusing me of being finicking and too good for the rest of you! What's got into you?"

"Nothing. You're the one something's got into!"

"All right. What have I done? Just tell me."

She didn't say anything and I jerked at her arm. "I said tell me!"

"And I'll tell you," she said then, almost spitting the words at me, "I'll tell you! I seen you with that Miz McDonald yesterday. I seen you standing there in the broad daylight with both arms around her, and I seen you take her kettle of water and pack it for her, leaving me and Ann to lug our own. There's no use your saying nothing, for I seen it with my own eyes, and so did Ann. We come out of the tunnel right behind her. And then first thing this morning Miz Coburn was over to see us, and she said you eat with them last night."

I was so flabbergasted I couldn't say a word for a minute, but I couldn't of got one in edgeways anyhow. She'd only paused for breath. "One thing is certain, you never eat with us last night. Nor sent word why. And then you've got the gall to show up tonight like nothing had happened. Just walk in and take your place and set down to be served! Well, I'm not serving you no more. Hear? You like that Ann McDonald so good, just go there and eat regular. Let her serve you and wait on you. I ain't doing it no more!"

"Now, wait a minute . . ." I started to say, but she wasn't in any mood to listen.

"There's no need your talking. Just go on your way and leave me be!"

"If you'll just listen. . . ."

But she wouldn't. "Listen to you make up a batch of lies to tell. I seen what I seen, and I meant what I said. Just go on your way!"

Well, I got mad all over again then myself. "All right," I told her, "if that's what you want, that's what you'll get," and I walked off and left her standing there.

I needn't to say, I reckon, I spent a miserable night, and a miserable three days following, for that's how long my pride held out. And the only way I could hold out that long was to get on Beck every morning and ride out, staying gone till past dark, so's I wouldn't even see Bethia. I tried to tell myself it was best for things to end so, for nothing could ever come of our feelings anyhow. But by the evening of the third day I knew I wasn't fooling myself at all. We were joined together against something bigger than Ann McDonald, and it was stupid for us to quarrel between ourselves.

I didn't go for supper, not quite daring to do that, but just after, I went. Ben was still using a blanket for a door, not yet having got around to hanging the one he'd been working on, and I just stuck my head inside. She was sitting by the fire, looking as droopy as I felt. I called her and when she raised her head she couldn't help letting a glad look sweep across her face, but she crimped her mouth down again in a second. "Will you come outside?" I asked her.

At first I thought she wasn't going to, for she looked around the room for something to busy herself with, and then from the corner where I couldn't see her, I heard Ann tell her, "Go on."

She came and I wasted no words. It was dusky dark and no one could see, but I wouldn't of cared. All I wanted was to hold her and kiss her and make things right again. And I guess she wanted the same thing, for her arms went up around my neck, tight, tight, and her mouth clung to mine, quivering and soft. I don't know how long we stood like that . . . long enough, anyhow, to still the misery eating within us. And then we drew apart, but like people who've been threatened with a terrible danger, we held onto each other, touching and clinging, our hands woven together. We talked, of course, and I told her what had happened and how it was, but I misdoubt it mattered a lot. The cause of the quarrel wasn't as important as the hurt it had built up, and that was eased by being together again.

I tried to tell her how it was that when you loved one woman so whole and so single-minded as I did her, it didn't leave room for any other woman in the world. That it was like none others breathed and lived, save as human beings, breathing and living in the same place you did. That when your whole heart and soul and body belonged to somebody you went around with a kind of covering against the world all over you, that none but that one person ever got inside. I tried to tell her how she was as much a part of me as my own hands and feet and head, and how could Ann McDonald have anything to do with me when I didn't even belong to myself?

She cried, then. "I'm ashamed. You make me plumb ashamed. I'd ort to of known better."

"No. I was thoughtless and careless. I'd ort to of known better. Jim can do his own courting from now on."

She laughed and shook her head and wiped her tears away. "I've not got this red hair for nothing, I reckon."

"I wouldn't change it for any other color in the world," I told her.

She reached out and took my hand again, and then of a sudden she laid her face against it. "It's a sin to say it, and a worse sin to feel it, but it's so. I love you. I love you, David, better than my own life."

She'd never said it before. I stood there, holding her, resting my face on the top of her head, feeling her hair against my cheek. Over the roof of the cabin back of us there was a little red star blinking . . . blinking and blinking, busier than a candle flame in the wind. It was the same star I'd seen many and many a night over the east meadow at my own place. Night after night I'd seen it, redder and busier than any of the others. I wished we could both watch it from the cabin doorstep, like I'd done. And the star and the wish made me sad. There was so little hope we ever could. But one thing was sure. As long as Bethia loved me and needed me, sinful or not, me and the life inside me belonged to her. I couldn't change that, and I wouldn't of, if I could. "I love you, too," I told her.

After a little she stirred and pulled away. "I got to put Davey to bed and redd up the dishes."

I let her go. When she drew back the blanket the firelight inside showed on her face. She looked back at me over her shoulder and smiled, and then she dropped the blanket and I stumbled off in the dark. But my heart was at peace.

# CHAPTER

# 17

J IM SPENT A RIGHT SMART TIME at our place after that. Hardly a week
went by he didn't show up, slicked and shined and his horse curried.
He always took supper with the Coburns, too. He went about courting Ann McDonald as steady and patient as he did everything else.

He was at the fort the night Billy Bush rode in with the news. Billy
was a kind of express between the country and the eastern settlements, but we'd not seen him for a time and a time. It was along in
March, a blustery, rainy night when he rode up to the gate, shouting,
shooting off his gun and pounding on the fence. Jim and Ben were
sitting with John Martin and me, talking, and the commotion displeased Ben. Thinking it some drunken traveler he went out to see
about it, and of course we followed. "Open up! Hey, open up in
there!" Billy was yelling.

"Who is it?" Ben asked.

"Me. Billy Bush. Hey, you Kentuckians!"

"All right, shut up," Ben said, and he drew the bars.

When Billy was inside he looked down on Ben kind of disapprov-
ing. "Well, seeing I've rid night and day to bring you the word, looks
like you could of let me in without keeping me waiting."

Ben grinned at him. "'Light and tie. Next time don't go shooting
off your gun and pounding on the gate. Just pass your name and you'll
get in quicker."

"I felt too good. Listen. Boys, Virginia has claimed title to the country and has set it up as a new county. Kentucky County! How's that?"

Lordy, but that sounded wonderful. We didn't hardly believe it. We
dragged Billy down off his horse and into the cabin and Ben sent for

the others so we could all hear the straight of it together. They came on the run and when we'd all gathered Ben set Billy down in a chair in front of us. "Now, talk," he said.

"Well, it's like I said. Virginia has claimed title to the land and has set it up as a county."

"When? When did they do it?"

"They voted it on December the seventh, and it was to go into law on December the thirty-first."

"Did it?"

"It did."

I couldn't keep from getting up and prancing around the room. "Man, man," I kept on saying, "it's just what we wanted! We've won, Ben. You hear? We've won!"

"Looks like it," he said, acting as calm as if becoming Kentucky County happened every day. But then this was no more than he'd expected to happen, and without all of us getting so stirred up, I remembered. Still, his face beamed as bright as Jim's or mine. Only something in Ben always kept him from acting roostery like the rest of us. "What about the colonel," he said to Billy.

"He's lost clean out. Oh, he fought to the last ditch, but when they voted, that ruined him. He's staying on at Williamsburg to see if he can't get some of his money back . . . some kind of compensation. He claims if they won't let him keep the land, they'd ort to pay him something for his trouble."

"Humph," Jim said, "he run his own risks. Don't see why the government would owe him anything."

Well, nobody cared about the colonel now. The big thing was we'd got shut of him and his company in Kentucky. What Virginia decided to do about him was their business. Billy was fumbling with his pouch. "I don't reckon," he said, pulling out some papers, "it'll hurt to show you these. I got the militia commissions here."

He handed them to Ben, and the way Ben took them you'd of thought they were made of lace. "Read 'em out," Billy told him.

David Robinson was named the county lieutenant . . . that was the highest militia office in a county. John Bowman was named colonel; Anthony Bledsoe was the lieutenant colonel; George Rogers Clark, major; John Todd, Benjamin Logan, Daniel Boone and James Harrod, captains.

I felt just a little disappointed. Not over me not being named. Lord, no. But because they'd put Virginians in the highest offices. We didn't even know David Robinson or John Bowman, and Anthony Bledsoe ran an ordinary over on the Long Island of the Holston. But before I could say anything, or any of the others for that matter, Billy took the papers back and said, "Now, let me tell you about these commissions. Those were the appointments made by the Assembly. But David Robinson didn't accept, and Bledsoe ain't going to. He's got too good a business where he is to give it up, he says. I've talked to both of 'em. And I've got here," and he flourished another paper, "the orders for Major Clark to take over the command till John Bowman gets here. I can't show you these orders, for they're sealed, but I know what's in 'em, and I know it's for Major Clark to take over. John Bowman, you'll like. He's aiming to come, and he's aiming to stay."

"When's he coming?" Jim put in.

"Soon. He's taking enlistments now for a company to bring out with him. He wants to bring a hundred men. Can you hold out till he gets here?"

The rest of us looked at one another, and then we busted out laughing. It went so foolish, that question. Less than two months before we'd voted to hold out not knowing if Virginia would ever help us. It wasn't going to take another vote for us to decide to hold out till John Bowman and a hundred volunteers could get here. Billy joined in the laughing. "Well, I reckon that's as good a answer as any."

He stuffed the papers back in his pouch. "I've not got the civil commissions with me. They'll be sent on directly. But I can tell you who's named. Ben, here, is named the sheriff, and Isaac Hite and Robert Todd and Ben and Major Clark is all to be justices of the peace."

Well, by grannies! Ben, the sheriff. "That calls for a drink," Jim said, and he broke out a jug of Monongahela and we all clustered around and pounded Ben on the back and shouted and lifted our noggins to the new sheriff. Ben was modest about it, saying there was many a one better suited than him to be the first sheriff, but knowing him as well as I did by now, I could tell it made him proud to be picked. It would of made anybody proud. The first sheriff of Kentucky County!

It was almost more than any of us could take in . . . what was happening. Fancy us with a regular militia, now. Fancy a company of Virginia volunteers coming out to help us. Fancy a sheriff and justices of the peace. By grannies, we had us a government we could put our dependence in, now.

We didn't have the ammunition to celebrate right, but we had to make a little noise, so we all filed out into the commons and shot off one round. Even Ben, cautious as he usually was, didn't object to that. We'd ought to of told the womenfolks what it was for, before we did it, though, for they all came running out thinking the redskins were on us, yelling and screeching like Indians themselves. Never did I see such a sight as that clutch of women in their night-shifts, hair hanging down their backs and younguns hanging onto their skirts, pouring out the cabin doors. It sent all of us whooping back to the blockhouse. But we might of known that being in her night-shift wouldn't shame Jane Manifee none. She marched right in on our heels and stalked over and got William by the ear. "William Manifee, you're coming with me. What in the tarnation's got into you men . . . shooting at the stars thataway with powder as skeerce as it is!" Her eye lit on the jug. "Humph," she sniffed. "I might of knowed! Drinking that raw likker again. Come on, William," and she gave him a jerk that nearly pulled his ear off. I got in front of her. "Janie, listen . . . listen. You'll make us a kettle of your best rum toddy when you hear. Let go of William, and listen . . ."

And I was right. She hiked up her gown tail and sailed out the door as soon as she'd heard. "I've got to tell the others! We'll all come, and I'll make you the rum toddy!"

Well, that was a night . . . that was a night. It was nearly morning before we settled down, and laying in my blankets with the toddy and the singing and the dancing and the news all whirling around together in my head, I gave up trying to get to sleep and just laid there and thought of it. Two years. Two years and a little over since we'd first come into the country to settle, and now we had won out over the colonel and were set up with our own kind of government. In some ways it seemed like a long time. But actually it had come mighty soon when once we made up our minds to it. Now, all we had to do was hold off the redskins . . . and the British.

Billy and Ben and Jim went on to Harrodstown the next day. Billy thought Ben ought to go, for it stood to reason Major Clark would be wanting to have a council with the ones who'd been commissioned officers. He wasn't gone but three days and when he got back he called us all together in the south blockhouse. "Everybody's to be mustered into the militia," he told us, "and we're to hold a muster day and drill soon as we can. Has anybody got ary business taking 'em outside tomorrow?"

None had so Ben named the next day as muster day for us. "Turn out with arms at sunup. You can pick your own lieutenant and ensign. But I'm to name two scouts to help with the patroling. The major aims to keep a watch up around the Ohio all the time from now on. I've been thinking on it since the major named it, and if it's all the same to the rest of you, I'd like to ask Dave and John Martin to serve as scouts. Saving them, you can pick who you like for the other officers."

It was a cold, blowy day but we turned out and lined up in the middle of the street next morning, the sun not yet clear of the stockade, and the ground froze as hard as iron under our feet. The women and younguns stood to one side and looked on. I couldn't help thinking, when we'd all lined up, that you'd have to go a long ways to find a less likely-looking batch of soldiers. Rag, tag and bobtail was what we looked like. All of us had on clothes that were greasy and winter-blackened. Some had bearskin caps pulled down over their ears, and some had on old buffalo-skin hats that were so weathered and battered that they flapped in the wind like sails. We were tall and we were short, we were old and we were young, and we were married men and single ones. Some looked as scrawny as pin-picked chickens, and some were solid and fleshened out. Some, like Billy Whitley, had a soldier's natural stance, eyes front and straight. Some stood with their stomachs paunched and their shoulders hunched over, and it wasn't likely any amount of drill would ever change their ways. But there was another thing I knew. You couldn't go by their looks. Most had served, one way or another, in Dunmore's War, and some, like Ben, had even served with Bouquet. But leaving aside any service in the army, there wasn't a man in that line couldn't bark a squirrel at a hundred feet, or couldn't slink through the woods without raising a sound. They might not of looked very tidy, but they could sure shoot tidy, and that was what counted in this country.

Ben looked extra tall and broad standing out in front of us reading off the orders. Listening to him, I was awfully glad he'd been named the captain. He might of held back some on the fight against Colonel Henderson . . . thinking it should be settled legal and peaceful by law. But he'd fight to hell and gone for his own against the redskins, and these in the fort, now, were his own. He'd make a good one to head them up.

When he'd finished with the reading he put us through a drill, marching us up and down the street. We got our feet mixed up and mostly forgot how to left-face and slope arms or even to step off on the right foot. But Ben was good-natured about it and kept his patience, and we all laughed and jostled one another and worked up a considerable steam, showing off in front of the womenfolks and parading around. The younguns got sticks and marched along behind us, like the tail of a dog wagging, and the dogs themselves capered around and barked at our heels and got in the way and howled when somebody kicked out at them. All told it was a kind of a joke, but one we enjoyed a heap and when Ben halted us and rested us we were all in a big humor. "I reckon that'll do," Ben said. "I wouldn't bank on you all taking no prizes for drilling, but you'll get better in time."

"Seems kind of foolish to me," Azariah Davis said, "practising marching and drilling thisaway. We get in the woods after the redskins it'll be every man for hisself amongst the bushes and trees."

"The time's acoming," Ben told him, "when we'll not be hunkered down in these forts, trailing out in the woods in little parties trying to come up on the redskins. We'll be marching, like an army, across the Ohio and on to the Indian towns themselves. We'll give them a taste of what it's like to sit hunkered down waiting for the enemy."

Azariah looked around at the rest of the men, and then he spit. "I don't reckon you're aiming to start marching very soon, though, are you?"

Ben laughed. "No. Likely not this year or next. But it'll come. In time."

And it did. It was five years off, though we didn't know it. But we commenced making ready for it that day.

Ben turned the men loose to hold their election, but he asked John Martin and me to go with him so he could give us our orders. Inside the blockhouse we sat down in front of the fire. "Major Clark says . . ." and he stopped to laugh. "It goes queer to be calling him major. Got in the way of thinking of him as cap'n. But I reckon we'll get used to it. Anyway, he says he wants all the country north of the Kentucky and to the Ohio watched. There's to be two scouts from each settlement. That makes six. You're to take turn about, two at a time, for a week. He's looking for the Indians to cross over in numbers from now on. The season's warming up, and it's his opinion the British will make a big strike this spring. But with scouts roaming the country between the settlements and the Ohio you'd ort to be able to give the alarm in time so's we can all make ready."

It was a good plan. We couldn't stop them from coming, but if we could just have warning it would give us time to make ready and to stand a better chance of holding them off. And with scouts on the Ohio watching all the time, it didn't seem likely they could slip over into the country without us knowing. No, it didn't seem at all likely.

"Want we should leave right off?" I asked Ben. I was well pleased with the part given to me. It suited me a lot better to be out, moving around, scouting and keeping watch, than it would of to be penned in the fort, drilling and standing guard. And it would be a lie to say I didn't know I was fitted for the part, for I was good in the woods and I knew it. Maybe not as good as Dannel or Simon Butler, and maybe just on an equal with Jim, but outside of them I reckon I was the best.

"Well, both of you ain't to go at the same time. So's not to take two men from one settlement together, the major says he'll pair you with somebody from one of the other places. Which one of you wants to go first?"

We both wanted to go, so we spit on a stick and tossed it to decide. I won. "All right, Dave," Ben said, "report to the major and he'll send you out with somebody from Harrodstown." He stopped and sat there, pulling at his chin and thinking. "I reckon it's overcautious of me, seeing as you'll be out all times of day anyways, but I wish you'd wait till night to leave. I'd feel a heap better, knowing you was on the trail between here and Harrodstown under cover of the dark."

Well, maybe it was a little overcautious, but it suited me as well, for as much passing as there'd been over that trail it was a wide-open mark for trouble.

I made ready to leave, which didn't take long, just seeing to Beck and making up a pack, and then I went over to Ben's. The sun had warmed up the air considerably and Bethia was outside the cabin cutting up some meat. Davey was with her, though he sure wasn't helping none with the butchering. He was riding a stick horse, playing like he was hunting buffaloes. He was such a spirited youngun that from the time his eyes flew open of a morning till they closed again of a night he was always on the go . . . never still a minute. And if he ever walked when he could run, I never saw him. I didn't know then that all younguns around three or four years old are as restless as the wind, and it used to make me tired just watching Davey fly around. "You'd better rest that horse of yours," I told him, "or you'll ruin his wind. Pull up and let him blow awhile."

But Davey always had an answer. "He just had a rest," he said. "His wind's good now."

I started in to help Bethia with the meat. It was seeing her using Judd's knife that called him to my mind. I'd given it to her some time back. I'd kept it awhile, thinking to face him with it, but then I'd got over being so mad about him firing the cabin, and she needed a knife so I'd given it to her. Watching her use it now I thought of Judd, and how there'd been no more word of him. I mentioned it. "It's queer, ain't it?" I said.

"I've been aiming to ask you. Billy Bush didn't bring no news either?"

"Well, I never asked, but if he'd had any word he'd of said so. Like he done the last time, he'd of passed it on to you, likely."

"Yes. Well, he never. I thought he might of said something to you."

"No."

Davey rode by. He had a stick for a gun and he lifted it to his shoulder. "Bang!" he yelled, passing us, "Bang!"

"Hey," I told him, "you can't shoot that fast without reloading!"

"I did reload. I can reload fast!"

"You sure can. About the fastest of anybody I ever seen."

He whipped his stick horse around the corner of the cabin.

"I reckon," Bethia said, "he's on his way." She lifted her hand and brushed her hair back and the blood from the meat left a little smear where her hand trailed across her cheek. I took my finger and wiped it away. There was nothing for me to say. She put the knife down and wiped her hands on a piece of skin laying on the bench beside the meat, bending over so her face was hidden. I thought she was crying from the way her shoulders shook, but when she flung around suddenly there were no signs of it. "Oh, I ain't going to pretend, David. It's been my hope he had went his way and left me to mine. I have been wishing I might never hear of him again. I have been praying there'd be no word of him . . . nor no sign of him, either."

"Well, I don't know," I told her, "as you could call what I've been doing praying, but I've been doing a heap of wishing right along the same lines. I reckon, though, there's nothing to do but wait . . . wait and see."

Her mouth trembled a little. "You needn't to wait, Dave. You ortent to. There's others, free . . . and we don't know. . . ."

Something just kind of boiled over in me, then, and I forgot everything but loving her so much and wanting to be with her and having to wait and not knowing. I forgot the country and its safety. I forgot Ben and Jim and all the others needing every man that could be counted on. I forgot all of them and my duty towards them. All I could think of was Bethia . . . and me. It's to my shame, but a man's only human after all, and I've not ever pretended not to have my share of human faults. "It needn't to be this way," I told Bethia, catching her by the arms and holding to her, hard. "There's no need to wait, and you can be as free as the next one. Not here . . . no! But if you're of a mind we can leave out of here tonight! We don't need to stay in Kentucky. We can go someplace else and make a start. I'd be willing to go any place you said!"

She didn't try to pull loose. She just stood there and looked at me, steady. "Where," she said, finally, "could we go that the shame of it wouldn't catch up with us?"

Oh, I knew she was right. The minute she spoke I knew she was right. Maybe I even knew it before I spoke. But I was too stirred up to listen. "I don't care for the shame!"

She took my hands off her arms then. "I do," she said.

I stared at her.

She picked up Judd's knife. "Not for myself. Not for myself at all. But for you. You're a man well thought of here in the country. And it's your country. You picked it and you made you a stand here. You've got no business leaving it, and you'd have no heart left in you to love or live with, if you left it. Besides, the folks put their dependence in you." As if that ended it, she turned around and went on with her work.

I stood there a minute, watching her hands move quick and sure, slicing and turning and laying aside the meat. She'd known the surest way to bring me to my senses. I would of cared, of course. I would of cared so much I'd never of had another hour of peace, remembering. And we'd of never had an hour of love. "All right," I said, going to help her, then. "All right, Bethia. But I'll wait till the end of time. Don't ever forget that, for I'm no more free than you are . . . and someday . . ."

She looked up at me, with her eyes misted over. "If the Lord intends it, Dave . . . someday."

Davey rode his horse between us then. "Bang! You're kilt, Bethia. Bang! You're kilt, Dave. You're old Chief Blackfish and you're dead. I shot you old red devil right betwixt the eyes!"

Ann came out of the cabin door just in time to hear him. She swooped down on him. "David Logan! Come inside this minute and get your mouth washed out! I'll not have you using such words!"

David struggled and howled. "Pa does! Pa says it!"

I grabbed the lad free and swung him up on my shoulder. "Don't, Ann. He's too little to know any better. Best scrub out Ben's mouth, instead."

She firmed her mouth. "I'll see to Ben, all right. Put him down, Dave. You come inside, David."

"Ann. . . ." Bethia begged for him, too.

The child clutched my hair tight. He was quick to catch on he had two of us on his side. "I'm too little to know any better," he told his mother, and then he commenced beating a tattoo on my ribs with his heels. "Come on, Dave. You're my horse. Let's gallop."

I figured it was time, myself, so we loped off down the street, leaving Ann standing in the cabin door yelling at us to come back. The last sound I heard was Bethia laughing. I remembered it later.

### CHAPTER

# 18

W HEN I LEFT THAT NIGHT Ben went with me to the gate. "Dave," he said, opening it for me, "I'm putting my dependence on you to warn us in time. If there's ary bit of trouble, don't fool around. Get yourself on back here fast. We need ever' gun we can muster. If you're tempted to help out the others, just recollect how few we've got here."

"I'll not waste time if there's need," I promised him.

I got to Harrodstown before daylight, but folks were already stirring and I found Major Clark having his breakfast. He invited me to join him and while we ate he told me of his plans. I'd heard them before, from Ben, but naturally I listened to the major go over them again. "We'll throw out a circle of scouts to watch the Ohio. In that way we shall guard against surprise attack. In the meantime each fort must work diligently to strengthen itself, and all the militia must drill and keep itself in constant readiness."

You could tell he was a military man, all right. He spoke his words short and quick, and he sounded sure of himself. We'll do this and this and this. And he had good plans, sound, sensible plans. The only trouble with them was, the redskins were already in the country.

We didn't know that, though, and anyway, Indians or no Indians it was the time of year when work had to commence in the clearings and folks had to take the chance of ambush to get out and see to it. To be as safe as possible, Major Clark had ordered that the men were to work in parties, or at least in pairs. After sunup they began leaving out, some going to their clearings and some going to the sugar groves to finish tapping the trees.

I made out with a couple of hours sleep and then I was ready to go. Hugh McGary was partnered with me for the first week. He was a little slow finishing up his chores and it was getting on towards the middle of the morning before we rode out the gate. "My boys and some others are working in my clearing at the Shawnee Spring," he said. "It's not far out of the way, so let's ride by there."

It was all right with me, but we'd not much more than reached the bottom of the slope leading up to the fort when a lad dashed out of the woods running towards us like a streak of greased lightning. Seeing us, he commenced yelling "Indians! Indians!" and motioning back of him.

"That's James!" Hugh said. He kicked his horse into a run and met the boy halfway, swinging him up alongside and turning the horse back with the same motion. I turned with him and we raced back to the fort.

Hugh had a voice like a foghorn and when he started bellowing "Indians" the minute we got inside the stockade, the folks commenced pouring out of the cabins like rats from a smoking corncrib. Jim came piling out and made for the gate and I slid off my horse and ran to help him. Then we ran over to the crowd that was gathering around Hugh and the boy. The lad wasn't rightly speaking Hugh's own. He was Miz McGary's oldest by her first man, and him and his brother had the name of Ray. But Hugh thought as much of them as if they'd been his own, and it was plain he was powerfully worked up over them being attacked.

The lad was winded and bent over, holding his side, which must of been cramped with the pain of running. Someone handed him a drink of water and we all stood about, waiting for him to get his breath back. Hugh kept rubbing his face and the back of his neck. Finally the boy could talk. "We was working, like you told us, at the clearing, but we got thirsty and quit awhile to go over to the sugar trees and get us a drink of sugar water. We was sitting around drinking and talking when we heared a whole passel of folks talking, but we never thought nothing of it, for we knowed there was several out thataway and just thought it was some of them. We didn't hardly have time to think on it one way or the other, for we'd not much more than heared 'em till they come in sight, a whole gaum of redskins, running down the path, talking and laughing."

"How many?" It was the major wanting to know.

James shook his head. "I never had time to count, but it was a heap of 'em. . . . I'd say forty or fifty."

"All right. Go on."

"They seen us right off. William had his gun with him, but me and Tom Moore and Billy Coomes had left ours at the clearing. Wasn't anything to do but try to get away, so I yelled at the boys to foller me and we lit out. But the redskins was right on our heels, firing and chasing us, and they must of got Tom and Billy soon, for the next thing I knowed there was only me and William running side by side. William kept losing time and I figured it was on account of his gun weighting him down so I yelled at him to throw it away and run faster . . . but he wouldn't do it. They was gaining on us and I knowed in reason we was going to be took. About that time William, he stopped and takened aim and fired, and just as he fired a Indian fired at him, too, and I seen him fall. I couldn't of done him no good, so I just kept on coming.My leggins got in my way and slowed me down, so I singled me out a good, big tree and run behind it and cut 'em off. Whilst I was hid there the redskins passed me by. I tried to sneak out without them catching on, but one tailing along behind seen me and let out a yell and they all turned and scampered after me. But not being hampered with my leggins I could outrun 'em. I reckon they give up when I got in sight of the fort."

Hugh was shaking like a leaf all over, and his face was the color of ashes. "I'd ort to take a whip to you," he told the boy. "I've cautioned you and cautioned you not never to lay your gun aside! A hundred times I've told you to keep it by your side. Now see what's happened!"

The lad ducked his head and mumbled something no one could hear.

Hugh shook him. "Speak up, if you've got anything to say."

"I just said it didn't look like William's gun done him much good."

"He's right about that, Hugh," Jim said, "don't be too hard on him."

But I reckon Hugh had to take his fear out on somebody. I've noticed that oftentimes when folks have been bad scared and commence to get over it their fear kind of turns to anger. Hugh walked over and took a straddled stance in front of Jim. When he began to talk he was so mad his voice shook with it. "This here is more your fault than anybody else's, Jim Harrod. Slack-handed, that's what you are. If you'd been the man you ort to be you'd of had men out to keep watch and the redskins couldn't of got this close to the fort. You're always out in the woods and never seeing to things. And them three boys, murdered and scalped, doubtless, can be laid right at your door!"

"By God," Jim shouted back at him, angered beyond caution himself, "no man can lay the fault to me. I've done the best I could. I've tried to get folks to stouten the fort and to keep out watch. You've heard me yourself, trying. It's been the careless ways of you and them like you, greedy to get your own clearings ready and not taking care for no others, that's to blame. You been sending them boys out to the clearing for a week, now. Whyn't you go yourself? Was you afeared you'd lose your own hair?"

Me and the major both was trying to reach them, but the folks were gathered in close around and kept getting in the way. Hugh had his gun up and his face had turned red and was mottled and patchy on the cheeks. "No man can call me a coward, Jim Harrod!"

Jim lifted his own gun. "If the shoe fits, wear it! You as good as called me one!"

I had a feeling that my feet were glued to the ground and I couldn't pull them loose, and those two damned fools were going to shoot one another, sure, before they could be stopped. And doubtless they would if it had depended on me, for I was wedged in tight. It was Miz McGary that broke out from amongst the women and flung herself in front of Hugh's gun. She was crying, for she was always a weepy woman, but it made no difference . . . she threw herself between those two men's guns. "Listen to me, Hugh. It's no time for bad blood. Them boys could yet be alive out there. Get out and see, and save 'em if there's a chance."

Hugh appeared not to hear her. He just stood there and glared at Jim and muttered, but she hung on, little and bent and teary-eyed. "It's my boy has been killed, Hugh," she begged, "see to him for me. You and Jim can settle this when you get back. You go and see if William is dead or alive."

It was Jim, though, that made the first move. He lowered his gun and walked over to Hugh and held out his hand. "I'd ort to be ashamed, Hugh. This is bound to gravel you a heap, and I'd ort to of knowed how you was feeling. We'd best have no differences with the redskins at our door."

Hugh kind of hestitated and then he put out his own hand. "Reckon my Irish was up, Jim. But it just come over me of a sudden. My God, when I think of them three boys!"

Lordy, but that Hugh McGary was a roostery one. Had a temper that went off quick as a trigger. But you couldn't help feeling pity for him that day. No doubt his conscience was graveling him for sending the boys to the clearing in the first place, and it but added to the load of grief he had to carry. There was a mite of truth in the things both men had said, but this was no time to quarrel amongst ourselves.

With tempers cooled now, they set about organizing the fort. Major Clark told me there'd be no scouting till this scare was over and I'd just as well get on back to Ben's with the news. He didn't know it, but even if he was the major and Ben just a captain that was what I intended to do anyhow, for Ben was counting on me. When I left, Jim and Hugh were heading up a party go out to the Shawnee Spring and see about the boys.

I rode as fast as I could without pushing Beck, but not wishing to keep to the trail on account of the redskins, I was slowed up a right smart by having to make my way through the country. And then, towards the middle of the afternoon it came on to snow, and that slowed me up still more. First it was just big, wet blobs that came down slow, like pieces of feathers floating around, and then it thickened till facing into it was like riding in a fog. If it had stayed like that I'd of had to bed down somewhere and wait for morning to go on, but the wind came up and the snow fined down little by little till it turned to sleet and I could see again.

The stockade was dark when I got there and I had to pound on the gate for what seemed like an hour before anybody heard me over the sounds of the wind and the storm. But finally I saw a light blink through the fence and then John Martin let me in. He was sleepy and stupid. "What you doing back?" He wouldn't of asked otherwise. He'd of known.

"Indians," I said. "Get Ben."

By the time I'd seen to Beck, Ben was in the blockhouse. He listened with a sober face to what I had to tell. It was a time to be serious, for there was no doubt it was a war party, and they were deep in the country already. No use blinking the fact, our troubles had begun. "We'll have a council tomorrow," Ben said, when I'd done telling. "Come on up to the house now and Ann'll fix you a bait."

"I'll make out," I told him. "I'd not like to trouble the womenfolks this hour of the night."

"She got up when I did. She'll have you something fixed time we get there."

When we came up to the cabin I noticed Ben had finally got his door hung. He'd been smoothing on that door off and on ever since they'd moved in, with Ann prodding at him to get it done. It was a good stout door, too. Ann was stirring around, laying out food, when we went in. "My," I said to her, teasing, "but ain't you getting grand with a big, fine door like this one. Likely you'll not be on speaking terms with them common enough to be using a blanket still." I looked around, but there was no sign of Bethia. She slept up in the loft with Davey, though, and I reckoned she'd not waked.

"It's high time we was getting a door," Ann said, sniffing. "Five weeks to a day we been in this cabin and still making out slack-handed. Here, set down. I'll bound you're famished."

I ate and Ben and Ann talked. There was no need keeping things from women who had risked as much as these in the country to go where their menfolks went. No matter how bad a man might want to spare them, he couldn't. An easy-frighted woman would of had a bad time of it. "I reckon," Ann said, "we can look for 'em here, now, soon or late."

"We'll have to count on it," Ben said.

"Well," she said, commencing to gather up the things, "it's no more than we expected, and there's no use borrowing trouble till they get here."

I'd been hoping Bethia would hear us and come down, but she hadn't, and figuring Ben and Ann would be wanting to get back to bed I stood up and said I'd be going. "Just sleep here," Ann said, "you can go up with Davey."

"I've not told him," Ben said, looking at her.

"Ben . . . you promised!" Ann dropped one of the wooden bowls and it rolled and clattered clean across the floor.

I picked it up and handed it to her. "Told me what?"

But I knew. As good as if I'd seen him I knew Judd Jordan had been, and he'd taken her away. All I needed to know was when and where. But I said again, "Told me what?"

"Dave, hadn't you better set down?" Ann said. "Dave . . . ?"

"No," I said. "What is it you've not told me?"

Ben finally spoke. "He come, Dave, right after you'd gone last night. And they left out at daybreak this morning."

"Where did he take her?"

"Back to Harrodstown, he said. He was put out at her for not staying there."

I thought how we must of passed, them on the trail likely and me off in the brush, unbeknownst to one another. For a time that was all I could think of, her going one way and me another, and neither of us knowing. It scared me to think of how things could happen to people that loved one another and thought of one another. It didn't seem like it could of happened that Judd could of come and taken her and me not known. It made me have the lonesomest feeling I'd ever had in my life . . . even worse than what I'd felt that time when I was a lad hiding in the bush and waiting for night to bury my folks. That was a time of grief and lonesomeness and loss, but this . . . this was like knowing for sure and certain that no matter how much you loved somebody, and no matter how much your thoughts dwelt with them, you were still all alone inside yourself. If your love and your thoughts couldn't tell you when something was happening to that person . . . if you could go along your way, and even pass in the snow and not know . . . nothing to tell you. It was like dying. It made the whole world such an uncertain place. It made even love so powerless. It scared me so bad I started shaking all over.

Ann put out her hand. "Dave, please set down."

"No," I said, "I'm all right." And then because the fear and the hurting mixed together were so bad, I lashed out at the two of them . . . at the two best people in the world. Like Hugh McGary that morning, I turned my hurt on folks that had nothing to do with it. "Why'd you let her go?" I said, not bothering to keep my voice down, not even caring or thinking if the younguns woke. "Why didn't you stop him?"

They understood even my shouting and stayed gentle. "We tried," Ann said. "Dave, we did try. We talked to him and told him it was better here and not so crowded. Ben even offered for him to stay here with us, too. He wouldn't."

Of course I'd known they'd done the best they could. It was just the hurt hitting out at the first handy thing. "Why did *she* go?" I said. "Why didn't she stand up to him?"

It was Ben that spoke up then. "She did. She tried to talk him into staying at first, and then when he wouldn't she said he could go if he wanted to, but she was going to stay."

"What did he do?"

"Told her it was no use her talking . . . she was going and that was the end of it. He got her cape offen the peg and put it around her and picked her up and set her on the horse and left. I don't know of ary other thing we could of done, Dave."

Ann had started crying. I'd forgotten how much she had thought of Bethia, and how all this was grieving her, too. Her crying called it to mind, but I was grieving too much myself to try to comfort her beyond patting her shoulder, and saying hush, now, hush, like you would to a baby.

Of a sudden I couldn't stand any more of it and I wheeled around and plunged outside into the dark and the storm. Fighting it towards the blockhouse was when I remembered that just the day before I'd left her standing there behind me and she'd been laughing. The remembered sound of it was like the wind blowing in my ears, with no more body or substance . . . just a thin wind blowing . . . and cold.

# CHAPTER

# 19

THERE WAS NOTHING TO DO but get up the next morning and go on. No matter what happens to a man, daylight comes, a snowstorm either quits or blows on, your stomach gets lank and you've got to fill it, and the hours of the day wear on. Indifferent and uncaring as it appeared to me then, I know now that the good Lord did a fine job when he planned it that way, for if all nature stopped to grieve with every troubled heart things would be in an awful mess right shortly. Wisdom, though, is the fruit of years, and that bleak March morning I had so little of it that the folks stirring and going about their chores as if nothing had happened, the day passing like every other day, seemed a mockery to me.

Ben called the men together and we talked over our position. We were the fewest forted up together, and our greatest danger lay in our being so few. Boonesburg had sixty guns, and Harrodstown had around sixty-five now that we'd left them. But our stockade was newer and stouter than theirs and that was in our favor. We had water handy and safe to get to. If we had to stand a siege, food and powder were the main things we had to worry about.

It was decided to start right off bringing in all the corn we had cribbed outside, and to drive the stock up close and keep it there. "And no man," Ben said, "is to go outside the fence by himself. Anyhow two must go to do any kind of work."

"What about hunting?" somebody asked.

"That goes for hunting, too. We'll hunt in pairs . . . of a night. That'll be about the trickiest job we've got to do, for it'll take us furtherest from the fort and there's the risk of firing drawing the redskins. If we take care, we ort to make out all right."

He counted off a watch for the gate and one for each of the block-houses. Then he told off a party of four to go with him to start bringing in the corn, and he asked John Martin and me to do the hunting the first week. We'd all shift and change about, naturally.

The rest of the month and the first part of April went by. Neither Boonesburg or Harrodstown hardly had a peaceful day. Not that the Indians laid siege to the forts. They don't work that way, unless it's a little station like McClellan's had been and they know they out-number the settlers two to one. They just seep around through the woods on the outside and pick off one or two folks at a time that dare to venture beyond the fence. Or they try to lure a party out by setting fire to a cabin or corn field and when they dash out, trap them in an ambush. They just hang on, like grim death, and you're never free of them. And of course there's always the chance they'll band together in sufficient numbers to pen you up. With parties ranging from fifty to a hundred working separately on Boonesburg and Harrodstown, any time they took a notion to throw their strength together they could of made a bad time for either place. But as long as they didn't, somebody could always slip out of a night and take word from one place to an-other.

Jim came down from Harrodstown that way several times, so, in a way we could keep up with what was happening. It was nearly always bad news. One killed, one wounded at Boonesburg. Hugh McGary and Archibald MacNeal hurt at Harrodstown. Hugh Wilson killed at Harrodstown, the man whose baby had been the first youngun born in the country. Archibald MacNeal dead of his wounds. Garrett Pendergrass and Peter Flinn killed and scalped in plain sight of the fort at Harrodstown. Dannel and five others hurt at Boonesburg. Jim said Major Clark kept a diary, like most soldiers I ever saw do, but that what he had to write in it nowadays was little more than a roll call of the hurt and dying. And every one the redskins picked off left us weaker and fewer. We were dwindling, one by one, using up our pow-der and being held inside our stockades. I worried about Bethia, of course. But Jim never named her or Judd and for some reason I dis-liked to bring it up myself.

Down at our place we couldn't help knowing that every day that passed brought our own time of trouble that much closer. All we could do was go on about our work. We brought in corn till it nearly crowded us single men out of the blockhouses. We kept the stock hop-pled down in the swale by the springs, and, taking turns we kept as good a store of meat on hand as we could, what with the weather warming and thawing and spoiling it. If we'd had salt we could have stored up more, but we'd long since been out of the last grain of salt.

Major Clark had sent a man, the Dutchman Michael Stoner, back to the Holston settlements right straight after the first attack to see if Colonel Bowman was on his way and to hurry him up if he could, and Michael got back as far as our place along the middle of April. He brought discouraging news in one way, for Colonel Bowman hadn't yet started, but in another way he had good news. For he had with him the civil commissions which hadn't come with the military ones. Billy Bush had brought news of them, and of course we knew who were to be the sheriff and justices, but we couldn't go ahead and organize the county government or do any business until the commissions came. It had been right worrisome, for under the Virginia law we were supposed to elect our delegates to the Assembly on the first Tuesday in April, which had now passed. It could be, we were afraid, the Assembly wouldn't recognize our delegates on account of them not being elected on the legal day. But we thought surely they'd allow for circumstances. "They'd ort to," Ben said, "seeing as it's their fault we couldn't hold the election in time."

"Man," I told him, laughing, "there ain't nobody going to ride into the country right now to bring commissions or powder or anything else. Not if they can help it. No telling how long them commissions has been laying over there at Arthur Campbell's."

"No telling," Ben said. "Well, I'll ride up with Michael tonight and see what the major thinks about having the election now."

"No," I told him. "You're in charge here and ortent to leave. I'll go."

"But I'm the sheriff . . ."

"You can appoint me to act for you, can't you? Just tell me what you want me to say to the major."

He commenced laughing. "You're bound to go, aren't you? And I'm thinking it ain't purely for the good of the country you're so set on going."

I laughed, too, but I didn't have to hide anything from Ben. "I'd just like to set my mind at ease," I told him.

"Go on, then," he said. "Just tell the major we'll abide by whatever he thinks is best about holding the election right away."

Major Clark was right put out over the Virginia volunteers not even being started yet, but he held his disappointment down. He just said it looked to him like it was taking them a powerfully long time, and why it should take all spring to raise and provision a hundred men was beyond all reason to him. "I'm more uneasy about the supply of powder than anything else," he said. "Give us the ammunition and we can hold the country. Well, there's nothing to do but meet each day as it comes. Now, about the election. . . ."

He was for holding it right away, "We can't have all the men meet together at once," he said, "for it would be too dangerous. But they can slip out at night in small parties. Neither place would be left undefended that way. We can take two or three days for it, if there is need."

We decided to start on the eighteenth, which was two days off, and would give me time to get back to Logan's, and would give a man time to take the word to Boonesburg. I thought we'd finished, then, and got up to go. I wanted to see Jim, and I wanted to mosey around and see Bethia if I could. But the major motioned for me to sit down again. "There's a thing I've been thinking of," he said, "and this might be the best time to get started on it. I've talked to Jim about it, but to no one else. . . . Dave, it's my opinion that we should strike at the source of this trouble."

"You mean make a drive on the Indian towns ourselves?"

"I mean more than that. The source, Dave, is the British. Left to themselves the Indians would only pester us by raiding and plundering. We have always been able to hold our own against them, and even to drive them off. But with the British behind them, they are a much greater threat. They will have an unlimited supply of powder, and in time the British may even furnish them with leadership. Now, where are the British in the western country?"

I thought. "Well, mostly over in the Illinois country. They've got that fort at Kaskaskia now, and one or two more."

"Exactly. And Hamilton is at Detroit, in charge of them all. Dave, if we can strike at the Illinois forts, and then drive on Detroit, we shall win our war in the west!"

Well, I thought he'd taken leave of his mind. How could we, less than a hundred and twenty men, now, and short of ammunition, holed up in three measly little settlements, strike out at provisioned and garrisoned forts! I must of looked as amazed as I felt, for the major started chuckling. "Oh, I didn't mean for us to do it alone. But it can be done, Dave, and I am convinced it is the strategic thing to do. This is what I've been thinking. . . . If we can send a couple of spies into the Illinois country to find out the strength of those forts, we can then lay the facts before Governor Henry. I am confident he will see the excellence of the strategy and will provision an expedition to accomplish it. If I am not badly mistaken, those forts are weakly held. Five hundred men, armed and provisioned, could run the British out of the Illinois country, I am positive. Then we should march on Detroit and the entire western country is saved to Virginia and the colonies!"

The boldness of his imagination took a man's breath away. Fancy having the kind of mind that, as hard pressed as we were, could see beyond holding grimly on to our three puny little forts and plan a move that would strike at the root of our troubles. If he was right, in one clean sweep we'd rid ourselves of our enemies and close the back door on the war in the east. And with him to lead it, I'd of bet my last acre of ground it would work. "I'm for it," I told him.

"Good. Now, tell Ben and no one else. Our hope of success lies in secrecy. This is what we must do. At the election, we'll have a drawing of two men to be assigned to me as aides. The people must think they are to work under my personal orders here in the country. Not even they must know any different until I tell them. They will go into the Illinois country, spy out the situation and report back to me. If it is as hopeful as I think it is, we shall then have a body of facts to lay before the governor."

Suddenly it came to me we had help in the Illinois country we'd not thought of. "If they'll find Johnnie Vann he can tell 'em more in thirty minutes than they can spy out in a month. He's out there now."

"Excellent! Excellent! I should have remembered that myself. Do you think he will lend himself to the plan?"

"I misdoubt he'll mind giving the British away," I said. "He'll likely shy off giving you any word of the redskins, but he's got no more love for the British than we have."

"Then I'll order the two scouts to find Johnnie Vann first."

He stood up, then, and I knew he was through talking. I had my hand on the door latch to leave, but I couldn't help turning around to tell him I wished I could be one of the two going. "Why don't you just pick two, anyhow?" I told him. "It's leaving a lot to chance, seems to me, having a drawing. You might get two that wouldn't be so good."

"And you'd like to be one that was picked." He grinned and shook his head. "There's not two men in this country I wouldn't trust with this errand, Dave. And the people wouldn't take kindly to picking and choosing. It would look as if I were showing favorance. No, we have to let it be done by lot."

"What if you get a man like Judd Jordan?"

"Judd Jordan?" He looked puzzled for a minute. "Oh . . . you mean that fellow you had the trouble with. Is he in the country?"

My hand fell off the door latch like the wood had got too hot to touch. "He's right here in the fort! Ain't you seen him around?"

"Here? You're mistaken, Dave. Judd Jordan is not here, and he hasn't been here. I'd have known if he had, for I've made up a militia roll within the last two days. What makes you think he's here?"

I told him, feeling like the bottom had dropped out of everything. If he hadn't brought Bethia to Harrodstown, where had he taken her? "He told Ben he was coming here," I said.

The major shook his head. "I am positive he has not been here, at all . . . not at any time lately. Do you suppose he would have been foolish enough to take his wife to his clearing?"

"He's fool enough to do anything," I said, "and likely that's just what he's done."

"Well, he's been out of the country for some time now, and doubtless he doesn't realize the straits we are in."

"That's no excuse," I said. "He was told. Ben told him. He's just bullheaded and stubborn. I wouldn't care if the redskins took and scalped him, but he's got no call to risk Bethia like he's doing."

The major raised an eyebrow and I thought likely he was recollecting some talk he'd heard, but he said nothing more than maybe I'd have time to ride by the clearing on my way back to Logan's. "I'll take time," I said, "and I'll not waste any getting started." I wasn't caring what the major or anybody else thought right then. If Judd had taken Bethia out to that measly little hut that passed for a cabin, with redskins overrunning the country and likely to come down on them any day, I wasn't aiming for her to stay there. Him and me had been bristling for a showdown a long time, and I decided it might as well come now.

"Don't forget to tell Ben what we've said," the major said as I went out the door.

"Oh," I said, "I ain't so worked up but what I'll remember."

"Well, I didn't know," he said, kind of dry like. I was already astride of Beck when he called to me again. "Dave, you can tell Jordan my orders are that he is to take his wife to one of the forts, if you like."

I just waved at him and went on. It was kind of him to make it official, but I didn't figure I'd be needing his orders. If she was there, I aimed to see to it him or me brought Bethia in.

She was there. It was drizzling a fine, cold mist and she was hunkered over what passed for a fire, trying to get it to burn. She had her cape pulled up over her head to keep the damp off. She looked white and sick and tired. When she saw me she pushed the cape back and ran her hand over her hair and even from where I was I could see her breast rise with the deep breath she took. She came to meet me. "Where's Judd?" I said, getting off the horse.

She motioned towards the woods.

"Gone?" I said.

"He's been gone most of the time since we come."

There's been few times in my life when I've cussed in front of a woman, but that was one of them. It was beyond all reason that he'd take so little thought of his own safety, to say nothing of hers, and I said so. "Oh, he says we're safe here," Bethia said. "He says we're safer than in the forts."

"I don't like his notion of safety," I told her. "Get your things. I'm taking you back to Ben's."

She didn't argue. She just walked over towards the horse. "I didn't bring none. He didn't give me time. I'm ready when you are."

I put her on the horse and led the way out, walking. Neither of us said so, but doubtless Bethia was thinking, as I was, that this would set the tongues of the womenfolks wagging at both ends. Not all, for I knew there'd be a few like Ann Logan and Esther Whitley and Jane Manifee that not only wouldn't talk themselves, but wouldn't allow it around them. This was no time, though, to be finicking about what folks might think or say.

It was no time, either, to be finicking about Judd Jordan. Had he been there I'd of had it out with him at the clearing. If he wanted to follow Bethia back to Ben's when he came back and found her gone, I'd still have it out with him. But right then all I wanted was to get her back inside the stockade walls just as fast as I could. Every step of the way I hoped and prayed we'd make it without trouble, and when the bars of the gate let down behind us finally, I heaved a big sigh of relief.

Ann wasted no time asking questions. She just folded Bethia in her arms and said, "Davey's been asking for you."

I told Ben all the major and me had talked about and he liked the idea of taking the Illinois forts just fine, except he was a little fearful that the major might get so worked up over it he'd draw on the country for more men and provisions than we could spare if Governor Henry didn't furnish him all he wanted. But he was willing to risk it.

We had the election the way it had been planned and John Todd and Richard Calloway were named to serve as the first delegates of Kentucky County. Both were from Boonesburg and I reckon all of us had the same idea. I know Ben and Jim and me talked of it and said it was a mighty good way of showing the folks at Boonesburg we held no grievance towards them for throwing in with the colonel in the beginning. Now that that quarrel was over and done with, they were as much a part of the country as any of the rest of us, with their part to take alongside of us. And we couldn't of picked two better men than John Todd and Richard Calloway.

We had the drawing for the two men to do Major Clark's errand, and it turned out that they were both from Harrodstown, which I thought was just as well for they'd be handy to the major. Not long after, Jim rode down with the word they'd left.

That was the time he brought the word about the bad raid on Boonesburg, too. Simon Butler and two other men had been standing in the gate making ready to go on a hunt when the redskins had fired on a couple of men working in the corn field just outside the fort. The men had run, not being hurt on the first fire, but one Indian, faster than the others, had caught them up and killed and taken the scalp of one of the men. Jim said Simon told him the redskin hadn't even hurried. He'd just taken his time, with all looking on. He'd made a mistake not hurrying with Simon Butler around, though, for Simon had shot him deader than four o'clock. Dannel, then, had formed a party and they'd rushed out. But there'd been more Indians than they'd figured and five of Dannel's party had been hurt, including Dannel himself. He came mighty close to losing his hair, for when he went down a big warrior, yelling like fury, had rushed on him. It was Simon's gun again that fired and put a bullet through the Indian. Lordy, but it would of been something, now, for a redskin to take Dannel Boone's scalp back to Henry Hamilton in Detroit! Ben commenced chuckling at the idea. "I reckon he'd of got double the bounty on it, wouldn't he?"

"Doubtless he would," Jim said. "You know what Simon was grieving about? He got three of the red devils but things was happening so fast he never had time to take their scalps. He's aiming to take one for every scalp the Indians have took, and he claimed them three would just about have evened it up."

Simon wasn't a bloodthirsty man commonly. Wasn't any of us. But it never set a bit good with us to have a bounty put on our hair by the British, and I don't see that we could rightly be blamed very much if we took to counting scalps some, ourselves. Well, that's the way it was at the turning of the month . . . down to a hundred and fifteen men, no word from Colonel Bowman, powder and lead being used up every day. Things were worsening, no doubts about it, and the summer lay ahead of us. Wasn't a one of us knew whether we could hold on or not.

But I don't recollect that we talked about it much. We just counted up who was left, from time to time, and went on about our business.

It was May, now and the days were lengthening and fair. The sky was high and deep and the sun was warm and balmy. The trees were leafed out thick again and the air was like silk against your face, smooth and fresh and clean. Down in the swale by the springs there were some little flowers blooming. They were purple and pink and yellow. When Bethia went to milk of a morning she generally picked a few. "If we can't get out," she said, "we can leastways bring some of the outside in."

Being cooped up inside the fort was hardest on the women those days. The menfolks could get out sometimes. The corn had to be planted and we went out by twos and threes to plant as many patches as we could. And we had to ride out and hunt for game, kill it and bring it in. Oh, there was a plenty of work for all, but us men could at least stir out and look at something besides the walls of the stockade. It wasn't like working our own clearings and seeing ourselves get ahead though, and Jane Manifee said it for all one warm, fair day that was a torment and a torture for wanting to be free and shut of the fort, when she went to the gate and shook her fist through a cranny. "Drat you red devils, anyway! Keeping us forted up here like a pen of animals and our places going to wrack and ruin! Come on and do your worst, so's we can either lose our hair and be done with it, or get out and make a crop this year!" It was a tiresome time, for a fact.

At first I'd looked for Judd Jordan to come storming in after Bethia, and I'd told Ben I didn't want any of the rest of them to get mixed up with him on my account. I said if he came I wanted it understood the trouble lay between Judd and me, and nobody else was to take a hand. Ben knew that was the right of it and he passed the word, but the time went on and Judd didn't turn up. There was no knowing where he was and what was in his mind to do. When I was out I kept as good care as I could, for I wouldn't of put it past him to take a shot at me from the bushes, and I never came back to the fort without thinking maybe he'd been while I was gone. If it was an anxious and troublesome time for all, it was an extra anxious and troublesome time for Bethia and me. But I reckon you can live with anxiousness till you get so it doesn't bother much, for when several weeks had gone by and there'd been no sight of Judd we kind of let down and quit looking for him every passing hour.

It seemed natural to go over to Ben's to eat of a night and see Bethia there, stirring around the fire dishing up the vittles, or coaxing Davey up to bed, or holding the baby for Ann. I don't know of anything that'll either draw folks close together so's they're forever after a part of one another, or split them so far asunder they can never come together again, as being housed all in a family inside a stockade. Ben and Ann, the two younguns, Bethia . . . they made up my family. They were my own folks, and all I wanted. Night after night we sat and eat and talked together, and if I live to be a hundred I'll never forget it. Sometimes the plain goodness of folks is enough to make you believe in the goodness of the Lord. The way Ben Logan and Ann trusted in Bethia and me, and believed in us and loved us was like that. Just plain good.

One night we were sitting there after eating and the talk turned to Jim and the way it was always him brought messages or word from Harrodstown or Boonesburg. "Humphhh!" Ann said, "he just makes excuses to come so he can see that Ann McDonald."

"How's he making out with her?" Ben said.

"She likes too good to have 'em all swarming after her to pick one," Bethia put in. "I wish to goodness she would marry Jim and he'd take her up to Harrodstown to live!"

It sounded a precious lot to me like there was some spite in what she said and I couldn't keep from teasing her. "You," I said, "are just afraid I'll eat supper over there with her again."

I might of known I'd get the worst end of it. Her skirt swished past me when she went by like she was afraid it might get dirty if it touched, and her nose went straight up in the air. "I don't think there's much to worry about," she said, "what woman would want you if she could get Jim Harrod?"

Ben just leant back and howled and Ann hid her face in the baby's neck and snickered. "I reckon," I said, kind of nettled, "you'd like to set your cap for Jim, too, wouldn't you?"

She was stacking up the bowls and things getting ready to wash up, but she stopped and looked over my way. "I don't know but what I would," she said, so serious it might near made my heart quit beating, "He's got the most land of anybody in the country I hear, and he's on the way to being a rich man. He's right down handsome to look on . . . not being bean-poley and fringey-haired like some I could name that ain't sitting too far away. It would be a common-sense thing to do, I'd think."

"Bean-poley!" I commenced sputtering, "Bean-poley! Who you calling bean-poley? And fringey-haired! My hair ain't no fringier than anybody else's, is it, Ben?"

But Ben wouldn't come to my help. He just sat there and shook and wiped his eyes. And then Bethia started laughing and I joined in and we all ended up making so much noise we woke up Davey. It took such a little foolishness to make us laugh.

Just the same, Bethia had put an idea in my head. My hunting shirt and leggings were skin-bare in places and stiff and spotted with grease and dried blood where, unthinking, I'd swiped my knife dry. They were pretty well smoked from the winter's fires, too. When I sniffed at them, there was no doubt they were getting a mite rank. I reckoned the warm days had brought out the oil and for a fact I was getting high as a polecat.

There was a little creek about half a mile west of the stockade and I decided next day, it being a Sunday, maybe I'd take a sashay out there and get myself cleaned up. Jane Manifee had made some soft soap not long before and I begged some of it off of her. "What you want it for?" she said.

"To get myself scoured up," I told her. "I'm going out to the creek and get free of some of this dirt I'm packing around."

She threw up her hands. "Lord love us, you'll come down with lung fever, washing all over this soon in the year. That water'll be as cold as December."

"I kindly doubt it," I said. "You going to give me the soap?"

"I reckon so." She scooped out a bowl full and handed it to me. "Don't go leaving that bowl at the creek, now. I got use for it."

I promised her I'd bring it back. I told Ben where I'd be in case of need, and then I headed for the creek.

May. May in Kentucky. All who want can have the heavenly city with its streets paved in gold and its mansions of pearl. Could I have my way, I'd have it forever the month of May, and a long meadow stretching down a little valley, high with grass, and the wind turning it and flattening it, and the sun shining on it, making the little seed-blooms look blue in the light. I'd have a creek flowing through the middle, clean and clear and green, swished into foam against the rocks and shoals. I'd line the creek with locust trees in blossom, with the bunchy, waxy blooms that hang droopy of their own weight and make the air heavy with their smell. And I'd rim the whole in with little hills, dropped helter-skelter and bunched together, to give it a homey, snugged-down feeling. No, I've never wished for anything more than this country that stretches all around us.

Jane was right, though. The water was a mite on the cold side, but after the first ducking it felt good. I splashed around until I'd got warmed up and then I set in and scrubbed myself good. You'd not think dirt could get so grimed in. I fairly rubbed myself raw in places before it all came off, and I didn't know but what there'd still be a stripe down the middle of my back where I couldn't reach too good.

Well, I thought, I might be streaked like a skunk, but I'd sure not be smelling like one. I took my knife and whittled off some of my hair, and then I scoured my head good, too. And I soused and scraped my buckskins. When I'd done I felt clean and unlimbered, stretchy and loose, like a winter-freed sapling.

I fished the rest of the afternoon and the stars were coming out by the time I started back to the stockade. It was still, like it always is just at dark, no wind stirring, and the leaves on the trees hanging quiet and moveless. It was like everything had stopped to rest. It was too soon in the season yet for crickets and katydids and jarflies. Too soon even for the frogs. But when I came up the rise by the fort and looked down into the swale I saw the first lightning bug of the year. Its light blinked in the gloom like a wind-stirred candle flame. I thought how soon, now, when you looked down in the swale there'd be hundreds and thousands of them, their lights down low, topping the damp of the weeds and grass. Of a day they'd hide there, hunting out the cool places. But come dark and they'd rise and fill the swale with glow. They've always been a mystery to me, but I've always loved to watch them.

A whippoorwill on yon side the swale sounded its call just then, timid-like and kind of soft. I was trying to think if it was the first one I'd heard that season. It waited a while then it called again, a little louder and a little clearer, like hearing its own voice had encouraged it some. After it had called several times it was answered from the woods. I couldn't help chuckling, for that's what it had been calling for . . . that answer. Now they settled down to it, asking and answering fast and overlapping. There's ways in which a whippoorwill makes the lonesomest listening in the world. Seems like it is a bird that's all by itself in the woods and come dark it cries for its own lonesomeness, trying to find its kind and whimpering at the night. *Whip-poor-will, whip-poor-will, whip-poor-will,* over and over again.

I was listening and thinking, and feeling the bird's own loneliness . . . but mixed in with it was something jarring on me. Something uneasy and fretful. Of a sudden I knew what it was. There was something wrong with the bird calls themselves. They were too clear and sharp-edged. They talked too plain. A bird always blurred his call a little, always hurried it some. I waited till they called again to make sure. And then I knew those weren't birds. They were redskins. An Indian can make a sound more like a whippoorwill than the bird itself. Or they can cry like a screech owl, or bark like a fox, or howl like a wolf. But they give themselves away, times, by doing it too good . . . making it too plain and sharp. That one down by the swale now, he held the cluck the bird gives just before he calls a mite too long. You can't roam the woods like I'd done all my life without learning the ways and the sounds of the animals and birds, and in time you get to where you listen without thinking, and the sounds are so known to you that the least falseness bothers and puts you on guard.

Well, we had Indians at Logan's Fort finally. As I went through the gate I recollected it was the eighteenth day of May.

◈

# CHAPTER
# 20

W E LOOKED FOR AN ATTACK the next morning, not knowing but
what the redskins were about us in numbers, and we got ready
for it. Ben posted men at every loophole and two on the corners, and when first light commenced showing we were pretty well
nerved up. But there was no raid. All that day we stood guard and we
got glimpses of them in the woods all around us, but they just slunk
behind the trees and bushes and there was no firing on the fort and
they never came out so we could get a shot at them. We couldn't even
tell much about how many of them were out there. They were to be
seen from all corners, though, so they had us penned up, for a fact.

Two days passed like that, and it gave a man the most exasperating
feeling, knowing they were there and seeing them, but them holding
their fire and making you hold yours. It tempted you to form a party
and rush them . . . but Ben was too shrewd to give in to such a
temptation. "We can last as long as our powder does," he said, over
and over when the men got restless. "Just let 'em set out there. We got
food and water."

But when two days had passed without the cows being milked they
set up such a bawling that none of us could sleep that night and the
next morning Ann Logan and Esther Whitley said they had to be
milked, redskins or not.

"It's too risky," Ben told them.

"Well, I aim to risk it," Esther said, speaking up peartly, "I ain't
aiming for my cows to be ruint."

She was just the one to do it, too, so we put our heads together and
finally Ben let me and Billy and John Martin sneak out to try and

drive the cows up closer to the fence. "Now don't do nothing foolish," Ben said. "They're likely just setting there waiting for something like this. We'll cover you the best we can, but the first sign of trouble, get back inside the gate fast."

We slid out, making a bold showing, but I'd not be telling the truth if I didn't say my heart was thumping like a drum, and I could of swore it had somehow got up in my throat, where it had no business to be and felt like it was going to choke off my wind any minute. I misdoubt Billy and John were feeling any braver.

But there's never any knowing what Indians are going to do, and we had a surprise waiting for us. There wasn't a sign of a redskin. Not a sign. The woods were as clean of them as if they'd never been there. They'd skedaddled, lock, stock and barrel.

When the women came back from milking, though, Esther was stormy mad. "One of my cows is gone," she said, "the little brindle. Best milker in the lot and the gentlest. Them red devils has drove her off and roasted her, doubtless. I wish I could get my hands on 'em! It would be a pleasure to roast one on a spit hisself!"

Mad as she was, and much as she had to be mad about, I couldn't help grinning at her. She stood there inside the gate, short-heighted but straight as a stalk of cane, with her face as red as a turkey cock's wattles and her words screeching out so loud had the redskins still been there they could of heard her. Instead of a bonnet like most of the other women wore, Esther fancied an old skin hat of Billy's and wore it all the time, inside and out, rain or shine. It was kind of Esther Whitley's mark. It had seen its best days before Billy discarded it, but Esther hung on to it, and while she talked it kept flapping in her eyes and she kept batting it back. "Plundering, thieving varmints!" she screeched, "don't know a good milk cow when they see one. Likely they hacked her to pieces without even hitting her in the head first. It'd be just like 'em. Pore little thing. Billy, you'd best see to your horses. Looked to me like some of them was missing, too." She picked up her pail of milk and stalked off to her cabin, spilling part of the milk in her haste and her anger.

Several horses had been taken, we found. A couple of Billy's, one of Ben's and one of Ben Pettit's were missing. We could ill afford to lose a one, and it went against the grain knowing the Indians had them, for few redskins ever learned how to take care of animals and commonly they abused and mistreated them pretty bad. But there was nothing we could do about it.

The next morning the woods were full of Indians again, but they'd disappeared by evening. That made me feel certain this wasn't any sizable party pestering . . . that it was just a dozen or so that had broken off from the main party and come plundering down our way. That many could scatter through the woods and slither around and look like thirty or forty. I said so to Ben. "There's no use us setting here and letting 'em steal and kill off the stock, Ben. If you'll give me leave, I can take four or five of the men and venture out and maybe drive 'em clean off."

He wasn't to say taken with the idea at first, but the more he thought about it the more sensible it appeared. Finally he said, "Well, take you four, but be careful and don't get too far away. Circle about, but if you come up on a sizable party don't try to make a stand. Get back inside in a hurry." I started walking off, but he called after me. "And don't let 'em trick you, Dave. Don't be lured off."

I promised him I wouldn't, for I knew as well as he did the redskins had a way of appearing to leave just so's a party would venture out after them, and maybe venture too far and be led straight into the hands of a war party. Even old hands at Indian fighting had been tricked that way, and it was right of Ben to call it to mind.

Five of us left the fort early the next morning. We circled to the north and picked up the Indians' trail, but we saw no sign of the redskins themselves. At the Flat Lick that evening we came across the remains of a camp where they'd killed a cow. There was nothing left of it but bloody bones and a skull already crawling with ants. One of the men poked at the bones. "I reckon," he said, "that's what's left of Miz Whitley's cow. It's just as well she can't see what happened to it."

There was a trampling of horse prints all around, too. We couldn't make out how many, but doubtless some of our own were in the bunch. We counted the spit sticks left from roasting the cow and figured there'd been ten or twelve Indians. The trail led north again and we followed it several miles before giving it up and turning back. "It's my opinion they've gone back to the main bunch," I told the others.

We went back and camped at the Flat Lick that night, and all the next day we prowled a short circle without seeing any fresh sign or any redskins. We'd done little good by venturing out, for while this bunch had left, there was no doubt more would keep breaking off from time to time to drift down and kill off the stock, burn the corn and steal the horses. And of course it was untelling but what the war party itself would come our way any day. There was no signs of them yet, though.

We'd just come back to the Lick along about the middle of the afternoon when Billy Whitley rode up in a tearing haste. He didn't even get off his horse. He just yelled at us. "Ben says get back to the stockade in a hurry. John Kennedy has just come from Boonesburg and he claims all hell has busted loose up there!"

The Flat Lick was only two miles from the stockade and we covered it fast. Inside, the fort was stirring like a bothered anthill, with folks running here, there and everywhere all at once. Ben had already told off places at the loopholes and I noticed Jane Manifee taking her stand at the one by the gate. When I went by I heard her telling one of the men to bring her a stool. "I ain't got but these two laigs," she was bawling at the top of her voice, "and I ain't aiming to wear 'em down to the nub standing on 'em. And get a move on!" She spied me and yelled. "Hey, younguns! I reckon you brung a passel of them red scamps in on your tail!"

"I did not," I yelled back at her, but not stopping. "They just took a good look at that face of your'n through the peephole and squandered out of the country."

"I'll fix you," she bellowed. "You just wait."

"Tend to your shooting, Jane."

"I aim to," she said, spitting onto the ground between her feet. "I'll get me a redskin for ever' shoot."

She would, too.

Esther was posted at a loophole, too, and the rest of the women were scurrying about with bullet molds and powder and lead, making ready for a siege. I saw Bethia and Ann with theirs, bringing it over to the south corner. They waved at me, but I had to go on.

Ben was still talking with John Kennedy when I found him. I told him what we'd found and he listened and nodded his head, and then he motioned for John to go on. "I was telling Ben," he said, "I'd just left the fort and had got about two mile, I reckon, when the redskins come scampering out of the woods. They made the most god-awful screeching and yelling you ever heard. Was a little hill close and I clumb up to the top so's I could see good and it looked like they was trying to fire the cabins. I seen little blazes shooting up, places, and directly some of the women clumb up and commenced trying to put 'em out. Was a heap of firing and yelling, and the redskins'd come on in a swarm and then give back to the woods. I seen 'em do it three, four times, and it looked to me like was considerable more of 'em than had been. Best I could tell was might near a hundred of 'em."

"What time was it they commenced?" I said.

"Just a little past day. John Todd and Richard Calloway had left out, just at good day, to go to the Assembly meeting, and they'd been gone an hour, maybe."

"They come back?"

"No. Likely they'd got too far to hear the firing."

"How long before you come on?"

"I watched the best part of an hour. Looked like the fort was holding out as good as it could, and I figured Ben had ort to know, so I come on then."

"You done right, John," Ben told him. "You get on over and eat something now."

John left. Neither Ben nor me said anything for a minute. "How many guns was it we figured they had last time we counted?" Ben said then, kind of slow-like.

"Twenty-two."

He rubbed his chin. "Todd and Calloway are gone, so that leaves twenty."

I reckon we both were thinking the same thing. Twenty men, and outside the pole fence of the stockade a hundred screeching, howling redskins. Twenty men with a scarce supply of powder, and a hundred redskins with the plenty of Britain to furnish them. It would be a miracle did Boonesburg hold out. Thinking of Dannel and Rebecca and the others I wished so bad we could help out.

But Ben shook his head, and he was right, of course. Bad as it would be to lose Boonesburg, and bad as it was to think of what was happening to the folks there, we had none to spare to send to their aid. "They'll be swarming out of these woods next," Ben said, pointing across the swale. "We got to see to our own, Dave."

We settled down to the same kind of exasperation we'd had before, save this time the redskins appeared to be a little bolder and there was some firing back and forth. But it was plain to see the main party was still busy up north, and Ben counseled everybody not to waste shots. "Save 'em," he kept saying, "we're bound to need 'em in time."

That's the way it was for several days, with us tightened up like fiddle strings, ready and waiting, wanting something to fire at and yet dreading it, Ben hoarding ammunition like it was gold and handing it out miserly and cautious. Then, like before, of a sudden the Indians were gone, the woods clean of them and so quiet after the firing and yelling that the quiet was full of noise itself.

I overslept myself the next morning, a thing I seldom did, but I reckon I slept extra sound on account of being let down a little. Anyway, it was Ben woke me up, shaking me. "Rouse up, Dave," he said, "it's broad daylight."

I was still groggy and he shook me again. "Come on, Dave, get up. We've done eat. The womenfolks wants to milk the cows. Take three with you and watch out for 'em. Come on now, they're waiting."

I finally rolled out and splashed myself awake with cold water. I rounded up Burr Harrison and Billy Hudson and John Kennedy to go with me and we went over to where the women were waiting at the gate. Ann and Esther were there, and Bethia. "Sleepyhead," Ann teased, when we walked up. But Bethia just smiled at me.

"I'm getting too old," I said, "to stay up all hours watching for redskins. Ain't the man I used to be. Need my sleep."

Esther batted her old hat down. "Just pure lazy is all," she snorted.

"Now, Esther . . ."

"It's the truth if ever I told it. You younguns is just plain shiftless. Don't know a day's work when you see it. Now, in my time . . ."

But Ben came up and slid the gate open. I stepped through and took a good look all around. It's on my conscience to this good day that I didn't do more. But I was still druggy with sleep, and even if I hadn't of been I reckon I'd of thought Ben had already ventured out. Anyway, I just stepped out and took a look and said it appeared to be safe enough.

The cows were cropping the long grass in the swale just down from the fort. The other men stepped through the gate and we made a kind of circling front for the women until they were outside too, then we squared in front, on either side and to the back of them as they walked down the slope. Wasn't but six cows giving milk left, and we singled them out and drove them into a huddle in the bottom of the swale. When they bunched and came together, us men fanned out in a kind of box around the women and the cows.

We'd no more than got set and not a woman had commenced milking yet, when a volley of fire from the woods raked across us. It came all of a sudden, astonishing and unexpected. One second there were just the cows and the women and us, and the morning chore of milking, all homey and quiet and peaceful. The next there was this raking volley of shots and Billy Hudson throwing his hands up over his head and falling where he stood, sprawling face down in the grass, his hands clawing at it and his legs twitching, and the cows snicking their heads back, milling and bawling and stampeding up the swale. There was just that second of disbelief, not taking it in, everybody frozen in their tracks . . . then we came to life, there was the knowing and the spasm of being afraid and the heart commencing to beat again. Almost without thinking I heard myself shouting, "Run! Fast, Bethia! Get to the gate!" And then there was the swirl of the women's skirts as they wheeled around and the clatter of their pails dropping to the ground, and they went flying back up the slope, us following them and shouting and hurrying them along.

Another volley caught us halfway up the slope and Burr Harrison went down. Esther's hat blew off, whether from the breeze of her running or from a bullet I didn't know. I saw her grab at it, and then she swerved and stopped dead still and looked back where it had lit. "God's sake, Esther," I shouted to her, "let it go!"

I caught her by the wrist, but she jerked loose and darted back, stooped over and picked up the hat, then clapping it back on her head again she lit out, the bullets thudding the ground all around her. I had slowed for her, but she'd moved so fast I'd barely put on my brakes when she was back up with me and making tracks up the hill. Ahead of us, Ann and Bethia were running fast, their skirts billowing out behind them, but I had the awful feeling that all of us were standing still, and that the slope of the hill was just sliding down underneath us, and that the fort was just barely coming towards us, of its own accord, like a ship hull up over the horizon. It felt like hours were passing.

I saw John Kennedy stagger and go down on one knee, dropping his gun when he lost stride, then he recovered, slowed down and limping in his right leg. I saw Bethia's bonnet, loosened by her running, slide back off her head and bounce by its strings down between her shoulders. I remember thinking what a target that red hair of hers made, and I looked to see it spreading in the grass any second. Then I was up to where John had been hit and as I passed I bent down and picked up his gun. Even then I recollected we needed every gun. When I straightened up I saw the fort gate flung wide open and Ben and Billy Whitley came tearing through. I knew they were both shouting, for their mouths were wide open, but not a sound carried down to us over the noise of the Indians' guns. Ben reached the women and he swung Ann up in his arms. In a flash he was through the gate with her, Bethia and John Kennedy on his heels.

I looked at Esther. She had her skirts gathered up past her knees to keep them from hampering her and she was churning her legs up and down as fast as they'd go. She had her chin ducked down against the wind to keep her hat on. Billy fogged on down the hill to meet her, but when he got to her she never even broke her stride. Like a horse in the last heat of a race she kept going, shaking off his arm. "God's sake, Billy," she heaved at him, "leave me be!" He swung around in back of her and ran on her heels . . . and then we were all through the gate and Ben was swinging it shut behind us, dropping the bar.

It wasn't till I leant against a post to get my breath that I knew exactly how scared I had been. For a minute I thought my knees were going to give way with me they shook so. All the folks in the fort were bunched and crowded around the gate, milling and circling and running about. Some of the younguns had begun crying and one woman was down on her knees sobbing, "Lord have mercy on us . . . Lord have mercy on us." It was Miz Coburn, her hands wringing their bones while she cried.

I looked for Bethia and saw her with Ann standing on the edge of the crowd. She'd straightened her bonnet, and though her face was still white she was calming. I made my way over to speak to her. "You all right?"

She nodded and ran a look clean over me. "I was afeared to look back," she said. "I was scared you'd been hit."

"Just luck we wasn't all hit," I said. "Just pure luck, and we can lay it mostly to the redskins' being such bad shots."

Davey was hanging on to Ann's skirts, his face buried in the folds that kind of muffled his crying. Black Molly was standing close by, holding the baby and patting it with a heavy hand, every limb of her body shaking and her eyes rolling around till nothing but the whites showed. Ann leaned down to comfort Davey. "There now, Davey, there. It's all right. Nothing to be afeared of now. Molly, quit that pounding little Billy's backside. You'll have the pore little thing beat black and blue. And quit taking on so. It's all right now."

"Yessum, Miss Ann, yessum," Molly said, handing over the baby. "But it don't sound much like it to me."

It didn't, for a fact. To the firing outside was now added the yowling and screeching of the Indians, crazy and wild and like something unearthly loosed on the air. For human beings they could make the unhumanliest sounds that ever come out of a mortal throat. Enough to send the shivering fear into every listening heart. Bethia gave a little shudder. "I hope," she said, so low her voice was but a whisper, "I hope pore Burr and Billy was killed straight off."

I hoped so too. The squalling outside meant the redskins had swarmed out of the woods onto the bodies like wolves onto a wounded sheep. If they hadn't been killed at once, they had poor hopes of living much longer.

"What was you and Esther poking along for?" Ann asked, Davey having finally quieted down.

"Either the wind blowed that hat of her'n off," I said, "or a bullet lifted it, and by grannies if she didn't have to stop and go back and get it!"

"The Lord have mercy! I reckon when Gabriel blows the last trump Esther'll keep the judgment waiting till she's got that hat on."

"She likely will." And we all laughed. The sound of it amazed me. To be laughing again, so soon. Ten minutes before, if I'd thought of it, I'd of swore none of us would ever laugh again. It made us feel better, though.

The crowd of folks was still huddled inside the gate, kind of shrunk together, the women bunched with the younguns hugging their knees and the men milling around the edges. Ben climbed up on a stump so all could see him and waved his arms to get them quiet. "Let's get to our posts, boys. Get to the posts. You womenfolks. You get the younguns safe in the cabins, then commence heating the lead. All keep steady now. Keep steady." He looked big and solid and heavy as a rock and he kept his voice down, and unflurried. "We'll stand 'em off," he said. "This is the stoutest stockade in the country and there's no way they can take it. We got plenty to eat and if we take care there's powder enough. Ever'body get to their posts, now."

The sight of him, big and steady himself, his words quiet and sure, was like salve spread on the burn their fears were making. He was the captain and the leader, and he was there talking to them, in charge of them and himself unafraid. And he set them their tasks to do. You could see the panic quiet, and the milling and shrinking ceased. The menfolks moved to the loopholes and the women herded the younguns to the cabins on the back side, and then brought their bullet molds and bars of lead to the blockhouses. Calm came where there had been fear, and purpose came where there had been confusion.

My post was in the south blockhouse alongside of Billy Whitley. We could see the whole slope of the hill and the swale down below. We could see Billy Hudson's body. The Indians had stripped him and scalped him. But Burr lay higher up on the slope and apparently the redskins hadn't ventured that close to the fort yet. We could tell, because Burr still had his hair.

All that day we kept to our posts, firing when we had a good shot. Ben came and went, passing each post time and again. "Make ever' shot count," he warned every time, "don't waste your lead. Wait till you've got a sure shot."

The Indians didn't storm the fort. They kept to the edge of the woods, but held to a steady fire. When the most of the morning had gone by and they'd not attacked, I told Billy I didn't believe there was as many of them as we'd first feared. "Waiting till dark, likely," Billy said, "or maybe daylight in the morning."

It could be, but I didn't much think there was enough of them to swarm out.

Little by little the fort settled down. The women with younguns went to fix food for them, and when they'd been fed and seen to, some of the others brought meat and bread to the ones at the loopholes. You could tell those that had never been through a siege before. Their faces stayed white and they were jumpy and nervy, but put it down that their crying was done and over with, and not one of them went around moaning because they'd ever set foot in the country and wishing they could turn back. To the last man and the last woman they'd settled down to hold on, now, and all that was left was learning whether it would take the last of them.

It was along about the middle of the afternoon Billy called out to me from his place. "Dave, look at Burr. I think I seen him move his foot."

I looked. Burr was stretched out, face down, long and limp, and he'd been deadly still all day. None but thought he'd been killed. I looked close, but I couldn't tell it if he moved. "Must of been a shadow, Billy," I said.

"Must of."

But we both kept on watching him and finally I saw his foot move, just a little, just a bare motion. "I seen him, Billy," I yelled. "He's alive! I seen his foot move!"

"I'll get Ben," Billy said, and he went out, running.

When Ben came we all looked until we saw it again . . . just his heel, balanced on his toe, wobbling from one side to the other a time or two, and then rested, like even that much tired him beyond endurance. "God, the pore thing," Ben said. He watched again and then he turned around. "We got to get him inside. Come night they'll finish him off, sure."

Billy didn't say anything, nor did I. Wasn't much use saying anything. All three of us understood. We couldn't leave a man, hurt and helpless, to the mercies of the redskins. But it was almost certain death to go after him. Whoever tried it wouldn't be likely to come back. We stood there and watched Burr and figured on it. "Best time to try," Ben said finally, "would be just before dark, wouldn't it? While there's still light enough to see, but dim enough not to make too good a target for the redskins."

"Reckon they might hit him kind of by accident and finish him off during the afternoon?" Billy said.

"Looks to me like we'll have to chance that," Ben said. "I don't see as we've got a right to take any more risks than we have to. You all stay with your posts till I give the word. I'll work on it."

The rest of the day passed, hot and eternally long. Seemed like the sun just stood still. Me and Billy kept an eye on Burr, but we didn't see him move any more and between us we decided he'd probably died. Late in the evening we could hear the cows bawling, at first close by and then getting fainter and we knew the Indians were driving them off. "That'll sure grieve Esther," Billy said. "Likely the next shot she takes at a redskin will travel a mite faster. Her temper'll hasten it some."

"Likely it will," I said. "There's one thing I wish. I wish Esther didn't think so highly of that old hat you give her. You'd best caution her it's liable to be the death of her one of these days."

Billy cocked his head and looked at me. "It's easy to tell you ain't a married man," he said. "None but one without experience would talk of cautioning a woman. In my opinion, there ain't nothing on the face of the earth as stubborn as a woman. As you seen for yourself, not even a redskin is going to make Esther part with something she's partial to. I ain't ever cautioned her, and I ain't ever likely to."

I couldn't help laughing, but at the same time I knew Billy wouldn't of talked so had he actually meant it. It was the kind of talk a man makes about his woman when he sets such a heap of store by her he can take a little leeway in speaking of her. Stubborn Esther Whitley might be, and set in her ways, but she was a power for dependence and stoutheartedness and none knew it better than Billy. Jane Manifee was another one like her, and in a quieter way Ann Logan was just as stubborn and stouthearted. Given her own chance I figured Bethia would hold up as good as any of them. All told, we had more of their kind in the country than the weeping, wailing ones. If we hadn't, we'd never of pulled through.

The sun had gone down when Ben came and asked me to go with him. He led the way to the gate. To one side there was a big bale of wool that belonged to Ann. "I'm aiming," Ben said, "to push that bale of wool ahead of me down towards Burr. You open the gate for me just wide enough to get through, then cover me as best you can. I ain't aiming to take it fast, so don't worry if it's a right smart time. If I go down, do what you think's best about coming after me, but don't take no needless risks."

I slid my gun to the ground. "It's your thought for me to stand here and wait whilst you roll that bale of wool down the hill and get Burr?"

"It's not only my thought, it's my orders. I am the captain in this stockade."

"Ben," I said, begging him, "you've got Ann and the younguns to think of, and all the others. It's on account of you being the captain you ortent to go. I can make it just as good as you."

But he wasn't even listening. He rid himself of his hatchet and knife and shot pouch and leaned his gun up against the fence. "See to Ann if I don't make it."

In a way I'd known there was no use arguing with him. He was doing just what I'd of done had I been in his shoes. When you're the captain you've got to be the captain, and you've got no call to send another man to his death as long as you're able to go yourself. So I just made ready myself. I saw to my gun and laid Ben's handy so I'd have two fast shots if there was need. "We've not seen him move lately," I said, "you'd best find out if he's still alive before you venture out."

"That's a good idea." He stepped to the loophole and looked and then he called out. "Burr? Burr Harrison. I'm coming for you. If you can hear me, move your foot again. You hear me, Burr?"

We waited, and watched. Burr didn't move. Ben tried again. "Burr, I'm coming after you if you move your foot. Try it, now. Move your foot as much as you can if you hear me."

This time we saw him lift his heel a little. He wiggled it just once, from one side to the other, and then it dropped down again. But that was enough. "All right, Burr," Ben called, "I'm coming now."

We rolled the bale of wool in front of the gate and I lifted the bar. I eased the gate open just far enough to let Ben push the wool through, then he stooped and slid out behind it on his stomach. "Close up, now, Dave. But keep watch. If I get there I'm aiming on making a dash back with him, and you get the gate open fast for me."

"You needn't to worry," I told him.

He had picked a good time. It was just coming on dusk, the time of day when there are no shadows and the light is so meager that things blur and run together without shape. The time of day when you think you see a thing and then you don't. Little at a time Ben made his way down the slope. He'd shove the wool ahead of him a couple of feet and drag himself up behind it, then he'd wait a spell before giving it another shove. That way its movement wasn't so plain.

It was maybe a hundred feet down the slope to where Burr was lying, and every foot of it I looked for a volley of fire to burst out. I listened for it so hard I felt like my ears were cramped back, and I watched so close my eyes watered and burned, and I held myself so tight that just getting another breath hurt. Ben moved so slow that it seemed like it took him forever to get to Burr, but I reckon it wasn't more than fifteen or twenty minutes all told. And by grannies, he got there without drawing a shot.

When he reached him, he wiggled himself around from behind the wool and then of a sudden he stood up, dragged Burr up over his shoulder and commenced racing back up the slope. That was when the redskins opened fire and the bullets thudded into the ground all around and plunked like a finger thumping a dead-ripe watermelon into the log poles of the stockade fence. I reckon Ben had told everybody on the loopholes to hold their fire, for there was no answering the redskins from anywhere. It was like they were all holding their breaths, looking on.

I swung the gate, wide so Ben wouldn't be hampered getting through, but I didn't expect him to make it. I didn't see how he could and once when he stumbled I made sure he was down. But he'd only hit a rough spot, for he picked up his stride and came on, and a few seconds later he was safe inside the gate and it closed and barred behind him. I reckon we all felt like we'd seen a miracle for the folks swarmed around, pouring out from the loopholes and crowding about Ben, pounding him on the back and yelling and whooping. It had been something to watch, for a fact. "By grannies, Ben," Billy said, hugging Ben and dancing around him, "you done it! You sure done it! You cheated them redskins out of Burr's hair, and right under their noses! Man, it was a sight to see!"

Ben had slid Burr onto the ground and he was standing there beside him, heaving and trying to ease his breath, but he was grinning all over his face. It was enough to make a man feel good, knowing he'd brought one of our own back amongst us, taking a risk the way he'd done and cheating the Indians not only of a wounded man, but of his own self as well. He had a right to grin.

Ann slipped through the folks crowded about and Ben's grin faded away. I misdoubt he'd told her what he intended to do, and likely he thought he was in for a good scolding. But she never said a word. Her face was so white even her lips had no color, but she just looked at him, and then she reached out a finger and poked it through a bullet hole in his sleeve. She pulled it back and poked it through another one in his hat brim . . . and another one in the tail of his shirt . . . and another one in his leggings. None of us had seen them before, but Ann did. When she'd found the last bullet hole, she pulled his head down and kissed him, in front of everybody. "I reckon the Lord was keeping watch over you, Ben," she said, and that was all. She just turned around and walked away then.

Burr was bad hurt. He had five bullet holes in him and he'd lost so much blood he just lay still, breathing heavy and deep, but unknowing of what went on around him. The best man we had at doctoring was Ben Pettit and he did what he could, but he didn't give him much chance. It seemed like a pity when Ben had risked so much to bring him in. But even had we known it, we couldn't of done anything else. And we got Billy Hudson's body inside, too. The next night me and Azariah Davis slid out in the dark and brought it back.

The redskins hadn't mutilated him, save for his scalp being taken. Apparently he'd been killed straight off, for had he lived till the Indians got to him, they'd of cut and carved him to pieces. We buried him inside the stockade that same night. Ben read a psalm over the grave . . . the one that commences, "The Lord is my shepherd . . ." and he said a prayer for the peace of Billy's soul. He was the first to be buried at Logan's Fort.

The days went by, hot and burny from the sun, and long with light for the redskins to see by. They kept up the same kind of steady firing they had on the first day, and when somebody poked a hat up over the fence in a lull, there'd be a volley that fair deafened you. We got glimpses of them sometimes, slithering from one tree to another the way they do, and once in a while a man would get a good shot and a howl would go up that told it had been a hit.

But they had us penned down, no doubts about it. We had to sit there and watch while they drove the cattle off, and listen to their bawling till they were killed, and see the smoke of the fires that roasted them. And we had to watch while they rounded up what few sheep and hogs we had, out of range of our fire, and drive them off too. From the numbers we saw driven off we knew there'd be precious few head of stock left, and we knew in reason what had happened to our corn fields and clearings. There'd be nothing but ashes to tell where they'd been.

Troublesome and fretsome as it was to lose our stock and our crops and cabins, though, that was the least of our worries. We could hunt and kill meat, and we could build our cabins again, and we could plant more corn. What eat at us and made us shrink every time we fired a gun was the dwindling away of our powder and lead. And towards the end of the week Ben had me to go over to his cabin for a talk. "We've got barely enough to last out another week, Dave, the way things are going. We got to get some, somewheres."

We had no way of knowing whether Boonesburg and Harrodstown were besieged or not. We thought likely they were, for no one had tried

to come through. And for their numbers, they were as short of ammunition as we were, so there wasn't much use in sending to them to
spare some. That left the Holston. Ann put food in front of us and we
ate and talked of it. "It's awful risky," Ben said. "The redskins'll be
watching the trails, likely."

"There wasn't no trails when we was here hunting in the old days,"
I said. "Why couldn't you and me just light out through the country
and stay off the path?"

"How'd we get over the mountains without going through the Gap?
You all used the pass coming and going, didn't you?"

I had to admit we did, but it looked to me like two men, traveling
light, could find a way over, and I said so. "It would be rough, doubtless, but that ain't saying it couldn't be done."

Ben ran his finger back and forth across the edge of the table, thinking. Finally he smacked his hand down hard, making the bowls and
plates clatter and dance. "Well, it's got to be done. Ain't no real use
thinking. We'll just have to chance it."

"When?"

"Tonight."

He called all the folks together in the square and told them what
our intentions were. He didn't try to keep anything back from them,
not even how little powder was left. He told them we'd make the
quickest trip we could and that Billy Whitley was to be in charge till
he got back, and they were to ration their shots and make out the
best they could.

Ann and Bethia fixed us a bait of vittles to take along . . . corn
pones and meat. None of us had much to say. No need of it. But I
took notice Ann kept looking at Ben like she was fixing his image in
her mind to remember when he was gone, and Bethia kept watching
me the same way. I reckon folks of our breed find it hard to talk when
our feelings are running strong. But it's just as well. There's times
when words don't have much meaning.

We'd picked the middle of the night to leave and Billy let us out the
gate. Right at the last Ben warned him again. "Now, don't take no
chances, Billy, and it's my orders you're not to venture out." There
wasn't a shrewder fighter in the country than Billy Whitley, but he
was given to boldness through his love for a wide-open fight. He disliked being penned up, and Ben was a little afraid that once he was
gone Billy would risk taking a party out. He promised he wouldn't,
though.

There's no need saying much about our journey, save that we made it. It's nigh on to two hundred miles to Sapling Grove, but by cutting across the country and staying off the paths and traces we pared that down to about a hundred and fifty. We never made a real camp the whole trip. We rode until we couldn't hold our eyes open any longer and then holed up to sleep an hour or two, and we ate riding. We made it there and back in eleven days, and we brought back better than a hundred pounds of ammunition. The weather was in our favor and we didn't have a single brush with the redskins, which helped a lot, too.

But we were a sight to see the night we got back. I could tell what I looked like by looking at Ben. He was gaunted and thinned down, with his clothes and face and hands briar-cut and torn, and a trail beard stubbling his jaws. Ann clucked over us like a mother hen, heating up water for us to wash and stirring around fixing us something to eat. She made us both get out of our clothes and wrap up in blankets while her and Bethia mended the worst of the tears. The flustered way they busied about was the only sign they gave of the uneasiness they'd had. It being past, their relief showed in an uncommon stirring around.

When we'd got settled down a little Ben sent for Billy, and Esther came with him. We had to tell of our trip first and then Ben wanted to know what had been happening while we were gone. "Nary a thing," Billy said, "ain't ary thing happened."

"Naught," Esther put in, "save the redskins is still clustered about, and Burr Harrison breathed his last the thirteenth day of the month and was buried alongside of Billy Hudson. And a traveler name of Lyon heading this way was either killed or took barely five mile from the stockade. And Barney Stagner was killed right outside the fort at Harrodstown and his head cut off and stuck on a pole for all to see. Outside of that, ain't ary a thing happened."

"Oh, well," Billy said, "things like that has got to be expected. I was meaning we hadn't had no . . ."

"You," Esther said, "was meaning you'd stayed put inside the fence like you was told to do. Which grieved you mightily that you couldn't get out and have a brush with the redskins. Now if you could of led a charge into the woods, you'd of had a sight to tell."

Billy laughed and we all joined in, but in a way Billy had been right. We'd expected to lose Burr, and to get back and find no one else had been hurt or killed was a big relief. "Someone has been from Harrodstown, I reckon, or you wouldn't of knowed about Barney," Ben said. "How are they making out?"

Billy nodded. "Jim snuck in one night. They're pestered about like us . . . redskins all about. So's Boonesburg. The country appears to be swarming with the red devils."

"How's their powder?"

"Scarce. Jim said the major was awful worried."

"I'll bound he is."

"Oh," Billy said. "I was near forgetting. Jim said tell you them two boys the major sent on that errand of his'n had got back. Somewheres they must of run into Johnnie Vann, for he come in with 'em."

He said it innocent enough, but he'd of been less than human if he hadn't been eager to know more than Jim had told. Ben looked across the room at me, but all he did was nod and commence grumbling to Ann. "This blanket hampers a man considerably," he said. "Ain't you got them buckskins mended enough?"

She handed them over. "The worst is fixed. You won't be showing through, leastways."

Billy and Esther left, but we were too worn-out and sleepy to do much thinking about Jim's news. Ben just said he reckoned the major would let us know what the boys had found out over in the Illinois country. I was fixing to bed down in front of the fire and I don't recollect saying a word, but I remember laying there and watching the firelight brighten and darken on the rafters after the house was quiet, and I remember thinking I'd be glad to see Johnnie Vann again.

O NLY I DIDN'T SEE HIM soon, after all. He didn't come down to our place like I'd thought he might, and the word trickled around that he'd left again. Ben and me, talking it over, thought likely the major was using him to scout, and if he was, it was the smart thing to do.

There was little passing between the three forts, for we all had our hands full. Unless you've been through an Indian siege it's hard to understand what it's like. Sometimes for a week or two we'd be penned up, then the redskins would drift away for a spell, then the first thing we'd know they were back again. But they never left the country and there was never a time that summer when the women and younguns got outside the walls, save early of a morning we'd drive what few cows were left right up to the fence and one or two women would venture out to milk. There was no more chance of working on the clearings than there was of sprouting wings and taking to the air. There was never a morning that just opening the gate wasn't liable to bring on a volley of fire.

We looked and looked for Colonel Bowman, but the days passed on and he didn't come. As the summer waxed we commenced to wonder if he was going to come in time to do us much good, for we all knew if we could last out the summer, not even the British could stir the Indians to pester us much through the winter. But lasting out was getting to be mighty chancey. In July Harrodstown got down to their last grains of powder and Jim made a trip back to the Holston and brought back what he could, but what we needed was a plentiful store, such as Colonel Bowman could bring into the country. Billy Bush had told us that the Assembly had set aside a thousand pounds to provision and arm the colonel's volunteers, and it stood to reason the most of it would go for ammunition. We'd of all been grateful for the help of the men, but what we were yearning most to see was a sizable amount of powder.

July went by and most of August with little change in our prospects. And it was a mockery that in such a worrisome time the country had never looked so fair. It was a good season, hot without being smothery, and with a plenty of rain which made a thick and fast growing of all things. The hills and the meadows and the valleys were heavy with green. It fretted us that in so good a season we had so little planted. We'd got out one or two corn fields kind of hid back in the woods, and that was all. Mornings the swale at the foot of the slope would be swirly with fog, and when it rolled away the sky would be as blue as a baby's eyes. Afternoons it would darken and sometimes there'd be a few scant clouds, white and drifty and so thin you could see right through to the blue beyond. When the sun set it was like being put down in the midst of a rainbow, all the air colored and set on fire with it. I reckon it must be on account of so much dampness, but no place in the world are the sunsets as pretty as they are in this country. Gold and purple and red, all smudged together, and the whole sky pink and gauzy looking. We had a sight of them that summer.

It was one morning towards the last of August that there came a banging and knocking on the gate and a shouting for us to open up. It was just before sunup, and I'd not been stirring long. We'd quit keeping a guard on the gate for it seemed useless. It was never opened save when Ben gave the word, and usually it was either him or me or Billy let folks through. I went to see. "Who is it?"

"We're from Colonel Bowman! Open up!"

I got that bar down in record time and three men slid through the crack so fast you'd of thought they'd been oiled. They were about as bad scared as men ever get to be. They all commenced stammering at once, but I hushed them and herded them into the blockhouse and sent for Ben, fast.

By the time he got there they'd quieted some and could talk with sense. "Where is the colonel?" Ben asked.

"He's at Boonesburg. He sent a party to Harrodstown, and he sent six of us down here to bring you the word he'll be reinforcing you soon."

"How strong are you?"

"Two companies."

"How much powder?"

The man who'd been doing the talking shook his head. "I wouldn't rightly know, but it's a plenty. That's mostly what we brung, for the colonel said we could provision off the country."

Lordy, but we could of danced a jig. In fact, we did so. We clean forgot for a little while what must of scared the men so bad, and that they'd started six instead of three. We were so pleased at the news that there was a store of powder in the country we just turned loose and pounded one another's backs, and shouted and yelled and acted like folks gone wild. It was Ben, of course, that brought us back down to earth again. "You all quieten down," he said, "these men have been in trouble."

We listened. They'd left Boonesburg two days ago and had come along without seeing any sign of Indians till they'd got within five miles of the fort the evening before. "There's a little creek along there, and that's where they ambushed us. Was a fellow guiding us, and he shouted for us to scatter and take to the bushes, but I seen three go down, him amongst 'em. I hid out, for he'd warned us to do that if we had trouble, and I commenced working my way towards the fort during the night. Them two," and the man nodded towards the others, "done the same and we run acrost one another just a piece down the swale. Johnnie had told us to foller the swale to the fort if we got separated from him."

I jumped like I'd been shot and fair shouted at the man. "Johnnie! Was it Johnnie Vann guiding you?"

He nodded. "That was his name."

"And he was shot?"

"He went down in the first fire."

I swung around towards Ben. "Ben, I'm going after him."

I reckon he knew I would, too, whether he said so or not, for he didn't argue. "Pick who you want to go with you," he said.

If I'd not picked Billy Whitley I believe he'd of drawn a bead on me, then and there, but Billy's boldness exactly suited my intentions and I nodded towards him. He gave a whoop and lit a shuck to catch us up some horses.

It was the Flat Lick where they'd been ambushed, and a good place it was. The trail widened where it crossed the run and a party following the trail would be in plain sight, whilst there was plenty of cover for the redskins. I was a mite surprised at Johnnie following the trail, but if he'd thought it safe I made no doubt he'd had good reason to think so.

There were two men lying on the ground in the clearing, and Johnnie was kind of half lying, half sitting, propped up against a tree to one side. He was still holding his gun across his knees. One of the men was already dead, but the other one was still breathing. Johnnie was bad hurt, I could tell, but he knew me when I went over and stooped down. He called my name and struggled to pull himself up. "Don't move, Johnnie," I told him. "We'll get you to the stockade soon."

I was bent over him and all the warning I had was the widening of Johnnie's eyes, seeing over my shoulder and past me. How he got his gun up and fired, all in the same second I whirled around and fired, I'll never know, but he did. At the same time I felt a sting like a knife blade being drawn across my left arm, and then a sudden pain went shooting clean down to my hand. Across the clearing in the edge of the bushes I saw a man, clawing at a limb and it giving under his pull. He sagged down slow . . . heavy and sprawling. The bushes swayed and parted, and then they shivered together over him, closing, and were still. My left arm felt paralyzed and I couldn't hold on to my gun any longer. It slid down to the ground and my arm dropped down against my side, nerveless and unfeeling. It surprised me to see blood trickling down on the back of my hand. I looked at Johnnie, and he'd passed out.

Billy was yelling and running across the clearing. "You got him! One of you got him, Dave! I seen him fall." He ran past me and plowed into the bushes. He thrashed around awhile and then he backed out into the clearing dragging the body with him. He dropped when he was clear of the bushes, looked at it, and then kicked it. "By God, Dave, you know who this is? You'll not believe it, but it's that measly Judd Jordan!"

But the woods around the clearing had commenced to whirl and the ground was tilting up against me, and it was funny but a kind of shade was pulling down in front of my eyes, making the sky and the woods and Billy and everything else dark. I remember thinking I'd best sit down by the side of Johnnie till things lightened up again, but about that time everything was blotted completely out, and there was neither dark nor light any more.

When I came to, Ben was bent over me. My sleeve had been slit and my arm fixed up and Ben was trying to pull my shirt back up over my shoulders. I felt the foolishest, for at first I had no recollection of where I was. Seeing I was awake Ben grinned at me. "It's a good thing you stayed asleep as long as you did. Give us a chance to gouge that bullet out without hurting you too much. Reckon you can set up, now?"

I thought so and tried. But I felt as weak as a kitten.

"It was losing so much blood made you so weak," Ben said. "You ain't bad hurt, but you got hit in the fleshy part of your arm and it bled a sight. You set there now and get your strength back. We got these to bury."

"Johnnie?" I said.

"We've done took him to the stockade. Him and the other one was hurt."

"How'd you know?"

"Billy come for us. Just you set there now, and we'll not be long."

He had brought Azariah and John Martin with him and they set about digging a grave. When they searched through the dead soldier's clothes, they found a piece of paper stuffed down inside his shirt. I saw Ben pull it out, but he didn't say what it was. Just gave a kind of low whistle when he looked at it, then put it away in his pouch and went on about his job.

They dug a place big enough to hold the both of them, the soldier and Judd. "Seems kind of an insult to put him in the same grave with Judd," Ben said, "but I got to, for it'll save time."

They put the soldier in first, then dragged Judd over to the edge. Ben bent over and looked through his clothes, too, and he pulled out a whole batch of papers like the one he'd got off the soldier. He barely glanced at them before he stuffed them into his pouch with the other one, and then they rolled Judd in on top the soldier. "I've a good mind not to say no prayer over that one," Ben said. "He don't rightly deserve it." But being a good Calvinist he couldn't bring himself not to do his duty. "No," he said, "that wouldn't be right. The Lord will be his judge, and maybe He can forgive him. I sure find it hard to do."

I couldn't make sense of what he was saying, but my head was still whirly and I felt dreened and sick to my stomach, so I didn't try very hard. My arm was paining me, too, and all I wanted was to get back to the fort and lay down in my own bed. Which was soon enough, for Ben didn't waste any time.

I must of slept most of the rest of the day, for it was dark when I came to myself again. I was in the blockhouse and Bethia was sitting by my bed. She smiled at me. "Could you eat now?"

Something did smell powerfully good, and of a sudden I was as hungry as a bear. "I believe I could," I told her.

She raised me up in the bed and propped things in back of my shoulders till I could sit, and then she brought a bowl of stew over. She wouldn't hear to me feeding myself. Instead she spooned the stew into my mouth like I was a baby. I didn't argue much, for it was too sweet to be fed by her.

When I'd eaten the whole bowl she laid it down and eased me back flat again. She started to get up then, but I caught hold of her hand and pulled her down to sit on the bed. "I reckon Ben has told you," I said.

She nodded, and then she leant over and kissed me. "Let's not ever talk of it again. You go on back to sleep now."

But I wouldn't let her go. I reckon it was just coming over me . . . what it meant to us. I took my good hand and pulled her head down and buried my face in her hair and smelled it and felt it, tickly and warm, against my skin. All the rest of my life I could do that when I wanted to. The top button of her dress was open against the heat, and a spot of skin, whiter than her neck and face, was showing. I kissed it, and she pulled away, her face reddening. I let her go, laughing. All the rest of my life I could do that, too. I didn't mind waiting if she'd rather. I felt so good I could of got out of the bed and danced a reel. "You go to sleep," Bethia said, buttoning her dress, "and quit being so frisky."

I was settling myself to do what she said, when of a sudden I remembered Johnnie. I asked about him.

Bethia didn't say anything for a minute, and I knew by her look she hated to tell me. "He's up at Ben's," she said, finally.

"But he's not got a chance, has he?"

"They . . . they don't think he's got much of one, Dave. But you can't ever tell. He's still living, and as long as he's living there's a chance."

"Does he know anybody?"

"Oh, yes, he's awake. He knows everything going on."

"I've got to see him," I said, and I commenced crawling out of the bed.

Bethia tried to push me down, but I'd got some strength back and could shove her aside. "There's nothing wrong with me," I told her, "but a shoulder hurt. I'm going to see Johnnie."

She helped me then and walked with me over to Ben's.

Johnnie was laying in Ben's own bed. He looked awful little and shriveled and old, flat of his back like that, more like a piece of dried apple than ever. He couldn't quite twist his mouth into a grin when he saw me, but he tried. Ben was sitting beside him and he got up and gave me his stool. He didn't fuss because I'd stirred out. Ann scolded a little, but Ben hushed her up. "I just come," I told Johnnie, "to lay you a wager that the next time we go hunting together I'll get more buffalo than you."

He shook his head, and it made me hurt all over to see he knew how bad off he was. He couldn't talk except in gulps between breaths, for he'd been shot low in the shoulder, tipping the chest. He motioned for me to listen, and somehow, dragging his breath through the words he told me what he wanted me to know. "He was took captive by the Senecas when he was just a lad, and raised up by them . . . the one you all call Judd Jordan. I've known of him ever since I commenced trading . . . but not by that name. His Indian name meant Tree With Strong Roots, but he was spoke of amongst the rest of us as Greasy John."

While Johnnie got his breath I was remembering Judd's knife. He'd carved his name on the haft . . . a stiff-limbed tree.

"He lived amongst the Senecas," Johnnie said, "and took to their ways till he was more Indian than ary one of them . . . he had a powerful hatred of the whites. He hated his own white blood."

"Why did he go amongst 'em then?"

"He never . . . save to spy on 'em and seek out their weaknesses to take back to the Indians. In his time he has led the Senecas on more raids that massacred whites than any of their own braves. . . ."

The story went on and on. Judd had been hired by the British to spy on the western country. He'd been sent to the Watauga to watch Colonel Henderson's dealings with the Cherokee. He'd been told to make out he was a settler and go into the country . . . I recollected that Bethia had been by herself at Joe Martin's. Where was Judd? "Amongst the Shawnee . . . it was him led the band that stole your horses when you all was journeying in."

"That limp of his . . ."

"That didn't come from you throwing him in the fire. It come from one of you shooting him whilst he was stealing your horses. It was your horse he set out to take, for after that fight you had with him he hated you worse than all the others."

"And he was to live amongst us and watch and take word to the redskins. . . ."

Johnnie nodded.

"Was it him," I said, remembering, "that knew about the powder Major Clark got from Virginia that time?"

"It was him."

The whole thing, the whole big scheme fell into place now. Judd had been at Harrodstown, of course, when Major Clark and Jack Jones had been elected, and he'd known when they'd leave for Virginia.

He'd gone there to find out what took place. "It was him," Johnnie said, "that led the party that pestered the major and . . ."

"And attacked McClellan's Station. You warned the major at Fort Pitt," I said, "but you never told him . . ."

"I didn't know he was in the country. I knew he'd passed the word about the powder, but I reckoned he was up north, and I didn't know ary thing about his connections with the British. It wasn't until . . ."

"Was it him led these attacks in the country this summer?"

"It was him . . . he could come and go as he pleased. You all took him for a settler and he could move about easy. You never thought nothing of it when he disappeared, thinking he was out on his own business."

Now it was plain why he'd told Bethia she'd be safer at the clearing than in the fort. He'd known the forts were to be attacked . . . had planned and led the attacks. My God, what a monstrous thing he'd done!

"When did you find out?"

"Not till two weeks ago," Johnnie said. "I went up to the Delaware town. I taken We-to-mah and the younguns there awhile back, and I went up to see how they was making out. Picked up the word then. I was coming to tell you. Passed through Boonesburg and the colonel was needing a guide so I offered to bring his men down."

"Why in tarnation did you stick to the trail, Johnnie? An old hand like you!"

He moved his shoulders. "They was all supposed to be up north of the Kentucky . . . pow-wowing. But it was careless of me, and I've paid for it."

"You'll be all right," I told him, trying to think so myself, "with Ben and Ann to take care of you, you'll see." I reached out and gave his hair a tug. "I thought you wasn't aiming to take sides in this thing."

He laid back in the bed. He was awfully white and weak and tired. He pulled the covers up under his chin like he was cold of a sudden, but he looked steady at me over them. "You put the mourning ash on your face when the least one died, and you wrapped him in one your own blankets to lay him away, and you buried him close to your own cabin. Like he was your own flesh and blood you did for him . . . brother. . . ."

The last words were said so low I could scarcely hear them, and fearing he was going I called out. Ann came running, pushing Ben and me out of the way. "You've let him talk too much. Go on now. He must rest." Bethia came to help her and they wrapped rocks they'd had warming on the hearth into the bed with him, and chafed his arms and hands and put wet cloths on his head. They shoved us aside and the two of them took him over.

Ben went over to a shelf and got the bunch of papers he'd found at the clearing. "I wanted you to see these," he said, handing them to me. "Them's what we found on Judd, and one of 'em he'd stuffed in the soldier's shirt."

The paper was a proclamation signed by the British governor of Detroit, Henry Hamilton, himself. I read it through, hardly believing what I read. He offered food, lodging and humane treatment to all who would desert the American cause and would present themselves to any British post. It promised that those who would take up arms against the Americans and use them "until the extinction of this rebellion" would be paid "adequate to their former stations in the rebel service" and could expect to receive two hundred acres of land.

I grinned at Ben when I'd finished. "What you reckon you and me would draw?"

"Nothing we'd enjoy, I'll bound."

I handed the papers back. "And Judd was to scatter these around."

"So it looks. They're sure proof he was in the hire of the British and that Johnnie's story is the truth."

"What you aiming to do with 'em?"

"Turn 'em over to Colonel Bowman. Reckon he outranks the major now."

Ben walked me back to the blockhouse. I couldn't get Johnnie's last words out of my mind. They grieved me and saddened me, and they even shamed me. "It was such a little I did," I told Ben. "Just made 'em welcome at my place and done what I could when the youngun was took. It was just human kindness to do what I could."

Ben steadied me over a rough place. "Maybe. But whatever you think it was, Johnnie thought it made you his brother . . . to protect and to stand by and to help."

"Yes," I said, with a bitter taste in my mouth, "and to get killed helping."

"Who's to go and who's to stay," Ben said, "is always in the hands of the Lord."

Well . . . of course. But I hated to think of Johnnie going.

# CHAPTER

## 22

Bᴜᴛ ʜᴇ ʀᴀʟʟɪᴇᴅ ꜱᴏᴍᴇ the next morning and our hopes went up. He ate a little bit of stew and Ben thought his color was better.

"If he just don't go to bleeding inside again," Ann said, "to my notion he's got a real chance." Her words sent my spirits soaring.

That afternoon Colonel Bowman and a right smart party of his men rode up. Lordy, I never saw such a man. He was as big as a mountain and even in common talk he had a voice that boomed out like a bass drum. "Heard you was having a mite of trouble," he said, getting off his horse. "Thought we'd come down and see could we help out."

"Well, that's right thoughty of you," Ben told him making him welcome, "and we're powerful glad to see you in the country. We got reason, though, to think the worst is over now. Just the same your men and your powder is as welcome as the birds in May, Colonel!"

They went inside the blockhouse and the women commenced scurrying around to cook up enough vittles to feed such a passel of men. Ben sent for me directly to tell the colonel how it was at the clearing where his men had been ambushed. When I got through he kind of grunted. "Obliged to you for seeing to 'em. They're volunteers and some of 'em ain't too sure of themselves in the woods. Lucky they wasn't all killed."

He went off to see to them.

"What'd he say about the papers you took off Judd?" I asked Ben.

"I couldn't to say repeat it," Ben said, grinning, "but the air ain't cleared up in here yet. No," he went on, sobering, "he taken 'em over and said he'd pass 'em on to Governor Henry."

The evening being slack and unbusy, some of Colonel Bowman's men commenced shooting at target just to pass the time. I was sitting on a bench looking on and Azariah was standing close by. He kind of snorted. "We ain't had powder enough to waste shooting thataway," he said. "We've spent ours with the redskins for targets."

The colonel and Ben were passing, and I reckon the colonel overheard Azariah, for he stopped. "There's none to spare," he said, "but there's enough for a little fun. I've heard how good you fellows can shoot out here and I'd like to see some of it. Here," he bellowed at the men, "put up a good target and let's have a shooting match. My men," he said, turning to Ben, "against Cap'n Logan's."

"All right," Ben said, "but you'll wish you hadn't."

They pegged a skin to the fence, the smooth side out and blacked a circle in the middle with a burned stick. "The one that's best," the colonel said, "gets all the bullets can be dug out of the target."

The men lined up to take their turns, all of them yelling and bragging and jostling one another. Around a dozen had shot, I reckon, when Billy Whitley pushed his way through the crowd and sat down on the bench by me. He'd been hunting and had just got back. "What they doing?" he said.

"Shooting match," I said. "Them's Bowman's men. We're trying to best 'em."

Billy handed his gun to Esther, who was standing there looking on. "Show 'em what some real shooting is," he told her.

She held back, though. "It's just for the men. I don't want to make a fool of myself, Billy."

"You'll not. You'll just make a fool of the rest of 'em. Go on."

I put in my word. "Go ahead, Esther. If you miss it'll be no more than most of 'em is doing."

She took Billy's gun and got in line to wait her turn. Some of the colonel's men commenced sniggering. "Thought it was your *men* was going to shoot."

But Ben quieted them. "She takened her place alongside the men at the loopholes this summer, and I reckon she's entitled to take her place shooting target if she wants."

When it came her time she batted her old hatbrim back out of her face and rested her gun, sighted, raised her head once and then squinted and sighted again. There wasn't a sound in the crowd when she squeezed the trigger, but as soon as the shot rang out the men broke and ran for the target. Big as he was Colonel Bowman got there first. "By grannies," he yelled, "she's hit it dead center, boys! Smack in the middle, not the width of a hair off! Now, there's a shot to put you on your mettle, if I ever seen one. And by a woman, too!"

Stung at being beat by a woman they tried until it was too dark to see to equal her shot, but none covered her, and when the target was lost in a blur they gave it up. They were good-natured about it, too, and all pitched in to dig out the bullets and pour them into her old hat. "You're entitled to 'em," they told her, "you won 'em good enough."

We had a shindig that night, for we'd not properly celebrated the colonel being in the country yet. My arm was stiffening and I felt a little lightheaded like I might be fevered, but I meant to go. I wouldn't of missed walking Bethia to the blockhouse, where the dancing was to be held, for two bad arms. This would be the first time we'd had the right to walk out together, bold and public in our intentions, and I didn't aim to pass it up if I could stay on my feet. It made me have a tingly feeling inside just to think of it.

Bethia hadn't ever looked any prettier. She'd washed her hair and it was still a little damp, and shining the way copper does under a bright sun. Her face was shining too, all sparkly and glad. I thought she had on a new dress and couldn't figure where she'd got it, but she said it was one of Ann's. "You sure you feel like going, Dave? Ben, he hadn't ort to go, had he?"

"He hadn't ort to," Ben said, "but I misdoubt you could keep him from it."

"I'm going," I said, "but I don't know as I'll do much dancing."

"Well, I should think not!"

Ann acted like Bethia had been her own little sister, straightening her skirts and pulling at the sleeves of her dress and fussing over her. "Now, you all take care and behave yourselves," she said finally, giving Bethia a little spank. "Mind your manners."

"I aim to," Bethia promised.

We went over to the bed where Johnnie was laying watching us. Seemed to me his breath came shallower, but he looked peaceful and quiet. "Just go with us," I told him, laughing.

The corners of his mouth crimped, like he was trying to smile. "I wish . . . you . . . well," he said, "you . . . and your woman."

He wished me well. Me and my woman. Those were the last words he ever said to me. They were the last words he ever said to anybody, for when Bethia and me came home along towards morning, glad and excited and happy, Ben told us how he'd died not more than ten minutes after we'd gone. Just, of a sudden, took a deep breath . . . and made it do for eternity.

We took the risk and laid him alongside of his youngun close to my cabin. The headboard is still there, weather-eaten and gray, but you can read his name yet, and the day he died.

COLONEL BOWMAN'S MEN stayed on at the fort for several days and then they left to go to Harrodstown. Ben went with them. There'd been such a flurry all summer with the redskins pestering that the militia officers hadn't ever been sworn in, and Ben hadn't yet been sworn in as sheriff either. The last court of the old county, Fincastle, had been held more than a year past, and it was high time Kentucky County was having its own court and commencing to tend its own affairs. Harrodstown had been named the county seat, so Ben went to meet with the others there and hold the first court. "Fancy," I said, following him to the gate when he left, "us having our own court in the country. We're getting plumb civilized."

Ben grinned down at me. "We are, ain't we?"

There was a thing I wanted to tell him, though. "Ben, me and Bethia don't want to wait overly long to get married. We thought a month, maybe, to be decent. When you're swore in you can marry us, can't you?"

"Why," he said, "I don't know. I hadn't thought. I reckon I could, though, seeing as I'll be a justice."

"We'd like it to be you," I said, "that binds us together."

He didn't say anything for a little while, just laid his hand on my shoulder. Ben's mouth could go as soft as a woman's when he was pleased or touched or at peace, and I've known it to quiver when his feelings have run extra strong. It did so now. "I take that kindly, Dave," he said. "And I'll be proud to join you."

I never knew a month could go so fast, and at the same time lag on its own swift wings. I had a plenty to do, making the cabin on the Green ready for Bethia. We'd decided to risk wintering there, though Ben shook his head over it and thought we were being foolish. "It's more'n ten mile off, Dave. You'd be hard put to get to the fort in haste."

"We got to risk it sooner or late," I told him. "One thing is sure. You can't get nothing done penned up in a fort."

I'd expected my place to be burnt to the ground, especially after finding out Judd Jordan had been in the country most of the time. But likely both him and the redskins had been too busy trying to take the forts. Then, too, if he hadn't never been back over that way, Judd must of thought he'd done tended to my place.

It wasn't much to look at, though, with the roof caved in and the grass and weeds matted around it. Still, it don't take long to clean things up, and I had help putting on a new roof. I smoothed the floor down again and scoured it white, and I trussed up a bed in one corner and hewed out a table and some three-legged stools. Later on I figured to make Bethia some nicer things, but for now these had to do.

Some of the men at the fort, handy with whittling, carved us out a set of bowls and platters, and the womenfolks divided up their pots and kettles with Bethia to give us a start. I packed them out one day and when I'd set the bowls and platters on the table and put the kettles on the hearth I thought the cabin looked right homey. Of course Bethia would want to change things around and put them where they'd be handier, and she'd have her own ideas about fixing the place up, but it was clean and it was roomy and it was ours . . . at least we wouldn't be cooped up inside the stockade. And I didn't think we were taking too much of a chance. Apparently the redskins had left the country, either because Judd had been killed, or because Colonel Bowman was at Harrodstown. Likely on both accounts, I thought, and it seemed reasonable to me we could look for a little peace during the winter. If there was fresh trouble next spring, we could cross that bridge when we got to it.

The last week before the wedding the whole fort was bustling and stirring for all the world like a hive of bees working. The men were out hunting for meat enough for the wedding feast, and the women-folks were busy cooking it. This being the first wedding at Logan's they all took a pride in making ready for it. Not that we expected many would risk making the journey from the other forts, but there'd be some, and the folks at Logan's wanted to make a good showing. The women turned out every cabin and scoured and polished and scrubbed till there was a mighty confusion of cleanliness. Man would start to take his kill in. "Don't you dast bring that bloody side of meat in this cabin! I got it all redded up and it'll make a mess," somebody would yell at him. Everything was topsy-turvy and it got so when they weren't out hunting the men just wandered around, not knowing for sure where they could lay the next foot.

Seemed to me like Bethia was busier than anyone else. I hardly ever got to be with her, for she was always flying about like a cloud of dust in front of a broom. She made me a new hunting shirt and a pair of jeans. The jeans were made out of nettle-woolsey and they itched a sight, but she was so proud of them I'd of worn them had they taken the hide off. Her and Ann made her a new dress, too. They had us to gather up some white walnuts and they took the hulls and dyed some cloth. Turned it a dull yellow. That was what we called butternut. Ann had a little smidgin of indigo and they dyed a little piece of the goods and put a kind of blue frill around the neck of the dress. Most of the women gave her little things to help out. Jane Manifee had a little piece of red ribbon she brought over and Bethia said she'd make a bow to go at the throat of her dress. And Miz Coburn had a set of buttons she'd saved over. They looked right pretty down the front. Esther Whitley, she brought over a real gold pin she'd packed over the Gap with her. Said she'd never need it again and Bethia might as well have the good of it.

Finally everything was ready and the day before the wedding folks commenced coming. There was a surprising number of them, too. I'd not looked for any to come from Boonesburg, but Dannel and Squire came, and John Todd and Simon Butler. None of the women from there came, but they all sent us presents. Rebecca sent a feather tick she'd brought into the country with her. Dannel chuckled when he handed it over to me. "It's Rebecca's birthing bed," he said, "and she allowed she'd not be needing it no more and you all, just commencing, would likely put it to good use." I reckon you could say we have done so, too.

The Poages came from Harrodstown, Ann with a coverlid she'd wove herself, and the McGarys and the Dentons and some others. Jim came, and Colonel Bowman and the major. Of course it was kind of an accident Major Clark was there, for he was on his way to Virginia to talk to the governor about the expedition to the Illinois country, but he stopped over for the wedding. He was sure in a good humor, too. He was bound that Governor Henry would be pleased with his news that Kaskaskia and Vincennes could be taken easy, and that he would provision and outfit an expedition right off. "After that," he said, snapping his fingers, "after that, Detroit . . . and the end of our persecutions."

Well, of course everybody knows now that it didn't turn out just like the major wanted it to . . . that after he'd taken the Illinois forts he couldn't get the backing to go on to Detroit, and our persecutions didn't end for many a long year, mostly on account of it. But our hopes were high that night and it looked certain. Sometimes it's a good thing you can't see very far ahead.

Great day in the morning, but the fence of the fort fairly bulged outwards with folks, and there was such a clattering and chattering of talk as you've never heard. Times when we could get together and forget for a little while about the redskins and the hard work and the everlasting struggle were so few we made the most of it. Everybody was lighthearted and gay, and we sang and danced and mixed and mingled till way into the night.

The wedding was held the next morning, with all gathered in the common to look on. There was a heap of joking and joshing right up to the last, but when Ben stepped out in front and held up his hand for quiet, the folks got so still you could of heard a deep breath. Then Bethia and me walked out. She was as pretty as a picture in her new dress and her hair shining like glory, and I reckon I looked as good as the Lord ever intends me to look. Only one thing bothered me. I was mortally afraid I'd have to scratch before Ben got done.

It was a nice wedding, if I do say so myself. I don't see how it could of been any nicer, for Ben made it solemn and just like we'd been in a church. At the end he prayed just like a preacher would of done. The minute he said amen, though, the solemnness was gone. The men circled around, shouting and yelling, and carried me off, and the women took charge of Bethia. I knew I was in for a rough time the rest of the day, but I'd had a hand in passing it out to others in my day, so I figured I had to take my own share now in good part.

Once Jim singled me out and came over where I was. "I reckon," he said, "you think you've got the lead on me now."

"It looks like it, don't it? Can't you get Ann to give you a answer?"

"I was just aiming to tell you. She says after the turn of the year she'll marry me."

I let out a whoop. "You just wait! Man, it's going to be rough! I'll not let you forget you've had no mercy on me today."

"I reckon I can stand up to it," he said. "It goes queer, though, me thinking of getting married. I ain't used to the idea yet."

"It scares me some, too," I told him. "But, comes a time when a man has got to decide whether he's going it on his own hook the rest of his days and end up a lonesome old man, or whether he cares to take the risk of pulling double. Me, I've done put on the harness."

He clapped me on the back. "If you rue it before the first of February you can tell me, and I'll back out."

According to the custom, me and Bethia were kept apart the rest of the day. The dancing commenced in the afternoon when the wedding feast was over, but we weren't even allowed to dance with one another, save the first set which we led. After that Bethia had to dance with every man who asked her, and I had to lead out every woman. It wouldn't of been mannerly not to. It sure was hard on a body's feet and legs, though.

The dancing stopped for supper and then commenced again, but now as many as could moved into Ben's cabin where me and Bethia were to stay the night. When dark began to come on and the women huddled together in one corner, giggling and whispering, I knew it was nearly over. I looked over at Bethia and she smiled back at me. I wondered if she was just trying to appear uncaring of what she knew was in store for us, or if she was so wore out she truly didn't care and would just be glad to get it over. I couldn't tell.

Of a sudden the women rushed and crowded around her, squealing and screaming the way they do, and they swarmed her up the ladder to the loft room which had been made ready for us. Downstairs us men all made out like we hadn't seen or heard a thing, but of course we could hear the womenfolks laughing and rustling about, and wasn't a one of us didn't know Bethia was being undressed and put to bed. A lot of sly looks came slanting my way. We'd been kept apart all day for this . . . this coming together in bed.

When the women came backing down the ladder, it was my turn, and with a heap of whooping and shouting I got shoved up into the loft room. Was a candle burning and I could see Bethia sitting up on the straw pallet that had been hers and Davey's bed until now. She had the new coverlid Ann Poage had given us clutched up under her chin. She was kind of white, but she managed a smile. I had just that one glimpse of her before the men clustered about. They were supposed to strip me and throw me into bed beside her, but Bethia fooled them. Before they got good started she reached out and pinched the candle flame and the whole loft went black dark. There sure was a howl went up and a lot of milling around, but it gave me a chance to slide under the coverlid. Safe there I yelled at them to get out now, they'd done their duty. There was some grumbling that they'd been tricked and they'd ought to make us go through the whole thing again, but finally they left. Which didn't mean we'd be left in peace. Lord, no. Off and on all night they'd be swarming up and down that ladder, bringing the jug and platters of food. A young couple has a poor chance of getting better acquainted on their wedding night, I can tell you. But we comforted ourselves we'd have our real wedding night at our own place.

It was noon before we got away the next day. The folks rode with us part the way, all in high spirits, racing their horses, shooting off their guns, yelling and shouting. But Ben wouldn't let them go too far, for fear there might be a few redskins left in the country and all the noise would lead them straight to us.

It sure was quiet when they turned back. So quiet it made me feel kind of awkward. We both had to ride on Beck, for my pack horse had long since been driven off by the Indians and I was just plain lucky not to of lost the mare too. Bethia rode in back, one arm around my waist holding on. She was quiet, too. It wasn't till we came to the river about midafternoon that I commenced loosening up and could talk. I reckon it was seeing the river and being reminded of how much I loved it and the country thereabouts freed me of my awkwardness. Anyway I told Bethia about my wanderings up and down the stream, and of my times with the Long Hunters, and of the hunts in the woods and hills all about. Bethia kind of let down, herself, and talked and laughed and asked questions.

When we got to the cabin we walked all about and I showed her what I'd done . . . the field where the corn would grow . . . the place near the house where she could have her garden patch . . . the grove where the pawpaws grew and the little hazelnut thicket. We talked of where we'd put fences and of the new buildings we'd need to shelter the stock. "Ann is going to give me a calf when the white-faced cow freshens," Bethia said, "if it's a heifer."

"And I've made a trade with Billy Whitley to work a month for a couple of shoats and a ewe." I told her. "We'll soon have us a good start of stock."

The sun was going down behind the hills when we went inside the cabin. "I'll change my dress," Bethia said, "and fix us some supper."

I built her a fire and then I went out to do up the night work. Beck was to be watered and belled and turned loose in the meadow. Wood had to be chopped and brought in. Water had to be packed up from the spring. It went natural to be doing up evening chores. I thought how I'd be doing them the rest of my life. Come sundown and it would be my job to make us ready for the night. To kind of wind up the day. There was a peace in thinking of it.

When I'd done, and I don't know for what reason, I went around
back to Johnnie's grave. The grass was already covering it over, new as
it was. And of a sudden I could hear Johnnie talking . . . plain as
day. I could hear him saying . . . "You'll all go there in droves, and
you'll cut down the trees and fence in the land and kill off the game,
and more and more settlers'll come, and in time there'll be villages,
like in the east, and what you come for will be gone. You'll kill it yourselves. You'll take the death of what you most want with you when you
go."

I could see the fire and the sandy beach on the Holston and Johnnie
on yon side the fire. I could hear his voice, rough with his grief. Well,
here we were . . . the settlers. Not so many of us yet, but a plenty to
make a start. And we were cutting down the trees, and we were fencing in the land, and we were killing off the game. We were making
ready for villages. But Johnnie was wrong. It wasn't the death of what
we most wanted. It was the life of it. What Johnnie hadn't known,
being a pilgrim and a wanderer, and what I myself hadn't known, it
being before Bethia, was that there were things to be treasured beyond
woods and trees and free-flowing streams and wild things, all living
wide and open and unhampered together. There were folks and their
ways, banded together, and their work for themselves and for one another. There were men and women to build a cabin and live in it, their
whole lives together, to raise up younguns out of their love for one
another and out of themselves. It wasn't chains that a settlement and a
roof-tree put on a man, but a bond that made him kin, in common-
ness and nature, to all those others he touched shoulders with, with a
duty towards them and a knowledge of them that made them all free
together. If we cut down the trees, more could be planted. If we fenced
in the land, more yield could be grown. If we killed off the game, better stock could be raised. I sort of told Johnnie that, standing there by
his grave. How folks would always find a way, and flow on, like the
waves of the sea, tide in and high, all upswelling and surging, afoam
with life and a mighty power. I reckon it was then, thinking it out for
myself and telling it to Johnnie, that I learned something pretty important. The ways of nature are fine and grand and wonderful . . .
but the ways of folks are better.

I went around the cabin then and sat on the doorstep. The knoll
slid down into the valley and I could see across it to the meadows
widening between the hills. It had been a time since I'd sat there in
gloaming, looking out over the valley. I thought of how long it had
been and of all that had happened in the country. We'd freed ourselves of the Henderson company. We'd built three forts and held

them against all attacks. We'd petitioned and made ourselves into a county, and we'd formed and set up our own county government. In a little better than two years we'd come a long, long way. We had a long way yet to go, of course. We weren't rid of the redskins by a far piece, nor of the British, but we'd made a start and likely we could hold onto and keep what we'd started. We had good leaders, good, strong leaders, and stouthearted folks to stand together. In time we'd dot the wilderness with settlements and people it with our younguns, and their younguns. Amongst them would be mine and Bethia's . . . those yet unborn that belonged to us. It was like giving over to them something great and fine.

Inside I could hear Bethia stirring about. I heard her feet shuffling over the floor, the moccasins moving soft and making only a little rustling sound. I heard the crane clank when she swung it wide of the fire. I heard the spoon scrape against the side of the kettle when she dipped up the food, and the bowls clatter when she set them on the table. I heard water gurgling when she poured it into the noggins. I thought how I'd be hearing them forever . . . all the little sounds a woman makes about her house, that come to be part and parcel of a man, like the woman herself. And I was content.

"You can come eat now," she called.

I stood up. The little red star, the busy one, was just blinking out of the night. I laughed, and went inside.